Angel in the house

John Mortimer

Published **by John Mortimer**

John Mortimer
37 Stock Lane
Whaddon,
Buckinghamshire.
MK17 0LS UK

ISBN 978-1-326-28637-8

CONTENTS

COVER. In Queen Victoria's gas-lit London, street sellers of hot pies and potatoes could be found cheek-by-jowl with fashionable passers-by and high-class jewellery shops. Part of an oil painting by Michael Matthews (1933-2014), this scene is typical of that which Elizabeth Susanna Browning, the heroine of this historical novel, would encounter as a young woman growing up in Brewer-street, just off Regent's-street in the 1850s.

YOUNG housekeeper Lizzie secretly begins to admire the master of the household, a slightly older but strikingly tall, handsome American newspaper editor working in Victorian London. Whisked to New York on the maiden voyage of Isambard Kingdom Brunel's giant steam-driven liner *Great Eastern* (pictured left in New York, 1860), the couple marry before returning to London to live in style near Regent's Park.

In New York, Lizzie discovered her husband's menacingly dark side, and there was more to come. Increasingly, Lizzy became subsumed as her husband's alcoholism and violent tendencies took firm grip of her life.

Desperately anxious for a solution, Lizzy took matters into her own hands, with a result she least expected. Then, after all the dark days, the sun finally shone and provided Lizzy with happiness.

This historical novel is deeply rooted in real-life drama. It is based on the petition for Divorce: Colburn vs Colburn of February 1870.

The book is written in the first person, recounting the events of Lizzy's turbulent years. It is a story of love and lust, and of good and evil.

John Mortimer, September 2017

ACKNOWLEDGEMENT
The author wishes to acknowledge Di Dean and Jack Hall Stephens for their expertise in reading the original manuscript; Deb Walker for her help with the families of Elizabeth Browning and Daniel Kinnear Clark; Roger D. Joslyn, CG, of New York for his assistance with the Colburn family in the USA, Jon Gregson for his information regarding Browning family history, and finally, locomotive expert Harry Jack, author of *Locomotives of the LNWR Southern Division*, for his knowledge of the London & North Western Railway, particularly with respect to James Edward McConnell.

FOREWORD

Jill Dawson's book *The Crime Writer*, published by Sceptre, an imprint of Hodder & Stoughton, is a novel about a novelist – Patricia Highsmith – writing a novel about a novelist planning a novel about a man plotting to kill his wife. Dawson writes: "Nosy little bitches, biographers, vultures all of them, trying to work their way into your secret heart, winkle out the darkness and deceit, take your life...and make it their own."

In this respect, I am guilty. This novel is about Zerah Colburn, a leading Victorian newspaper journalist and editor. Through research, I have winkled out Colburn's darkness and used it to write a novel about Colburn and his English wife, Elizabeth Susanna, who provides the story of their life together.

And the darkness in Colburn's life? This can be found at the National Archives in Kew, Surrey, UK in the form of 'Colburn vs Colburn. The Petition for the Dissolution of Marriage', filed on 16 February 1870.

This documents the traumas that befell Elizabeth Susanna Colburn at the hands of husband Zerah Colburn. The Petition has remained a closely guarded secret ever since, it being required by law to be held 'closed' for 100 years.

Set against the background of the great and the good of Victorian engineers and their colossal life-changing projects, this novel unlocks Elizabeth's (Lizzy's) terrible secrets as she searches for justice, peace of mind and, eventually, love.

Chapter One

Growing up

THOSE who befriended my late husband, a successful public figure, without exception had no idea of the extreme depths to which he would sink to humiliate and ill-treat me, or inflict his snarling opprobrium.

For, while I knew him better than anyone, even I would not have known the full depth of the waywardness to which he would sink were it not for the diligence of Mr. Bentley, a most persistent private enquiry agent.

As you will discover, my husband, a prominent engineer and recipient of wide public acclaim and generous tributes, nevertheless developed into a devious, cunning and treacherous bully who, in the eyes of the law, engaged in criminality yet managed to escape public ignominy. He created wounds that refused to heal.

Memories of past events have not faded with the years, particularly the torment of syphilis; the utter shame, subsequent pain and disgrace it inflicted on an innocent woman. Even today, I suffer after-effects, physically and emotionally. While now deeply in love and happily married, there were occasions in my darkest days when I had wished myself dead.

However, I have reached the point in my life, with the shadow of death nearby, where I have no excitement for the future, and I find myself inevitably dwelling on the past, which explains why I have chosen to unfold my story on paper. It is not my intention to blacken my husband's name – he managed that on his own account – but to tell the truth as far as I am able. In doing so, I shall not guard his reputation for future generations.

It began in late in 1859 when, aged 22, I replied innocently to an advertisement in the Personal Columns of *The Times*. The prospect of new employment offered an exciting opportunity. However, I did not know what to expect having previously relied entirely upon my parents to find work.

Our family lived in Brewer-street, St James, close to magnificent and fashionable Regent-street. A most pleasant part of London, it contrasted favourably with the rough horrors of the densely packed terraced houses of the East End, its occupants drawn from all corners of the world.

Regent-street, with palatial shops and residences, served as a dividing line between aristocratic London of the West End and the more impoverished Soho with its poor housing. It formed part of John Nash's plan to connect Regent's Park with Carlton House.

Born the eldest of six children, seven if you include a stillborn, we lived near to Golden-square, a beautiful square with magnificent houses. Further away to the west lay the equally engaging Berkeley-square, and beyond that stretched Hyde Park, a walk of one mile distant. There I enjoyed walking among the trees with my parents.

I arrived on 3rd November 1836 and on New Year's Day 1837 my parents took me to St George's District Church, Camberwell to be baptised Elizabeth Susanna Browning by the Rev'd Samuel Smith. At the time my parents lived at No. 6 Leicester Place, Albany Road, Camberwell. The event marked the beginning of my association with the Church of England. As a small child, mother taught me to say my prayers. From my childhood memories she provided the family's strength. As soon as old enough, probably six, I would accompany my parents to church and I did so until of sufficient age to attend alone.

Whenever my parents moved house, and they did so several times, they quickly found churches to attend. I could also recite the Lord's Prayer, as well as other prayers. At age six or seven, mother taught me to read and write. Well before eight, I enjoyed reading books.

Living in Brewer-street, we regularly attended nearby St James's Church, though occasionally we would walk along Regent-street, with its beautiful curved quadrant, then across Regent's Circus to All Souls, Langham-place, opposite the

Langham Hotel. This required a much longer journey, one we made usually only during fine weather.

With a traditional and uncomplicated faith, my parents brought me up to trust God, to love Him, and show loyalty to Queen and country. We always attended Church of England despite growing awareness of the Evangelical movement. The evangelicals believed they could find a Christian path in all their actions, including the details of daily life. Christianity taught me compassion; and to love others as I would love myself. Each night, I would kneel by my bed, praying for myself and family. Mother taught us, as a family, always to say 'sorry' should we make mistakes or offend others, and resolve any differences before retiring at night. 'Before the sun sets,' she would say, 'make sure you have settled your differences, and become friends.'

My father, Thomas Browning, a shrewd accountant, provided well for the family; many other families experienced a far worse plight. Yet my upbringing gave no hint of dramas to come.

As I grew up, London expanded. To my knowledge we moved at least three times and always westwards. In 1851, then aged 14, I arrived with my parents at No. 25 Brewer-street. Previously, we lived at No. 19 Clifford-street, off Bond-street where, besides my parents and me, the family comprised younger sisters Harriet Augusta, Margaret and Maria, and the latest arrivals, the twins, Thomas John and Henry Charles. The arrival of twins at No. 19 Clifford-street on 14th April 1849 provoked my parent's move to the larger house in Brewer-street. The twins were christened at Saint. James's church in nearby Piccadilly where Edward later was also christened on 9th March 1851.

Margaret is eight years younger than me, having arrived on 14th April 1845. At that time, the family lived at No. 9 Myddleton Square, off Saint John-street, Clerkenwell. Following Margaret's birth I had no choice but to help mother about the house doing various "jobs", as she called them. Margaret was christened at Saint Mark's Church, Myddleton Square by the

Rev'd Dolman on 8th June that same year and the same church where Maria would be christened some two years after, but then by the Rev'd Hill on 23rd May 1847

Clerkenwell changed from being a fashionable area of London a hundred years earlier to one, when I was a girl, of breweries, distilleries and print works providing much employment. Clerkenwell even had three prisons and became famous for the Clerkenwell Outrage of 1867.

Little wonder father wanted to move house for the sake of his wife and children.

I would be almost five years old when mother had a stillborn, a little girl. The stillborn arrived on 24th September 1841. Did my parents give her a name, I often asked myself? It took mother some years to recover from that experience, which explains Margaret's arrival some four years later in 1845. Had the stillborn lived, mother would have given birth to six girls in a row. Unaware of it at the time, it was only much later that mother explained how the arrival of a stillborn so greatly upset her, and how she would not let father even go near her. Later, I would find out to my cost what it would be like to deliver a stillborn. Even now, I do not know where my little sister is buried.

Our house formed the bedrock of mother's world. My mother, rather than my father, controlled our daily life, given her strong will and stoic character. Father generally occupied a peripheral presence, maintaining his distance from most matters involving children. Only as I became older did he exercise more discipline, then he took a deeper interest in my welfare.

Father came from a local family in Bermondsey and grew up living on the south side of the River Thames, with the Tower of London visible on the opposite bank. I have heard it said, though I do not know if it is true, that one of his relatives, William Browning MA, was the Rector of St. Mary Magdalene in Bermondsey from 1723 to 1727 as well as High Sherrif of the County of Surrey in 1740. However, I do know for certain that my grandfather, William Browning, worked as a fellmonger in

Bermondsey.

Bermondsey's grimy and melancholy streets, with loan offices and pawnbrokers, hardly differed from those in the East End on the other side of the river, the exception being the tanneries. These turned hides into leather, and caused evil stinking smells to fill Bermondsey's air.

For Bermondsey, although a slum, was London's main leather working centre. Every factor necessary for the expansion of the trade could be found in Bermondsey: open countryside, a constant supply of water and oak bark from surrounding countryside; hides from the butchers of London, a plentiful supply of cheap labour and a market for finished goods in the city.

The tanning pits of Bermondsey received a plentiful supply of water from the tidal Thames and used as motive power by tanners and leather-dressers.

Many other related trades flourished alongside the leather trade – wool and hair were separated from the skins and sold for hat-making, as were horns which were used to make combs, spoons, knife handles and musical horns.

To my father, Bermondsey and the East End were areas to avoid; while both wallowed in dirt the West End enjoyed money. Leisure too abounded in the West End. Bermondsey and the East End were good for nothing except the sweat of labour.

The East End stretched eastwards to the River Lea and north of the River Thames to the fringes of Hackney. To father it was no place to escape to; an unhealthy area of filthy, densely-packed labyrinthine streets, poorly constructed courts and alleys. Many were those crowded into old houses garbed with soot, or confined to dingy rooms. With its atmosphere of general disgust, menace, poverty and human misery, it is not surprising the region spawned criminals, thieves, robbers and villains. There were few work prospects of merit; a place to be avoided with a family. Life for the poor was one of hopelessness and squalor. With children sickly and half-starved, many died from cholera in the various outbreaks.

He had no wish to raise his family under such conditions. Be that as it may, even Brewer-street could not escape the cholera outbreaks that severely tested London's graveyards, prompting demands for new cemeteries in the countryside.

London's river and docks exerted a powerful influence. Bermondsey and the East End offered no escape from slate coloured skies and repetitive drudgery. The area painted a stark contrast to the tree-lined avenues of his longed-for West End.

I grew to know father as a proud, puritanical and respectable man, a disciplinarian, and one not easily tolerant of other people's views. Determined as a young man to leave Bermondsey, he searched for a better life north of the river, but far from the East End. His 'better life' did not come easily, first finding work near Camberwell, an area still south of the river. It was there he began his journey in married life, with the West End remaining as his main goal.

Gradually, he made his way in the commercial world before the family moved to Clifford-street. In 1851, he advanced further to become a merchant's accountant and moved with his wife and children to Brewer-street close to his work.

As its only accountant, the business valued father's skills, and he quickly earned their respect. Aged 60, he believed his family deserved a larger house.

Mother, some 20 years younger than father, spoke little of their early life together. I do not know how, when, why or where they met. They never discussed private matters in my presence. I took it as their secret. My mother's parents lived in Walworth, a mile and half from Bermondsey. Perhaps my parents met at a dance or musical soirée; I like to think so as father liked music – all kinds of music, but especially music by Bach. He loved J. S. Bach's Orchestral Suite No. 1. BWV 1066 – I always remember the title of that piece because of the date of the Battle of Hastings. I like to think they were deliriously happy together.

My mother bore six children spread over 14 years; she also

miscarried and experienced a stillbirth. She did not discuss miscarriage or stillbirth. Only later, when I had left home, did father tell me the news; he asked me to keep it to myself.

Mother must have been 26 when she gave birth to me. At the time poor but happy, the couple lived in Camberwell, itself a mile from Walworth. Mother acted as a vital and trustworthy family linchpin. She made the house a happy, family home. Despite this, as one by one more sisters and brothers arrived I felt less close to her. We were a large and respectable family, though not as large as some I knew. I envied those without brothers and sisters. As an adored only child, each would enjoy the full love and attention of their parents. Even so, I could not say my childhood was miserable. And indeed, I shall never forget my mother who, through her love for God and her devotion to the church, etched the sign of the cross on my soul that will remain until I die.

By the time Harriet arrived, three years after me, my parents had moved from south of the river to Clifford-street. It marked a turning point in their lives, having left the squalid, unhealthy conditions of south London for the West End, so much favoured by father.

Maria followed Harriet and Margaret in 1847 and two years later, my twin brothers Thomas John and Henry Charles arrived. Mother regarded Edward de Lacy, the last to arrive, as the 'baby' of the family. Aged two months in March 1851, when the man from the census knocked at the door, Edward cried all the time the census man asked questions of my mother. He even asked her why she had given Edward the unusual Christian name of de Lacy, which sounded not only superior but French also. Our move to Brewer-street occurred in January 1851, so we were not completely settled in the house by the time of the census.

As the youngest, Edward received most attention. Not surprisingly, I envied him, especially as Harriet, Margaret, Maria, the twins and I all slept in the same room. With few possessions, including clothes, one drawer of a chest had to suffice for me.

When younger, I went to school for mornings only. At the

time, my parents could not afford to employ a housemaid. One word sums up what I most remember of home in those years: work. As the eldest, I saw myself as the family skivvy. On arrival home from school, I would put on my apron and immediately begin helping mother. Even from first thing in the morning, she found various tasks to complete, including washing dishes and some cleaning. I soon identified mother as house-proud and meticulous; she believed in a strong family but I received no payment for work as father earned just enough to go round.

The move to Brewer-street brought transformation to my life in more ways than one. Mother expected me to leave school and help with housework. With this came the loss of the simple truths of early childhood, some of which made me happy and others caused sadness.

And so I stayed at home to care for the youngest. Harriet would be 11 and still at school, leaving Maria four and the twins two at home. Larger than the house in Clifford-street, No.25 Brewer-street involved much more work. Even though father worked hard, my parents took in lodgers to increase the family income and provide further assistance with housework. Mother described housework as 'unending'.

One lodger gave her name as Mary Parker; she brought with her a son, Charles born 10 months previously in Hartlepool. I never saw Mary's husband, or even knew if he existed. Mary, born in Newcastle, did not speak of him. Father simply said she was 'disadvantaged'; for this reason she assisted with household work in return for a much reduced rent. This reflected my father's caring and philanthropic attitude; he also endeavoured to punctually settle his bills.

Other lodgers included two Italian artists: Guiseppi Bertini, 25, and his sister Maria-Rosa Bertini, 21. A French woman, Louisa Doha, joined us from Paris in search of work. I think her parents must have been quite well-to-do, because while she lodged with us she never did find work, yet she paid rent regularly to father. During her stay, Louisa improved her command of English, so maybe that explained her reason for coming to London. I recall she celebrated her 21st birthday in 1851 with us. She kept her room tidy, mother used to say.

The Italian artists kept to themselves; however, from them I learned some words of Italian. I liked Louisa; she taught me some French words and phrases. I wondered if by taking in foreigners as lodgers, father deliberately sought to expose us to other languages and peoples as part of our education. In reality, he struggled to make ends meet and the lodgers provided valuable income; at the same time he extended more than passing sympathy to people in need, like Mary Parker and Louisa Doha. Even as I write this, father and mother (who live at No.36, Endlesham-road, Clapham,) enjoy income from Cordelia Hornbrook, a lodger, born in France.

The larger house at No. 25 Brewer-street inevitably required more housework and for this father employed Mary Scanlon, aged 27. Mary worked as a servant to help mother and me.

Mother did the washing and cooking, leaving Mary and I with much of the cleaning, including raking out fires, laying wood, blacking and polishing the fireplaces. Monday was washday; on Tuesday we ironed the clothes, a duty occupying most of the day, sometimes longer. I became proficient with the iron; cleaning was my least favourite task.

Gradually throughout my childhood, conditions at home improved as father progressed at work. I saw little of him during my early years. He left for work early in the morning, returning late at night. Father also worked on Saturday, leaving Sunday as the only day on which the family enjoyed his presence. We saw him more when we lived in Clifford-street and Brewer-street.

I liked father. I used to think he thought of me as the apple of his eye; he certainly spoilt me should mother be out of sight. From time to time he offered warnings, one being I should be wary of those who lived beyond their means. He wanted me to do well for myself. He would call me his "dearest daughter", which upset Harriet.

Many, many years later I discovered that father kept a notebook in which he recorded in his elegant and neat handwriting all kinds of information.

Perhaps, because I spent so much time with mother, I did not feel particularly close to her. Mother's tongue could be sharp. I, as the eldest, felt it most, I thought.

I much enjoyed reading – it provided escape from daily routines. Among the monthly periodicals were a number produced by Mr. Charles Dickens, including *Household Words* which of course were of great interest to father. From the pages of any books and journals I could lay my hands on, a magic world could appear. These formed an early part of my education. Father firmly believed in the power of the published word to advance our understanding. Gradually I discovered a good memory for words and numbers.

Mother ensured we looked presentable; she made her own clothes and ours. Driven by a strong sense of tidiness, she worked hard and frequently appeared tired and drawn.

Mother's sharp tongue kept us all firmly in our place, father included. She often said 'If you had as much housework as me, you would not make such a mess.'

Although 14 of us lived at No. 25 Brewer-street, we enjoyed a happy family atmosphere and I have pleasing childhood memories.

I recall 1851 for two reasons. Firstly, I took notice for the first time of the census and all involved with it. Secondly, the Great Exhibition opened to the public in the glass palace in Hyde Park designed by Joseph Paxton, head gardener at Chatsworth House, seat of the Duke of Devonshire. The grand exhibition, a great celebratory occasion, marked the biggest spectacle London witnessed since the coronation of the Queen; it brought together more people than ever before in one place. Designed to reflect British genius, the exhibition seemingly contained everything, from steam locomotives – my first sight of one – to steam hammers, scientific instruments, and many, many other wonderful machines and artefacts.

Father took mother and me to see the exhibition while Mary Parker looked after my brothers and sisters at home. That summer the weather was hot. For us, father said, to visit the exhibition would be an education in itself – a wonderful experience of art, beauty, and mechanical devices. We watched displays from all over the world in the great palace and, for the first time, I witnessed a lavatory on display.

We spent a whole day at the exhibition yet did not see everything on show. Large crowds attended, many attired in fine clothes; some people visited two or three times before the exhibition closed. By comparison we looked rather drab, albeit clean and tidily dressed. I read that over six million people visited the exhibition. Later, in 1854, workers removed the glass palace and erected it as the Crystal Palace at Sydenham where they enlarged it by half as much again.

For me, visiting the exhibition ignited a feeling of restlessness. It opened my eyes to the world. The work of helping to look after my brothers and sisters proved hard, especially when mother was taken ill on a number of occasions. I wanted to earn money; father told me to wait a while but I remained restless, eager to experience more of life.

Increasingly, as I grew older, I appreciated father's company and sought his approval and support. One day, aged 16, I repeated my feelings. He said mother would be 'most upset' to see me leave, as she would lose a willing pair of helping hands. Indeed, when father told her my news she was most unhappy, quickly making her feelings known with three infants under four to care for. I asked what she had against me wanting greater independence. She told me employment would not be easy. Even if I could find it, work could be far worse than working at home. She tried to dissuade me from leaving.

Father must have reassured her, for while she remained obstinately disapproving she gradually relented. Father said that while I might find work, it would not be well paid as I could offer only limited experience and that only in domestic work and care of infants. As for cooking, I had only watched mother, occasionally baking a few items under her strict guidance to gain confidence. She had no wish to waste food through my errors. I could not describe myself as a cook.

In terms of my knowledge of children, I regularly cared for twins Thomas and Henry. My mother brought up Edward, who she loved dearly; later I helped care for him too. All this proved good experience to stand me in good stead for my first job.

One day on return from work, father purchased a copy of *The Times*. In the evening we searched the Personal Columns. Father used a black pencil to circle positions he judged suitable. Most advertisements for a nanny required at least one reference. I, on the other hand, possessed none.

One advertisement, from a professor of gymnastics living in Golden-square, sought an assistant for a children's nursery-maid.

As it happened, the opportunity my parents took to move to Brewer-street occurred when father was offered the position of accountant at Messrs Ganière, fine silk and woollen merchants. The business occupied No. 34 and No. 35 Golden-square. It was Father's improved wages that enabled him to rent No. 25 Brewer-street, a short walk from Golden-square.

On his journey to work the following day, father made enquiries. He discovered a Professor Braithwaite lived at No. 37 Golden-square with his family. However, although the professor was head of the household, his wife took charge of the children and servants.

Father took the opportunity to pay a short visit to No. 37 to seek further details of the vacancy. In the ensuing discussion, he put my name forward, offering the professor his personal reference. Father arranged I attended for interview next day.

That day I put on my Sunday-best clothes and travelled with him to Golden-square – as a young woman, father would not allow me to travel on my own, whether by cab, omnibus or on the new railway. I did make several journeys by horse bus with father, but I hated the jostling and foul smells from other passengers, many of whom looked bedraggled and tramp-like. I disliked horse buses too because they shook from side to side as they rattled over the uneven streets, throwing passengers around on their bench seats. Whenever possible I avoided such journeys as the air inside could be fowl smelling. Only men would travel on the upper deck to enjoy the 'fresh' air.

At the door of No. 37, a housemaid greeted me. She escorted me into the drawing room to await the professor's wife. It seems father submitted good recommendations on my behalf; that he worked within a few doors almost acted as a reference.

The children's nursery-maid, Emma, had requested permission to leave in three months' time. As the professor's wife shortly expected her fourth child, she required the assurance of a suitable replacement well in advance to guarantee there would be no break.

The three children ranged between the ages of one and five; it would be my duty to help care for them, and assist with their education. The professor's wife, Mrs. Braithwaite, asked many questions of me and my family, including my experience with infants. She outlined my duties and proposed that should I prove myself worthy within three months, she would raise me to the position of nursery-maid. After a short while, she seemed to make up her mind, even though my experience as a nursery-maid at best could be described as 'only limited'.

She asked if I would like to work at the house. She explained my wages; while only modest, at least I knew I would receive some payment. Mrs. Braithwaite appeared kind and I accepted at once; it appeared foolish to refuse.

She said I would have my own room, eat in servants' quarters with Emma, Mrs. Meadows the cook who also acted as housekeeper, Gladys the housemaid, Edith the parlour maid, Katy the scullery maid, and Robert the footman. Mrs. Meadows, a professed cook, frequently received assistance from Gladys. Mrs. Braithwaite told me to address the housekeeper as Mrs.

Meadows.

At first, I found myself in the company of strangers but within a short time we were all on friendly terms. Later, as we became on very good terms, Mrs. Meadows said I could call her Doris. Doris would rise first each morning and she made sure everyone of us followed soon after.

She asked if I would like to be known as Beth; I found the name strange at first but it became familiar. Mr. Meadows, Robert, was Doris's husband. He called Doris his 'bit o' jam' as he was sweet on her. Fortunately, we all fitted in well together. In the snug at night we discussed all manner of things, but not religion; belief is something personal to everyone.

Doris would remind us of the world's unkindness to women, and not only in the house. A married woman's duty was to provide her husband with a clean home, food on the table and raise their children – and to be usable. In return, according to Doris, a woman relinquished ownership of wages and any personal property to her husband who could exercise power over the home and 'his woman'.

Nor was the world kind to women who strayed beyond normal boundaries; even men too. She told us of a young man by the name of James, recently apprenticed as a butler. He did not stay long at the house. His departure resulted from his penchant, when out on errands, for keeping his eyes open for pretty street girls and, as Doris called it, placing his hand inside the bodice or up the skirt of Katy, the long-suffering scullery maid. Mrs. Braithwaite, when she heard, dismissed him instantly with a sharp tongue. According to Doris much worse happened below stairs with men being warned against the 'solitary vice'.

In some houses of which she knew, the 'master' would regularly 'interfere' with one or other of the maids without any question or rebuke from anyone, simply because he was 'the master of the house'.

Doris had the highest regard for Mrs. Braithwaite and for the master – the Professor. Doris said that Mrs. Braithwaite had told her: "All good breeding includes kindness, courtesy, unselfishness, respect, tact, gentleness and modesty of deportment." I could discern that from mistress's behaviour.

As for dress, Doris, Gladys, Edith and Katy wore white dresses with grey aprons in the mornings for heavy cleaning; they wore black dresses with white aprons during afternoon and evening. Emma and I wore black dresses with white aprons throughout the day.

Golden-square proved a wonderfully pleasant experience, though my task of looking after the children and assisting their education proved work hard once Emma departed. I found the children somewhat constraining, though I managed to remain self-sufficient.

Compared with my life at home, the house offered every comfort, quite apart from being well-appointed and situated in a delightful location. In several rooms, pictures of Queen Victoria and Prince Albert hung from the wall. Mrs. Braithwaite had chosen all the furnishings, including the sweeping window curtains, long lace curtains to adorn the folding doors, and elaborate draperies over the mantelpiece to match the heavily fringed tablecloth. Expensive papers covered the walls with all the furniture built to a high standard; many pieces carried the most intricate of details.

At meal times, when family sat around the dining table, Doris would lay white tablecloth, napkins and white bone china tableware. Doris told us Mrs. Braithwaite adopted 'turning the table' whenever she had guests to dinner. Doris explained that you would talk to the person in your left for the first course, and the person on your right for the second course. And so on.

'The rule is that you keep changing for each course,' said Doris. I never forgot that.

We lower orders were required to wake at 5 o'clock with breakfast taken at seven following completion of certain tasks. Throughout the day, each person's work must be completed. In her first task of her day, Gladys would rake out fires, and black and polish fireplaces.

Luncheon, at 1 o'clock, consisted of three main courses, usually pies and meats, followed by dessert and tea. Supper at 9 o'clock comprised cold buffet and damson pie, or something similar. The days for the most part were long and hard; mine slightly less so though the children could prove tiresome. It might be argued that as servants we were deprived of our liberty, however no one discussed it.

We could eat only when master and mistress completed their meals. And, after the meat course, we invariably retired to Doris's room, called 'pug's parlour' where we relaxed, laughed and often engaged in girlish giggles. With no men present, and the room to ourselves, Doris would engage in what she called 'women's talk'. I learnt much from these, far more than I might ever dare to relate here.

And so with that, at Golden-square, I gradually realised life had become more complicated and difficult than I initially and innocently imagined.

For her part, Doris maintained a stern formality over the entire proceedings below stairs, instructing everyone to be habitually clean, and declaring it our duty to keep secret any of the master and mistress's daily habits. Doris acted as a Leviathan below stairs.

I could not help but notice how the professor and his wife much admired their children and their home. Mrs. Braithwaite treated us kindly yet firmly; she in return expected loyalty and hard work for long hours. Doris, whose experience extended to other domestic situations, confided she had not worked in a better house. I should count myself fortunate mistress engaged me, she once said.

Doris's tenure at the house outlasted any of those below stairs. As housekeeper, she held an important position. She carried a large bunch of keys which she laid down whenever she was cooking. Invariably she misplaced them, often asking me to help retrieve them. Doris made no social distinction. She believed in one for all and all for one.

Often Doris would say 'things are not what they used to be'. Only some 10 years previously, Golden-square comprised highly desirable houses; homes to artists, solicitors, surgeons, diamond merchants, attorneys and accountants. She told us that one by one, owners of the fine houses turned them over to letting for lodgings. She considered this 'awful'.

We who worked in the servants' department below stairs and beyond the green baize door, though classed as servants by the professor and his wife, were well respected. Doris claimed mistress, having found good workers, required that no one should leave, unless from misbehaviour. In some houses, below stairs workers ate frugal meals and generally were badly treated, often bullied or exploited.

Each week, Mrs. Braithwaite brought down the previous week's copies of the *Illustrated London News* and other journals for us to read in any spare time; often I would be first to take one to my room. Mrs. Braithwaite allowed me to borrow books from her library, as I so enjoyed reading. She made one proviso: I should always wear white gloves to handle books. Of course, I read stories to the children during the day, and invented some tales of my own.

Mrs. Braithwaite extended her kindness to me in several ways; she seemed to have a liking for me. In return, I tried hard to fit in with other people's lives. After a while, I also took on the added responsibility of lady's maid. Once or twice, I received good clothes to wear when mistress finished with them. Some were almost like new; they required only minor alteration to fit. The mistress even made some of her own clothes.

In the evenings, I read, played patience and engaged in needlework and other fancywork when the children had retired to bed; my mother had taught me how to sew. It did not concern me to wear 'cast offs'; I had no money to buy smart new clothes. Other servants also received items of discarded clothing, even footwear.

Mrs. Braithwaite provided ample food for all of us below stairs, usually made from leftovers, such as puddings, vegetables and meat. No one went hungry. I would say we enjoyed more 'meat and veg' than others similarly employed. And, anyone below stairs could go to church once a month, given Doris's approval, which was usually forthcoming

At first, I missed my parents even though they lived almost round the corner. I hardly saw them. No. 37 proved to be such a friendly house I soon settled in, playing my part in its running. In addition to Robert, who handled dirty and heavy work around the house, an occasional gardener would be employed. He worked in spring, summer and autumn; his accommodation always arranged elsewhere.

Next door, No. 36 was a private house until 1856 when the owners sold it to become a hotel. In 1863, the same building became part of the business employing my father, by which time he had finished work. In the meantime, I discovered No. 37 once served as the home of Samuel Cooper, a 'surgical writer'.

During my employment at Professor Braithwaite's house, numerous outbreaks of cholera occurred. Brewer-street, Broad-street, Poland-street, Vigo-street and Warwick-street did not escape. By the grace of God, my parents eluded illness; mother took special care. Living in Golden-square we missed the outbreak, caused mostly by people using water from street-pumps. Doris told us of deaths nearby. I found it a deeply worrying time.

Mrs. Braithwaite endeavoured to reassure us. She explained that the Grand Junction Company, which supplied the sub-district of Golden-square, extracted water from the River Thames at Kew. She said the company claimed its water to be almost entirely free of animal and vegetable impurities before distribution, and as such safe to use.

London, a city based on work, labour, power and commerce, also assumed the mantle of a great centre of leisure. Living in Golden-square, it soon became obvious which periods of the year were most popular with visitors. April, May, June and July served as the main 'season' with a large influx of people. For the well off, the period offered almost non-stop gaiety, parties and amusements.

In my head, I can still visualise the shouts and yells of the muffin man and other street sellers of London – Doris's favourites were the baked potato man and the hot elder wine seller; and the sight of lamplighters with their torches, the clatter of hoofs and the clink of harnesses as cabs with their iron wheels rumbled over the cobbled streets. On occasions, we would notice the appearance of some squalid ballad-singers; they appeared out of place in Golden-square.

During evening we could not miss the echo of passing footsteps, which some declared to be the true sound of London, while throughout the night could be heard the various striking clocks. Whenever it rained and before going to sleep, I would listen to the blustery raindrops on the windowpane. And on Sundays we could hear the tolling and pealing of parish bells as they summoned their flocks to church, while on warm summer evenings, sounds of music from practising flute or violin players floated in through opened windows. During the day, London gave out its own sound; more like a great growl.

Doris would frequently declare 'I don't know what the world is coming to.' She would claim 'we stand witness to the lowering of morals as folks become less prim and proper.' And she grumbled about young women becoming increasingly restless as they spoke openly of 'emancipation'. Somewhat restless myself, I kept quiet.

Sometimes, in the evening, we gossiped about young men, love and marriage. Doris opened my eyes to the world; in my innocence they had been securely closed. I learnt much from her. She said women should never 'trust a man who does not shine his boots or shoes'. As for true love, she described it as 'strong, unselfish affection blended with desire'. She said that to marry into wealth 'ought to be every girl's ambition' in order to escape the drudgery of the vulgarly working class. To her, a wife's duty was to please her husband, act as moral guardian, and provide love and comfort for the children. Doris saw it as a wife's responsibility to create a cherished family home; money did not always bring happiness, she would tell us.

She acted like a mother to us younger ones, and discouraged any 'followers' to the house. On a personal level, in quiet moments during our evening 'talks', I learnt more about womanhood from Doris than ever from my mother. Later, I remained grateful for her remarks, like her sensible advice that women should not venture out in the rain because of the time it took to dry clothing. Also, although I had learnt such matters from my mother, Doris never failed to impress on us the common belief that any woman who fell pregnant outside even an unsatisfactory marriage would never be able to redeem herself from the disgrace. As such it was 'better to be careful than sorry'.

One particular night, I had a dream of unlimited love from a young man who pledged to devote his whole life to me, without any regard to himself. Unlike most dreams which quickly fade next morning, that one has remained with me.

I worked at No. 37 for over six years; they were almost the brightest years of my life. Then, like a bolt from the blue, in late summer 1858, the professor sprang a surprise for all of us employed below stairs.

The master called me into his study to inform of the family's planned move to another part of London, some miles further north of Golden-square. My services would no longer be required. The professor expected the family's next residence to be smaller, not larger; they would thus not require as many staff.

The master said I could take time off to find new work; as a reliable employee, he would write an excellent reference. His news came as a great shock. As I assumed my employers found happiness where they lived, I never gave any thought to leaving.

No. 37 provided my first employment. As I lived in the same house as my employers, I would need to find work and somewhere to live. I could return to my parents, though I now wished to stand on my own two feet in search of work.

I did as father suggested when first seeking employment and purchased a copy of *The Times* in Oxford-street. In the evening, when work with the children finished, I returned to my room and settled down to scour the Personal Columns.

Page two of *The Times* usually contained the Wanted Column. I noticed some advertisements in French; while I knew some words of the language I did not fully understand the entire text. Two-thirds down the first column I read six lines which changed my life forever.

I have retained the item since; it provided my first employment obtained through my own effort.

WANTED. Respectable young woman of about 20 years and of good character as Housekeeper to a newspaper editor. She must be obliging and capable of cooking plain food and serve at table. Excellent references. As her master travels the country from time to time, she will need to take charge of the house. Wages £12 and beer found. Own room. Apply by letter only, with real name and address to Zeta, 12 Red Lion-court, Fleet-street.

I do not know to this day what attracted my attention. The advertisement seemed quite ordinary. One word stood out, 'Zeta'. Who or what did 'Zeta' represent? Father described Zeta as the sixth letter of the Greek alphabet; the origin of the most common pronunciation of the Roman letter Z. Father considered it a strange address to apply for a vacancy and urged caution. And why did the advertiser ask for 'real name and address?' Otherwise, it appeared an interesting position as it would allow me to progress. To be in charge of a household would be a new experience.

I began to draft a letter. Of course, I learned to write at the various schools I attended; indeed teachers praised me for the clarity of my script. I gave my age and experience, making alterations here and there. When satisfied, I wrote out the letter in neat, clear handwriting, keen not to make a single mistake.

The following day I posted the letter early. The next morning I received a reply from a Mr. Colburn. He requested I attend for interview at No. 7 Gloucester-road, north of Regent's Park, and Regent's Canal. I pondered: No. 37 and No. 7; would seven prove to be a lucky number? The letter required me to attend next morning at nine o'clock punctually, with references.

That morning I rose early, putting on my best outfit. It looked almost new. I brushed and pinned my hair and chose which hat and gloves to wear.

At nearly 22, I could offer more experience than when first seeking work. By that time, women increasingly were going out to work and, as Doris said so many times many people spoke out about greater emancipation for women, while active campaigners in Sheffield had formed their own society for female suffrage two years previously.

Father did not wish me to travel alone; he preferred instead my sister Harriet accompany me. I refused. After much discussion, he insisted I took a growler to ensure I arrived neat and tidy. My father, when wishing to appear dignified, much preferred to travel by growler, a four-wheeled cab drawn by a single horse with two people seated inside. He provided enough fare to permit return in safety by cab.

I arrived at 15 minutes to the hour, with ample time to inspect the exterior of the house. It gave every appearance of a large, imposing, three-storey building, suggesting the occupant as either a wealthy merchant or professional. The front door looked newly painted in black, giving it a crisp appearance. Steps to the side of the house led down to a cellar or basement. I walked some way down the road before returning. I climbed the four York stone steps and knocked on the door. I trembled: in fear or in excited anticipation? I stepped back to view the house again. A tall man with imposing features opened the door.

'Miss Browning?' he asked in a precise, but pleasant tone.

I have not forgotten his first words. They live with me

forever.

One word described him – imperious. I remember too his grey eyes. I could not help it. They contained a sparkle – even a hint of excitement. Could it be danger? Perhaps even then I should have taken notice of my own reservations.

I noticed he dressed fastidiously, with an air of vanity too. As to his question, I nodded my head, feeling myself blush slightly.

Service with Professor Braithwaite taught me to be polite to those above and below my station. I suddenly became extremely shy.

The man invited me into the hall where stood a grandfather clock; it was striking nine o'clock. After closing the door, he led me into a room at the front of the house dominated by a large desk and an equally large bookcase almost full of books. The number of books astounded me. They reminded me of one of father's sayings: 'There is as much glory in a kingfisher's feathers as in a whole shelf of books.'

The man sat down behind the desk; he asked for references. I could produce only one, from Professor Braithwaite. I handed it to him. While he read it, I looked around quickly. The furnishings alone gave every suggestion of a successful man. I noticed an upright wooden chair in front of the desk, a large fireplace with a fancy coalscuttle and two deep, comfortable armchairs. Around the room, on the walls, several pictures took pride of place. Unlike ordinary pictures, like those of family groups or landscapes, they illustrated locomotives discharging large clouds of black smoke, some with carriages. They looked strange.

On finishing he told me to be seated, asking me to explain myself and my duties at Professor and Mrs. Braithwaite's house.

Surmounting the first hurdle of starting to speak, although nervous, I found it easy to talk to him. I briefly described my family and the nature of my work for the last six years. I cannot postulate how quickly those years with the professor passed. It seems quite strange that I spent so much time in one house. I had almost become a member of the family – albeit a member very much at arm's length.

When I finished, he explained what would be required. Gradually, I became more accustomed to my surroundings. I realised the man seated at the desk could perhaps be only a few years older than myself.

He told me his name – Zerah Colburn. He gave his birth country as America. I noticed his accent was different; in fact, quite discernible. His American voice, though hard, seemed friendly, almost homely. It carried an air of excitement. His eyes, still with a sparkle, I found somewhat penetrating. He did not stare exactly, though he fixed his gaze on me. They compelled me to avert my eyes, looking instead down at the desk. I might become used to his eyes should I work for him, I remember thinking.

I noticed how crisply he pronounced the name Colburn. He did not sound the 'l', putting instead emphasis on the 'burn'. It sounded like Coburn. He carried an air of immaculate self-importance: his shoes, highly polished, protruded from the desk; above them sharply creased trousers. That would please Doris. Wavy hair and carefully manicured fingernails added to a fastidious appearance. From time to time, he removed a pocket watch from his waistcoat, as if he regarded time as important. Professor Braithwaite wore a similar timepiece.

He gave mention of the previous housekeeper who departed her employment without notice; then he asked how soon I could be released. He offered no explanation for the housekeeper's hasty withdrawal. I assumed she must indeed have left quickly; I could not see any sign of dust or dirt. Indeed, a strong aroma of beeswax on furniture and floor pervaded the air.

As I could begin immediately, I replied 'At once, Sir.'

'Hmm,' he said.

He described himself as editor of a weekly London newspaper devoted to engineering – that was a new word that I would hear much of during my life with Mr. Colburn. He travelled first to

England in 1857, and repeated his visit later the same year accompanied by his friend Mr. Alexander Holley, and a colleague, Mr. George May.

'Simply to live and breathe England's air at that time I then regarded as the climax of my life,' he said.

The trio's visit lasted some three months. During the period, he and Mr. Holley travelled to Paris, their first sight of the French capital with its wide avenues. It became clear to me that the two men, presumably Americans, had breathed another world to my lowly one. The city of Paris much impressed them, especially Mr. Holley. He described it as a city of beauty, elegance and fun while Mr. Colburn praised its intellectual energy, highlighting also his admiration for England, its rich heritage and its royalty. He wanted to return as soon as possible. London, its capital, in particular drew his attention; he called it the 'city of words'. He saw London as the 'capital' of books and newspapers; his love of writing drew him to seek employment in London as editor and journalist.

He added something I did not then appreciate: Britain led the world in harnessing power from coal, water and steam to drive heavy machinery. He said the industrial life of Britain he found fascinating, especially the steam-powered pumping stations, railways, coalmines and spinning mills; he believed railways accounted for the most outstanding invention of the century. Advances in industrial activity generally proved far wider and deeper in England than in America, he said, adding how much he admired the economic energy powering Britain at the time.

'Nothing can eclipse the railways for their great movement of people and commercial goods,' he told me. 'Their arrival marked the real beginning of Britain's greatness.'

From his remarks, I judged his interests extended far and wide, including many subjects about which I had never, even for a moment, given any thought.

He further described his fascination with London.

'No greater industry is concentrated more in London than the writing, making and distribution of the written word. It explains why I have come to London; for here there has been spectacular growth in the manufacture of words in books and newspapers.'

He added: 'Fifty years before I first stepped foot on this capital's streets, London offered nine morning newspapers and seven evening papers published daily. A further 17 appeared two or three times a week, three in French, can you believe. In 1853, publishers produced 3,000 books.'

As to my employment, he expected I would be 'much occupied' with my work on occasions; at other times I would be on my own for two or three days and nights at a time, with less to do. Would this be of concern? I recall telling him it would not. Sometimes, at No. 37, the housekeeper and I would be alone in the house. With such a large house, if we felt lonely in the evening, we observed from upstairs windows the sight of passers-by in Golden-square.

Mr. Colburn said he viewed punctuality and cleanliness as matters of great importance. I should not have been surprised at mention of punctuality; the house contained several clocks.

'There is never a finer quality than punctuality, Miss Browning.'

Then, for the first time, he referred to his wife and daughter in New York; he expected them to join him some weeks later. On their arrival, he planned to employ a housemaid for cleaning and other tasks. While this arrangement would entail less work for me, my responsibilities would increase in other directions, especially helping to look after his wife and child. He suggested a butler might be employed later.

As he planned to invite important people to dinner, he expected me to provide good, wholesome enjoyable fare. He enquired if I could cook to a high standard. I told him I would try my best to please.

'I am reliable and hard-working, Sir.'

'Can you cut thin slices of bread?' he asked. His request caught me unaware; a trick question perhaps? 'I will try my best,

Sir.'

'And are you clever with a needle?' he asked, and then without waiting for a reply added: 'Now that I live in England, I have acquired a passion for oysters,' he added. 'I have them at least once a month. Please ensure too you use Breton sea-salt butter. It slips down the throat with unbelievable silkiness. And we must have champagne at the ready. Oysters and champagne are most delicious.'

I reassured him on such matters. His desire for Breton butter completely foxed me; it might prove difficult. I did not then know where I could obtain such butter. The professor's cook, Doris, excelled in the kitchen. I often stood watching her at work; I even helped occasionally. I took the liberty of making copies of her best-liked recipes in a small notebook to show my mother; all tasted delicious. I lacked Doris's experience though occasionally, in the event of a straightforward meal, I did prepare and even cook one course while she hovered over me. We shared the secret; 'below stairs' always shared secrets. Doris behaved as a mother to me, I don't know why. Without children herself, she regarded me as a friend.

As Mr. Colburn spoke, I grew concerned; there would be much to occupy my mind. What he said next still resonates.

'Miss Browning, would you like to work here? Your wages are £12. I require you provide uniforms.'

It surprised me I did not have to convince him as to my efficiency. Presumably, my single reference provided evidence to meet his requirements. It amazed me how quickly he drew his conclusion. I could but say 'Yes, Sir. Thank you, Sir.'

'Good. You have one month's trial. It is now July. My wife will be here in August. You will start tomorrow at nine o'clock; punctually. You have one half day a week for yourself; I expect you in by 10 o'clock in the evening. Remember: no men here. I find a well-kept house directs a woman towards the path of virtue; the opposite leads them astray. I believe it is customary in this country that servants do not speak until spoken to. Is that true?

'Yes, Sir,' I replied.

'Good. Well, then I will now show you the house.'

He astounded me with his immediacy. Surely, he would have received other applicants. As to my wages, I knew good West End housemaids could command £17, whereas in the East End they received £13. However, as a concession he did grant me coals and candles, though he said he would remain firm and maintain a tight grip on everything that mattered to him. What he offered me did not match those rates and yet he would expect me to be a maid-of-all-work. Presumably, if I did not like the work, I could leave after one month.

He strode out of the library, as he called it, leading me into the study. He opened the door and said proudly: 'This house is quite famous. Not many years ago, the Mexican ambassador to London lived here. I am privileged. We are privileged. The house is well equipped as you will see if you look about yourself.'

A large desk with an equally large chair occupied the centre of the study. The burnished fire irons looked resplendent. A large table shared the room, covered with sheets of what appeared to be drawings.

'Remember the house must remain neat and clean, and when you polish in here do not disturb any papers or drawings on the table. And I mean any drawings. These are engineering drawings of national importance associated with my work. Drawers are always locked.'

'Of course, Sir.'

The study contained another large bookcase, with shelves piled high with papers. On the walls, illustrations of locomotives took prominence. On the fireplace mantle stood an imposing slate and marble mantle clock. I decided Mr. Colburn had made the house an extension of his place of work.

He led me to the dining room where a commanding mahogany table with chairs occupied the central position - it was quite usual to have mahogany in the dining room and rosewood in the drawing room. A large sideboard almost filled one wall. There I noticed decanters, glass and china; the heavy curtains were of velvet. Both rooms represented further an expression of Mr. Colburn's achievements.

He took me to the parlour and then to the basement with its voluminous kitchen and large pine table, two chairs and several large cupboards. We briefly looked into the scullery. A previous resident, an ambassador, had installed hot water, he told me. The scullery had a floor with red floor tiles and a stove in one corner.

'Watch for vermin in the scullery. I have observed them occasionally,' said Mr. Colburn. Then he added: 'I shall not require you to sleep in the kitchen; your room is at the top of the house, as I believe is customary in some houses.'

He pointed to a door leading to the cellar. He said I would find a garden to the rear of the house. He said the previous occupant of the house, a Mr. William Lamond from Edinburgh, displayed a keen interest in gardening. He had lived in the house for several years with his wife, young son and daughter. Mr. Lamond, an esteemed member of the Stock Exchange, employed a cook, a nurse and a housemaid.

I discovered much later from some documents that the house's most recent occupant had been a Mr. Lamond, 45, his wife Cordelia, 37, their cook Mary Read, 33, and nurse to the children, Mary Ann Farmer, 29. The documents gave the housemaid's name as Lucy – Lucy Taylor, aged 20. Although unknown to me at the time, this name would reverberate in my head for years to come. I also noticed the document sited Gloucester-road as being in the 'Ecclesiastical District' of St. Mark's, Regent's Park, a church later I visited regularly.

'I may employ a gardener,' said Mr. Colburn. 'It is quite a large garden; I have no interest in such pastimes. My work is my pastime.'

The downstairs rooms were relatively small and intimate compared with those at No. 37 Golden-square. The house, although sparsely furnished, contained furniture of high quality.

The rugs, deep and comfortable, emphasised the highly polished wood flooring.

The first floor contained four bedrooms, two large and two small, one of which appeared to be used as a dressing room. As we entered the principal bedroom I noticed first the good quality carpet. The surrounding handsome mahogany furniture comprised wardrobe, table, toilet table, a small bookcase and a chiffonier. The washstand held a basin, ewer, soap dish and another dish for toothbrushes. I noticed particularly the large bed took the form of a brass half tester with curtains only at the head, lined to match the furniture. The bed appeared much simplified against the four-poster Doris told us the professor shared with his wife. Gas jets illuminated the dressing mirror. A pair of candlesticks held prominent position on the mantle while a third stood on the dressing table.

We moved to a further room on the half landing with contained bathtub, hand basin and water closet.

He pronounced: 'It is for our use, you will be pleased to learn. The geyser to heat the water before use is powered by gas. Geysers are noisy, expensive and dangerous. So be careful. I will instruct you as to its use. Clean the pan closet meticulously and keep the door closed at all times. You may not be aware of it, Miss Browning, but a 'halting station' or public lavatory was installed in Fleet-street in 1851. You may not be aware of it but the first women's lavatory opened in the Strand, quite close to my work, in 1852.'

'Yes, Sir,' I replied, not knowing what else I could say.

We climbed a further flight of stairs to a floor with two rooms, a box room and a small attic-like room, containing travelling cases.

'This is your room,' said Mr. Colburn, showing me into one room with a fireplace; it contained a single bed, small wardrobe and dressing table with mirror. A chair stood by the bedstead, while a small hand basin and jug rested on a white wooden stand.

The previous occupant must indeed have departed quickly;

ashes remained in the fireplace. This would be my future sanctuary, a refuge.

We retraced our footsteps to the hall. At the front door, Mr. Colburn gave one final instruction: 'I shall leave the running of the house to you until my wife arrives. But the house must be neat and clean, with everything arranged to suit my taste.'

Then, before allowing me to speak, he bid goodbye, repeating he expected me the following day, promptly at nine o'clock.

Outside, I crossed the road, making my way to Regent's Park. I sat on a park bench. It had all happened far too quickly. One minute, I sat attending an interview; the next, a Mr. Colburn had offered me the position of housekeeper. Would I regret my decision to embark on this part of my journey through life?

There would be much work in contrast to life at No. 37, as I would be combining the tasks of housekeeper and housemaid, both of which I had not undertaken previously. On the other hand, I would shortly receive additional help to meet the requirements of two further people, mother and daughter, of whom I knew nothing. What would they be like? Would they like my plain cooking? Indeed, would I be able to manage to cook on my own? Untested by anyone, would my cooking be found pleasing?

The more I considered my new employment, the more my doubts gathered momentum. And, as I would learn to my cost, my employer's secrets would emerge later.

Had I made my greatest mistake?

I walked to the cab rank; I instructed a waiting driver.

'Number 37 Golden-square, please,' I said.

'Yes, ma'am,' replied the driver. 'At once, ma'am.'

Chapter Two
My new employment

ZERAH COLBURN arrived in the world on Friday the thirteenth. This might have been looked upon as an unlucky omen for an infant whose uncle, as a boy, had been one of the cleverest in the world. And, as if that was not bad enough, the baby arrived in January 1832, the third coldest winter ever experienced by the states to the north of New York City. The birth proved far from easy. So much so that the infant's mother, Sarah, aged 40, vowed never to give birth again.

And so it was on Friday, 13th January 1832, a child was born to local farmer, Zebina Colburn and his wife Sarah who lived adjacent to the small township of Saratoga. With a population of around 2,500 it nestled in the countryside upstate of New York city. Zebina, one of nine children, had the benefit of being Sarah's junior by nine years. His parents, Abiah and Elizabeth Colburn, lived many miles to the north in Hartford, Vermont; Vermont could be much colder than New York State.

Zebina lacked some of the unique attributes of his younger brother, 'clever' Zerah, who became famous as the 'calculating child'. Indeed, brother Zerah proved to be so clever that his father took him to England and France to earn money performing in front of noble gentry and audiences in theatres and halls. As a mathematical 'freak', Zerah could solve the most difficult problem any member of the audience might throw at him.

Zebina and Sarah hoped their much-prized son would become a genius like his uncle and so chose to call him Zerah, after Zebina's famous brother who, by then, had become a devout Methodist preacher in Cabot, Vermont.

Abiah's money-raising expedition to England did not please Zebina, or elder brother, Green, who both were given the task of supporting their mother during their fathers' absence by working on the land. Zebina and Green were just 12 and 15 respectively when their father and Zerah.

So prolonged was the father and son's absence that Zebina had reached the age of 24 by time the duo returned. Zebina's first marriage, having faltered and eventually dissolved, had prompted a move to Hillsborough, New Hampshire, to begin a new life.

Hillsborough, on the banks of the Contoocook River, had become into a thriving industrial activity following the construction of a cotton mill with its adjacent river providing the power.

Zebina, drawn by the prospect of work, easily found work in the growing town. It was in Hillsborough that he met and married Sarah Ayer, daughter of William and Mary Ayer, then residents of Hillsborough with its population of 1,800. Following their wedding, Sarah and Zebina decided to leave Hillsborough – Sarah had no wish to live in the same town as her parents. In any case, more accustomed to farming, Zebina did not enjoy working in the mill where he found the noise of the machinery deafening. The couple decided to move Saratoga, New York, where Zebina could started yet again and become a small time farmer.

The happiness that Sarah and Zebina enjoyed on the arrival of a son, however, proved to be short lived. Aged just 37, Sarah's husband Zebina died when their boy was only five years old. Sarah felt understandably 'robbed'. Not only had her husband failed to at least match his father's lifespan of 61 years, and who ironically died in London, but Zebina's death left Sarah destitute, so much so that she had no alternative but to return 'cap in hand' and live with parents William and Mary in Hillsborough.

Sarah, poor and somewhat infirm, remained resolute that her young son should have the best she could manage. She arranged for him to attend a district school where his attendance was strictly limited. However, although Zerah lacked his uncle's extraordinary intelligence, Sarah soon discovered her son possessed above-average intelligence. With a head for numbers he also demonstrated an insatiable appetite as a reader, devouring every book he could find in the remote country town. He seemed able to remember everything he read.

As soon as she could, Sarah searched to find work for her 12 years' old son. As he had expressed a fervent desire not to take up farming like his father, Sarah found him something more appropriate; a job keeping monthly accounts, invoices and payrolls in the offices of the Sugar River Manufacturing Company in Claremont, New Hampshire. There, later, it was not uncommon for him to be found paying the hands, who then numbered some 200.

At the Sugar River Manufacturing Company young Zerah, for the first time, witnessed the sounds and motions of machinery in operation, in this case cotton machinery. This proved to be Zerah's introduction to mechanical engineering.

As it happened, Sugar River Manufacturing Company, a new business having started in 1831 – a year before Zerah's birth – had received a charter to manufacture cotton and woollen goods using the energy resources of the nearby Sugar River. In 1846 the name changed to Monadnock Mills and for a century the mills were an important factor in the growth and prosperity of Claremont.

Meanwhile, long before his untimely death, Zebina had known from Colburn legend that the family could trace its lineage back to one of the early New England settlers. Edward Colburne, aged 17, had crossed the North Atlantic from England with his elder brother Robert on the sailing ship *Defence* which, under the command of Captain Edward Bostock, departed from London in September 1635. After a 54-day voyage against prevailing headwinds, just 15 years after the famous voyage of the *Mayflower* with its complement of separatists, the sailing ship with passengers and cargo duly arrived in Boston.

Passengers described the voyage as not only frightening but extremely dangerous; it was not uncommon for ships to flounder on the hazardous trans-Atlantic journey.

Consequently, Zerah Colburn grew up with great admiration for young Edward from Colchester, England. Indeed, Zerah (whose mother died aged 85 on Tuesday, 13th June 1876 in Bradford, New Hampshire) was so taken by Edward's exploits that he made a pact with himself – that one day he would leave the wilds of New Hampshire and journey to England to witness the treasures of his forebears' country.

In his early teens, Zerah joined Locks and Canals Company in Lowell, Massachusetts. This cotton machinery maker prompted his fascination with steam and locomotives. He then worked voraciously with several locomotive builders before joining *American Railroad Journal* in New York as a writer.

In New York, he married Adelaide Felicita Driggs, a woman many years older. Following a disagreement with the editor of *American Railroad Journal*, Henry Varnum Poor, Colburn created his own weekly paper, the *Railroad Advocate*. After a while, and ever restless, he sold a half share to Alexander Lyman Holley, a like-minded young man, the son of a banker and Connecticut governor. Colburn's attempt to operate a saw mill failed, as did selling locomotive tyres in competition with Lowmoor's tyres made in England.

Disillusioned, Colburn returned to writing. He developed a passion for travel and in England learned at first hand the spirit that fired the Industrial Revolution. A short spell as editor of a weekly London engineering paper, *The Engineer*, rekindled his interest in publishing his own newspaper. He returned to New York to breathe new life into the *Railroad Advocate*, but without success. A three-month study of locomotive practice in England and France by Colburn and Holley provided material for a substantial report for Presidents of American railroads.

This reaffirmed Colburn's love of England to which he returned as editor of his previous paper, *The Engineer*. Settling down in London in 1858, Zerah Colburn became a man about town, drawing satisfaction from the most important city in the industrial world.

OOOOOOOOOOOOOOOOOOOO

SITTING back in the cab I reflected on events. Again, I remained surprised how quickly Mr. Colburn concluded his decision to employ me. Could I be leaping headlong into a lion's den?

On my return to Golden-square, I paid the cab driver. Once inside, friends below stairs asked of my progress. I gave them my news; they seemed genuinely pleased.

Later that day, I went to see mistress to inform her of my intention to leave immediately for my new employment next day. She paid my wages, adding a small surplus as a token for the quality of my work. She gave praise for my honesty, and for being dutiful and hardworking. She offered good wishes for the future, and informed I could retain uniforms and clothes given me.

She told me I could expect to find the work very hard and demanding, quite different from anything I had so far undertaken. She again added her best wishes that I would not be taking on too much

'You will find new surroundings strange to accommodate for a while,' she told me. 'The hours will seem long and the work unremitting. And you may feel lonely and isolated, but persevere. Try not to worry. I am sure you will succeed.'

Mistress also handed over a thick journal with 'Best wishes for the future' written inside the cover, which I found touching.

'You might find this useful in your new position,' she said, suggesting I make various notes in it, or turn it into a diary. She asked my address and promised to write. She shook my hand, bidding me farewell. Collecting belongings and saying goodbye to everyone, I left for my parents' house where I spent the night.

My parents, pleased to see me, took opposing views as to my new employment. Mother required a description of the house and the 'Master', as she called him. I told her as much as I considered appropriate. Her words said it all: 'It sounds to me as though you will have your hands full in more ways than one.

You'll be working from morning till nightfall, I'll be bound. Those floors will require much scrubbing. You'll be on your hands and knees; polishing too, more likely.' Nevertheless, she expressed some pleasure in my success at gaining work.

Father appeared less happy, accusing me of knowing nothing of my new employer. I would be alone in the house with a stranger, at least until his wife arrived. Although he described himself as editor of a London newspaper, my employer nonetheless was a journalist. To father, all journalists were naturally curious and as such untrustworthy.

Father promised to make enquiries; meanwhile he instructed vigilance. At the first sign of trouble I was to return home.

The following morning I awoke early, packing clothes into a case. I would be within relatively close distance of my parents, so should I need anything more I could return home to collect it. Although father showed concern as to what the future might hold, he handed me some coins to add to Mrs. Braithwaite's. He also offered my fare for a cab.

I caught a growler in Regent-street at a quarter past eight; I arrived ten minutes early.

After paying off the driver, I looked at the outside of the house, for the first time taking stock of my surroundings. The house, I recalled, had 12 rooms on three storeys, a basement and attics presumably, and a garden at the back. There could much lot of work for one person. It stood amongst similar handsome brick houses. The villas on 'our' side of the road looked magnificent. I would be living in a respectable area. In my mind, I was already calling it 'our' road. Perhaps one day I would have time to explore it further. Father told me Regent's Park Canal could be found nearby.

I mounted the steps to the front door. Would I be scrubbing these very steps one day soon?

'I am pleased to see you bright and early,' said Mr. Colburn, answering the door. 'I am keen to be at work; I have much to occupy me today. Come. Make yourself at home, Miss Browning.

You will find food in the pantry.'

Once inside, he continued: 'Please busy yourself as best you can for your first day. You will find my study door locked. I shall be out all day; I will return early evening. I will not require a meal tonight, however when I return we can discuss your duties more fully. Meanwhile, please be sure to water the potted palms.'

And with those few words, he disappeared through the front door, banging it behind him.

Alone in my new employment, the deathly silence seemed almost eerie.

I carried my case upstairs to my room and unpacked; I noticed one or two of the steps creaked. I explored the house. It seemed as tidy as before; as if no one lived there.

What would I do? Would I have enough work to keep me occupied all day, seven days a week? Of course, I soon found out to my cost. For my first task, I decided to clean my room, including the fireplace, to make it look smart.

Left alone, I realised that while the house appeared quite large, first impressions could be deceptive. Although by no means as large as my previous employer's house in Golden-square, I found a great deal to occupy my time. I was now in sole charge; a big responsibility for someone inexperienced in housework for such a dwelling as this. In the scullery, I found implements for house cleaning. In the pantry I found bread and cheese. They appeared fresh.

Changing into my uniform I began work. Deciding to follow Mrs. Braithwaite's practice, I wore a white dress and grey apron for morning work; a black dress with white apron for afternoons and evenings.

I set myself the task of scrubbing the floors. My white dress soon became filthy dirty – I would have to wash it. The floors looked as though they had not been cleaned for weeks. The scrubbing brushes were worn out. I would need new ones to be effective.

I quickly realized that without Doris I no longer had anyone to give advice, or to wake me each morning. At first this caused me great concern, but I settled soon into a rhythm as I listened for the striking of nearby church clocks.

I soon became familiar with my new surroundings. The house appeared spotless with nothing out of place. The previous housekeeper must have been thorough in her work with the exception of the cellar. To my horror, on opening the door, I immediately detected an air of mustiness. On further investigation, with the aid this time of a candle, I could see spiders and black beetles in corners, and fungus on the walls. I reminded myself one day to ask my employer what, if anything should be done with the cellar.

Doris taught us how to move silently – to be neither seen nor heard. I knew too I should adopt strict routines to complete all my work satisfactorily.

In the evening, as the clock in the hall approached seven, I heard the bell clang in the kitchen. I made my way quickly to the hall door, and recognised the outline of Mr. Colburn.

'Good evening, Miss Browning. Has it been a good day?'

'Yes, Sir,' I replied, wondering why he did not use his key. "But I need a new scrubbing brush and other items."

'Come. In the study we can discuss that and your duties. You can tell me of yourself and I likewise. I have taken the liberty of purchasing a copy of *Mrs. Beeton's Book of Household Management* in Charing Cross-road. You will find it useful. It is published by her husband, Samuel Beeton. By presenting you with this has no reflection of your capabilities as housekeeper. However, at some point in the future you might like to aspire to *service á la francais* where food is the main display feature of any table sitting. But that can come in good time.'

'But before that, I offer you another: *A Plain Cookery for the Working Classes*, by Charles Elmé Francatelli, a former chef to the Queen. It has over 200 simple recipes, some you may not have seen. Books are essential for all our education,' he added.

I thanked him, proudly holding my new books but concerned

about future expectations. I followed him to the study where he instructed me to sit.

'Come, explain yourself and family again.'

With little more to tell, I had soon finished. His slight drawl gave the impression of a man of relaxed disposition, though I noticed he sat on the edge of his chair, as though wishing to be elsewhere on other business.

'I know few of your customs here in England with regards to servant staff; you must forgive me if I am not as practiced as your previous employer, Professor Braithwaite,' he said. 'I will tell you of myself, and from this you will understand my purpose in England.'

His openness surprised me. Usually, those of us below stairs heard only indirectly of their employer's personal matters.

'First things first, you tell me your name is Elizabeth Susanna Browning. I shall call you Lizzy. I could call you Eliza, but I do not like that name for a young woman such as yourself. Lizzy reminds me of Jane Austen's *Pride and Prejudice*, which I have read twice; it contains a lady by the name of Lizzy. You will address me as Mr. Colburn, or Sir. Do you understand?'

Lizzy? I did not much like the name Lizzy. I preferred Beth, but could not bring myself to say so. My parents always called me Elizabeth. Not content to use my own name, like Doris Mr. Colburn had given me a new one.

'Do you not like it?

'Oh, yes, Sir,' I replied, guilty of having told a lie. 'It will take some getting used to, Sir. I was known as Miss Browning or Beth.'

'That is fine, Lizzy it is.'

Then by way of explanation, he added proudly: 'This house is quite famous, as I mentioned before. I have read the deeds of No. 7 Gloucester-road; in the early 1850s the building housed no less than the Mexican ambassador and the Mexican consulate. At that time, the majority of the houses in the road served as private dwellings, occupied for the most part by important people, including architects and surgeons. That helps explain this fine house.'

He quickly changed the subject and spoke of his upbringing. Born in Saratoga in the state of New York, his mother and father worked a smallholding, but were poor. Aged five, any security attached to his childhood ended following the death of his father Zebinah; he and his mother Sara returned to Hillsborough, her parents' home town in another state, New Hampshire, to continue their impoverished lives.

His uncle, Zerah Colburn, shared the same name. Because of his uncle's remarkable gift for mental arithmetic and extraordinary memory, his father brought him to England to be exhibited on stage in return for money. The money they received helped the poverty-stricken American family.

'Most Colburns are poor. Through his remarkable gift, uncle could make large calculations in his head. He later became professor of Latin, Greek, French and Spanish at Norwich University. I share some of my uncle's genius for mathematics and appetite for knowledge.'

After a difficult relationship with his mother, Mr. Colburn started work, aged 13, at a machine shop owned by Mr. L. B. Tyng in Lowell, close to Boston, in Massachusetts. Mr. Tyng proved a valued friend.

As he explained this, I found it difficult to recall peoples' names; later, I overcame this when it became necessary to do so for my work. Even less did I understand the purpose of a machine shop.

My employer seldom attended school, except for an occasional week or so. Nonetheless, he would read any book he could lay his hands on. As he spoke, I began constructing a picture of his young life; it must have been a struggle without a father.

Mr. Colburn continued with his compelling litany of how in 1846 he received employment as a clerk from Mr. A. L. Brooks, an extensive lumber manufacturer and dealer in Lowell. With him he studied machinery, especially stationary and locomotive steam engines.

At that point, I blurted out: 'I saw my first steam locomotive at the Great Exhibition.' He appeared impressed.

His intense interest in steam-powered machines, as well as locomotive steam engines used as a means of transport, acted fortuitously to bring him to the attention of Mr. William Burke, superintendent of the Lowell Machine Shop. Through Mr. Burke he received grounding in skills that later formed the basis of future work, particularly as he became a persuasive advocate of steam power.

He told me Mr. Charles Dickens, who he described as an English genius', visited America in 1842 where there was great enthusiasm for his work. However, the writer had no love of the country where Mr. Colburn was born and raised. Of the many places Mr. Dickens attended, the Lowell Machine Shop stood prominent and where, I was told, he was much impressed with the well-educated mill-girl workers.

'My pen and ink sketches appeared of such merit to Mr. Burke, he at once employed me in the drafting room. I was 15 at the time. Mr. Burke considered it remarkable I understood all the principles of machinery at such an early age. In short, machines were my passion.'

At the time I thought this rather boastful.

He enjoyed the work so passionately that eventually he became superintendent in a locomotive works. Though he took great pleasure in designing these machines, his real fulfilment emerged as a writer about machinery.

'Above all else, I am a sophisticated writer,' he repeated confidently, adding 'It gives me such great thrill to write and to be aware that others will read my words.'

He admitted his success as a locomotive designer did not develop as he expected; a rare admission of weakness in the years I knew him.

By the age of 20, in 1853, his activities had covered many

employments, though his next employer changed his life, he revealed. Mr. Tyng introduced him to the editor of a weekly New York newspaper, the *American Railroad Journal*.

As soon as he mentioned this, I knew at once how close we were in years; of course, his worldliness made him substantially more mature. Throughout his frank explanations he stared at me, as if trying to look through me. I knew to return his stare was impolite and, feeling uncomfortable, from time to time I lowered my gaze.

'Joining the paper required my move to New York where I met and married my wife. Soon, I disagreed with the editor. We did not see eye to eye. When that happens, someone has to yield. I decided to leave.'

He looked hard at me. I no longer held his gaze. I looked to one side. I can remember his words even now, as they hold such special significance. Someone had to yield. I could not believe his forthrightness. Did he have an inflated sense of his own worth? And did his previous housekeeper have to depart quickly?

Working at the newspaper gave him the idea for his own weekly 'railroad' newssheet, aged 21. And that word appeared again – 'railroad'; it came as a new word to me. I looked puzzled.

'What is a railroad?' I asked, forgetting myself.

'Well, over here you call them railways; we in America call them railroads. Many years ago, coal wagons ran on plate ways – metal plates attached to timber baulks. When rails took their place, the word railway was naturally used. Your Mr. Dickens, in his description of the coming of the railways in *Dombey and Son*, described them as railroads. It is common.'

Once again, his enormous breadth of knowledge came as a surprise. My sense of inferiority immediately deepened.

'Coincidently, my wife gave birth to our daughter,' he went on, quickly changing subjects. 'She is now on holiday in Weymouth with Sarah Pearl; their health suffered greatly during the voyage from New York. They will join us here when they are ready,' he added by way of explanation, before continuing.

Meanwhile, at about the same time, a partner joined him in his publishing venture, a young man of similar age with a deep understanding of locomotives. He gave his name as Alexander Holley.

I looked at the clock on the mantelpiece. It showed nearly eight o'clock. How time flew. He noticed my glance.

'Are you tired? I will finish soon.'

'Somewhat, Sir,' I replied.

'Well, I found the job unexciting. Holley agreed to buy a share of my newssheet and edit it, while I took up land warrants in Iowa. These proved unsatisfactory; likewise the saw mill I bought into. I returned to New York to sell railroad tyres for Ames Iron Works. I worked with Ames for some months and eventually lost interest.'

I began to consider whether his life had been cursed in some way by its early promises of success. Then he continued.

'Missing writing so much, I returned to New York to work with Holley. And, because of Ames, I longed to visit England. At the time, Ames's railroad tyres competed with Lowmoor tyres imported from your country. I convinced Holley to pay part of my trip to England. While in London, in early 1857 I met Mr. Edward Healey, owner and editor of a weekly newspaper called *The Engineer*. He began the paper in 1856. That year marked the end of the Crimean War but, more important for him, a year earlier the government had abolished the penny newspaper stamp that prompted so many new newspapers. Mr. Healey urged that should I work for him, however as Holley needed me more, I returned to America.'

The visit to England, including the cities of Birmingham, Newcastle-upon-Tyne and Manchester, made a lasting impression on Mr. Colburn. He described Birmingham as a city of 1,000 trades. He told me if something was not made in Birmingham, it was not made anywhere. In Newcastle, Mr. Stephenson's locomotive works acted as one of the largest employers in the north-east of England. Of London he described it as the city of Mr. Charles Dickens, the famous English writer. He recommended I read his works. He praised Mr. Dickens as a journalist and as an author, and for these he commanded his respect.

While in England, and shocked by the brutality of men's labours, Mr. Colburn pledged to expose the many sweatshops housing 'creatures who lived in the wilderness of mean hovels of the manufacturing towns'. He yearned one day to return to England.

'The poor have no childhood,' he said. 'That is tragic.'

Among those he met on that visit was Mr. James McConnell, widely respected in Britain at the time for the part he played in the founding of the Institution of Mechanical Engineers as well as for 'Mac's Mangle', a locomotive that could swiftly and neatly trim edges from station platforms. Mr. Colburn said he was born in Fermoy, Co. Cork.

Mr. Colburn also said Mr. McConnell had become known as 'Handsome Mac', for obvious reasons. His name I did not forget. On our first meeting later, I had to admit his nick-name most appropriate.

By the time Mr. Colburn arrived back in America, panic among the banks compelled the two partners to close the *Railroad Advocate*.

'I implored Holley we should travel to England to detail the country's railroads for a special report,' he told me, continuing to call them railroads, not railways. 'As I had read so much about England, I wanted to see more of it and meet some of its famous people.'

'My family, the Colburns, sailed from England two hundred years ago. They left behind a country now home to an entire industrial revolution that has spawned huge engineering works for armouries, bridges, ships, steam engines, locomotives and railroad lines. Britain is the most advanced country in the world. You must be proud to be English and live in England, Lizzy.'

'We spent three months in England in 1857. We arrived for

the planned launch on 3rd November of the steam ship *Great Eastern* from David Napier's yard on Burrell's Wharf, on the Isle of Dogs. The shipyard laid her keel in December 1853. Due to a three months' delay to the launch, we had to return to New York without witnessing the epic event. We published our report the following year. I loved England so much I vowed to return and work at *The Engineer*. And, well, here I am.'

He described it as ironic he should journey to England while many poor people from Russia, Italy, Germany and France were sailing in the opposite direction to seek their fortune in America.

'America is the favoured destination for French and Germany in search of a new life. For me, the engineering profession in America is less respected, less profitable. That is why I have come here. In England there are those with vision, intellectually curious people wedded to the notion of progress; they are determined to improve their own lives and those of others. Did not the English win at Waterloo?'

'Thirty years before my arrival here, the Rainhill Trials triggered the birth of the Liverpool to Manchester Railway. Since then the railways have spread throughout Britain and the world. The railways now criss-cross this country, opening it up in a manner not previously thought possible. People are no longer tied to working within walking distance of their homes, while residents of inland towns are able to eat fresh fish,, delivered straight from the sea. They represent a marvellous achievement by the engineer.'

As a child, I never gave a moment's consideration to railways, let alone ever saw one move, though father briefly mentioned them from time to time. Mr. Colburn said the railways played a large part in all our lives. They affected the entire population, even those who never travelled by train as the railways transported food and goods, transforming their lives.

Mr. Colburn explained that just before he and Mr. Holley returned to America he had the pleasure of riding on the footplate of an important locomotive, called a Patent, from

Euston to Bletchley. Designed by Mr. James McConnell of Wolverton Works, he briefly had the pleasure of meeting him, but Mr. Colburn assured me the famous engineer would be one of many important men he would invite to the house for discussion and dinner

I managed to keep pace with his life story; it spilled from his lips with such speed as he appeared to show such ferocious ambition and undiminished self-belief. Here indeed I witnessed a man who, through his own energy and exceptional gifts, had raised himself from poverty.

Then, with what I considered a degree of frankness, Mr. Colburn repeated his inexperience of dealing with servants. He knew servants were common amongst better-off households as several well-known engineers, friends of his, employed them.

He said something else quite extraordinary. He spoke of slavery in America; how black people served as slaves to white people. I have forgotten the details; I can only recall his reference to the relationship between master and slave. I wondered if perhaps mention of slavery ought to hold some hidden relevance for me. Did he perhaps liken servants in England to slaves in America? I did not agree with slavery, although it seemed widespread in America.

Even today as I write, I do not know why he made reference to slavery in America, unless in some way he wanted to give me some kind of signal. If they were signals I did not notice them; they went over my head. He said simply: 'Soon they will be free.'

Were slaves the same as slaveys in England? I thought at the time.

He then mentioned a man he admired. The name of Mr. Samuel Smiles meant nothing then; but I have not forgotten it. Mr. Smiles published a book with the title *Self Help*; Mr. Colburn told me he read it twice from cover to cover. He counselled I should read it, but I did not.

He praised Smiles, who preached self-improvement, the discipline of hard work, dignity of labour and a desire for self-improvement.

'That I have been successful is due in no small part to my obsessive zeal for engineering and writing. I hope you have a passion for work, Lizzy. I have also known humiliation; that is a feeling you do not forget.'

For the first time, he used my abbreviated name. It surprised me to hear it. For a moment, I wondered to whom he referred. Plainly his writings made him proud, but did his humiliation make him humble or angry? That was something I would find out. Mr. Colburn said that at *The Engineer* he spent much time writing, acting as a 'clear-sighted guide' on engineering matters.

It seemingly required much effort to fill the newspaper each week with information. In this respect, his insatiable appetite for newspapers, journals and learned papers, and his travels throughout the country to manufacturers and so on, provided the editorial material he needed.

'I may leave the house early some mornings to visit the provinces. I also attend meetings; sometimes evening lectures. I shall not be here much. As I explained, my wife and daughter Sarah Pearl will arrive shortly. Then there will be more work for you. My wife is widely travelled; as a young woman she visited Trinidad many times with her parents. She comes from a large family – the Driggs family.'

He expected I would keep the house scrupulously clean, wind clocks and 'process' his clothes through washing and ironing. He would require clean shirt and underwear every day. Finally, he reminded me to wind the hall clock once every seven days.

'I am fastidious,' he reminded me. 'I demand cleanliness and orderliness; I want all things in places I can find them. In other words, young woman, I expect to be looked after efficiently.'

He requested I light a cheery little fire in his bedroom during winter months before retiring, especially when he took early morning rail journeys to the north of England or Scotland.

He required luncheon on Saturday and Sunday, unless otherwise instructed. He would provide housekeeping each week, out of which I would deduct my wages. If I needed more, because of lavish dinners he might arrange, I should ask. Otherwise he would settle accounts personally. He said I would find housekeeping a source of strength.

He would not require dinner in the evening, unless he instructed otherwise; he planned to attend the 'Gentlemen's Club' he had recently joined.

'Those are the mechanics of it, Lizzy.'

'Yes, Sir,' was as much as I could say.

'If you need anything, ask. You may not see much of me each day; we will be as ships that pass in the night. Do not be afraid to speak Lizzy, should you need help. As to your cleaning equipment, I shall leave money in the hall tomorrow for you to purchase your needs. See to it.'

Abruptly he added: 'You can leave.'

I left the room, saying, 'Thank you, Sir. Goodnight, Sir,' and closed the door. Later, in the privacy of my bedroom, I reflected how difficult it had been to stave off a sense of relief when he finished, but also how much he revealed. With much to absorb, I made some notes. It pleased me to have Mrs. Braithwaite's journal although I realised the challenge of maintaining a record of my new employment. As to the work itself, I became concerned I had indeed taken on more than I could deal handle.

For the next little while, life settled into a routine. With a very small amount of time to myself; only in the evenings could I add to my journal. And, as I spoke with few people, except when shopping, I was left free to do my work.

On some occasions, when his study was not locked, I gave it as thorough a clean as I could. I tried to move the large table in the centre of the room, in order to beat the carpet beneath it. But I could not dislodge it. I then glanced at the large drawings on the table. According to wording at the top of various sheets, the drawings depicted locomotives. As I carefully lifted the corners of the sheets, I could see other illustrations of rolling stock, bridges and ships' engines.

One day, Mr. Colburn returned early; he caught me inspecting the drawings. He offered to explain. That started my journey of discovery into a new world. I learned some aspects of engineering from him, though only at the fringes. While I considered him well equipped with knowledge that would make him a good teacher, he could be impatient, impulsive and easily distracted. Yet I learned much.

Concerned always to achieve high standards with my cooking, it pleased me to find Mr. Colburn consumed everything I placed in front of him. He clearly enjoyed a healthy appetite. I varied his meals using meat, fish and poultry. He provided ample money for my needs, though I never spent more than necessary.

He mentioned, should I so desire – he did not make it compulsory – an arrangement for me to attend the National Training School for Cookery.

'It is not a reflection of your cooking, Lizzy. I will pay your two guineas fee. I can easily arrange matters; the experience will assist with the forthcoming rather lavish dinner parties I plan.'

I trembled at the prospect of preparing food for 'lavish' parties. Would I be able to satisfy my master's expectations?

We exchanged only small conversation, mostly concerning the rudiments of daily life. He went to work, returning sometimes long after I retired to bed. His energy appeared boundless. From time to time, he paid compliments as to the food I prepared. Above all, he demanded perfection; he required everything in its place. Increasingly, as I soon discovered, he would control me too beyond measure.

As time went on, I became friendly with the housekeeper next door; during spare moments, we met and spoke briefly. She occasionally joined me in the kitchen for a cup of tea.

Life turned out to be quite humdrum, though I did attend the school for cookery (for which Mr. Colburn did indeed pay the fees) where I met other young women in service. From time to time, I asked Mr. Colburn if he found my housekeeping satisfactory; he replied always, 'everything is fine, Lizzy.'

Increasingly, I placed him on a pedestal as admiration for his wide knowledge deepened. It proved a new experience to be in such close contact with a man who clearly had struggled to educate himself and who brought his work home. He did however keep the most irregular working hours.

On one occasion he informed me, seemingly for no particular reason, *The Engineer*'s offices occupied 163, Strand, on the corner with Norfolk-street. At the beginning of the paper's life, the owner, Mr. Healey entrusted printing of *The Engineer* to Mr. Samuel Taylor of Greystoke-place, Fetter-lane where Mr. George Reveirs worked in the composing room.

Infrequently, Mr. Colburn would walk from the house to his office; most days he made the journey by cab. Once or twice he mentioned the desirability of a pied-à-terre as a means of escape; somewhere where he could dress before attending formal meetings or dinners at one or other of the institutions. I guessed that 'other life', the life at the office, allowed him to enjoy life as a bachelor; dining well, drinking, and who knows, what else. But such properties were expensive to maintain, he would complain. He always used a cab to and from the printers to meet Mr. Reveirs with whom he would pass the newspaper for press each week. Mr. Reveirs typeset the original prospectus heralding the arrival of *The Engineer* in 1856.

Sometimes, when Mr. Colburn returned to the house with large rolls of drawings, he might explain one or two. Gradually, I took more interest in his activities, understanding a small part of what engaged him so much.

Subjects of most interest included the theory of steam, boiler explosions, iron and steel, a possible trans-Atlantic cable, proposals for a canal at Suez and, as I learned later, the *Great Eastern* steam ship. Each topic formed part of a closed book nevertheless I gradually became familiar with some aspects.

I found time to visit my parents. If careful with the remains from housekeeping, I could travel by cab; this I much preferred. I began to feel quite content; even happy. I became experienced in handling money and my confidence grew.

The first major disturbance to our routine occurred when Mr. Colburn announced his wife and daughter would arrive shortly from their protracted holiday on the south coast.

Unsure of quite what to expect, I imagined it would be strange to have another woman in the house; a child too. I almost regarded the house as my own; just Mr. Colburn and me. Soon there would be two more women.

Mrs. Colburn might have different requirements. I considered my standards high. My mother and Doris between them gave excellent grounding; I would need to tread carefully.

I need not have worried. At our first meeting Mrs. Colburn appeared pleasant, with unaffected manners. She was much older than I expected, possibly by as much as 10 years older than Mr. Colburn. Smartly dressed, she exuded confidence. She spoke with quite a strong American accent.

Perhaps at one time she might have been a dressmaker; she had so many clothes. There must have been three large cabin trunks delivered next day following their arrival.

I liked Miss Sarah Pearl, a sweet, though rather a frail-looking child. Three years old, I could see her mother spoilt her. She too could select from a large choice of clothes.

When I saw the measure of the clothes – I helped Mrs. Colburn unpack – I realised the amount of washing I might be required to handle.

I anticipated Mrs. Colburn would wish to discuss my work. Expecting a change of routine, it came as a great relief to be allowed to continue as before; she would see how I managed the household work. She asked me to address her as Mrs. Colburn, or ma'am. I preferred ma'am.

I could not understand her demeanour. She did not seem happy in London. I did wonder if she had come under sufferance. Also, while Mr. Colburn acted as head of the household, Mrs. Colburn made the decisions, with firm instructions that I change the bedding every week. Mr. Colburn was no longer as pliant or as friendly with his wife on hand.

Soon, I mentioned to Mrs. Colburn I had too much work; that Mr. Colburn said if I required help I should go to him.

'Ask me, Lizzy,' she instructed.

I said it would be of great help if we could have a maid to assist with some of the work. As I cooked, cleaned and handled all clothes washing, I had enough to do. The increased work left little spare time – something I had grown accustomed to, although I did not mention that to her.

She said she would talk to Mr. Colburn. Mrs. Colburn clearly intended I should not have any conversation with Mr. Colburn, with whom I enjoyed a bond – albeit at arm's length.

Within a week, Mr. Colburn engaged Alice, a young maid. We became friends. With my help, she soon found her way round, quickly adjusting to the routine. Although Mr. Colburn made the final choice, ultimately Alice became my responsibility. I found it a comfort to have another person below stairs; one of her duties would be to light the fire in the master's bedroom.

I continued to act as cook, though occasionally I sent Alice out on errands. At the time, when best meat cost nine pence a pound, Dover soles one shilling and sixpence the pair, rabbits one shilling each and oysters seven pence a dozen, I did not have any problem placing good food on the dining-room table.

However, gradually over the coming months, I began to notice a change in the mood of the house. I sensed an atmosphere of tension and coolness had developed between Mr. and Mrs. Colburn. They were unlike my parents – or the professor and his wife. Tension and a strained atmosphere pervaded the house.

Occasionally, I heard heated conversation followed by a thud as the front door slammed shut. Sometimes, I feared the glass in the door might fall out. I became worried and made enquiries locally where I might obtain the services of a glazier, lest we should need one instantly.

In my mind, I knew who slammed the door – Mr. Colburn. I

sensed he could be erratic because, weeks before Mrs. Colburn arrived, if I asked him something he would say, 'Not now, Lizzy. Not now.' The tone of the second 'not now' was substantially more severe, curt even. His temper could quickly boil.

One evening, while serving dinner, I was about to walk into the dining room, laden with tureens of food. I heard raised voices as Mr. and Mrs. Colburn remonstrated, using insults and recriminations. Someone grasped a glass of red wine, and hurled it at the wall. The glass smashed into a hundred pieces and red wine splashed everywhere. I knew it must be Mr. Colburn.

'Damn it, I won't,' I heard Mr. Colburn say.

'Put the tureens on the table, Lizzy. Fetch cleaning materials, quickly.' ordered Mrs. Colburn. 'Mr. Colburn has knocked over a glass of wine.'

'Yes, ma'am. At once, ma'am.'

I hurried to the scullery, returning with cloths, and brush and dustpan to clear the mess.

'Goodness me,' I said to myself. 'Here's a to-do.'

I knew it to be no 'accident'. Something exasperated the master for him to lose his temper. I wondered what it could be. And did he lose his temper in public? For, while Mrs. Colburn would appear ready to challenge or argue with her husband, in my presence he had grown accustomed to my deference. I did not have long to wait what matter troubled the master; the answer came from a most unexpected quarter.

Miss Sarah Pearl always rose early and she often crept down stairs to visit me in the kitchen where I might be having a cup of tea. Sometimes, when she woke very early, she would creep into my bedroom. I would tell her to return to her bed. More often than not, Mrs. Colburn could sleep, or stay in bed, until 10 o'clock in the morning.

That particular morning, I recall it might be May 1869, Miss Sarah Pearl came down early to the kitchen. I was giving her breakfast at the table. With a knock on the door, Mr. Colburn walked in.

'Sarah Pearl, go upstairs and see Mommy,' he said. As the youngster toddled off, Mr. Colburn closed the door firmly. I remember his words now as clear as daylight.

'Lizzy, Mrs. Colburn is not happy here. She and Sarah Pearl are to return to America shortly. I shall remain here for some time. I require you to stay here. I will have no need for Alice. I will pay her off. She can leave at the end of the week.'

'Yes, Mr. Colburn.'

Mrs. Colburn and Miss Sarah Pearl departed within days. Mrs. Colburn thanked me for my work as I helped with packing. And with it, daily life resumed the somewhat monotonous routine prior to Mrs. Colburn's arrival. I wondered what, if anything had happened between the two to cause Mrs. Colburn to return so quickly to America.

Many weeks later, a most unusual envelope arrived addressed to Mr. Colburn, marked 'Most urgent'. I did not know quite what to do. With Mr. Colburn out of the house, I handed him the envelope at night when he returned. The next thing I knew, Mr. Colburn knocked on the door leading into the kitchen.

'Can I come in? I have bad news.'

'Certainly, Sir.'

Mr. Colburn's face carried a solemn appearance.

'Lizzy. I have something to tell you. I have heard through the telegraph of a dreadful shipwreck in the North Atlantic. All hands on board the vessel which sailed from Southampton to New York have been lost without trace, including my wife, Adelaide, and Sarah Pearl.'

'Oh, Mr. Colburn, I am so sorry,' I replied, genuinely crestfallen.

I could not hide my shock, or my sadness. I do not like to hear of anyone's death, whether by railway, horse, war or any accident. I do not even like to see animals die.

'Is there anything I can do to help?'

'You are kind, Lizzy. I appreciate your concern. My wife and I were aware of the dangers of the Atlantic passage. Some 20 years ago, the White Star ship *Naronic* carrying cargo with 74 passengers disappeared without trace. In the following seven years, four more vessels have vanished in the North Atlantic ice fields. It can be a perilous journey. Even Mr. Dickens, on his journey from Liverpool in Britannia, Cunard's first wooden paddle steamer to be built, experienced the vessel running aground before docking in Boston in 1842. It was then a perilous crossing; it is now, except in the safest steam vessels.'

'I may journey to New York to arrange family matters, in which case I will be absent for some time. Mrs. Colburn has a sister, Miss Julia Driggs; she may manage matters on my behalf. I do not need any help, thank you.'

Mr. Colburn did not appear grief-stricken; I sensed no searing sense of loss, anguish, distress, shock, anger or even sadness. At least, I would expect a distraught man, one having lost wife and child in tragic circumstances. To drown at sea in the icy waters of the North Atlantic is unthinkable, with no one to hear their cries of terror or for help. Their end was beyond my understanding. Mr. Colburn on the other hand appeared unaffected. Why so, I wondered? Was he a cold, ruthless and calculating man without feeling for human loss?

In his absence, he expected me to maintain the house 'ticking like a clock,' until his return. Could the same fate befall him? He brushed aside any of my concerns for his life as 'foolish'.

As it turned out, Mr. Colburn did go away. He said he would be absent for many weeks, repeating his need to travel to New York to arrange Mrs. Colburn's affairs. There would be no family funeral as all on board were lost at sea. In my mind, I questioned how *The Engineer* would manage in his absence. He gave me more than enough money for essentials. He requested firmly I never mention Mrs. Colburn's name again, or that of Sarah Pearl. Once again, I did not detect any anger or sorrow expressed through the great loss of either Sarah Pearl or Mrs. Colburn; he remained calm and matter-of-fact.

After six agonising weeks in which I feared all manner of

catastrophes befalling my employer, Mr. Colburn returned. In his absence, I meticulously kept house and maintained the fires. Generally, there was less to occupy me, so I had time for patience, which I played many times over in the quiet evenings. At times, the house was eerily silent, save for the striking of clocks.

On his arrival, Mr. Colburn appeared more content; a different man, happier, slightly more jovial and more relaxed. He quickly resumed his previous routine. I saw almost nothing of him, except at weekends. He gave the appearance of working hard, occasionally spending part of Saturday and Sunday in his study which I kept tidy, making sure not to dislodge papers. If he had a pastime, beyond playing chess, which would require a partner, I was not aware of it.

Sometimes, he could be absent for a week. I recall on one occasion he spent one week in Cornwall where he examined pumping, winding and stamping engines – whims and stamps, as he called them. Funny names, I thought. The engines numbered over 600, some as tall as houses working in deep mines extracting tin, copper and arsenic. He mentioned Richard Trevithick. He explained how 'Captain Dick', as he called him, had developed these steam engines and created the first self-propelled locomotive engine. Mr. Colburn took special interest in three locomotives at Redruth. Called Miner, Smelter and Spitfire, they undertook work previously undertaken by horses.

He also visited Mr. McConnell at Wolverton Works. He said Mr. McConnell was a devout member of the Church of England.

Mr. Colburn also began to arrange evening dinner parties of important engineers. Those in attendance were always men – ladies were not invited. Ladies remained apart from the intellectual engineering world in which men lived and excluded from their interests and activities. In this respect I proved something of an exception as I began to show more interest in Mr. Colburn's work; later I had the privilege to overhear some of the best conversation on matters concerning engineering.

For Mr. Colburn's dinner guests I remembered Doris's advice: 'The servant should offer everything at the left of the guest, so that the guest may be at liberty to use the right hand. The exception is water, which is poured at the right side.'

For, from what I could gather, most men were engineers of one kind or another. They would stand huddled around a table, discussing large plans or drawings. Mr. Clark attended the most frequently. A Scotsman, polite, studious, conscientious, quietly-spoken yet he displayed a twinkle in his eyes; he enjoyed his meals – and a glass or two of Macallan's Scotch whisky. I estimated Mr. Clark would be some 10 years older than my employer. He possessed a large beard that extended to his ears, as was fashionable at the time.

My employer described Mr. Clark as a *bon viveur* and a connoisseur of fine wines. Mr. Clark always acted most courteous and friendly towards me and I responded accordingly, within my capacity. I approved of him.

Both men played chess using Mr. Colburn's fine set which took me ages to dust. Mr. Colburn admired the well-known American chess player, Mr. Paul Murphy, who competed in Europe.

I discovered, quite by chance, when I observed an envelope addressed to Mr. D. K. Clark, that he lived nearby – at Broadstairs, No. 1 Park Village, East Regent's Park and well within walking distance. Mr. Colburn gave this as his principal reason for selecting Gloucester-road to live; he Mr. Clark numbered among the first engineers he met on his arrival in London in 1857. He held an office at 11 Adam-street, Adelphi. Park Village East is many yards from Gloucester-road – between the London & North Western Railway and Regent's Canal.

Mr. Clark, it seemed, had visited America some years previously to study locomotive design; a subject he held in common with Mr. Colburn, of whom I heard Mr. Clark once describe as an 'industrious young man'.

I discovered some time later that the reputation that Mr. Clark achieved in America by his book *Railway Machinery* secured his introduction to Mr. Colburn in 1857; the same book sparked a joint volume and through which the two men became great friends.

One topic united them. They declared British locomotives as simple, strong and carefully finished. American locomotives, on the other hand, reflected the 'incarnate spirit of opportunism – intended to meet the needs of the moment with long life neither desired nor sought'. In Europe, especially Germany, engineers favoured complication and excellent workmanship, with simplicity the last item on their minds.

In particular, Mr. Colburn had great respect for his older friend, a former locomotive superintendent at the Great North of Scotland Railway. He too had designed locomotives for both passenger and goods use.

Mr. Colburn told me: 'I am a great admirer of Mr. Clark; he fills my life with great pleasure. He is most assiduous and an authority on railway machinery and about which he can be most persuasive.'

I judged from their talk that each man had found a perfect soulmate; amazed by their good fortune, each appeared almost greedy for the other's company and delighted by the brilliance that flashed between them. They spent much time together and later would work together on a book, such was their mutual respect.

Other visitors included Mr. John Scott Russell, Mr. William Siemens, Mr. W. Bridges Adams and Mr. Edward Charles Healey. I remember all their names clearly as one evening, all the men attended together and Mr. Colburn gave instructions to prepared place settings in my finest writing. It took some time before he was satisfied.

As to social standing, these men occupied a far loftier position than I had previously associated, with the possible exception of Professor Braithwaite. From what Mr. Colburn said, the men played an important role in shaping the country's destiny. Slightly uneasy in their presence, I usually departed the room quickly. Mr. Colburn, as a self-assured editor, however could enjoy the company of clever people of any class. Like him, his friends were driven by a desire to achieve.

Mr. Colburn described Mr. Bridges Adams as an important locomotive engineer, an inventor and prolific technical journalist. He founded Fairfield Locomotive Works in East London building steam carriages. It enjoyed Eastern Counties Railway as its most important customer. Mr. Colburn described Mr. Bridges Adams as a 'larger-than-life' gentleman; a South American adventurer. His wife, with the unusual name of Sarah Fuller Flower Adams, he described as a poetess. Their daughter, with a Christian name of Hope, later became a doctor.

Mr. Colburn met Mr. Scott Russell first when Mr. Healey invited both men and other prominent engineers to dinner at his house, Sidmouth Lodge, during Mr. Colburn's first visit to England in 1857.

It was at Sidmouth Lodge that Mr. Healey introduced Mr. Colburn to English style table manners, to which he readily adapted. Mr. Colburn clearly delighted in high-born company. For my table settings I followed Doris's example, placing soup at one end and fish at the other, separated by corner dishes; for these I received his appreciation.

I noticed how Mr. Colburn, with his huge frame, often towered over visitors, dwarfing some of the men. Yet, despite his size, he possessed tireless energy and agility. And, as far as I could tell, he saw no need to raise his voice to be heard above other men in the room.

It required almost the whole morning to prepare table to my satisfaction. As for the meal, I deemed it the largest thus far, with four courses, in addition to cheese and port. And, when dinner was about to be served, I would sound the brass gong to summon everyone.

Together with obtaining provisions, preparation for the meal required two days. I had no wish to undertake such a meal all too frequently. It was hard work.

Another visitor was Mr. Joseph Bazelgette. Mr. Colburn described him as engineer to the Metropolitan Board of Works. He created a sewer network for London that helped relieve the city from cholera, a virulent outbreak of which occurred in 1853. Another broke out in 1854 when people drink water from a pump in Broad-street, Soho. Later, new sewers further improved the River Thames following the sultry summer of 1858, when London's putrid river caused the 'Great Stink'.

Between 1859 and 1865, almost 100 miles of Mr. Bazelgette's sewers appeared in London, carrying the contents of over 450 miles of other sewers; it was not until 1875 they were completed. Mr. Bazelgette (he received a knighthood that same year) created the Thames Embankment, which rose high and dry above the river below. It opened in July 1870. Mr. Bazelgette also displayed great interest in the expansion of railways and this interest made Mr. Colburn proud to offer him hospitality.

I enjoyed preparing meals when Mr. Clark attended. He appreciated food and complimented me accordingly. Perhaps he did not receive a square meal at home. He described my cooking as 'excellent'.

It was on only his third visit when, after the meal, in a private moment he drew close to me. He put his arm round my slim waist and pulled me closer He whispered: 'I always enjoy your cooking, especially your puddings. I wish my cook could put together a feast even half as good. If I may be permitted, I would describe you as the angel in the house. You appear tirelessly patient and self-sacrificing. Mr. Colburn is indeed fortunate to have found you. I wish you would come and work for me, but that would destroy my friendship with your employer.'

To such profuse flattery I blushed, of course. I felt my face go a deep red and I had to hasten from the room, but not before he pinched my bottom. No one had called me an angel before; not had anyone pinched my bottom.

Mr. Colburn would sometimes say 'I expect Mr. Clark for

dinner tonight, Lizzy. Prepare something special. Please bring up a few bottles of red burgundy from the cellar. Mr. Clark and I are compiling a book together and we shall compare notes long into the night. Bring the Macallan – it is Mr. Clark's favourite; being he from Scotland finds it most alluring. Oh, and glasses. We have much to do to pass on our knowledge to those less fortunate than ourselves.'

Only then did I glean an inkling of the master's work away from the newspaper. On Mr. Clark's departure, Mr. Colburn thanked me for my efforts.

On one occasion, Mr. James McConnell, locomotive superintendent of the London & North Western Railway, joined Mr. Colburn and Mr. Clark at the house for dinner. They engaged in lively discussion about express locomotive design. Both Mr. Clark and Mr. McConnell had produced designs for locomotives with large diameter driving wheels. At times, laughter emerged from the dining room; clearly not everything in discussion was of a serious nature. Sometimes I heard ribald conversations and on other occasions voices became quite heated as each man had his own views; for example about firebox design – quite above my head at the time.

Mr. Colburn portrayed Mr. McConnell as having many of his own characteristics: strong and determined; clever and full of energy. Some men described Mr. McConnell as 'cunning', he added.

Many months later, Mr. Colburn attended Mr. McConnell's works at Wolverton to study manufacture of 'Bloomers'. I recall saying at the time what a strange way to describe a locomotive. Mr. Colburn explained 'Bloomers' had seven feet-diameter driving wheels – far taller than a man. Wolverton Works built at least 10 of such locomotives He said they had six feet six inch driving wheels – taller than a man.

On that occasion, Mr. Colburn stayed overnight at Mr. McConnell's house, Park House, Wolverton, there being no accommodation available at either the Cock Hotel or the Bull

Hotel in nearby Stony Stratford. At the house, he engaged with Mr. McConnell's wife and after dinner participated 'vigorously' of the locomotive engineer's extensive wine cellar. I recall Mr. Colburn seemed much impressed with Mrs. McConnell (her Christian name was Charlotte, I was told), describing her as an 'admirable' wife, particularly as next morning she ordered cook, Ruth Dyres, who Mr. Colburn described as 'very pretty', to provide her guest with an ample breakfast before continuing his tour of the Wolverton Works. Much later, I was told that Mr. and Mrs. McConnell eventually had eight children, some with unusual names: Quentin, Edith, Edward, Ronald, Elizabeth, Helina, Charles, and Florence. Ronald was but an infant, one of three children then, when Mr. Colburn attended Park House.

Later in life, when I read in *The Times* of the death of Mr. McConnell and his subsequent burial in the churchyard in Great Missenden, Buckinghamshire in June 1883, the item recaptured memories of the occasions Mr. McConnell visited the house in Gloucester-road. Like Mr. Clark, he too could be effusively complimentary. Again I read somewhere of his grave being accompanied by an imposing monument; a white, winged marble angel pointing upwards. That reminded me of Mr. Clark and his description of me as 'the angel in the house'.

One particular evening, following Mr. Clark's departure, the master entered the kitchen. He caught me seated at the table, reading the previous day's *The Times* – a copy of which arrived daily through the letter box, with the exception of Sunday. As it was the end of the day, I had removed the cap I always wore in daytime; my hair hung freely.

Without warning, he moved quietly to stand behind my chair.

'You are a wonderful influence on this house, Lizzy. I am grateful for your work these past few months. I do not know how I would have managed without you. Your presence helps to secure the happiness, comfort and well-being of this little household. I shall soon entrust you with household accounts as an extension of your duties. You are indeed my household general.'

'It is why you pay me, Sir,' I said, immediately recognizing the latter phrase from *Mrs. Beaton's Handbook*. I had read the book from cover to cover and tried to take its contents to heart, where I thought they applied. At times, I considered myself underpaid, but dare not ask for more.

Silence descended on the kitchen; a dangerous silence. I heard the clock tick. A tap in the scullery dripped as if in accompaniment.

He ran the back of his forefinger down the nape of my neck. A shiver passed down my spine. I froze as my body stiffened. He placed his hands on my shoulders, squeezing gently. I detected alcohol on his breath.

'You are a good woman, Lizzy; a figure of beauty. And your cooking tonight excelled. Mr. Clark and I thoroughly enjoyed it; most enjoyable.'

Father's words echoed in my head; would his warning bear fruit? Why did the previous housekeeper leave unexpectedly?

I sat glued to the wooden chair as if paralysed. A figure of beauty. I wondered what would be coming next. As he maintained his hands on my shoulders, he gently moved his thumbs up and down the top of my spine. He had suddenly become quite different to the man I saw regularly; a man I considered ruthlessly competitive, a man with irrepressible confidence, a man with a temper.

'Does this upset you, Lizzy?' he said softly.

My mouth went dry; I could not speak. I did not know what to say. A strange heat flooded into my face. I blushed; my pulse quickened. Although nothing more than an ingénue at the time, I sensed my body respond to his actions. No man had ever touched me in such a manner.

'You and that Mr. Clark drank too much red wine Sir,' I ventured boldly, half-laughingly, avoiding a direct reply whilst trying to make light of it.

'I am sorry, Lizzy. I should not offend you. You are a good

young woman. I like you. I should not touch you. I am sorry. Do you know why I chose you to work here?'

'No, Sir,' I replied, wondering what he would say.

'Well, by strange coincidence, my wife used a milliner in New York City by the name of Eliza Browning. She and her family emigrated from England. Occasionally, I collected millinery from the premises of a hoop skirt maker, John Seller. Eliza, then aged 19, lived in the same dwelling at 76 Henry Street in New York City. She used a corner of his shop for millinery work. Henry Street was but a half mile from the offices I used for the *Railroad Advocate*. You remind me of her youthful looks. And I knew of another Browning; I have read Elizabeth Barrett Browning's works. When I saw your name, I recognised a coincidence I could not ignore; my good omen for the future. Now run along. Get some sleep. Do not be concerned, I am absent tomorrow night. Tomorrow will be quiet. Good night.'

'Good night, Sir.'

Suddenly he left the room, closing the door quietly. I sat dumbstruck. I wiped my eyes with the back of my hands. His gestures turned my life upside down, changing it forever. The master would not have touched me in such a manner unless he held some feeling for me.

And Eliza Browning? Where did she fit into the master's life?

What of me? Did I have some remote affection for him? I thought of him as 'the master'. Now the relationship was different. Was a stronger bond being forged?

I put *The Times* away. With plates, pots and pans already washed and dried, I tidied the kitchen. I pushed the chair against the table, closed the door and went to bed.

I could not sleep. Should I confide in my parents? What would father say? How would mother react? What will happen when the master returns? How will I control matters? Will I be able to take control? Do I want to take control? Or should I let matters control my life?

As I lay awake, I considered that in our relationship of master and housekeeper, I had grown to like him. I had to confess to myself that I was proud to be noticed by him; and to receive his recognition. I had not experienced that before and felt flattered. Our ages differed only slightly, yet in the way he asserted himself, he clearly occupied the position of 'the master'; he pursued life with energy and vitality. I had become accustomed to his comings and goings. He made few demands that were beyond me – until now.

Everything changed the moment his finger touched my neck; I felt an exciting tingle. My face flushed. The division between master and housekeeper no longer existed.

Like the wine glass hurled at the wall.

What caused their argument? Did Mrs. Colburn perhaps want the family to return to New York? And did Mr. Colburn yearn to remain in London; to be here – with me? Did he already have feelings for me when he threw the glass at the wall? Or was his anger directed at someone else?

Did I have any feelings for him? I did like him. Tall and reassuring, his manner exuded confidence. His temper could quickly spark into life. I did not like that. I hoped it would not be directed at me.

I eventually fell asleep; next morning unusually, I overslept. Events of the previous evening circulated in my head, giving cause for unease. I rose quickly and dressed but when I reached the hall I knew he had already gone, leaving me alone.

I began work. I could not concentrate; my thoughts turned to the previous night. What should I do?

When he returned the following evening, he said nothing. Life resumed as 'normal'.

Weeks later, he returned from work one evening at seven o'clock. I heard the front door open. He seemed somewhat merry; maybe on the way from work he had called at his club where he met with his circle of friends. He knocked on the kitchen door and walked in.

'Good evening, Lizzy, how are you?'

'I am well, Sir. Everything is in order, Sir.'

'Carry on with your tea, Lizzy. Do not concern yourself. I have endured a difficult day with the journal. All that could go wrong today has gone wrong.'

'I am sorry to hear of it, Mr. Colburn,' I replied as he sat down on a chair beside me.

As I ate my meal, he launched into a diatribe of the day's events. I did not understand the significance of many of the names and words, including some completely strange ones. He continually referred to a man called Bessemer involved with making steel.

The one-sided conversation continued for what seemed like half an hour. I finished eating and remained seated at table – tea plates in front of me. Without warning, he rose as if to leave the room, and moved to a position behind my chair. I felt a repeat of the shiver down my spine, not knowing what to expect.

'You are a good worker, Lizzy. I am grateful for your efforts. And you pay attention to what I say. And you keep this house spotless.'

'It is my duty, Sir.'

As before, he ran the back of his forefinger down the nape of my neck. He placed his hands on my shoulders as before and squeezed them again, gently.

'You are a good woman, Lizzy,' he said softly, before adding 'I admire you for being painstaking in the manner of your dress, modest though it is. That you are conscientious in performing your duties also pleases me.'

I sat glued to the chair.

He continued to stand behind me. He put his fingers and thumbs on the lower part of my head and began movements. He removed my cap and laid it on the table. His actions flummoxed me. I was lost for words. He began to massage my head, with deft movements of his fingers. He bent down, tenderly kissing the back of my neck. He bit into it gently. Still I said anything.

Without warning, I saw Mr. Colburn in a new light. How

would this end?

He removed his right hand from the top of my head and unfastened the top button of my uniform. Starting at my neck, he slid his hand gently inside my uniform. His action took me by surprise. I still did not move.

'Mr. Colburn,' I said, as firmly as I could muster. The words were as much as I could utter. I could think of nothing else to say.

His warm hand did not stop. It went inside my bodice, his palm resting gently over my left bosom. It remained there, gradually closing round me, tightening.

'As your housekeeper, you have no right to touch my body in that way, Sir,' I declared with unusual boldness, recalling the wine glass as it struck the dining room wall.

'You are sweet, Lizzy. I'm sorry. I wanted to feel the softness of your skin. I am sorry. You are lovely. It was presumptuous of me.'

He slowly withdrew his hand, placing it on my shoulders in a paternalistic way, as if to make amends.

With one movement he crossed the divide. We crossed the divide. He touched my body intimately. As for myself, I admitted to some affection towards him, though no more than friendship. I also spoke my mind.

I rose from my chair, my pulse still racing, turning to face him. Should I slap his face?

'I must clear things away from the table, Sir,' I said weakly.

Before I could do anything, he moved a step closer.

'Do not be angry with me, Lizzy. I have long admired your beauty and your small waist, not to mention your devotion to your duties.'

I looked into his eyes for a fraction of a second, before pulling away. A hint of humour crept into his lips. Was he playing a game? The easy-going charm and courtesy of this man touched my heart. It heralded my first experience of any feeling towards a man. I still did not know what more to say.

'Say something, Lizzy.'

'I do not know what to say, Sir.'

He put his arms round me and pulled me closer. He must have detected the firmness of my breasts through his shirt. I could not escape the tenderness with which he kissed me on the lips. He kissed again, with more fervour this time.

I pulled my head away.

'I think we should not be doing this; if I may say, Sir.'

'There is no one here, Lizzy. Just us two. You are safe with me. There is nothing more beautiful than a young Englishwoman.'

'I have work, Sir. I must prepare for tomorrow.'

He put one hand behind my head, guiding my face towards his lips, and kissed again, more firmly this time.

'Do not be angry, Lizzy. You do like me, don't you?'

'Yes Sir.'

'Give me a chaste goodnight kiss I can remember.'

He kissed again; this time I responded. My head said 'No' yet my pounding heart gave way under the strain. He held me for what seemed a long time.

'Please let go, Sir,' I pleaded, pulling my head back.

'I need someone like you. You would be good for me. You are shy and beautiful; I admire the flush of your skin. I would like to kiss your whole body.'

Then, instantly, as if someone pulled a lever, he changed completely.

'Clear away your dishes and enjoy a good night's sleep. Be ready to wake fresh for another day. Tomorrow I shall be away to Gorton in Manchester to visit Beyer, Peacock & Co.; the company builds fine locomotives. It is a workshop closed to Americans, but I have gained access. For I have found hidden in the darkest parts of this land, some of the brightest innovations of industry. They say Manchester is where engineers go to see the future. It is why I am heading there tomorrow. The hundreds of thousands of spindles of the cotton mills remind me of Lowell and its many mill girls – my first contact with young women at work. For four months of the year, the windows of the mill were closed and, with some 50 solar lamps burning morning and evening, they made the air impure. The only ventilation came from the opening of doors as workers came and went. There was much disease.'

He added: 'I shall witness again at first hand the dangerous work of factories, even those sweatshops I have mentioned. I shall meet working people; people like me with very poor parents. Do not expect me to return for two days; you will have time to complete your work. I shall rise early and be on my way with Bradshaw's.'

'Yes Sir,' I said. The master never spent a day in bed through sickness or ill-health; each day he rose early to begin work. I was to discover he could exist with very little sleep.

Mr. Colburn placed great emphasis on his edition of *The Railway Companion*, a well-thumbed copy of the railway timetable he used to plan his rail journeys. He did not travel without it. He explained once why he held Mr. George Bradshaw in such high regard. A printer devoted to producing maps of canals, rivers and railways, Mr. Bradshaw later branched out into producing timetables following the growth of the railways. In New York, Mr. Colburn previously sold maps of American railroads; he admired Bradshaw's descriptive cameos of various industries across Britain.

That night, in bed, many issues required resolving. Up to that evening, Mr. Colburn had discussed matters of business only. Without warning, his guard slipped to a public face and a private face.

I heard talk years previously of the common practice for a master to 'fondle his kitchen maid'. Now I knew the reality. Were his intentions serious or just to amuse himself? I found myself attracted to him and charmed by his intelligence. Kind, well spoken, well-travelled, indulgent and knowledgeable he may be; and aware of his poor origins he was determined to transcend them. Yet, I knew also of a harsh temper.

Did the master fully intend going to Manchester? Or did he plan to travel to Liverpool and take a liner to America with no plans of a return? What would I do then? A variety of frightening possibilities unfolded in my head; I endured them for two days.

On some days, work at the house proved unrelenting. Each day the routine was the same: cleaning the main rooms first followed by the kitchen and scullery, before changing into a clean uniform for the evening meal. Often too tired to do anything else, I climbed into bed at the end of the day, exhausted. Other days I had more time to myself. I could not ignore my good fortune. I found time to write my journal. I had good reasons to be thankful for Mr. Colburn and life in a modestly furnished yet comfortable house.

Mr. Colburn returned in a few days. I heard him enter the front door; he made straight for the study. Even now I recall my relief at the time. After a while, Mr. Colburn came to the kitchen and knocked.

'Come in, Sir.'

'Lizzy, I expect you have read in *The Times* of Mr. Isambard Kingdom Brunel and Mr. John Scott Russell. They are constructing the biggest ship in the world, called *S. S. Great Eastern*. I told you Mr. Holley and I missed her launch. Brunel has already been responsible for two of the world's finest ocean liners, *S. S. Great Western* and *S. S. Great Britain*; now he has embarked on a third. I have shown you drawings. Built for the Eastern Steam Navigation Company, they named her *Leviathan*. Her new owners, the *Great Eastern* Steamship Company, have changed her name to *Great Eastern*. She is truly magnificent – an engineering masterpiece. She is to take 4,000 passengers and a crew of 400 to Australia in 36 days, half the time of present-day steamers. The voyage is 22,500 miles. She has space for 5,000 tons of cargo and 12,000 tons of coal. I want to sail in her.'

Carried away with enthusiasm, Mr. Colburn spoke as if nothing took place between us several evenings previously.

'Mr. Alexander Holley is here. I met with him in Liverpool, our second largest city after London. He is to chronicle the maiden voyage of *Great Eastern* for *The New York Times*, as well as for my paper. He will remain in this house for a few days, maybe even several weeks, until the ship sails.'

So Mr. Colburn not only visited Manchester, but Liverpool too, I thought.

'Please prepare a bed for Holley in the spare room at once. He will arrive shortly. Make provision to serve luncheon and dinner this weekend. He may require breakfast; please make ready. Holley and I are old friends. He must feel welcomed in England. It is the least I can do. Prepare your best table.'

He then admitted, somewhat surprisingly I thought, the two men suffered differences in the past. Mr. Holley believed Mr. Colburn owed him money from copies of their report Mr. Colburn sold in England; this claim Mr. Colburn disputed. Mr. Holley even engaged a lawyer in New York to reinforce his claims. Mr. Colburn now regarded it as 'water under the bridge'.

He continued: 'When Holley and I travelled to England in 1857 we visited Mr. John Scott Russell at his family house in Sydenham, Westwood Lodge. From them I gained an insight into English aristocracy. It made me determined to become part of it. Scott Russell has a beautiful house.'

As an afterthought, he said 'I will arrange a repeat order of Burgundy wine and cognac from Hedges & Butler, and Bordeaux wines from Berry Brothers in St. James's-street. I shall also order green ginger wine from Thomas Nunn & Sons of Conduit-street. Holley enjoys claret. And he can try Clark's Macallan malt whisky. It will be like old times.'

I knew Hedges & Butler's establishment from when I lived in Brewer-street. At No. 155 Regent-street, the shop specialised in 'golden sherry' as well as port and champagnes.

Mr. Colburn changed the subject swiftly.

'While in Liverpool, Birkenhead to be precise, we witnessed an invention by fellow American, George Francis Train. He is laying a track for a tramway to carry passengers. Train said he plans a similar tramway in London next year,' he said excitedly. 'I shall write on the matter.'

'Really Sir,' I replied, not knowing quite what else to say.

Within the hour, I heard a loud knock at the door. I went to open it and a young man with curly hair confronted me. His face carried a wide boyish grin. He looked happy, relaxed and carefree.

'Does the great Mister Zerah Colburn live here?' he asked, emphasising the word Mister.

'Indeed Sir,' I replied.

'Well, my good woman, please instruct Mister Colburn that Mister Alexander Holley has arrived from America.'

'I will, Sir. He expects you. Come in please.'

Chapter Three
America beckons

A S SOON as Mr. Holley emerged through the front door I sensed a change to the atmosphere. His friendly, somewhat jolly countenance contrasted with Mr. Colburn's haughty grandeur.

I noticed Mr. Holley's curly hair. Not as tall as Mr. Colburn, though bulkier, his face carried an air of fun. He appeared happy and content with life; he had the look of boyish insouciance.

When Mr. Holley arrived in early May 1860, London looked splendid with trees in full bloom. I loved that time of year, with the heavy scent of blossom. As the sun shone on houses nearby, everywhere looked bright after the grimness of winter.

With two men living in the house, would I be expected to handle the washing of Mr. Holley's clothes? As my work would increase for a few weeks should I expect extra payment?

As it happened, Mr. Holley created no inconvenience. He requested his clothes be cleaned by laundry, using the best that could be found nearby. Mr. Holley, who wore fine clothes, settled his own account at the laundry. His clothes gave every appearance of being expensive; made by an exclusive tailor in New York

Each morning, the men would depart the house together each morning. From what I overheard, Mr. Holley spent much of his time meeting various important engineers, including Mr. Scott Russell. He visited Mr. Russell at Westwood Lodge, close to the rebuilt Crystal Palace.

Mr. Colburn told me earlier, that in August 1859 Mr. Brunel took a furnished house in Sydenham with the purpose of regular visits to his ship, *Great Eastern*, during final stages of commissioning. On Monday, 5th September, the assiduous engineer stepped on board his ship for the last time. Following a stroke, he died 10 days later aged 53.

My employer deemed Mr. Brunel as the engineers' hero. Both Mr. Colburn, as editor of *The Engineer*, and Mr. Healey, owner of the publication, attended the grand funeral of Mr. Brunel in October 1859. A large number of important people were present. Years later, in 1864, Mr. Colburn visited Bristol for the ceremonial opening of the Clifton suspension bridge, designed by Mr. Brunel.

Mr. Colburn showed me his long eulogy to Mr. Brunel. I considered it somewhat critical of the engineer's achievements while awarding credit to Mr. Scott Russell for the construction of *Great Eastern*. Mr. Colburn concluded:

'Whatever may have been the imperfections of his character and the disadvantages of his peculiar temperament, Mr. Isambard Kingdom Brunel was nevertheless a man of talent, and, as an engineer, well versed in the intricacies of his craft.'

In October 1859 also, Mr. Colburn attended the funeral of Mr. Robert Stephenson. He held Mr. Stephenson in high esteem and openly spoke of his creative genius. Mr. Colburn admitted to enjoying special attachment to the railway engineer. For, in the same year as Mr. Colburn's birth, the Locks and Canals Company in Lowell, where he served as an apprentice, took delivery of two of Mr. Stephenson's *Planet* locomotives with plans to build them in America.

'Mr. Stephenson has to be one of England's greatest railway engineers,' he told me. 'He not only built locomotives, railroads and bridges, he also undertook major engineering works.'

Others Mr. Colburn held in high regard included Mr. Michael Faraday. Mr. Colburn described Mr. Faraday as an eminent natural philosopher. It meant nothing to me yet it sounded important. Mr. Faraday much approved of a Mr. William Grove who had discovered a means to generate electrical energy by combining hydrogen and oxygen – I think they were the words mentioned. Mr. Colburn also told me how, in April 1860, he had written to Mr. Faraday on the topic of boiler explosions, a subject of great interest to my employer. A suggestion from Mr.

Clark led Mr. Colburn to develop his theory of the method of boiler explosions, known later as the Colburn Theory.

Mr. Colburn handed me his letter to read before posting it to Mr. Faraday. I remember it finished with the words: "I am Sir, Your obedient servant, Zerah Colburn." I then recognised my employer as a well-educated man who wrote very polite English, bearing in mind he originated from America.

He further explained how some of Mr. Faraday's lectures provided the basis for articles in Mr. Dickens's *Household Words*, the periodical to which my father subscribed from time to time, together with the weekly installments of *Hard Times*. I mused that it was indeed a small world or, as Mr. Colburn would say, 'wheels within wheels'.

Mr. Holley found particular friendship with Mrs. Scott Russell, an Irish lady who took the young American gentleman to her heart. I caught snatches of conversation as the two men discussed the lady over dinner one evening. The Russell family comprised three daughters (most notably Rachel, the eldest, a musician and an artist) and a son Norman. The two men described the children as intelligent. I thought how fortunate to be intelligent.

On their return to the house that evening, the two men spent much time in discussion; both enjoyed wine, judging by the number of bottles consumed. They enjoyed humour together and I could not fail but to observe their mutual admiration. I detected a mutual bond.

I heard snippets of their discussion of Mr. Holley's 'trial trip' on *Great Eastern* from London to Weymouth (before her maiden voyage). A huge explosion occurred during the journey, giving rise to some discussion. I gained the impression Mr. Holley might be compromised for lack of money; he wrote also for Mr. Colburn's paper to help cover the cost of his visit to England.

One day, the men travelled to Birmingham to visit Boulton & Watt at the Soho Manufactory in Smethwick. The company had installed hundreds of steam engines and built the screw engines for *Great Easter;* the company enjoyed historic associations with Mr. James Watt, with whom Mr. Matthew Boulton had shared steam-engine patents. Mr. Colburn was writing on the subject for *The Engineer;* Mr. Holley accompanied him to gather material for *The New York Times.*

During Mr. Holley's stay, I again overheard the name Bessemer repeated. I think Mr. Holley visited Mr. Bessemer for some reason, for I overheard snatched conversation when I attended the dining room to serve dinner, and again collecting dishes. Mr. Holley mentioned his wife, Mary; she remained behind in New York where they lived.

Both men could not contain their enthusiasm for *Great Eastern's* forthcoming maiden voyage to America, a ship seemingly created against the odds within London's dynamic riverside activity. It would be a spectacular event, they said. Five times larger than anything ever built, *Great Eastern* represented the biggest vessel afloat. She could accommodate 800 first-class passengers, 2,000 second-class and 1,200 in third-class. Some would regard a journey to America to be the height of endeavour. As the two conversed, I might just as well be listening to two excited schoolboys – not grown men!

Although he displayed the same enthusiasm, I sensed something deeper lay behind Mr. Colburn's zeal. Sometimes he seemed distant, as if his mind wandered to other matters. Could he be planning some conspiracy or intrigue with Mr. Holley?

Later, Mr. Colburn informed me Mr. Holley would embark for New York on *Great Eastern's* maiden voyage, due to take place in June. Mr. Holley developed a close friendship with Mr. Scott Russell, so much so I heard the shipbuilder had placed a state cabin at his disposal for the voyage. Mr. Holley also became well acquainted with Mr. Scott Russell's son; he would accompany Mr. Holley on the voyage.

'I am trying to secure a passage too,' Mr. Colburn added. 'It is proving difficult; nevertheless I shall succeed. Holley is popular with all Scott Russell's family; more popular than I.'

'What will happen to me?' I asked.

'You will remain here and take care of the house in my absence.'

A few days later I received the shock of my life. Returning from work, Mr. Colburn entered the kitchen without knocking.

'How would you like to go to America, Lizzy?'

'America, why would I want to go to America? How will I travel? I have no money. And whom would I travel with?'

'You must see America,' he replied without answering my question. 'Many young women would give their eye teeth just to step on its soil and breathe its air. I have convinced Mr. Scott Russell to make available my passage to New York. I will write articles for *The Engineer* describing the maiden voyage across the Atlantic, while Holley will describe the ship's principal engineering details for *The New York Times*. Holley's reputation is to ask searching questions. As for you, Lizzy, you will work your passage as a member of the crew of 418. You will engage in assisting the small number of women passengers. I can then close the house until our return.'

His suggestion made me flabbergasted. No other word could describe it. My employer had a scheme for the entire adventure. His proposition filled me with complete amazement. How audacious. In principle, I could raise no objection; it could be extremely exciting, and dangerous. Would I receive wages? Would Mr. Colburn allow me to turn down his offer? I remained wary of Mr. Colburn; while I witnessed no repeat of any over-familiarity, his temper I knew as something to avoid.

What would my parents say? Father would not be pleased; the prospect of his daughter sailing to America could meet with fiercely spirited resistance. He would think I had taken leave of my senses to embark on such an experience. Here I was, aged 23, torn between staying in London with my parents and possibly having to find another position, and embarking on an unknown adventure across a wide ocean with a man, or men I hardly knew.

'Will we return to England at the conclusion of the voyage?

How long shall we be away?

'Of course, of course,' he replied without hesitation, ignoring my second question. 'Why do you ask? I have my articles to submit and an important position to maintain in London.'

'Shall I receive my weekly wage?'

'Of course, why not? Will you come? You must come?'

I remained mystified. Should I regard this as a spontaneous invitation by Mr. Colburn, or part of a much greater plan? How would a journey to America be of benefit? What would life be like as a member of the crew at sea? And what of the Atlantic itself? Might I perish on the journey? I had heard of the Atlantic only as an unseen and unknown spectacle. As to working on a ship, would I be seasick? Who would instruct me as to my duties? Indeed, what would be my duties? I might be lonely. I could see nothing but uncertainties ahead.

'Will we be safe? Is *Great Eastern* a secure vessel?' I asked, thinking of Mrs. Colburn. Of late, Mr. Colburn seemed to have forgotten the death of his wife and child.

'Without doubt she is as safe as houses. She is the largest ocean-going vessel in the world. She is the pride of Great Britain; built with 10,000 tons of best quality Lowmoor iron. Come now, give me your decision.'

I paused for some time to give the matter my consideration.

'As you wish, I will come,' I said, immediately regretting my decision.

'Excellent. You do not seem excited,' said Mr. Colburn. 'It will be a great occurrence; the greatest experience of your life. I will make arrangements.'

Goodness me, I remember thinking, there is never a dull moment with the master.

As expected, mother and father declared grave misgivings. Both looked shocked when I revealed news of sailing alone to America with the editor of a London newspaper. Father expressed deep concern; suspicion even. I knew instinctively he opposed Mr. Colburn's proposals. He looked angry; one comment conveyed his attitude: 'Watch that man Colburn and what he gets up to. I don't trust him. Either you both display prodigious bravery or foolishness in your desire to cross the Atlantic in an iron steamship of all things.'

Father ominously added that he could remember the sinking of the iron ship RMS *Tayleur* of the White Star Line in January 1854 when 360 of the 650 on board died. The vessel, bound from Liverpool for Australia, sank off Ireland.

What would happen if the ship hit an iceberg? What would happen should the vessel sink? Will we ever see you again? What if there is a fire aboard the paddle steamer - *Great Eastern* has already experienced a fire during her trial trip? My mother raised all these questions and many others. To make matters worse, I could not give any answers. Before long she became too upset to talk further on the matter. I tried to reassure her, yet some questions I was unable to answer – I did not know the answers. I was as much in the dark as they. Mr. Colburn did not even consider such eventualities. My own doubts re-emerged.

'That Mr. Colburn of yours seems to feature much in your life,' said mother, eventually. 'Is something going on between the pair of you?'

'Nothing, as you say mother, is going on. He offered an opportunity to visit America and I took it. I expect us to return; he has a position in London to fulfil.'

Towards the end of my visit home, our conversations – mother and I – became tearful. The parting was quite sorrowful.

Within weeks, Mr. Colburn laid plans. Before departure, he engaged a part-time butler and his wife, Mr. and Mrs. Jenkins, to act as temporary caretakers during his absence. A neighbour, who employed them, spoke highly of their work. Mr. Colburn sought the neighbour's permission for the couple to observe the house. I had met Mrs. Jenkins from time to time though we seldom engaged in long conversation.

Meanwhile Mr. Holley, already in residence in a boarding house in Southampton, participated in the trial trip to Holyhead;

the trip lasted 24 hours from Saturday, 9th June to Sunday, 10th June. In a letter to Mr. Colburn, he stressed the importance of his early arrival the following Friday. Mr. Colburn gave me his letter to read. Mr. Holley wrote "She is advertised to sail on Saturday. The passenger list reached only 25, as the management so persistently and unnecessarily disappointed the public in times past."

I did not know it then, but father recorded the event in his notebook. Many years later, when able to read it, I saw: "Friday, 16th June, 1860. My dearest daughter Elizabeth S. Browning left for Waterloo to sail to New York, U.S. in the *S. S. Adriatic*." How did he confuse *Great Eastern* with the *S. S. Adriatic*; a name I had not heard?

Early on Wednesday, 14th June 1860, Mr. Colburn locked the door behind us. Our journey to America had begun; but first he told me to 'empty out'. We took the early train to Southampton to join the *Great Eastern*. We travelled First Class; for Mr. Colburn anything less would be unsatisfactory. The journey, my first by rail, proved at first terrifying. As I grew accustomed, I enjoyed it as a new and exciting means of travel. I had not travelled so fast in all my life, whereas for Mr. Colburn the journey contained not a single vestige of novelty. As I looked out of the window at passing scenery, I noticed the flying white breath from the locomotive as we made our speedy progress. How could I forget it?

For almost the entire journey, Mr. Colburn conducted a running commentary about places we passed, including the enormous Bagshot Heath. He knew the journey by heart. On his first visit to England, London & South Western Railway gave permission to travel on a locomotive footplate on that same line. The journey presented a great thrill; travelling at high speed he could experience the wind against his eye preservers (protecting against flying ash) and through his hair.

As we approached our destination, some five miles ahead lay a vessel looking like no other. I caught glimpses of Southampton, the waterfront and the sea. The strangeness of it I found captivating.

'That is *Great Eastern*,' said Mr. Colburn proudly, as we neared our arrival, pointing ahead to a large ship. The station clock registered 12 noon precisely as we pulled in.

We left the train behind as Mr. Colburn hailed a cab to take us to the ship. As we journeyed, *Great Eastern* gradually loomed before us, filling the horizon. For me, such a large, single piece of machinery created its own novelty. On arrival, we found other people standing around, passengers I assumed. They gazed at the huge vessel in amazement. In an instant, the ship's enormous size overwhelmed me as it towered above us.

We made our way to the gangplank to join the ship. As we did, for the first time I experienced butterflies in my stomach; I grew fearful, realising for the first time the enormity of the task to which I had agreed. It was too late to turn back. How would I find my way around such a large ship? By comparison my slight figure paled into insignificance. Would I ever see Mr. Colburn again? Would we even meet at some time on the voyage? The more I considered it, the more frightened I became. Fear must have been etched on my face.

As we reached the head of the gangplank, Mr. Colburn consulted the passenger list nailed to the structure. As if reading my thoughts, he said 'Our small company will be quite lost in this cavernous vessel intended to cater for many hundreds more.'

'I will communicate with you during the voyage. Do not speak or approach me. I have no wish for Holley to know of your presence. If Holley observes you, ignore him. If he asks me as to the coincidence, I shall inform him you are working your passage. Moreover, I do not want a member of the ship's crew, such as you, troubling me. Holley and I have important work to complete, as well as reports to write. Mr. Norman Scott Russell is here to compile a journal of information for his father's benefit.

'Yes, Sir,' I replied, meekly. Completely isolated, he confirmed my worst fears.

'And do not call me Sir,' he commanded, sternly. 'I will find the chief steward. See, wear this on your left hand. The crew will believe you to be attached.'

And with that he ungraciously thrust a slim gold ring with a small diamond into my hand. Its presence shocked me, the more so that eerily it slid easily onto my ring finger. How did he know the size of my hand? Before I knew it, Mr. Colburn disappeared.

I looked at the ring. I had not before received such a personal item. Was it for me to keep – or to borrow? At the time it seemed such a thoughtful and considerate gesture I did not know what was yet to come.

Before long, Mr. Colburn returned with a uniformed man.

'This young woman seeks the chief steward,' I heard him say. 'Mr. John Scott Russell has arranged her passage as a crew member. I understand Mr. Scott Russell will leave the ship shortly to return to London.'

Mention of Mr. John Scott Russell drew the chief steward smartly to attention. He seemed a cheerful enough fellow.

'When do you expect us to depart, chief steward?' I heard Mr. Colburn ask. 'And when shall we arrive?'

'All of that is in the hands of Captain John Vine Hall. Our planned departure is on 16th June. Captain will time his arrival at New York to secure the highest tide possible,' he replied. 'More uncertain is how much time will be lost in running south to clear ice.'

Ice? Ice? Mention of the word frightened me. What did he mean, ice? Did he mean icebergs?

'My fellow passenger, Mr. Alexander Holley, tells me weeds, and barnacles have adhered to the ship. They may remove 60 miles a day from her speed, increasing her sailing time of less than nine days to more than 10. Is this true, chief steward?'

'I have heard also, Sir. Nevertheless, we will arrive in time to celebrate 4th of July.'

'Come with me, young lady. What is your name?' the chief steward asked.

I accompanied him to find five other young women – cabin maids – including four young Irish women. I suddenly experienced a feeling of loneliness and isolation. The young Irish women who, it later transpired had decided to start a new life in America, made me feel welcome; we became good friends. The Irish women shared a four-berth cabin; another young woman and I were each allocated a single cabin each, there being so few passengers. I was so pleased to have my own cabin. Had that been arranged?

The cabins and saloons – five on the upper deck and five on the lower deck – were completed to a high class; of course, I had not seen anything like them. The brilliant apartments, thanks to their gilt mirrors, appeared expanded as if multiplied into suites of saloons. They would befit the Queen herself, especially the ornate dining room with its chandeliers, wood panelling, luxurious carpets, deep comfortable chairs with their elegant patterns and drapes at the windows.

I saw from the passenger list, posted in several places, the total of passengers numbered only 43; a small number surely for the first voyage of *Great Eastern*, a vessel I once heard Mr. Holley describe as 'the most splendid ship on any ocean'. Why so few passengers? I heard later some passengers were dissuaded by an expected rolling of the ship in Atlantic storms; that I found worrying too.

From the passenger list, I could see Mr. Holley, Mr. E. Skinner and Mr. N. Scott Russell all allocated to State-room No. 18. Their names were missing from the guest list, which numbered eight; I assumed they enjoyed a private understanding with Mr. Scott Russell's father, like Mr. Colburn.

According to the chief steward, the men in the sailing department numbered 172. The steward's department, which included me, comprised 51. This left the engineer's department with 194 men; including 23 officers and 23 engineers. The chief steward informed us Captain John Vine Hall would have charge of the ship for the voyage.

The chief steward instructed we meet in cook's galley in one hour's time. He briefly interviewed us one by one, explaining what he expected of each one. I could judge from our conversation that, of all the young women, I offered most experience; as such I ranked myself competent enough to complete any domestic task asked of me.

At night, alone in my cabin, I found sleep difficult. Eventually, I tucked my head into the harsh cotton pillow, tightly closing my eyes. I drew deeper and deeper into myself, trying to isolate myself from the surroundings. I began to cry quietly. What had I taken on so glibly? I found myself in the care of complete strangers, and amidst alien noises. The Great Ship still remained in dock; it had not even begun its epic journey. Would I be safe amongst so many sailors? Would Mr. Colburn come to my rescue should any ill befall me?

Early next day, as the huge vessel readied, long lines of sailors and firemen formed on deck to answer to their names. We were told that with fires lighted in the boiler room the night before, and boilers kept under steam overnight, at 12 minutes after 8 o'clock, the captain would signal the engines to turn over, launching the start of our journey to the New World.

The day passed and nothing happened with the exception that the many visitors who had come to view the huge vessel ahead of her departure were ushered ashore. The chief steward went to great pains to make sure there were no stowaways. That evening we waited for instructions of our departure. But no instructions came. Only very late, before we turned in did the chief steward explain.

'Captain has announced he will not be sailing until the 17th,' explained the chief steward. 'It would seem the crew have been enjoying themselves and consumed too much drink.'

The chief steward dropped his voice to a whisper. 'I have heard tell Mr. Daniel Gooch, a director, is not best pleased.' Much later I heard of Mr. Gooch's further displeasure by the southerly route taken by the ship; this was even further south of the regular steamer routes. Mr. Gooch wanted the journey completed in nine days; in the event, it took 10 days 19 hours.

And so it was, as the giant vessel eased from the quay on 17th June, I glanced at the disappearing shoreline. While Mr. Colburn's future seemed assured; I did not know what mine would bring.

By three minutes to 10 o'clock, we passed the Needles.

The chief steward required, as our principal task, to make up cabins of guest passengers, with any remaining time allocated to assisting in galleys, peeling vegetables and fruit, washing dishes and helping where necessary. Later in the voyage, we cleared public rooms after banquets.

The chief steward had already found much work for us; he acted as a father figure; he had presented us with uniforms to wear. And, working in the galleys, we did not go short of food – although not at the best time of day, and sometimes food had gone cold. The sea air made me hungry; I found it a long time between breakfast and something to eat after luncheon. As we prepared food, we sneaked morsels.

Later, I re-examined the passenger list; at the head of the list appeared a Miss Herbert, followed by Mr. and Mrs. Daniel Gooch, and Mr. & Mrs. Stainthorp.

One crew member confidently informed me that Mr. Isambard Kingdom Brunel recruited Mr. Daniel Gooch as locomotive engineer to the Great Western Railway; the two men were great friends. (Mr. Colburn much later explained Mr. Gooch, a director of The Great Ship Company, owners of *Great Eastern*, had urged the captain to take a more southerly route of only nine days' duration. He said Mr. Gooch had designed 'broad gauge' locomotives with giant eight-foot diameter driving wheels. Some trains took only 208 minutes running time for the 194 miles between London and Exeter.)

The list of names showed Mr. A. L. Holley as affiliated to *The New York Times*, Mr. Z. Colburn (with no affiliation), Mr. N. Scott Russell, the son of Mr. Scott Russell and a friend of Mr.

Holley, and his friend Mr. Skinner. I mused why Mr. Skinner should travel with Mr. Russell; an old school friend perhaps? I once heard Mr. Holley shout 'Skinnee' – I assumed that to be Mr. Skinner. I noticed three other names: Mr. Woods from *The Times* newspaper in London, Mr. Mckenzie, representing various London newspapers, and Mr. Geo. Wilkes, representing the American press. My personal association with Mr. Colburn, and seeing his name in print, provided me with a small thrill.

The three lady passengers travelled without maids, so we cabin maids took turns to offer assistance with their private duties. For example, at night we dismantled their elaborately pinned and padded hair, unlaced stays and helped them dress for bed.

The few passengers became lost in the *Great Eastern* amidst its cavernous public rooms with their magnificent interiors and its long decks. Some men stood mesmerised for hours on the guard walks topping the huge paddle wheels on each side of the vessel. The walkways measured five paces wide; they could accommodate many people. They proved a favourite rendezvous; from there passengers could watch the churning of the paddle wheels as the ship's giant hulk slipped through the calm waters of the North Atlantic.

Sometimes, when I took a peep through the windows, I could see Mr. Holley and Mr. Colburn seated, making notes and deep in conversation. Another day, I saw Mr. Holley a top the main mast, braced counter to the wind and observing the horizon. To scale such heights amply demonstrated to me the level of his bravery. I thought of his wife Mary; she would be greatly concerned if she but knew of it.

Some passengers stayed up half the night admiring the phosphorescent wake as it receded into darkness. Bar stewards accordingly worked late, serving drinks and cocktails.

On the second day, in the middle of the night, I awoke from a crash; it reverberated throughout the entire ship. Next morning, I discovered hundreds of empty ale bottles broken loose from their moorings; they discharged down the paved flooring of the passage between fore and aft saloons.

Another night, a howling gale caused the vessel to roll from side to side. I heard shouting from 100 or so sailors away up on the foretopsail, not mention the loud noise generated by sails as they collapsed thundering on deck. A huge expanse of canvas still flapped in the wind.

In the evening, musical concerts alternated with artistes performing in the Ladies' Saloon. Passengers, few in number, soon became comrades-in-arms and, according to one steward, the placing of bets formed their most common topic of conversation. Sometimes, he said, they would wager 'whole vineyards' on guessing the speed of the ship, and devised games to prevent the onset of boredom during long daylight hours.

A good sense of camaraderie developed also between kitchen and housekeeping staff, though generally I kept myself to myself. However, we women grouped ourselves together and looked after one another.

Most crew members took it as a privilege to be selected for *Great Eastern* duty. Some of the crew, aware of three tragedies, feared the ship ill-fated. The death of its creator, Mr. Brunel, coupled with the explosion on the trial trip and the tragic drowning of Captain Harrison, *Great Eastern*'s first captain, ignited rumours the ship carried a jinx. Some claimed to know of two men unaccounted for during construction, their bodies seemingly entombed in the hull.

Other crew members did not agree with the presence on board of company executives; crewmen called them 'dead heads' because they did not pay their passage. With eight on the 'free list', including Mrs. Gooch as the only lady, this reduced the paying number to 35, less than generally attributed to the *Great Britain* on her first passage.

Some of the crew I witnessed only once, at the start of our voyage. They worked in shifts day and night stoking the ship's boilers. Steam from the boilers powered the engines to thrust the leviathan through the ocean. The chief steward called these men the 'black gang' – black from shovelling over 200 tons of coal a day. It reminded me of the iniquities of class divide on the vessel – men working below decks to provide the power to propel everyone else on board to their destination.

Crewmen working above decks anticipated their employment also might offer an opportunity to glimpse the rich and famous, and maybe benefit from handsome gratuities. Such life might also offer boisterous social activities in their quarters as compensation for hard work. Alas for them, with crew greatly outnumbering guests and passengers, their mood remained understandably subdued.

On 21st June, for the first time, dinner was served after cocktails in the first after-saloon with passengers seated together at table. The dinner service I would describe as most splendidly elegant with its silver covers. I made close inspection of the white dinner plates; each resplendent with a cable pattern arranged around the edge, the image of *Great Eastern* under canvas benignly observed from shore by Britannia and the Lion. Dessert plates carried the same motif in gilt.

I observed too how passengers lived in their own opulent private world; strangers became friends as they quietly crossed the ocean from England to America.

As we neared the conclusion of our voyage, I grew increasingly concerned. At no time had Mr. Colburn attempted to make contact. What would happen to me?

I suppose I saw Mr. Colburn in the distance no more than six or seven times on the entire voyage. On the day preceding our intended arrival in New York, I rose early to lay table for breakfast in the dining room. He walked into the room, bold as brass; he quite ignored me. I might be invisible. About to walk past, he stopped and whispered in my ear: "I have fallen passionately in love with you". Then he thrust a piece of folded paper into my hand and marched on, energetic as ever.

I tucked it into my pocket to read later in a quiet moment. I continued my work. His manner overwhelmed me. I hastily retired to a corner to open the note. A message, written in the large, unmistakable handwriting I had long come to recognise, carried six words:

I have great plans
Marry me

As soon as possible, I retired to my cabin and bolted the door. With my back braced against it, I re-opened the slip of paper. I read the words again; only two mattered: 'Marry me.'

Only then did I realise the significance of the ring he had so lamely thrust into my hand at the outset of the voyage. He wanted to marry me!

I could not believe it. Up to that moment I had given no thought to marriage, it being only an abstract.

I folded the paper and placed it in my pocket. 'Marry me'. Did I misunderstand? There must be some mistake. In one simple message, I felt humbled, yet confused. I withdrew the note and read it again. 'I have great plans. Marry me.' How brash. In my shyness and innocence, I failed to know how to respond to the man.

The immense size of the ship ensured I dare not venture far on deck, especially during evenings when work finished. That night, I left my cabin and went up the nearest companionway to the deck in search of fresh air. I needed it with so much happening so quickly. I looked over the side at the frothing ocean. What was Mr. Colburn up to? What an outrageous request: 'Marry me'. At times the man's ideas appeared wild and reckless. Was his idea born of arrogance? Had he had too much to drink to make him uncommonly romantic? And did he really love me? And what were the great plans?

I found the sight of the ship's outline, gliding so effortlessly through the Atlantic swell under a moonlit sky, a thrilling experience. As I stared at the sea, two words pulsed through my brain repeatedly. Marry me. Could he be serious? I could not take it in. The enormity of what lay ahead I found frightening. The elation of a marriage prospect to a successful man became heavily clouded with fears of the unknown. My emotions varied this way and that. Marry me. What were his real thoughts? Marry me. Why me? That night, I lay in bed in the dark and tried to assess my predicament, I tossed and turned. I prayed to God before falling asleep.

Early on the morning of Wednesday, 27th June, one or two of the older crew members believed they could smell land. I could not. Later a pilot boat, sent from New York to meet us and fire a salute, confirmed the men's sensitive nostrils. At 8 o'clock in the evening, the passengers unanimously met to present a memorial to the captain to record his successful voyage. Great applause accompanied the presentation.

The same night, the captain held a small, celebratory party below decks for senior members of crew – at least as many as could leave their duties. He made food and beer widely available. Each cabin maid received an invitation from the chief steward, and while I joined the others, I remained preoccupied with my own thoughts.

Before the party formerly ended, I returned to my cabin, packed some clothes and prepared for the next day. What would happen to me now? When would we return to England? Mr. Colburn gave no indication of when or how we would make the return journey. Who would pay for it? Indeed, would we even return to London? And what of that note?

Worried by many unanswered questions, I took a long time to fall asleep. I lay on my back, staring into space, the noise of throbbing engines dimly in the background. What would become of me, so inferior compared with the likes of Mr. Colburn? Like it or not, the presence of Mr. Colburn made life interesting and exciting. My doubts continued.

Even the steady thrashing of seawater from the paddle wheels on the ship's side failed to lull me to sleep. With so much to weigh up, I tossed and turned, without even giving any thought as to what New York would look like. Could I visit the city and would it be like England?

I could think only of the two words on the scrap of paper. Marry me. I still have the scrap of paper as I write. With the passage of time, it is now creased, crumpled and fragile.

Why did he want to marry me? Did he love me? Did I love him? What was love anyhow? I had read of love in romantic novels. What is it? How do you know when you feel it? Yes, I liked him; did I have enough reason to marry him? Did I know him well enough to make a lifelong commitment? Did I have an alternative? I could not forget his bad temper, and the smashed wine glass.

There appeared no end to Mr. Colburn's plans for my life? I detected an element of ruthlessness; a sense of determination in his scheming to win my hand. It could not be otherwise; miraculously we found ourselves together on Great Eastern in the vast expanse of the Atlantic. How would I address him? Would it be Zerah? Would I be housekeeper turned mistress of the house?

My new life posed so many questions and no answers. There were other questions. Did he have real feelings for me? Should I take this as a genuine feeling of love? Or was it lust driven by infatuation? Did he now want a woman younger than his first wife as his new bride? Would feelings for me evaporate once we wed?

I thought again of the crash of the wine glass as it struck the wall. Should I regard that as an omen for the future? Something caused Mrs. Colburn great unhappiness; enough for her to leave England. Yet she and her daughter died at sea. What really happened to them in the icy cold waters of the North Atlantic? How dreadful. Would I too be unhappily married after a time? Would I suffer the same fate? Even now I found myself sailing in those same chilling waters that claimed their lives; a sailing organised by Mr. Colburn. Was I safe?

I must have drifted into shallow sleep for I was wakened by a gentle knock. I sat up. It happened again. I threw back the covers and went to the door.

'Who is there?' I whispered. 'What is wrong?'

'Mr. Colburn,' the reply came. 'Open the door quickly.'

I obeyed, pushing back the bolt. I peered through the smallest crack. Dressed only in nightclothes I became worried as to what might happen.

'You are safe with me, Lizzy. I must speak with you.'

His voice, in whispered tones, expressed urgency. Was the ship sinking? I opened the door a fraction more. He pushed it wider, and slipped through. He closed it behind him. I reached for my coat behind the door and put it around my shoulders to conceal my nightwear. The only source of light came through the glass above the door, but it was enough to see his face. His rheumy eyes suggested he had been battling the Atlantic weather.

'My note. What is your reply? Will you marry me?'

'I have not yet fully absorbed it,' I replied. 'You surprised me; I need more time. What is your hurry? We hardly know one another.'

'While on board ship, I have given much thought to our future,' he said in hushed tones. 'I have great plans, Lizzy. You are a beautiful young woman; a woman of great charm and generosity. I find you irresistible. I love you. I cannot imagine life without you. There is nothing more beautiful than an English rose. Lizzy, you astound me. You are my English rose.'

Mr. Colburn seemed very excited; as he spoke his voice assumed normal levels.

'Speak softly,' I implored, surprised by my own authority and by his passion and intrigue. 'I wish no one to hear.'

'Tomorrow, Thursday, 28th June, according to the captain, the ship will pass Sandy Hook, off the New Jersey coast,' he said, almost ignoring me. 'Our arrival in New York will mark the official conclusion of the voyage. However, a thick fog has enveloped us; it will slow our pace. The Captain is confident it will soon disperse. Watch for the lighthouse when the fog clears; they built it 30 years ago to warn of dangerous rocks.'

'It will take some time before we arrive at the Port of New York. There are formalities to complete. I shall leave the ship as I have business to conduct in New York. You will come with me. When I have finished we will take the railroad to Philadelphia, a large city and the country's capital for 10 years up to 1800. Just we two; afterwards we will marry.'

No other word could describe how I felt: dumbfounded. At the start of the voyage he said we would return to London; now we were heading for Philadelphia. And marriage!

'Be in your cabin exactly one hour after ship docks. By such time, all passengers will have disembarked. Although I must examine the ship's paddle and screw engines, I will collect you. I want to tell you more about my plans.'

He kissed me on the cheek, and disappeared. I locked the door and repaired to bed. I could not sleep. With my head spinning, I lost all sense of reality. Could this be a dream?

Mr. Colburn's change of plan caused great concern. His new ideas worried me. How would I find him if he did not reach my cabin? He clearly planned not to return to London. After New York, our destination would be Philadelphia; most confusing. I had not then heard of Philadelphia, or where it was located. What would happen if I wished not to travel to Philadelphia, and had no wish to marry? Would I ever see London again?

His plans made me even more hesitant in yielding him an answer to his provocative question. His plans changed constantly.

I found his phrase bewildering: 'I am deeply in love'. Love can be blind. What would happen should I not wish to marry? How did I know if I liked him sufficiently to marry?

In addition, I possessed few clothes. Where would we live? How would we live? What would I call him?

Eventually I drifted into sleep. Next day we heard from the chief steward that *Great Eastern* completed 3,242 knots in 11 days and 2 hours; a journey somewhat longer than expected. During the voyage, the vessel burned 2,876 tons of coal. We heard too the result of the ship's lottery. The captain pronounced it decided by *Great Eastern* passing the lighthouse at Navesink Highlands, overlooking the entrance to New York Bay. One of the officers drew the prize of $120.

Due to the fog, it took a day longer to reach the Port of New York. On Friday, 29th June the ship finally docked. Beforehand, the crew decked out *Great Eastern* fore and aft (I did learn some nautical language from them during my passage) with flags and bunting. A large crowd gathered on quayside, many having travelled long distances to see the famous steam ship. For them its arrival marked a gala occasion. Passengers and some crew observed the proceedings from the deck. Steamers and small boats loaded with sightseers likewise appeared, braving the mix of sunshine and showers. As we approached, they began to cheer and wave flags. I saw hundreds of admiring eyes.

I gazed at the buildings; they differed greatly from those of London I knew so well, and so far away. Many seemed tall, and almost new.

As promised and an hour after the vessel docked, Mr. Colburn appeared. He knocked at the door; I opened it. He came in and shut it behind him. He placed his back to the door, barring my exit should I attempt to escape.

'Will you marry me, Lizzy? I will not leave here until I receive your answer.'

'Where will we live?' I asked, trying to gain time and appear practical. 'I have few clothes apart from these I stand up in.'

'None of that matters as long as you and I are together. You do love me, don't you?'

'I like you. I don't really know you.'

When we were in London, I began to know him more. Some might consider him handsome, distinguished with good manners and certainly knowledgeable and fastidious with regards to everything; so fastidious indeed that the word itself became the *mot just* for most aspects of his life. His temper on the other hand I could not ignore.

'We are made for each other. I have watched you. See how well you looked after me in London. You kept house meticulously, proving yourself an accomplished cook,' he replied.

'Getting married is much more than cooking,' I protested. 'You must know. You have been married – I am sorry; I did not mean to refer to it. You know what I mean. I am unmarried. I know very little about men.'

'I am going to start again. The most amazing idea came to me as we sailed the Atlantic. No one knows of it, only you. I shall create a new weekly newspaper out of Philadelphia.'

'You are editor of a newspaper in London,' I countered. 'Is that not enough for you? Mr. Healey awaits your return – and your articles.'

'Be gone with Mr. Healey. I will write him, informing of my plans to remain here. He will find a new editor.'

'You cannot. You have an obligation. He is your employer,' I pleaded.

'Well, I am here now. We are here. That is what matters,' he stated firmly. 'My plan is to publish a newspaper. If it is not successful we will return to London.'

It would be foolish to reason further; I remained quiet. I remembered the crash of glass on wall, something never far from my mind. Would it forever haunt me?

'As to getting to know more of each another, Lizzy, we will spend time together in Philadelphia. We will marry in New York. How about that?'

It appeared I had no choice. I thought: 'You could knock me down with a feather', as my mother would have said.

'How will I return home?' I asked.

'You have no need to return home. You will be married to me. We will live together. Sometime we can visit your folks in London. Now I must inspect the paddle engines – the screw engines I have done. The crew will disembark later.'

He took me in his arms; he pulled me tightly against him. He kissed me gently on the lips. I responded, kissing him in return, warily. It was a strange experience. It all seemed so matter of fact and remote; just like organizing the editorial contents of next week's *The Engineer*, I imagined.

'I will wait on the quayside. Inform chief steward of your plan to remain in New York. You will not be returning to England. Be firm with him; very firm.'

'I have forms to complete for the ship's manifest of passengers. It seems there are 43 passengers, including two Russians – brothers John and Michael Juraveloff. I found talking to them a great pleasure, learning much from their experiences. Eight passengers originated in the United States; the other 33 came from Great Britain,' he said.

He then left. Alone again with my thoughts, I could not shake off my grave misgivings. What would life be like with Mr. Colburn, as Mrs. Colburn? What would my parents say once they knew? They would say: 'You are too young. You should wait awhile.' They might even have their own plans as to whom I should marry.

I could not escape the image of the wine glass hitting the wall. He threw the glass with unbridled, almost deranged anger. I saw red wine trickle down the wall, like blood. Surely, I should take that as a warning, a sign.

I would have to understand him much better. What could be his motives? Because he asked me to marry him did not imply I should accept. Yet he left me with little choice. He assumed I would travel to Philadelphia. Did I have an alternative? Would I be sufficiently brave to disobey and make the return journey to England alone?

I found chief steward and explained my plans. I would not be available for excursions to Cape May on 2nd and 3rd August, nor would I return to London.

'You young women are much alike,' replied chief steward grumpily. 'You make me cross. Over 300 passengers are booked for the trips to Cape May. Not only are there insufficient berths to accommodate them, but we lack the crew to look after them.

The wine steward is on the verge of collapse – and the passengers have not even arrived.'

'Now I have to find new cabin staff – and right quickly. I am not happy. You are a nuisance. You think nothing of the consequences of your action. Each one of you is staying here. What is it about this place? Are you set on marrying the same man?' You must watch your step; New York is a dangerous place.'

'Never mind,' he said with sudden change of heart. 'Good luck to you. Here is a guinea. You have been usefulness itself. The voyage has been good for your complexion; the sea air has put brilliance into your face. Now be off with you, afore I change my mind.'

Carrying a small case, I went to find the gangplank. I most likely looked a pitiful sight as I searched for Mr. Colburn on the quayside.

Someone touched my arm.

'Mr. Colburn. You took me by surprise.'

'It is Zerah from now on, not Mr. Colburn. Understand? You now stand on American soil.'

He wanted control of me; he liked to be 'in control'.

'Yes Sir.'

'And none of the Sir business either. We are to marry, are we not? It is Zerah and Lizzy from now on. Or would you prefer to be called Eliza? We could even marry now, here in New York. We could obtain a special license.'

I could not believe it. And Eliza? I did not wish to have the name Eliza.

I became overwhelmed with a strange emotion; a deep feeling of having just crossed the ocean and was about to move my entire life away from all I had known to be with this 'new' person with whom I would spend the rest of my life.

'Mr. Colburn, I hardly know you. I have nothing in which to get married! As to my name, of the two I prefer Lizzy.'

'I accept that. And it is Zerah now, not Mr. Colburn. It will not be long before we wed. As you say, we have to get to know one another first. That is what you said; it is as you wanted. Personally, I know you well enough to marry now.'

He went on: 'First things first. We must find a bank to arrange money. Remind me tomorrow to purchase *The New York Times*. I must read Holley's report of *Great Eastern*'s maiden voyage. We will travel to Philadelphia to find rooms. I know the city from years back. On the way I will outline my plans.'

We made our way to a bank. I walked close at his side, frightened lest I lost sight of him. I wanted to hang onto his coat. Everywhere I turned was strange. Even people around me looked strange; some had dark skins, almost black. Never before had I witnessed a dark-skinned person.

I waited outside while he entered the bank, remaining nervous throughout his absence. He must have been away for what seemed an hour. I became concerned lest anything should happen to him. When he finally emerged we made our way to the railway (he called it railroad) station. From time to time, he took my hand, as if to hurry me along the street or the platform. He walked fast. We eventually caught a train to Philadelphia.

The train could not have been more to different to the one we took to Southampton. Noisy and dirty, it belched out thick black smoke. Smoke enveloped passengers on the platform, causing them to cough. Zerah enjoyed the experience, the motion, the clatter. I could barely hear him speak.

I recall he made mention of American railway engineers not fitting fishplates to their rails; how they accounted for the big difference between English and American railways. I did not understand his explanation.

As we sat side by side on the carriage seat, he held my hand reassuringly. He gave an almost boyish grin of satisfaction, of victory. Eventually, we reached Philadelphia after changing many times. In the evening darkness he seemed to know his way. Making for a nearby rooming house, he requested two rooms. Tomorrow, he told me, we would find an apartment, and buy me some clothes. He gave every appearance of being kind and thoughtful.

I suddenly realised my hunger, having not eaten anything since breakfast on *Great Eastern*. The rooming house keeper brought bread and cheese, placing them on a table in the dining room. Zerah asked for a bottle of red wine and two glasses. Must I drink it? He wished no doubt it would loosen my inhibitions.

'I do not drink wine,' I declared emphatically.

Father would not allow alcohol in the house, except for special occasions. He forbade it on principle. I did not even know how they made wine. Secretly, I tried tiny sips from Mr. Colburn's opened bottles at No. 7, Gloucester-road; some wines tasted bitter. I could not imagine how anyone could like drinking wine. Of course, I knew Mr. Clark and many others enjoyed their wines. I took wine at communion, and only in sips; that was different.

'This is good. You will feel better.'

I could not protest. The waiter brought the bottle of wine. Poured into glasses, the wine took on a deep red colour, almost bloodlike in appearance.

Surprisingly, the warmed bread and cheese tasted good. The wine affected me somewhat. I soon began to feel light-headed. Surprisingly, I enjoyed its taste. Maybe anything would have tasted as good in my state of hunger and after such a bewildering day.

We made our way to our rooms. Before leaving, he put his arms round me, pulling me tightly into him. I realised again his strength. He kissed me hard on the lips. Again, I found myself yielding and, after giving him a brief kiss, I pulled away.

'I love women, they take my breath away. Why did I receive so little love from my mother? Now it is you I love. You are my English rose. Learn to love me, Lizzy,' he said, bidding 'good night'.

'Tomorrow, we start our new life together,' he added. For the first time, I detected an air of physical vanity about him.

I closed the door, quietly easing the bolt into place. I sat on the bed; if felt lumpy and the creased linen did not look clean. I wondered who slept in it last night. Seemingly, having come out of nowhere we had become part of a secret, completely self-contained world, anonymous to those outside.

I recalled his words: 'A new life together', 'I love women; they take my breath away'. And 'you are my English rose'. So now I am his English rose; twice he told me. Would I learn to love him? Could I be expected to love him, simply because he loved me? Did I understand the meaning of love? Did it really exist? Did it matter?

I found his manner captivating. Would I become as a moth fluttering around a candle's flame? Still shy, and unaware of his deep feelings towards me, I remained unsure of my own. Maybe already he had placed me, like a bird, in his cage and locked the door, never mind what would happen to me later.

I looked around again. How did I come to be in the room? The shabby rooming house Zerah selected lacked respectability. A strange smell hung everywhere, the stairway, the landing and rooms. Who else shared our little universe? For reassurance, I rechecked the bolt on the door. I heard noises from other rooms, strange noises. As I stood stock still, could I hear amorous groans, squeaks and giggles of a couple next door? Anything might happen during the night and no one would know; murder or suicide.

I went to the window; looking out I saw a few streetlamps break up the darkness. Several people walked along the street; one or two shouted or sang. In contrast, my cabin in *Great Eastern* was luxurious. I longed to be back there; it seemed a safe haven. I treasured its privacy where I could say my prayers privately. In Philadelphia that night, God seemed so far away. And yet, in some strange way, I knew I was not alone.

London also seemed in another world. I longed too for home and the security of my parents. What had I let myself in for by agreeing to *Great Eastern*'s voyage? I did not even know how to make the return journey. Powerless, I lacked the necessary money to reach England, and London. What little money I received from the chief steward amounted to English coinage – shillings and pennies. They held no value in a country using dollars and cents. *Great Eastern* already seemed half a lifetime away. Now far from home, I had put my life at risk, placed in the hands of someone else; a man who would become my husband.

Completely dependent on Zerah Colburn, I felt under his spell. I could detect some feelings for the man, but enough to marry him? Moreover, he carried an uneasy sense of threat. I faced an impossible conflict: one expects to love the person one is marrying; yet I hardly knew this man, except as my master.

I felt wretched and uncomfortable; isolated in a strange, smelly boarding house. Eventually, I undressed warily and crept gingerly into bed, exhausted. I prayed quietly for God to take care of me.

The next morning, I splashed my face with cold water from the hand basin, dressed and went downstairs. Zerah sat at table reading a newspaper. I would have to become accustomed to calling him Zerah. He consulted his pocket watch.

'Eat and we can be on our way. We must find an apartment so I can begin work.'

He immediately took control again. Would this be my future, with someone else in control? After breakfast, of sorts, Zerah settled with the rooming house keeper.

'First, I must buy a copy of *The New York Times*,' he said, darting off to a newsstand.

He scoured the pages intently for Mr. Holley's article before declaring 'Ha-ha'. Silently he read the newspaper intently for some time. I stood at his side in the middle of the 'sidewalk' as people passed on each side.

'Look. Read this,' he said pointing triumphantly to a paragraph:

'Before closing the narrative of the trip, I am happy to be able to express my thanks especially to Mr. MCLELLAN, Chief

111

Engineer, Mr. N. SCOTT RUSSELL and Mr. ZERAH COLBURN, for the important information and assistance given in preparing an abstract of the engineering results. It should be remarked Mr. MCLELLAN was on board the *Great Western* and the *Great Britain* on their Atlantic voyages. He has now risen to be Chief of the *Great Eastern*.'

'No. Not that,' he said testily. 'Read this. Good eh? Notice how Holley writes under the pen name Tubal Cain. Clever, eh?'

'Only one other soul is admitted to the mystic seclusion of this sacred apartment – Mr. ZERAH COLBURN – who is immediately pounced upon to figure out difference of time and horse power, which are accomplished with an agility that does credit to the mathematical shade of his logarithmic uncle.'

I nodded approvingly and asked: 'Sacred apartment. What's that?'

'It was State Room No. 18. It had two large portholes on the sea side and four berths opposite. Well done, Holley. Thanks to my pocket watch I timed the engines.'

He appeared to know our direction as we headed towards Washington Square. On the way, we walked down long, straight streets with high buildings on each side. Exactly how tall I found difficult to judge; certainly much taller than anything I had witnessed in London. When I looked down the side streets, even more high buildings appeared.

He explained some of the history of Philadelphia. I have forgotten much of it, with the exception of the Liberty Bell. He said it most famously rang in 1776 to summon citizens for the reading of the Declaration of Independence. A bell foundry in the East End of London cast the bell over one hundred years previously. I readily recapture the foundry's location in Whitechapel, to the north across the River Thames from Bermondsey where my father spent his boyhood. Some described Whitechapel as the worst district in London. Its dwellings housed all conceivable filth and wretchedness. Many Jews lived there too.

Mention of the Liberty Bell reminded Zerah of The Bell, a poem by Edgar Allan Poe, an American born in Boston who travelled to London before returning to marry in New York. Zerah, admired Poe's poetry. Poe died many years earlier when, on 3rd October 1849, a man found him in a delirious state on a street in Baltimore, Maryland, days before his death.

The sun shone – I could tell that by the deep shadows cast by the buildings, yet I could not see it. Eventually, after a long walk, we arrived in Washington Square.

'This is where we will live. I saw it advertised in a newspaper. It is a swell district. You will enjoy it here. It is like London.'

He left me outside with my small case as he disappeared into No. 204 Washington Square; such a huge building. I looked around. It seemed a beautiful and fashionable district, spaciously laid out with gravel walks, ornamental trees and shrubbery. Far different from the rooming house where we spent the previous night.

In the centre of the square, a circular grass plot accommodated an equestrian statue. Taking my case, I walked across to read the words: George Washington.

Iron railings enclosed the square; a notice declared it open from May to November. As I looked around, maids took charge of infants. It must be a good class district.

It reminded me of Golden-square. I felt homesick. I thought, what would father be doing? What would he be thinking? Would mother be worrying for me?

I looked again at No. 204 Washington Square, a red brick building, near the Philadelphia Savings Fund Society. I discovered later two adjacent streets, Lotus and Walnut; they ran from the Schuylkill River in the west, to the Delaware River in the east. At right angles to these streets ran Front Street, and 24th Street. I thought it strange to have numbered streets.

In selecting Washington Square, Zerah made a fine choice. The apartment he chose comprised two sparsely furnished bedchambers, a front living room and kitchen – both had the minimal of furniture. Along the passage I saw the communal bathroom.

I insisted we slept in separate rooms until our wedding, which now seemed a foregone conclusion. He promptly announced he would use his room also an office until he found one.

Zerah did not like separate bedchambers. He let it be known he wished that we share the same bed; to be intimate the moment we moved into the apartment. My strict Christian upbringing accounted for a sense of responsibility and I stood firm.

I already had fears of meeting father and face his probing questions. He would require an understanding of why I married Mr. Colburn; and why I married a foreign man, a non-Christian foreigner at that. Were there not plenty of Englishmen available? And was I really in love with the man; sufficiently in love to cross the high seas to marry him?

Or, had I married without love on the pretext of getting away from home? Both parents would find these, and others, unsound reasons for not proceeding.

As for myself, dare I tell father a lie; that I had fallen in love, when in truth I was completely unsure? Father and mother seemed so far away. Not for the first time did I feel lonely and afraid. Just as some children I had read about might on their first week at boarding school.

Chapter Four
Marriage and all that

ERAH, desperate to begin his new newspaper, worked all hours of the day, either scratching away in his long scrawl, or alternatively gathering news or subscriptions in the city and around. I wondered what he would call his paper. The feverish activity almost mirrored his life in London; an invisible force driving him ever onwards.

As Philadelphia newspapers carried articles hinting of civil war, Zerah claimed any hostilities would drive up trade for locomotives, so increasing his new paper's chances of success. When I heard it mentioned, the prospect of war frightened me; I wanted to leave for London but I knew that to be out of the question.

From Zerah's standpoint, he had replaced London with Philadelphia, with the exception that where we lived he worked alone, whereas in London many others provided him with assistance. In Philadelphia, as he explained many times, besides gathering editorial material, he trailed from one railroad works to another, 'touting,' as he called it, for subscribers and advertisers.

He quickly identified a small office situated at the north-east corner of 5th Street and Walnut Street from which to launch his publishing activity; it required but a short walk from Washington Square. I did not visit the office, but from Zerah's description it could not be large, as he continued to write most of his editorial 'copy' alone in his bedroom.

Zerah viewed Philadelphia as a mechanics' paradise; a place of great industrial activity. Many businesses were associated with either engineering or locomotive manufacture, with Baldwin Locomotive Works being the largest. One day, Zerah took me to the works, with its many huge cathedral-like buildings devoted to manufactory. I had not witnessed anything like them before. The size of one alone reminded me somewhat of the Crystal Palace, however, the noise and clatter of many men at work I found both deafening and intimidating. As we entered, men nearest to us halted their activities and stared. I found their interest in us embarrassing; I blushed and turned to Zerah, wanting to leave. Zerah, on the other hand, unmoved by such clatter and banging, almost lovingly absorbed the atmosphere.

He endeavoured to reassure me. 'As a rule, Americans are honest and kindly people; most believe in the natural superiority of everything American over everything English,' he said.

Mr. Matthias Baldwin, the owner, had known Zerah almost from the day the journalist arrived in New York; the two men met first in 1855. He much admired Zerah's work both as a locomotive engineer and for his written work. Not many men could combine such work to his high scale.

A subscription to Zerah's paper cost $3 a year or $10 for those who purchased four copies. Baldwin Locomotive Works, being a large employer, took out many more subscriptions than four. As Zerah later explained, the benefit to him of subscriptions materialised as readers 'paid up front'. In this way, Zerah received his income ahead of completing a year's worth of copies. To encourage businesses to subscribe, Zerah wrote short articles about them and placed them in his newspaper.

Baldwin Locomotive Works was typical of such companies. In March of the year we arrived in Philadelphia, Mr. Baldwin secured a flood of orders for locomotives, causing the works to be extremely busy. Under normal conditions, two draughtsmen were considered enough for such a big locomotive workshops, their duties confined to making large-scale skeleton drawings. However, with so much additional work, Mr. Baldwin engaged Zerah to assist with engineering designs. The work suited Zerah and he performed it well.

Mr. Baldwin, aware of Zerah's financial plight, paid handsomely in cash, and regularly by all accounts. Some evenings, Zerah sat in the tiny kitchen counting his dollar notes. However, faced with a fierce workload Zerah had to burn his candle at both ends.

Despite previous reservations, I enjoyed sightseeing; Philadelphia offered many new experiences. I felt secure, venturing out a little further each day. As to understanding more about Zerah, I had little opportunity. We sometimes talked in the evening; he wanted to learn more of my family. He had many distant relatives yet, even with his mother still alive, he revealed little about his family, with the exception of his uncle Zerah and his extensive travels as the 'calculating child'. Subsequent to his visit, his uncle wrote a book documenting his life on public display in England.

Most of the time, Zerah was preoccupied with work. He spent most of daylight hours out and about, meeting important men in Philadelphia; other days he travelled much farther afield to engage with presidents and senior engineers of railroads. Occasionally, he stayed overnight. He left me to fend for myself, preoccupied as he was with his work. More often than not, he would then write his editorial text in the evenings, sometimes rushing with it to the printer to be set next day in type. Then he proof read pages and made any corrections.

The apartment had a small kitchen, which I used for cooking. I also engaged in shopping for food. The apartment required only a small amount of housework; nothing like as intensely labouring as my work at No.7 Gloucester-road. Zerah handed money as and when I needed it – but only just enough for food, not much else. He could be quite frugal. If careful, I could make a small surplus and, visiting one of several bookshops, I could buy second-hand books. I wondered if our life would always be like that.

Meanwhile, whenever I could, I continued to make notes in my journal; by then it contained details of life at No. 37 Golden-square and No. 7 Gloucester-road, as well as events of the voyage.

After a month's hard work, the first issue of the paper appeared on 16th August 1860. Zerah appeared pleased with his endeavours, though he found one mistake; this annoyed him immensely. I considered the issue looked just like *The Engineer* newspaper in London, but when I said so he smiled, and gave a wink. The paper's title was: *The Engineer!*

It contained just five pages of editorial text and three pages of advertisements; it carried no illustrations, which I considered strange. Zerah said pictures wasted space. It did not look a large publication considering the amount of work involved.

For the next issue he made yet more visits, so once again I found myself alone for days on end. When Zerah returned, he would scribble furiously, often long into the night. I wondered if the end justified the means. We continued as before, with little opportunity to become more acquainted with each another. We were as ships passing in the night.

Gradually over the coming weeks, the amount of work eased and we saw more of each other, especially at weekends when Zerah took me sightseeing. We ate meals at cafes. By then he did not appear hard up. I gradually warmed to him as the closeness of our contact played its part.

His clothes were smart, though not as sharp as those of Mr. Holley, who clearly loved to cut a dash. I had almost forgotten him: it seemed so long ago that we were on *Great Eastern.* I particularly noticed Zerah's belt, a thin black leather belt measuring about two inches wide with a gold buckle. He always wore it.

As my feelings for him began to develop, I had to admire his diligence, determination and enthusiasm for hard work. Seemingly starting from nothing in Philadelphia, he soon made his presence felt as his paper grew in importance.

From time to time Zerah said how much he loved me. Did he love me more than his work? Or did he love his work above all else?

He spoke little of marriage; he knew my views on that sensitive subject. We continued to sleep in separate rooms, and he always gave me a goodnight peck on the cheek. He caressed his fingers through my long hair; it seemed to give him enjoyment and his touch also gave me a thrill of excitement.

We had travelled far since that evening in Gloucester-road when, in the kitchen, he first touched me. However, I remained haunted by the image of the shattered wine glass.

He never once spoke of his wife and daughter or his freedom to remarry. And I did not ask.

He confessed that he fell in love with me the first moment he saw me standing on the doorstep in London.

One morning, in the middle of September, Zerah asked: 'Lizzy, have you a better understanding of me now? You have lived with me for many weeks. That must be long enough for you to decide if you love me sufficiently to marry.'

I said nothing.

'Whatever you say, Lizzy, I will marry you this month. A September wedding in New York will be just swell. And I have picked Monday, 24th September, as the special day,' he announced. 'It will be our special day.'

Monday; for a wedding? What on earth did he mean? And what a strange day on which to hold a wedding! I asked why he picked Monday, and how many people would be present.

He explained that because of his publishing schedule (those were his words, except schedule sounded more like skedule) he could spare only Monday and Tuesday from work. Also, the New York City registry office was fully booked on Saturdays for weeks ahead.

'We will have a couple of witnesses,' he added. 'Mr. and Mrs. Baldwin are in New York City that weekend for an important railroad function. They have kindly offered to stay over and act as witnesses. Mr. Baldwin is a religious man. You will like him. He's been like a father to me.'

I must have appeared dismayed.

'Mr. Baldwin is a good man. He and others like him set up the Franklin Institute to encourage young men isolated from technical education,' Zerah elaborated. 'He is a gentleman. He is genial and an exemplary churchman. As a philanthropist he has helped many local institutions, and he has supported me. You will like him. I am sure of that. He is well known and admired; he is a Christian man. I believe he nears 65 and is widely respected. We are honoured to have such an important man as a witness. He is very busy.'

Zerah explained how, in September 1857, he and the presidents of several railroads had agreed to form The Railroad Association for the improvement of railroad machinery. Mr. Baldwin played an important part in helping establish that association.

Zerah intended his comments as reassurance. Nevertheless, not only would I not have a formal weekend wedding, but the witnesses would be complete unknowns. I felt lonely; I had no friends or family in America. And what of the wedding night itself?

Once more, Zerah had everything planned.

'We will marry at the Metropolitan Hotel,' continued Zerah pragmatically. 'It is one of the best and newest hotels in town. It is not only a swell place for a wedding, but it is ideal for a honeymoon. We will travel to New York on Saturday and return on Wednesday.'

'You will like it. Alex and Mary Holley married with minimum fuss at the same hotel in December 1855. No one knew they had gotten married. They eloped to New York as both parents banned the marriage. Mary was only 16 years old at the time and her father judged her far too young for marriage. Alex's father likewise thought the same of his 23-year-old son.'

'Perhaps Mary's parents were being protective,' I suggested, wondering what my own parents would say if they knew of Zerah's plans for me. 'Fathers do worry about their daughters. Perhaps they wanted them to be certain of their love for each another.'

I did not make the acquaintance of Mrs. Mary Holley. She would have been about 20 when we married. Mr. Holley always spoke lovingly of Mary; he had so much respect for her. I remember how he praised her delightful personality, and her bubbling chatter. Such was Mary's devotion to her husband she followed wherever work took him.

'You seem to have it all organised. All I have to do is turn up,' I said with an air of resignation.

'That is what husbands are for,' replied Zerah.

'Why could we not have Mr. Holley and his wife as witnesses? Mr. Holley is a pleasant gentleman from what little I know.'

'Mr. Holley is far too busy. He is writing a new book titled Armor; it details iron and steel used to build ships and guns. He could not spare the time.' Zerah's dismissive tone suggested further discussion of the topic would be out of the question.

'I require new clothes,' I said, defiantly.

Zerah reached into his pocket and pulled out a roll of notes.

'Here is a bunch of notes for you. Make sure you spend wisely and return me the change. And choose some of silk; I like the feel of silk.'

Clearly, he did not expect me to spend it all, but there appeared to be more than I might need.

'Look after those notes. Keep them safe. There are many here who would take them from you quicker than they would rob their grandmother. And get a travelling case for yourself.'

By that time, I had become familiar with the centre of Philadelphia, and could find my way. So while Zerah worked, I did some shopping. I spent time each day collecting items for my trousseau, but experienced difficulty finding the correct clothes. They were not a suitable fit, and materials too were different from my normal wear. I became puzzled as to what I should put on.

Eventually, I found a store with a tailoress engaged in the workshop behind and they took my measurements. I found them most helpful and they made some of my clothes.

On the Saturday before the wedding, we rose early for the journey from Philadelphia to New York. It proved tiring, requiring a combination of steamships, 'railroads' and ferries.

The journey took four-and-a-half hours; we changed 'railroad' lines several times. The railroads we used were: Philadelphia and Trenton Railroad, the Trenton and New Brunswick Railroad and finally the New Jersey Railroad. The trains clattered along the rails and belched out smoke; their pace was variable. Sometimes the train would hurtle along at breakneck speed, making an awful clatter; at other times, it crawled along before gaining speed again.

By the completion, I had grown quite weary of travelling. Eventually, we made our way to the Metropolitan Hotel. I did not know what to expect, but I was overawed with what I saw.

The huge six-storey hotel stood on the corner of Broadway and Prince Street. Zerah told me a man by the name of John B. Snook of Trench & Snook designed the building in the Italian palazzo style. I did not understand, but palazzo sounded grand, like a palace – and so it was. Swell, as Zerah described it.

The hotel had opened for business eight years previously, making it the second largest hotel in New York City after the Astor House. Its lavishly furnished public parlours and 500 guest rooms, each with hot and cold running water and steam heating, offered every luxury imaginable. The entire atmosphere I found new and exciting.

We were, seemingly, to live in some style. Zerah's generosity amazed me. The manager directed us to our suite; it contained a bedroom with one very large bed, and a lounge. Zerah must have made arrangements with the manager at reception.

'Remember, we do not sleep together until we are married,' I impressed on Zerah.

That did not stop him from caressing my hand, and looking at me in a way that every woman would understand.

He knew how much marriage vows meant to me. My parents trusted me to uphold Christian values. I had an obligation to them, even though they were far away with no knowledge I was about to be married.

'Fine, one of us can sleep on the chaise longue in the lounge while the other has the bed,' said Zerah. 'I can wait a while longer for my conjugal rights and personal needs. We will toss a quarter.'

I lost and had to sleep on the chaise longue. I believed he still thought of me as the maid or housekeeper, and not his wife-to-be. Despite this, I mused that the delicacy of Zerah's continued self-imposed abstinence reflected his affection for me; I also found that pleasing.

The suite had a delightful bathroom. I had not seen anything like it, nor so splendid. I enjoyed the novelty of hot and cold running water and use of the most unusual bath. However, I found the room infernally hot; not at all like anything I had previously experienced, even in Golden-square.

The hotel's entertainment area included theatre, ballroom and refreshment rooms. Outside I noticed a large garden. With every amenity, residents had no cause to leave the hotel.

Even so, we went sightseeing in New York though did not venture far from Central Park. In the evening, after a meal we went to a theatre. I found it exciting to walk along Broadway; I stayed close to Zerah as he held my arm, hurrying me along as usual. We saw many strange-looking people, some of them dark skinned. I would not have felt safe unless accompanied.

Sunday also we devoted to sightseeing; Zerah knew the city well. The following day we met with Mr. and Mrs. Baldwin. The wedding, at 11 in the morning, took place before a Justice of the Peace. We arrived with five minutes to spare. The moment had finally arrived. Would I be marrying out of duty, love or fear?

The ceremony took place quickly; I could hardly accept it had taken place at all. I expected it to occupy half an hour; not just a few minutes. The ceremony was formal and routine, and quite austere without my family.

Following an exchange of vows and a few brief words, the officiator asked Zerah to place a ring on the bride's left hand.

"You are now man and wife," he declared.

Then we engaged in one simple signing of documents; this together with the wedding ring were the only tangible signs of an event I previously expected as the happiest of my life. In spite of the ceremony's brevity, I did take my vows seriously.

While our wedding took place, outside other couples waited in turn for their few moments in front of the JP.

It crossed my mind to ask if the marriage was *bona fide*, but I knew better than to do that.

Then I had the opportunity to read the document. Simple and to the point it read: "New York. Sept. 24th 1860. This is to certify that I have this day joined in the bonds of holy matrimony Zerah Colburn of Philadelphia and Elizabeth S. Browning of London according to the laws of the State of New York. R. S. Hammond." Nothing more; nothing less.

We then took luncheon, during which Zerah and Mr. Baldwin engaged throughout in business conversation, leaving Mrs. Baldwin and I to talk. Given she and I had not previously met we conducted ourselves well. As we conversed, the men drank beer.

She asked if I had met Zerah's mother. I said not. Was that something I should ask Zerah later?

As expected of a president's wife, Mrs. Baldwin had every confidence and knew how to conduct herself. She occupied much of the conversation, speaking mostly of herself and her children. On the subject of marriage, she declared that getting married was the biggest decision in a woman's life. It could influence her and her children until the moment she died. From time to time, as we talked, I fingered nervously my new wedding ring.

'Is Mr. Colburn someone you wish to spend the rest of your life with? Does he bring you happiness?' she asked inquisitively at one point. Too inquisitively, I thought. But without waiting for a reply, she put forward advice I have not forgotten.

'The secret of a happy marriage is great friendship – and complete frankness; and a caring, sensitive and understanding husband who knows how to ensure his wife enjoys a pleasing arousal.'

'You must learn to keep counsel until the right moment, and never dispute. Men are always right. You should be aware also of your husband's weaknesses, but never broach them. Remember that. Finally, you only begin to know a man properly once you have lived with him for many, many years. Possibly you will never fully understand him. They can be secretive.'

'Thank you, Mrs. Baldwin,' I replied. 'I hope to prove a loving and dutiful wife, and have my husband's love.'

Mrs. Baldwin's words of wisdom proved correct, but not before I had to absorb a dismal lesson several times over; that tyranny walked close beside me. Looking back after all these years, at the time I was completely unprepared for marriage; far too nervous and possibly even a little reluctant. I had no vision of what the future might hold, except that of longing to be loved and cherished. Would I be disappointed?

As it turned out, it transpired to be a marriage of opposites as I discovered to my cost. Two quite different people from humble beginnings thousands of miles apart, now joined as one. As an only child, Zerah would be accustomed to having his own way; as one of a large family I had to take my part in household duties, such as frequently caring for my brothers and sisters.

I had no wish to be seen with sister Harriet, three years my junior, as it looked as though I had no friends of my own – not that I did have many, as mother made me work so hard cleaning the house and looking after her children. My childhood and that of Zerah could not have been more different.

Back in New York, Mr. Baldwin paid for luncheon; he reached first into his back pocket to retrieve a roll of notes that were held by a gold clip.

I noticed how everyone at the Metropolitan Hotel seemed to be rich; they were certainly expensively dressed. Perhaps it was a swell place for a wedding; it just appeared that our wedding was not 'swell' at all. I had no one of my own family to share my momentous occasion.

By the middle of the afternoon Mr. and Mrs. Baldwin had bid their farewells and we were alone: Mr. and Mrs. Colburn.

'You will have no requirement for a chaise longue now, Lizzy. You can sleep in comfort – that is, if you will be able to sleep at all.'

We returned to our room and Zerah locked the door behind him.

'Just to keep the maids out,' he explained. He went to the window and drew the curtains. 'It is time to undress Lizzy and see what you really look like. This is no time for any private reserves.'

I said that as we were married I much preferred to be called Elizabeth. As Lizzy, I was his housekeeper; now I was Zerah's wife.

'Just as you wish, Lizzy, sorry, Elizabeth,' he replied. 'But I shall find it hard. I shall always think of you as Lizzy. As I have told you before, there is nothing more beautiful than an English rose, and you are my English rose – Elizabeth.'

I found myself embarking on a strange experience; an initiation into adult pleasures. I read once that the honeymoon provided a golden opportunity for young couples finally to be alone and express their love for one another. But here was an experienced man with a virgin woman. Now, when the moment had finally arrived, I felt shy and uncomfortable, even though I had known Zerah for some time. I was uncertain of my true affection for him; and his for me. I went to the bathroom to undress, locking the door.

'No need to undress in there,' he shouted. 'Come here.'

What happened next proved most difficult – making the transition from housekeeper to mistress of the house. How would I rise to the occasion? I knew little if anything about men. I hoped, vaguely recalling various conversations of mine with Doris, I would not disappoint. When I returned, he was already in bed.

'No need for clothes, Lizzy. It is warm enough here; just the two of us. Remove your nightwear. Don't feel nervous.' He had forgotten.

As to not feeling nervous, my long-held innocence spawned its own nervousness as to what might happen. No previous experience of mine could prepare me for what followed. My parents brought me up to understand that we minimised any bare skin. Indeed, when I lived in Golden-square, Doris would tell us young women that while married couples might be ardent lovers, they would never see one another without clothes. Zerah seemingly did not agree with such prudish behaviour. In America everything was different.

Zerah already had removed his clothes and could not wait for his to hands roam my body even before I finished removing mine. He was already aroused but I then found the sight repulsive and disgusting. As he struggled, he almost tore the material. Soon I was naked. I had not been so uncovered, even in summer when London was at its hottest.

Once in bed, he leaned towards me. At first it was an exploratory kiss, but the kisses extended beyond my lips. Using the fingers of his right hand, he caressed my throat gently, delicately and almost reverently, before moving to my bosom. His kisses became more passionate and gradually I became more at ease. Zerah's fingers expertly began again to manipulate my skin, one moment gently caressing me and the next taking flesh between finger and thumb and squeezing as he whispered gentle allurements into my ear. He was strong yet gentle, assertive yet considerate, so much so that my amorously aroused body yielded to entirely new emotions.

Zerah whispered how much he loved my slender body and enjoyed the feel of my skin; he had not touched such soft, delicate skin.

As I lay on my back, unexpectedly and deftly he took each leg in turn. His hands, like iron manacles around my ankles, forced my legs back against my body as he placed me in an undignified position. I then saw his lean, muscular body arching over me. He held me in that pose for some time, stroking and caressing my most intimate regions.

I knew what small boys looked like from twin brothers, Charles and Henry, when I gave them their baths. Zerah's instrument was huge, stiff and upright. As Doris had once confided to us in the snug during an evening of 'women's talk', "It stood out like a chapel hat peg".

In the wake of my repressed upbringing, I regarded Zerah as very adventurous. My parents brought me up in a religious home with puritan values, and little or no show of affection. I had had no experience of another life outside a sheltered home, thanks to my parents' beliefs. Even at Professor Braithwaite's house, my exposure to any intimacy was minimal. Zerah's sudden and overwhelming passion I found surprising and unsettling, so much so that even Doris's sometimes florid descriptions offered no inkling of what was to come.

Zerah, clearly experienced, pushed my legs down and began to kiss again, seemingly reaching every minute area of skin. His kissing intensified; my entire body tingled with excitement. His tongue began to probe my most intimate regions. I knew something was about to happen. I enjoyed his attention. He seemed loving and caring. As we embraced and kissed, my warmth for him as man and husband deepened. We wrapped each other with our arms. I believed that here, as he precipitated matters further, was passion, tenderness and kindness. Would this be the beginning of unlimited love?

As his sinewy fingers again explored my chest and lower regions, relentlessly stroking and massaging my body, my pulse began to race. I felt myself yield. He again squeezed my skin, rolling it between his fingers. It appeared he could wait no longer. He parted my legs again and before I knew it he moved inside and, with repeated thrusting actions, unleashed a tidal wave of energy. He pushed and pushed; suddenly my body experienced an intense, sharp pain. When almost on the point of bursting, I thought was I on the point of being torn apart? I gave a cry. It made no difference; he had spoilt the occasion.

All at once the thrusting subsided. He lay exhausted at my side, leaving me with a feeling of utter confusion. Was that how it felt to be deflowered? Doris had told us once: "It weren't up to much for us women." I experienced a sudden deep sense of shame; I had just taken part in an unsanctified sexual relationship. Father and mother would be deeply saddened.

With this thought, my violated body had been rendered worthless; discarded like a rag doll. His action had been almost brutal. The tops of my legs ached and I could only feel relief the ordeal had finished.

"Do you enjoy this as much as I?" he asked.

I did not reply. I no longer took pleasure from being close and intimate. Zerah, perhaps sensing my feelings, edged nearer. I attempted to gain control and tried to push him away, but as I did so, he whispered in my ear: 'I love you more than words can say. I am a spent force, but you can send another powerful force through my body.'

I pulled the sheets to my chin. After a while, he threw back the covers and struggled to his feet; he began to dress. I looked to one side and witnessed traces of blood on the sheet. My face blushed instantly.

'The maids will replace them with fresh bedding. They are accustomed to such events,' said Zerah comfortingly.

I washed and, finding fresh clothes, dressed. From the window; the sun shone on the street below, busy with people going about everyday matter. Later we went downstairs. I felt uncomfortable and embarrassed; I imagined people were staring at us, especially as I experienced difficulty walking. We went to the restaurant in search of a meal. After making our choice, the food quickly arrived. Zerah enjoyed his usual appetite, consuming everything on his plate. He also drank his favourite red wine. I was not hungry and picked at my food. During our meal little was said. We returned to our room, alone again.

I noticed the bed at once; spoiled sheets had been removed,

the bed freshly made and the counterpane turned down. My blushes returned.

'There, I said you had nothing to worry about,' declared Zerah.

That night in bed he satisfied himself twice, and on each occasion I found myself in strange positions. Once, he tied my wrists together behind my back using a short silk rope he retrieved from his suitcase. He had come prepared. He described it as just playful fun. I did not believe him. I felt humiliated. To do this, he rolled me over on my stomach and folded my arms behind my back, tightly tying my wrists together before rolling me on my back. Not only revulsive, I felt most uncomfortable and painful until satisfaction on his part was complete. A pattern of repugnant behaviour had begun to develop. The reason for our hasty marriage seemed all too apparent.

Next morning when I awoke, Zerah was already caressing me tenderly; his lovemaking already active. He was so energetic. Within a short while I found myself beneath his huge frame as his weight forced every ounce of breath from my body. His action left me powerless.

'Were you like that with the first Mrs. Colburn?' I whispered.

In a fraction of a second, his body stiffened. His face turned deathly white as blood drained away, becoming immediately contorted. An evil, sour smile betrayed a decayed tooth I had not witnessed before. His grey eyes flashed and instantly became furious. He appeared frozen in a sudden, frothing rage. I had not seen him so angry.

He grabbed my hair in one sweeping, violent action, held me down, and twisted me over with my head face down in the pillow. I struggled to breathe. He pushed what felt like a knee into my back.

He beat me on the buttocks at least a dozen times using the palm of his hand. I might have been a child. His actions stung so much I became numb. Cruel and vindictive, Zerah's behaviour revealed a vicious element of his character I had not witnessed previously.

'Do not ever, I repeat ever, mention Adelaide Colburn again. Do you hear? Do you hear me?' he screamed, glaring. 'Or you will receive more punishment – only next time with my belt. Brutality is what women understand. I will not have Adelaide's name given out loud.'

He rose from bed and strode across to reach for his trousers; as he returned, he withdrew his belt. As if to reinforce his message he held it aloft above his head between his hands, the gold buckle glinted in the light. He brought the belt down slowly and deliberately, holding it tightly against my throat. I my heart thudded; I soon gasped for breath.

I grasped his wrists tightly and dug my nails into his skin for all I was worth. He removed the belt. I burst into tears. He not only hurt me physically, but I became suddenly lonely and frightened; my pride once more deeply wounded. No one had ever subjected me to such a beating before, or so viciously. Father had occasionally gently smacked me lightly for simple wrongdoings, but never hard.

My remark about his wife had been made in innocent jest. My attempt at humour touched a raw nerve. He inflicted a thousand times more pain than father ever did. I feared for my future; for my life. How could we continue together? I yearned suddenly to be rid of the icy shroud of marriage that now enveloped me.

I was completely unprepared for his sudden outburst. One minute he was loving and caring, the next he acted like a mad dog, his mouth foaming. His savage anger emerged as more than just a temperamental outburst; his reaction had been that of a madman, keen to initiate the fault line in our marriage.

Many words flew instantly through my head: bully, cruel, evil, nasty, vindictive and violent. Put together, they did not adequately describe the repugnance of the man with whom I was destined to spend the rest of my life. My marriage had ended within hours of our wedding.

I could only think something deep-rooted in his nature had

been provoked. But what? Why did speaking out of turn in jest deserve such a beating? Why would mention of his wife's name spark such vitriol? Did he have something wrong with his mind? Had his father's death affected him more than he cared to admit? He once declared as his aim to exceed his father and his uncle in every respect. And did his mother have some part to play; did she starve him of affection?

Like a cunning fox, he had lured me to his den to be his prisoner, then to overpower and ill-treat me. Now in his thrall, any hope of further romance would be out of the question. Already disquieted by Zerah's coarse values, I dare not even consider what my family would think if they knew?

In an instant, life became joyless and without purpose; at that moment, confused and resentful, I wished myself dead. I had no reason to live. Most of all, I felt completely unloved, unattractive and fearful of my future. Any confidence I had gained through knowing Zerah seemed to ebb away with my tears. I felt like a lonely sentinel holding out against an unknown enemy; for at that moment, part of Zerah's character was a completely unknown quantity.

For the first time, I knew the real meaning of isolation: isolation from home, family and my below-stairs friends in Golden-square.

Zerah finished dressing and banged the door; the curtains remained drawn across even as the sun shone outside. He turned the key in the lock, making sure the person left behind was a prisoner – his prisoner.

Almost too sore to move, I struggled to replace my nightclothes. Eventually, unable to sit, I lay supine on the bed, only later to bury my face in the pillow. Sobbing, I pulled the sheets over my head.

Carried along in the euphoria of my new life, I had abandoned my long habit of saying prayers at night. In America, with so much to see, it was as though I had forgotten God. Was I paying the price for that? Surely, God would not do that?

What could I to do? Instinctively I asked God to guide me in my hour of need. I needed His help.

A prayer I had heard many times before came to me:

God grant the serenity to accept the things I cannot change, the courage to change the things I can change, and the wisdom to know the difference.

Most of all, I wanted someone to love me; care for me. I was so lonely. I wondered how I came to be in that position. We began as servant and master; we then became friendly, and while I had not liked him so much at first, I found him personable, his manner attractive and captivating. He had a certain charm but a dark side also clouded his character. For, as I gradually began to know him more, so I discovered that while he was fastidious, he could be good-natured. His first kiss took me by surprise, but strangely it felt natural.

Amiable and loving at first, he became the man who now confronted me; the man who would determine my future. How different from the writer whose eloquent English and beautifully-crafted sentences of engineering text I had read from time to time. His flowing words put my own writing to shame.

I now witnessed for myself Zerah's evil side, and so soon into our marriage. Hitherto I had seen only the veneer; his darker side passed unnoticed. And yet, of course, I had witnessed it: the glass he smashed against the wall. Did he direct that same violence at Mrs. Colburn? Was his violence directed at her, or himself? I wished to talk to her. Could she reveal the secret?

Then I began to question recent events further. How convenient for my husband that his former wife and child died by accident, allowing him to remarry. Did he arrange their deaths? I dismissed this. Nonetheless, I recalled Doris's words. She told how men, after a night out drinking on payday, went home and beat their wives black and blue. I too now had experience of that. Doris would be shocked.

After a while, the pain subsided, but my damaged pride went unhealed. I could not believe what took place. What kind of man had I married? Though Zerah never gave a hint of heeding Christian values, I did not expect such evil treatment. I lived with a man I could neither understand nor control. For the first time, I would be wary of any happiness. Fear replaced affection.

I thought the ill-treatment meted out disproportionate to my misdeed. What was my misdeed? Clearly, I should not mention his wife's name. What happened between them? Why did it have any bearing on me? Perhaps Mrs. Baldwin was right.

Was this how all men treated their wives? Did they beat them into submission? Had Mrs. Baldwin tried to warn me?

And what would father think of me? Did he behave similarly to my mother? If father did beat mother, she never raised it with me; she could be too frightened to speak. Those incidents would be private to both. I never even dreamt father capable of such acts. He always seemed kind. Could he be two persons in one body?

And Professor Braithwaite and Mrs. Braithwaite; did the professor beat his wife? I always presumed they respected and loved one another.

Did Zerah shelter dark, terrible secrets and lies? I tried to reconcile the friendly man I met in my first interview with this now violent ogre.

I had no idea of the time, but later I heard the door open. It was closed quickly and the lock engaged.

'We have a train to catch. I must return to Philadelphia. Our stay in New York is over. I have work to complete. Dress and pack your clothes. We leave now.'

Zerah spoke as if nothing had happened. His tone was clipped, severe and precise, as if giving orders to an engine driver.

He came over and dragged me out of bed.

'Get dressed woman, I said,' he ordered.

My eyes brimmed with tears. I had no escape. Being a woman, I had to obey my husband. I had no alternative. I meekly collected my clothes and limped into the bathroom – the lovely bathroom with hot and cold running water I would see no more. I locked the door and tried to dress, shivering with fear. Still feeling sore, I rubbed my skin to restore circulation before continuing to dress. I brushed my hair and collected my things. Dare I refuse to come out? My wedding day over, I would never forget my stay in New York. What a horrible city.

'Hurry up, woman,' Zerah shouted. 'Make sure you empty out.'

I emerged cowering; then gathered the remainder of my clothes into my case, folding them to gain time. Why did he now call me 'woman'?

'Do not waste time,' ordered Zerah. 'We will miss the train.'

The journey to Philadelphia was more terrible than before. Whenever we had to catch a train or ferry, he would grab my hand like that of an uncooperative child and haul me along. That made matters worse. His temper continued to bubble within. I was tempted to scream. No words were exchanged on the journey; the silence spoke my punishment. I yearned for an explanation for his behaviour, but dare not ask in those circumstances.

Back in Philadelphia, life took on a strange routine. I was now Mrs. Colburn, but Zerah remained withdrawn, perhaps driven by events in New York. Conversation was restricted to bare essentials.

I tried to continue as if nothing had happened, believing it my only solution. Yet I had no money and nowhere else to live; I could not escape. To be as amenable as possible seemed the only course of action. Living in fear, I had no wish to antagonise him further as his moods could change from day to day without warning. I questioned how anyone could generate friendship when he was in that state.

I had no idea of what the future would bring. I hoped, and prayed, we could return to London, but I saw no sign of that happening.

One evening, after two days of sleeping in separate rooms,

Zerah apologised for his behaviour in New York. He implored me to forgive him and become friends again; claiming that concern for the business had sparked his anger.

I forgave him but feared his words rang hollow; that all he wanted was intimacy? Was that what marriage meant to him?

He moved closer and caressed me, lovingly, then began to kiss me. Zerah's sexual senses were keen and real, fired by a vivid imagination. He coaxed me into bed and began to be intimate. I knew it foolish to resist, but I was not strong enough, physically or emotionally to tangle with him. He was so powerful and controlling.

My feelings towards him, which previously had grown warm and friendly despite his desire to control me, had become cold and mechanical. I despised him; even to the point of loathing.

If he was aware of how I felt, he seemingly took no notice. Could he be so insensitive to all that had happened?

He persisted with intercourse but I did not enjoy any of it. How could I? He was now much rougher. He expected me to show delight and gratification. The experience, for me, lacked all enjoyment, leaving me lifeless and humiliated, all because of something I had said.

And that was how it continued for some time.

As October drifted into November, and November into December, Zerah became moodier by the week. As for me, I had no life at all. Quite apart from anything else, Philadelphia turned out to be a cold and windy city; the weather already wintry

Occasionally, I would wake in the middle of the night from intense nightmares of despair, with dreams expressing my inner fears; there appeared to be no escape. What would become of me, of us?

Then one day, out of the blue, Zerah spoke of a financial crisis, a panic, as he described it. No one would lend money and some banks were closing permanently. In one or two instances, a 'run' had taken place on a bank.

Although I knew none of the details, I sensed trouble.

Towards the end of December 1860, Zerah said he would close the paper; on 23rd December, he published the last issue of *The Engineer* from Philadelphia. He could no longer support the newspaper; for, as railroad businesses drew in their horns, new subscriptions dried up too.

Zerah must have been in touch with Mr. Alexander Holley because he told me that Mr. Holley's father, a governor of Connecticut state and with a financial stake in the Iron Bank (a bank formed by several iron works), had taken measures to ensure there was no 'run' on his bank.

And what of Zerah's dream? He became even gloomier, warning of increased prospects for war between north and south in the wake of Mr. Abraham Lincoln's election as president.

'I have little money, Lizzy. I have enough for our fare to England. That is where we are going now,' he informed me grumpily. 'Pack your clothes. We will leave on the last day of December. I will book our passage.'

His words came as a shock; a pleasant shock, even though he had reverted to calling me Lizzy. My prayers had been answered. There was at last a glimpse of light at the end of the tunnel. We were returning to England!

'What will we do in England?' I asked, my voice trailing away.

'Why, I will return to *The Engineer*, you stupid woman. Mr. Healey will re-instate me. In his letter, way back, he wrote that if I ever returned to England he would find work.'

'Besides,' he went on, 'England continues to boast a great industrial revolution. We must play our part, make a difference. Some people live like animals but our destiny is greater. If you did but remember Samuel Smiles you would know about self-improvement.'

That was wonderful news. We were returning to my home country – I would see my parents again. I could not believe my good fortune.

Nevertheless and not for the first time, I encountered Zerah's sense of entitlement. His attitude of self-denial, which implied he never made a mistake, could just as easily slide into one of arrogance; so much so that he believed Mr. Healey had no alternative but to re-instate his former editor. Why would that be so?

Meanwhile, I could not wait to see my parents. I knew then how much I loved them both even though I would have to admit to having become married – and not happily. Would I dare tell them? There would be much to explain. It would not be easy. Father would be angry. I had good reason to fear what might happen in the future.

As to returning to London, I was not looking forward to that. While I found America very cold, in London we would again encounter the fog and smoke which at times could even pervade the house. I had heard that in winter some streets of London could be so full of dense brown smoke that scarcely anything could be seen. In spring and summer, coal smoke, dirt and dust would pour out of the multitude of chimneys which, together with the mist, frequently prevented the sun from shining through.

Even when there was no fog, such as early in the morning or on warm summer Sundays when factories were not working, there remained a bluish grey haze to dampen any spirits. But I would not let that cloud my own joy of seeing both of my parents as well as my brothers and sisters again.

And I had to remind myself that I would be returning to England with a new status, that of Mrs. Elizabeth Colburn.

Chapter Five
Mistress of the house

O N our arrival at Liverpool mid-way through January 1861, Zerah immediately dispatched a letter to inform Mr. Jenkins of our expected arrival in London. He gave instructions to secure basic provisions and light fires in all principal rooms downstairs, including the kitchen and scullery. He also requested Mrs. Jenkins prepare light food in preparation for our appearance.

The journey by railway from Liverpool to London was long and tiresome. For the final part in London, Zerah hired a cab to accommodate ourselves and our luggage; including a large trunk containing paper and books acquired in America.

We could not have arrived back in London at a more inappropriate time. Frost and snow seemingly paralysed the city and surrounding areas in that savagely cold winter. Newspapers reported how the principal mail route to France, the London, Chatham and Dover line, was affected by up to nine feet of snow for some 48 hours. In London, many water pipes were frozen and Zerah congratulated himself on his presence of mind to engage the services of Mr. Jenkins to care for the house in our absence.

In some places, as we passed, shivering groups queued for water in the streets, the pavements already slippery with ice.

One upheaval since our departure the previous year we could not ignore from the vantage of the cab. In our absence, work had started on the Metropolitan Underground Railway with construction planned to occupy three years. Destruction of property to make way for the railway could be seen everywhere. Many lost their homes in the upheaval while whole areas of London underwent continual change. Zerah said it reminded him of parts of Paris.

I cannot find words of my own to adequately describe the

extent of that upheaval. I can but refer to Mr. Dickens's book, *Dombey and Son*, in which Polly walked through the terrible aftermath of the great destruction in Camden. He wrote "Here a chaos of carts, overthrown and jumbled together, lay topsy-turvy at the bottom of a steep unnatural hill; there, confused treasures of iron soaked and resulted in something that had accidently become a pond."

Zerah read *Dombey and Son* more than once, praising it as one of the first great novels of the railway age where trains are used as symbols, but he disliked intensely how the author dwelt on the destruction of the rows of small houses and gardens in Camden, changing the neighbourhood and patterns of life forever.

We could vouch for this from our experiences. In the Euston Road, thoroughfares became wholly impassable; walls remained unfinished and houses were in all manner of disrepair. To say the least, confusion appeared to be everywhere.

Zerah, as one might expect, found work of the new railway exciting, even exhilarating. He admitted that coal mines, industrialisation and the growth of the railways created havoc and degradation to people and places; yet they were the inevitable price of progress.

He praised the Metropolitan, describing it as the world's first underground railway. First proposed by Mr. Charles Pearson, solicitor to the City of London, engineers used what Zerah called 'cut and cover' methods to achieve their success in constructing the line. From what little I saw, it created huge disruption, as well as much noise and immense clouds of dust.

The railway ran close to the south side of Regent's Park, and followed the line of Marylebone-road and Euston-road. At that time, London not only experienced its coldest winter but the hottest summer for many, many years. A worse time to undertake such work could not be imagined.

The new railway left London with an indelible mark, displacing over 12,000 people, many of whom lived in abject poverty; it caused demolition of over 1,000 houses. However, when eventually completed, the underground railway proved popular, as six million used it in the first year. In winter, people adopted the railway as a shelter from the cold.

That harsh winter caused the most tragic calamity. Close by, in Regent's Park, the frozen ornamental water opposite Sussex-place, known as Broadwater, drew many ice skaters. However, so many were on the ice at one time that the ice cracked, sucking many under water, itself some 12 feet deep in places. At one time, 200 people fought for their lives in freezing water and over 30 died; meanwhile many thousands – between 3,000 and 4,000 – crowded the shoreline to watch proceedings, causing much commotion.

I took great pleasure from my return, even though no one could hide from the rising stench from sewers, horse manure and urine in some of London's streets as we passed. I had not noticed such smells in Philadelphia. Also, the sickening smell of coal gas clung to the atmosphere; however, Zerah seemed unperturbed.

On arrival, the house looked comfortingly familiar. That Zerah retained the property in the event of his unexpected return to London proved a wise decision. He obviously expected to return at some point in time. But did he make the decision to wed me and remain in America on the spur of the moment?

In our absence, little had changed in Gloucester-road, an avenue of imposing villas and terraced houses, which someone described the standard as much higher than in many other streets of London.

To compound that, the long engine shed that faced the beautiful terraced houses of Fitzroy-road, adjacent to Gloucester-road, remained a troublesome burden for residents.

We were but a short distance from the London & North Western Railway, which ran close by from Paddington. To the north end of Gloucester-toad stood the large Camden goods station with its marshalling yards and the offending engine shed. To our good fortune, all were located sufficiently far away that neither noise nor smoke troubled us. Smuts and blacks proved such a nuisance that few people wore white; both marked every item they touched, making it impossible to keep clean.

This proved so for houses to the east of Gloucester-road. Here, the soot and grime given off by locomotives as they idled at the shed continually hung over the houses like a giant cloud; so much so that smuts and blacks quickly grimed washing hung out to dry. Even before our departure to America, women in those houses complained bitterly. Zerah saw no evil in the locomotives or their smoke smuts; indirectly smuts provided his livelihood, a source of interest and comment to be accepted as everyday occurrences.

As for myself, I had left the house as housekeeper but returned as Mrs. Colburn. Such was the speed with which Zerah Colburn implemented change. However, although I may have returned as lady of the house, I felt at no great ease in the wake of the beatings and abuse admonished by my husband.

Did Zerah secretly enjoy beating me? Did he carry a secret malady of which I knew nothing? I am sure my father would not have hit mother; so why did Zerah beat me? I hated him for what he had done, but as a Christian, I knew that to hate was wrong. I should forgive my enemies.

Mr. and Mrs. Jenkins' preparations made us feel welcome. As we entered the house, the warmth greeted our faces and, unlike some people's houses, there were no frozen pipes.

I hoped our return to No. 7 Gloucester-road might herald a new beginning; that I could overcome my apprehension and Zerah and I could become friends again and enjoy good fortune. I hoped above all to feel comfortable in my new role in England as Mrs. Colburn. Should the worst happen, I could see my parents and confess all. I hoped they would forgive.

On arrival, my first task required me to lay and light a fire in the bedroom, then place warming pans in the bed. The huge bed with its brass bedstead that Zerah used previously caused me to think. If this bed could speak what tales would it tell? Now I would sleep in it too. Zerah and his previous wife had slept in this bed; I longed to exchange it for a new one. Of course, that would be out of the question.

It would be our first night of sleeping together at No. 7 Gloucester-road; our first night in England as man and wife. Would the enforced closeness wrought by our return to London rekindle any romance?

Not surprisingly, after unpacking some luggage, weariness set in; the journey across the Atlantic had been so much different from that which we had undertaken in *Great Eastern*. The crossing and the subsequent rail journey from Liverpool – Britain's busiest port – had been taxing in the extreme. It seemed we had been travelling for months. I lost all measure of time.

Someone on the voyage said that out of all the passenger ships crossing the Atlantic, one soul in thirty lost their life. It may just have been an ugly rumour, but it was an unhappy prospect for any Atlantic traveller. It reminded me of the fate that befell Mrs. Colburn and her daughter, Sarah Pearl – though I kept those thoughts to myself. I hoped no further crossings of the Atlantic would be required of me.

Outside, the January cold gripped London, but in the bedroom the fire blazed heartily, thanks to my earlier efforts.

The relationship between Zerah and me remained somewhat cool, as recollections of life in America lingered. Should I show more affection than I felt? Zerah could be engaging, generous and even humorous. However, I could not rid memories of his cruelty. I looked forward to seeing my parents – but not to revealing my news.

The house was quiet and lifeless, and soon we would have to consider hiring domestic staff; Zerah would interview each in turn first. He made all decisions.

In the evening, following a small meal, I soaked in a hot bath for a short while. Before my bath, I first removed the warming pans, allowing the bed to air.

As I emerged from the bathroom, I found Zerah waiting,

naked. He came close, took me in his arms and squeezed me, giving me long and clinging kisses, growing ever more passionate in his embrace. He carried me into the bedroom and lowered me onto the rug in front of the blazing fire. Our bodies glowed in the flames. He caressed me and removed my nightwear.

'I do love you, Lizzy,' he said.

'You have a peculiar way of showing it sometimes,' I replied.

He then picked me up from the rug and laid me on the bed.

With the gas lamps already turned right down low, only the flickering flames of the fire lit the room. Then, all at once, he came back to the side of the bed where I lay.

'What is it you have to remember now we are back in London, Lizzy?' he said with flint to his voice, his tone no longer affectionate. It had changed in an instant to become stern, with a cruel twist. I shivered despite the heat of the bath.

I could smell the red wine he had consumed earlier. His grey eyes had turned to pebbles. The malice of his demeanour frightened me.

I saw, as he stood over me, he had reached for his black leather belt. He held it menacingly, taut between his hands. Then, he raised high his right hand, belt in hand, as if to strike.

'Do you want a beating like you received in New York?' said Zerah roughly. 'Remember – no word about Mrs. Adelaide Colburn to anyone, repeat, anyone here in England, and that includes your parents. Do *not* discuss our private life. Do you understand?'

He then bent down, putting his left hand round my throat and, squeezing hard, hissed menacingly in my ear.

'Do you understand?' And don't even think of running away. Your family will despise you – they will want nothing to do with you. And don't think either of straying into the arms of another man, or you will receive some of this belt. Do you understand?'

It was useless to scream. With no one else in the house, I was alone with a devil. One moment loving, the next he had become an evil giant.

Again, he attempted to control; even isolate me from family and friends, but this time in my home country

'Do not hit me,' I cried out. 'My baby. Do not hurt my baby.'

'Baby? What baby? You did not tell me about an infant,' he shouted. 'How long have you known?'

'I am expecting a bairn,' I replied. 'Our child. I think I am about four months gone. I have just discovered it.'

'Do not jest, woman. You deserve a good whipping,' he shouted.

'No, Sir,' I cried. 'I am with child. Our child; your child. You would not wish to hurt our first born, surely.'

He came near and felt my stomach with his right hand. My belly was a little larger than normal, but hardly so.

'If I find you are lying, Lizzy, I shall beat you to within an inch of your life,' he warned. He put down his belt.

'Dress for bed,' he ordered. 'Think yourself lucky. Take this as a warning. Remember. Never mention Mrs. Adelaide Colburn in this house. And never speak her name in this country. Do you hear me? Do you understand? Speak her name and you will regret it. The last beating you had will be as nothing to what you will receive.'

Quite abruptly, his voice changed again becoming softer. 'I hope it is a boy,' he said. Out of the blue, his love appeared to overflow, as if desperate to mend a broken heart.

'Now come to bed. Let us be friends. You will see the doctor tomorrow.'

I went to dress. The room was warm, yet I shivered with fright. My hands trembled as I put on my nightwear. All previous memories flooded back. The evil man I knew in New York had not departed. He was there at my side, unpredictable as ever. I had no wish to be there; to live in the same house. I craved the ground to swallow me whole.

I climbed meekly into what would be for me the marriage bed. He followed shortly afterwards. I turned my back to him, brought my knees up to my chest and put my arms round them.

He lifted my nightdress, fondled me and was intimate, but he was more careful, gentle even with an air of renewed tenderness. For me the lovemaking was mechanical, with no enjoyment. Was I to be grateful; show gratitude? He turned and faced the other way, soon lapsing into asleep with a clear conscience.

After a while, I turned over and I lay on my back for what seemed an eternity. How many times had I felt like this – lonely? I stared into blackness, the fire long since having extinguished. Rigid with fear, I knew not what to do next. I gripped the mattress so tightly with my left hand I could feel the stitched edges. Outside, cabs rattled by with their fares, perhaps returning from a theatre or concert. Why did Zerah not want mention made of his first wife? What had happened between those two?

I was not only confused and bewildered but also angry; angry in my heart and not just in my head; angry that he had placed me in this position, beholden to an evil man and carrying his child.

Storm clouds gathered once more over my life. At night, I would have unmanageable dreams that caused me to wake with a jump; I had found myself in a trap. In the turmoil I could conceive of two reasons the first Mrs. Colburn might return to America. She hated England. Alternatively, if she had not been exactly afraid of Zerah, she sought escape from his fiery temper. Now she was dead. If she had remained in London, she would be alive. And, adding further to my turmoil, were two more questions: was she the first Mrs. Colburn? Or were there others?

I had been looking forward to holding a baby in my arms; it would be a new experience to be responsible for something so tiny. But would ours be a happy home for it? If not, how could I end my misery; our misery? Should I kill the infant and myself? How would I do that? Cut my wrists? I was too frightened for that. I hated the sight of blood; seeing the presence of it caused me to faint. I could drink alcohol and drown in Regent's Park Lake. I thought of all those who had died in the frozen lake. That was not for me. Perhaps I could gas myself. Hang myself. Maybe I could take mercury; many died from mercury poisoning.

Alternatively, I could run away. Where could I go? I had no money – Zerah held firm control of the purse strings. My parents, although loving and caring, would have little sympathy, I imagined. I had made my bed and now I had to lie on it.

I could move away completely and start again, but with a child to rear that would not be easy.

As I stared at the ceiling, I retreated more and more into my private thoughts. Which, if any, of his father's flaws had Zerah inherited? Finally, I devised a plan. I would humour Zerah as best I could for baby's sake, until the right moment came to escape the demon.

My parents had taught me from an early age to forgive others for whatever they inflicted. I recalled the Lord's Prayer. It was my task to forgive Zerah – and find a means of escape.

I turned over and faced Zerah's back. I put my arm round his body. He emerged from sleep in better temper.

'I am sorry to make you angry. It was my fault,' I told him. 'Please forgive my foolishness. I gave no thought to your feelings. You will enjoy the baby when it arrives. They need all the love their parents can give. We should love one another, and love our baby.'

He turned over and faced me. Had his anger subsided?

'Forgive me too,' he confessed. 'I am sorry. My blood boils over in a flash, like the witches' caldron in Macbeth. But you must never ever mention my first wife.'

I was not yet bold enough to ask why, despite his unusually contrite manner. I knew from bitter experience how quickly his temper could flare. I dare not rise to the bait.

Of concern to me would be Zerah's reaction to this baby. He had been independent as a child and many years since he had been father to a baby. I knew of his daughter, but I had little insight into his relationship with her. Did he really want this child? He hoped for a boy, presumably to carry through the Colburn lineage; much different from wanting a child.

Next morning, following Zerah's departure to present himself at *The Engineer*'s offices in his effort to resume his position, I visited Dr. Graham's surgery nearby. He occupied No. 15 Gloucester-road. He could not attend to me immediately, so I made an appointment for the following day.

On my return, I tidied away newspapers and resumed unpacking. Later, I composed a short letter to my parents advising them of my return to London and how much I would like to see them.

Not knowing of their movements, I asked for a convenient date to visit. Whenever I went, the meeting would be the most difficult of my life. I would have to eat humble pie and explain my marriage to Zerah.

On his return that evening, Zerah informed me that Mr. Healey, the owner of *The Engineer*, grudgingly expressed gratitude for his editor's return. Mr. Healey nonetheless was angry that Zerah had absented the journal without warning.

Mr. Healey, as I may have mentioned, was a proud man; Zerah's sudden and unexplained absence had made him appear a fool. Zerah's decision to remain in America, following the maiden voyage of *Great Eastern*, infuriated Mr. Healey. However, by the time of Zerah's return to London, Mr. Healey's anger had subsided, but it quickly rekindled when Zerah marched through the door, bold as brass, asking to meet Mr. Healey.

According to Zerah, and I had to accept his words, Mr. Healey had little alternative but to re-engage him. No other technical editor in London, it seemed, could match Zerah's skills as engineer and writer.

However, during Zerah's absence, Mr. Edward Healey had taken into partnership his elder brother, Mr. Elkanah Healey, allowing Mr. Healey to act as temporary editor.

Mr. Healey was compelled to re-engage Zerah; he found work of editing the weekly journal time consuming and mentally arduous. He was not a writer by nature. The appointment not only restored Zerah's pride, but provided him with a good income – at least he said so.

Mr. Healey had said that while there were many 'penny-a-liners' to fill the columns of *The Engineer*, or indeed many other newspapers, there were insufficient writers of stature and authority to meet his needs. There were always more writers than columns to fill, Zerah told me, but none who could write as well as him.

According to Zerah, a respectable 'man of letters' could command an income equal to that of any doctor or lawyer. And, he added, the quill-pushers who characterised much of London's literary output, earned only a small reward, so Zerah was indeed fortunate to receive a good income. Mr. Healey must indeed have held Zerah in great respect for his extraordinary stream of specialist words to justify such a senior position in his business.

Zerah returned that night to the house overjoyed. Not only had he resumed his position as editor, but also his authority remained undiminished as he regained his dominance at the newspaper. Zerah made no mention of any ultimatum, never again to transgress. Perhaps both men needed each other if they were to be successful.

Mr. Healey had handed Zerah a new opportunity. Only many years later did I learn that while Mr. Healey judged Zerah an 'erratic genius' – brilliant intellectually as a writer – he also regarded him as an eccentric, impulsive and painstaking worker, ever confident of his own importance; a man who envied – and resented – no one.

Consequently, Zerah exuded a renewed air of destiny, as though on the road to greatness. For, whereas prior to his visit to America, he had not been appointed specifically to the editor's chair (even though he called himself editor) but instead given an 'influential position on the staff', on his return from America he became editor. Even more than before, Zerah approached everything with an air of entitlement and embarked all that he could to burnish his image in the engineering fraternity, almost as though he had never been away on the other side of the world where he produced a perfect replica of *The Engineer* newspaper.

Zerah set his heart on fulfilling his dream as the 'perfect' English gentleman: the pleasing prospect of marriage by 35 (Zerah was 28), a house in Belgravia for the happy couple (Zerah's house was close to Regent's Park), a footman in splendid uniform, and at least a brougham. While Zerah still had some way to go in reaching his goal, he remained convinced his new appointment set him on the right road.

And so he resumed the style of living befitting a London editor. Among his first actions, he placed an order for daily newspapers and journals to keep abreast of world news. Besides *The Times*, we received the *Illustrated London News* and the *Illustrated News*, both of which I found most interesting.

Zerah purchased clothes and shoes from high-class outfitters; his shirts were handmade, usually having been 'put out' for making. He wore a tailcoat with waistcoat and trousers to complete his morning dress. His overcoat he used for winter and, to protect his shoes, he wore galoshes newly arrived from America.

A rule imposed by Mr. Healey required men to wear silk hats. Made of plush sewn silk covering a stiff blocked base of canvas, he always wore it on his journey to and from *The Engineer*. It required much care.

He also acquired an umbrella, considered essential for a man of Zerah's standing. He purchased it and a stick from James Smith & Son. The business, founded in 1830, moved in 1867 to New Oxford-street, but it also had an establishment in Saville-row. At one time, an umbrella would have been seen as effeminate, but men of Zerah's standing considered an umbrella essential.

For financial transactions, Zerah employed Coutts & Company; it occupied an office in the Strand, almost opposite the offices of *The Engineer*.

I noticed too he purchased a pocket watch. He had long wished to own this particular item; a sterling silver full Hunter. He obtained it from E. Dent & Company of No. 61, Strand, the company that supplied the Great Clock for the Houses of Parliament. Dent pocket watches were much prized by gentlemen for their high quality.

Zerah regarded his attire as indispensable to a gentleman. To me they reinforced his assurance and added to his style of living. In keeping with this, he described himself as 'inimitable - "after your Mr. Dickens", he said - as he saw no other man at work who could surpass his command of English and knowledge of engineering, heat and steam. And who else could match his energy and ambition?

That night, as we sat at table and ate the modest meal I had prepared, the talk reflected the day's occurrences at *The Engineer*.

Undertones of tension remained ever present. For me, Zerah's earlier threat to beat me remained uppermost, given my pregnant condition. The atmosphere was difficult. Was this a further widening of the divide between us? Fine cracks had already appeared in our marriage; would they become chasms? I sensed the strain; perhaps Zerah, following his new appointment, was insensitive to it. He regarded it as important to be back in control of *The Engineer*'s editorial department; and he controlled me. He spoke of the privilege for us to live in London at a time of exciting change. Why then had he been so keen to live again in America?

Despite his reassuring comments, I felt uneasy and unsure of the future. Someday, I would have to learn to stand on my own two feet. I longed to imbue some of Zerah's self-confidence into my own rather timid attitude. I lived life half expecting an eruption to take place at any moment; such was my wariness of him. I equated it to living with a coiled spring, awaiting its instant and unpredictable release.

Following his acceptance at *The Engineer*, Zerah drafted an advertisement for a housekeeper. He placed it in *The Times*.

'We shall both inspect the candidates,' he told me, as if trying to show friendliness. 'But I will make the final decision.'

I became more aware of our neighbours. Living in a large

house – Park House – at No. 1, was a respected surgeon, Mr. Joseph Blackstone. His son, also a surgeon, Mr. Joseph Blackstone Jnr, lived next door to us at No. 8. The Rev. Edward Hayes Plumptre, MA, lived at No. 4.

Another curiosity of Gloucester-road took the form of the occupant of No. 2. This was a Mr. Robert Browning. Though he shared my maiden name, as far as I am aware he had no connection whatsoever with my family. His fine residence enjoyed a coach house and stables. The house next door to us also enjoyed stables.

Mr. Charles Culliford (Charley) Dickens, the eldest son of Mr. Charles Dickens, resided in Gloucester-road too. Years later, on 9th June 1870, when his father died from a stroke, he continued at the same address, namely No. 46 Gloucester-road. His father occupied Gad's Hill Place, Higham, Kent until his death. Another resident of Gloucester-road, Mr. Antoine Claudet, an authority in photographic circles, occupied No. 11.

The following day I attended Dr. Graham. By then I ceased to be unwell and sickness in the morning had begun to take its effect; also there were signs of quickening. I discovered the doctor to be a youngish man who asked many questions, including my address and my husband's occupation. Being young, he was not as fashionable as some more famous in the locality. I explained we lived but a few doors distant. He took my pulse and checked my breathing and, following a cursory examination, confirmed my pregnancy.

'You appear to be a healthy young woman, look after yourself and you will have no worries,' he said. 'See me in two months' time.'

His words offered some comfort, giving a slight spring to my step.

Zerah quickly resumed the momentum he displayed at *The Engineer* prior to *Great Eastern*'s maiden voyage. He could be absent for several days at a time; in the evenings he attended meetings at various engineering institutions.

On his daily return from *The Engineer*, Zerah would often visit No. 65. He would arrive at our house and say 'I called in at No. 65.' Such was his humour. Because, located at No. 65, was The Engineer public house. I did find this a rather peculiar and bizarre coincidence. That Zerah Colburn, the editor of *The Engineer*, should live at No. 7 Gloucester-road and there, at No. 65 Gloucester-road, was situated The Engineer public house.

Zerah said the public house, one of three in Gloucester-road, was intended for thirsty enginemen and other employees of the railway. The building, in brown stock brick, he claimed had been constructed between 1845 and 1850. The name, The Engineer, had been given in recognition of Mr. Robert Stephenson who supervised the nearby London & Birmingham Railway.

Zerah told me that on the day the London & Birmingham Railway opened, the four biggest towns in England – the main political, commercial and industrial centres - were for the first time brought within a few hours of each other. By joining the capital to Birmingham, the rails linked those already running through the Black Country and onwards for 100 miles to Lancashire, Manchester and the great port of Liverpool (with which in future I would be briefly acquainted). The London & Birmingham Railway became the main artery of England.

Railwaymen and enginemen frequented two other public houses on Gloucester-road, the Lansdowne and the Pembroke Castle, but these hardly ever by Zerah, unless he sought particular information.

Zerah could spend one or two evenings a week in The Engineer. Inevitably, he developed friendly terms with the publican. I imagine that one reason why the two men became so well acquainted was the one subject they had in common – The Engineer. Zerah also found it absorbing to meet railwaymen; they provided valuable technical details of the running of the railway, as well as of new locomotive developments.

I did not once step inside the public house – indeed, no one invited me to do so, nor would I have wanted. My father told me they were places of evil; dens of iniquity. Certainly, I would not have walked in on my own account. Public houses were a man's domain.

However, I was aware of some of those who frequented the place. I knew that only because of those Zerah met on a regular basis – sometimes he would discuss these men with me.

Meanwhile, the advertisement in *The Times* proved successful; before long we engaged a new housekeeper, a woman in her early 50s who, we found, to be exceedingly thorough in her work. Her name was Mrs. Betteridge.

It pleased me that Zerah did not choose someone of my own age. A few of the applicants were young and, I thought, pretty. However, Zerah passed over them in favour of Mrs. Betteridge.

She wished to be addressed as Mrs. Betteridge, her name in service. But Zerah did not like that name for some reason and insisted we use her Christian name. Margaret however soon became shortened to Peggy. It took time for Peggy to welcome her new name. She and I adjusted well, though I sensed she knew I did not come from 'good stock'. She slept in the room I once occupied at the top of the house. She proved an understanding and knowledgeable woman; one I came to respect, trust and even admire.

Peggy used the term 'good stock' when speaking of some of her former employers, who had come from 'good stock'. She once declared taste was not a personal matter but something sanctioned by society. Peggy proved an excellent cook and competent with her shopping. She had excellent references, having at one time also been a nurse. Clean and tidy in her manner and well organised, she was the antithesis of many domestic servants who could be untruthful, lazy and indifferent. Zerah had made a good choice.

However, before too many weeks, Peggy complained of too much work and required assistance. She requested we employ a housemaid. She could be quite forthright; she even sought permission to interview prospective candidates. I knew Zerah would not accede; indeed, he declined with a firm No. Peggy however voiced her own requirement: housemaids should clean the house without being seen and heard, hoping their work would be noticed.

Shortly afterwards, having looked intently through the Personal Column in *The Times*, Zerah selected three applicants he deemed suitable to attend for interview. From these he picked Rose. Fortunately, Rose had a quite meek and mild nature, and settled in well with Peggy, who immediately took her under her wing.

Rose, a single woman with a gamine figure, was some 10 years older than me; her most striking feature was her luminous blue eyes. Did I detect that Zerah found her attractive? For I could see that while she was perfectly civil, always calling me ma'am, she seemed to have reservations towards me, perhaps from knowing (having talked to Peggy) that I had 'come up in the world' through marriage. As for myself, I remained outwardly the demure 'angel in the house', as Mr. Clark once so flatteringly had described me, knowing when not to speak out of turn when Zerah was present.

With the passage of time, I felt baby moving inside, sometimes even giving gentle kicks. I paid regular visits to the doctor who told me he knew an excellent nurse able to provide care at the appropriate time.

I looked forward to its arrival and holding it in my arms, warm and soft; a new living being. But would this be a happy home?

Peggy (I do not know to this day if she was indeed married and if so, what happened to her husband), had experience of babies she told me. She did not say if they were her own, or whether the experience came through nursing practice. It reassured me to have her nearby.

The visit to my parents proved to be less dreadful than I feared. Father was not at home when I entered. Perhaps that was deliberate; possibly he was out in search of another house, as mother had said they were considering moving further west in London.

I confided as much as I dare in the circumstances, keeping to details of the Atlantic crossing and some of life in Philadelphia. Then I revealed my marriage to Zerah. There was a long silence.

Eventually she asked the question I most feared: 'Why did you marry?'

Lamely, I replied: 'I became caught up by events out of my control. It seemed I had no alternative.'

She gave a grunt. I had worse news yet to break to her.

Then she wished to know why I had not waited to marry in London where family could attend and meet the bridegroom.

'Was your plan never to return?' she asked. 'How could you do that to your loving parents?'

Beyond that there was no form of rebuke, as I had expected.

I told her of Zerah's desire to marry in New York in his home country. Afterwards, I again wondered if my parents had someone else in mind I should marry, perhaps a young accountant who could offer advantage of some kind, even a fortune.

I admitted to one untruth: I expressed my fear that father would refuse to sanction the marriage. Mother ignored this; instead, she said that according to some, a large family offered the best recipe for happiness in marriage. She hoped we enjoyed each other's company, and would be happy.

At that convenient moment I told mother of my pregnancy. Of course, the prospect of becoming a grandmother pleased her. It would be a new experience for her too. She expressed 'great happiness' for us and promised to do all she could to offer support, without being intrusive. Should I require, she could visit the house and care for mother and baby, but as she often said, 'only if you really want my help'.

I was unsure how Zerah would react to her presence and was accordingly non-committal. On the other hand, I knew that I might need her support and assistance; I did not want to offend her. I had known my parents far longer than Zerah, and I knew they loved me.

While mother no doubt saw it as her business to ensure that I 'married well', as she put it, she also wanted me to marry at the altar. While she saw this as unbreakable, it could bring couples great unhappiness.

Mother expressed her wish to meet Zerah, and invited us to the house one evening when father could be present. I told her I would talk to Zerah and write. I did not look forward to that.

Later, when we visited my parents, I could sense Zerah was not enthusiastic to join me, but he knew his obligation as father to our child. I found it difficult to judge father's opinion of Zerah. He said little; maybe he regarded himself as the underdog. That did not prevent his visceral repulsion for Zerah, as mother later revealed to me privately.

The evening however passed off almost uneventfully; my father caused one difficult moment when he asked if our marriage in New York was valid in England. Zerah replied quickly that 'of course' it was. After that, father had little to say, but I sensed his unease.

We talked of many things but mostly of the voyage in *Great Eastern*, life in Philadelphia and the financial 'panic' that engulfed businesses and forced our return. Father, being an accountant, pricked up his ears at the word 'panic' but remained silent.

Zerah made mention during conversation of the immense disruption caused by railway construction in London, including the Metropolitan Underground Railway line. As the first attempt to build a railway beneath a large city, it was an obvious talking point, the more so with Zerah's intense interest in railways.

In my heart, I knew exactly what Zerah permitted me to discuss with my parents, and I saw it as my task to steer conversation away from anything that might be controversial.

Meanwhile, at No. 7 Gloucester-road, life gathered a new momentum. I became increasingly aware of the infant growing inside as I became larger and larger, and more self-conscious.

Zerah meanwhile was intensely preoccupied. With his far-reaching capacity for work, he re-engaged with *The Engineer* with even more vigour, his own business failure in Philadelphia quite forgotten.

With a natural gift for languages, it was quite usual to see him reading French and German newspapers brought from *The Engineer*'s offices. He occasionally used French words in daily conversation; au contraire were two of his most frequent. Notably, he would write letters in French to engineers in France; and generally he had much appreciation of and respect for the French as a people.

Zerah developed a liking for French wines, in preference to German white wines. He regularly visited Berry Brothers in St. James's-street. On one occasion he disclosed that on his visits to Berry Brothers he would use their coffee scales to reveal his weight, and of which he would make a record.

During our absence in America, Mr. William Gladstone in his budget of 1860 dramatically cut excise duty on wine – especially French-made wines – as the Cobden-Chevalier treaty reduced tariffs between France and England. Mr. Gladstone intended to encourage people to drink wines in preference to spirits.

According to Zerah, the 1855 classification of the wines of Medoc (Bordeaux) split the top Chateaux into five classes: Ch. Lafite, Ch. Latour, Ch. Margaux and Ch. Haut Brion were defined as the First growths; Mouton (Rothschild) was omitted and included as a Second Growth.

So, while Zerah became knowledgeable about French red wines, he developed a taste for them too. In the following years, he drew attention to some good vintages, like those of 1863 and 1864.

Peggy and Rose increasingly undertook more work as Zerah renewed his custom of entertaining prominent engineers at dinner. Both women were engaged in house cleaning duties, as well as shopping, cooking and washing dishes. My principal task was to plan the courses, while Zerah would issue invitations.

Occasionally, Zerah invited me to join, but mostly the occasions were 'men's affairs', opportunities for an exchange of *their* views. I gave some thought to introducing Mrs. Braithwaite's practice of 'turning the table', but considered it inappropriate; it could cause an argument.

Increasingly with these events, and on other occasions, I became aware that Zerah maintained an only child's certainty that his own ideas ought to be given priority; an opinion of mine that persisted for many years thereafter, and one confirmed by Mr. William Maw, of whom more anon. I had not noticed it in our early acquaintance; but as time by it became more apparent.

Mr. John Fowler, consulting engineer to the new Metropolitan Railway, attended several times. Construction of the line across London began in 1860; it eventually opened on 10th January 1863 with free rides for many people. Zerah spent much time in the tunnels during the opening day with Mr. Daniel Gooch. For Zerah, the grand banquet marked a highlight of the opening ceremony. The railway company invited Zerah and Mr. Healey; over 700 people attended.

Zerah held Mr. Fowler in great awe, partly because of the importance of his task to provide London with its first underground railway. Mr. Fowler later received a knighthood. Aside from the Metropolitan Underground Railway, Mr. Fowler gained fame for the design and construction of the Forth Bridge, alongside Mr. Benjamin Baker and Mr. William Arrol. He also built the Albert Edward Bridge at Coalbrookdale, Shropshire and the Victoria Bridge at Upper Arley, Worcestershire.

Zerah explained that Mr. Fowler had designed a fireless locomotive; it ran experimentally on the Metropolitan Railway. He intended it should be smokeless but according to Zerah, ever outspoken, it was 'a dismal failure', while railway workers called the locomotive 'Fowler's Ghost'.

In the spring of 1861, London's trees were in blossom and the grass in London's parks lush and green; everywhere looked much brighter after the grimness of winter.

In April of that year, civil war erupted in America when the Confederates attacked Fort Sumter in South Carolina. From that moment on for some four years, Zerah closely observed developments in the war through the pages of *The Times*.

My main preoccupation remained with the infant within. I wondered what baby would look like; would it be boy or girl. If a girl, would she look like me?

Meanwhile, the house became a well-known meeting place for many engineers of similar standing to that of Mr. Fowler. Indeed, it was through Mr. Fowler's kindness that Zerah received permission to make a 'trial trip' on the Metropolitan Underground Railway. The first, just a short journey, took place in November 1861; a full-length 'trial trip' occurred the following May. Men of great importance attended, including Mr. Gladstone.

Mr. Fowler lived at Thornwood Lodge, Campden Hill, on the west side of Kensington Gardens. Mr. William Maw (who later became Zerah's associate, as I will include later) and his wife Emily, years later lived in Addison Road, close to Campden Hill.

Such 'trips' were intended to impress potential travellers of the safety of underground railways. Zerah however criticised the damp and smoky conditions in the tunnels, even though the trains used Mr. Fowler's supposedly 'smokeless' locomotives. Eventually, these locomotives proved unreliable and engineers discontinued their use.

In 1861, Zerah also renewed his acquaintance with Mr. Train who laid three demonstration horse-drawn tramways in Bayswater-road, Victoria-street and Kennington-road. Only one of these, from Westminster Bridge to Kennington Gate, eventually proved successful. Zerah approved of the whole idea (was that because Mr. Train was an American?) though he suggested an improved design of rail.

While Zerah's dinner parties made Peggy feel important and kept her extremely busy, they offered me time for needlework, reading and knitting clothes for baby. Zerah found the standard of Peggy's cooking pleasing and gave praise in front of guests. Indeed, the dinner-parties and soirées proved so successful, with guests fulsome in their praise, that Zerah began to repeat them more frequently.

Zerah's explanation for these soirées – sometimes there could be one or two dinner-parties a week, depending on the extent to which business took him away from the house – was their opportunity to provide him with material from which to write articles for *The Engineer*. He stressed that while he could not report directly what guests told him, the information he gathered offered essential background material for leaders (opinion columns, he once explained) and news and features.

It was then that I cast my mind back to Golden-square and *Great Eastern*. So much had happened since the voyage, but what would the future bring?

At Golden-square I recalled how in summer the cherry and lavender girls would bring their wares to the door in the hope of a sale; in winter we heard the muffin man with his bell and shouting "three for a penny", and the roasted chestnut seller. Teas could improve by catching the cockles-and-mussels man who did his best business in late afternoon. In the morning, we would witness the milkman with his covered pails hung across a yoke, doling out milk to mothers with children. We were told of a cow in St James's-park to supply milk on demand for nurses and children out for a daily walks. Occasionally, the potman delivered strong drink, like porter and stout. Sometimes, Doris caught sight of Robert the footman peeping out of the window with the hope of stopping the potman for a pint of mild porter.

With so many people in the house there was always sound of movement and voices. But as to 'our' house, there were no sounds of music as there had been at the Professor's house. There, we would hear Mrs. Braithwaite playing the piano both during the day and in the evening. At times she would entertain the children who, occasionally, would accompany her with their singing.

At No. 7 Gloucester-road there was a complete absence of music. The house seemed dead despite all the activity that took place there. Of course, outside the lamplighters remained as ever active day and night with their ladders and lamp lights, while during the day I noticed the passing chimney sweeps with their rods and brooms on their shoulders, announcing their presence by shouting 'sweep'. Occasionally, the sweep might enter into conversation with the regular costermonger who plied his trade of fruit and vegetables or a 'peeler' might stroll by.

And we had the occasional pedlar-woman attend the door, quickly rebuffed by Peggy's sharp tongue. There were also gypsies shouting 'chairs to mend? Any chairs to mend? Once again Peggy gave them short shrift unless we had a chair in the kitchen or scullery in need of repair. They often sold brooms and brushes while the women told fortunes. I wished sometimes to be brave enough to ask if they could predict my future.

Chapter Six
The doctor calls

IT WAS early May 1861 I first became unwell. I raised it with Zerah one morning before his departure to attend *The Engineer*. So preoccupied with events on the Metropolitan Railway, Zerah could suggest only that I visit Dr. Graham.

'Remember, he costs money,' was all I recall him saying.

Remarks such as these from Zerah were not new. To Zerah, life was work; and work was life. He lived for work. He had to work to satisfy at least one of his innermost feelings and, in this respect, he was fortunate to have something on which to focus his precocious talent.

I mentioned my ailment casually to Peggy. She probably had no wish to commit herself, though I suspected she might have had an idea as to what might be wrong.

'If I may be allowed to say so, ma'am, I would advise that you see a doctor,' she said simply.

I agreed to visit the doctor, in case something there really was amiss, and made an appointment with Dr. Graham for the following day. On my return from the doctor's surgery, I took a cab and visited my mother. I could not explain to her how I felt, but I was weak and listless with pains in my stomach; I had difficulty walking. Baby must be nearly due. I thought: 'One day mother I may be able to tell you hardly I have been used by my husband'. Did I but know it there was more to come.

My mother had had six children; she may have had more, but if she did and they had died, she never discussed the matter. She could not offer much help, except to tell me that it gave her pleasure to talk to me and offer support, as she shared my general misery. I knew then how much I valued her. It comforted me that we had had to return from Philadelphia to live in London.

The following day I attended Dr. Graham. He examined me

thoroughly. He did not speak for some time as he used his stethoscope. He looked concerned.

'Mrs. Colburn, I am very, very sorry, but I have to tell you that I cannot detect the baby's heartbeat. I feel no movement. I think it best if you retire immediately to bed. It may be a matter of life and death. Perhaps you can arrange for your house-keeper to care for you. From what you say, she seems a responsible person. I will visit you.'

Dr. Graham's news horrified me. I had come to the surgery expecting another routine examination, but instead I learned that Dr. Graham could not hear the baby's heartbeat. I felt numb. I had known something was wrong. I had not felt movement for some days, but considered this a natural stage of childbirth. Now the baby lay lifeless in my womb.

Dr. Graham told me that I had no alternative but to let nature takes its course. He explained that the alternative to home delivery was a lying-in hospital. He told me that lying-in hospitals had a poor reputation for epidemics of childbed fever. I knew exactly to which he referred. I had heard rumours to that effect.

'Most women avoid them at all costs,' he told me. 'There are some that accept married women. And if you so desire I can make enquiries.'

I could not bear the thought of attending hospital. I had to avoid that. I returned home immediately and described my dilemma to Peggy. She understood, having cared for a number of women in childbirth. She was most sympathetic and took me under her wing. We began to develop a new bond of friendship.

Zerah was most annoyed not to see me as my usual active self. He offered little sympathy. He had never been ill, and expected everyone to be the same.

The days were long; all I could do was lie on my back, occasionally reading a book. Dr. Graham came to see me and occasionally spoke a little of his work.

He had said that delivering babies was an important part of his practice. Almost all were home deliveries. He explained briefly of the growing practice among doctors to administer chloroform in a titrated dosage. This would be administered by placing only a few drops on a cloth for the mother-to-be to inhale. He said that I would be free of the pain but would be able to follow his commands, moving my legs and pushing hard when the time came for delivery. My mother later told me no such practice was available when she gave birth.

The experience, when it occurred, remained for me unbelievably painful and physically distressing. I had never experienced such pain before. I wished mother had been present.

Peggy was a wonderful source of support and practical help, taking on the task of bringing ewers of hot water and removing the afterbirth and disposing of bloody towels. I gripped her arm tightly throughout. Dr. Graham declared he could not have managed without her.

Almost as soon as the ordeal was over, I saw Dr. Graham briefly leave the room; he carried a small bundle. Peggy held my hand. I gripped it tightly. When he returned Dr. Graham and Peggy glanced briefly at one another. Neither spoke; however, I could read their faces – that was enough. I burst into uncontrollable tears. Despite her many attempts, Peggy failed to halt the torrent of tears. That night, a deep shadow fell across the house with the passing of my first born.

The next day, Peggy sought my permission to leave the house; she returned with a posy of pale flowers. After thanking her profusely, I took to my room and placed them in a small vase. Later, before they drooped, I pressed some of the flowers between the pages of a large book. For weeks thereafter I dressed in black and never ventured out.

Even now, after all these years, I can still feel the pain; not only the physical pain, but the emotional anguish. I had the extreme agony of giving birth, knowing that my baby was no longer alive. It had come into the world lifeless.

Dr. Graham explained that as a stillbirth we were under no obligation to register it. Nor had the stillborn any baptismal rights. However, he said that if we wished, he could arrange through an undertaker for its burial in St. Pancras Cemetery, a cemetery started in 1852 on what was then Horseshoe Farm on Finchley Common. It would be placed in an unmarked grave with an unrelated adult, although it was quite common for a stillborn to be placed in an already open grave with a dozen other infants. Dr. Graham described the location as a delightful setting for a cemetery. He informed of a small fee for burials on consecrated ground.

I left the matter to him. I wanted nothing to do with it, and told Dr. Graham so, adding that my husband would settle his fee .That night I prayed the infant's soul had travelled to heaven to find eternal peace.

I knew of course of the custom for a black crape to be tied with white ribbon and placed upon the front door; an indication that the grim reaper has entered the house, and borne away another prize. But I had no desire to broadcast my distress.

And so I heard no more. Later, Peggy told me that in some cases, to avoid the burial fee, it was common to discard a stillborn with the household rubbish, bury it on private land, or in unconsecrated parts of burial grounds to be treated as if it had not existed. I told her I could not do that.

To the outside world, my baby had not existed. But this did not stop me from grieving. My thoughts were all I had left. I sensed an overwhelming feeling of loss; and however much I detested it, the emergence of hatred and contempt for Zerah. Feelings of hope and expectation had withered with the birth of the dead child; my child. How would I recover from this?

Dr. Graham tried to explain, telling me it was common for mothers to lose babies at birth, or even shortly after birth. However, his words were of little consolation. I was distraught. All I could do was to sob, curling up like a ball in bed.

Had I deserved this? Was God angry with me? And if so, what had I done to attract his wrath? And how could I make amends? It occurred to me: God gives and God takes away.

Equally, what had we done? Why was our baby unwilling to enter the world and meet us? Why did it not want to join us? Had we been so horrible to it that it could not face us?

In my heart, I could not escape the image that Zerah was at fault. The way he treated me in the early days of our marriage offered a grim omen for the future. The baby must have detected, through the walls of my womb, the unwelcome atmosphere outside, and taken fright.

The more I thought about the implications, the more I felt deeply sad. One day, I looked forward to a baby emerging into our lives – the next day I had nothing. I had prepared a nursery for the baby. Now it would stand empty, a temple to failure.

I had entered the doctor's surgery reflecting on some trivial ailment, only to be given the heart-breaking pronouncement that my baby's heart had stopped beating. Part of my soul remained behind in the surgery to mourn.

An air of sadness hung over the entire house. As I lay in bed, staring at the ceiling, the anguish of the baby's death was unimaginable. I could find no words to describe the pain of my loss. In my heart of hearts, I had not wanted the child, but only because of the relationship that had developed between Zerah and me. We were not the best of parents; our home not an ideal place in which to bring up a child.

All I could think about was the baby; a baby to keep me busy. I would never hold or feed the infant; nor would I rock, wash and dress it. The baby that who would not grow up.

Peggy described the baby as only tiny – she must have seen it. To me, no matter what its size, it had been a living creature coming from our union; a precious life, just as I had been a precious life to my mother. The difference was that I lived and my baby had not.

I spent most of the next few days in bed as Peggy continued to administer care. She was so kind. She could see the birth experience had proved a physical and mental drain, and so she just sat beside me at times and held my hand.

'Hold me,' she told me. 'And cry if necessary.'

She gave me words of encouragement; perhaps what happened had been for the best. Perhaps there had been something wrong with baby such that it would not have grown to be a healthy child. Perhaps there may be another opportunity to make amends for what had happened, and we could start again. A time would come when I would feel ready to replace the little one.

After a while, Peggy departed and I was alone again. All I could do was to pull the sheets over my head and sob.

That evening, Zerah came home as usual. I could see that he was concerned, even perhaps a little annoyed. I was afraid to speak out about my loss for fear of his judgement.

I think Zerah's concern was in seeing me white-faced and lying in bed, with Peggy administering to my needs. That he was annoyed suggested the birth was more a disruption to his daily routine, and less about his concern for my well-being. Such was the state of our relationship.

He said he was sad that we had lost our baby, but I could see his sorrow was superficial. He had not grasped how much the experience meant to me.

'Was it a boy?' he asked.

'I do not know,' I told him. 'I did not ask. I am sure Dr. Graham will tell you when you settle his account. I just know I have lost my baby; whether it was a boy or girl is immaterial to me. I cannot believe my baby is dead.'

I had had a living being inside me – and somehow I had killed it. I suddenly recalled my mother's own stillbirth and the heartache it brought her. I had never killed anything in my life; not even a spider. When mother had told me to tread on a spider scuttling across the room, I could not do it. Instead, I caught it between my hands and placed it outside. To me, all animals were entitled to life. I had killed my baby.

Zerah was unmoved as to where they buried the infant.

For me, the delivery was the start of a long grieving process

168

that has not disappeared. I still mourn today for the child I lost. I later learned that it was a boy, as Zerah discovered when he further questioned Peggy. To me, it was my baby; I was inconsolable.

Something must have had gone seriously wrong within my body to cause baby's death. I repeatedly returned to my first thought: that it had sensed evil vibrations from outside my womb. These were so violent in nature that it had no will to live.

I did not think that Zerah, even for one moment, grieved; to him death was a natural event; an event over which he had no control. It had been a medical occurrence, a scientific event, perhaps. Something had happened within my body and I carried the blame.

Yes, I am sure Zerah was disappointed the boy he wanted was now no more. He had always been distant about the baby. He had his writing on which he could focus. I had nothing.

Throughout my illness, Peggy had been particularly kind and caring, making cups of tea and acting as a mother. Her experience in nursing proved invaluable; without her help, I would have been lost. For, with Zerah absent all day at *The Engineer*, and sometimes away for two or three nights, I felt lonely, almost invisible.

Mother was the only person to whom I could open my heart. I had no one else to whom I could talk about my loss – the one subject forever on my mind.

Even to Harriet, then grown up and a young woman of 22, I could not fully unburden. Mother warned to be on my guard talking to Harriet lest I gave her my innermost secrets; she might inadvertently release them to her friends. And there were secrets I could not even reveal to mother.

When I went to see mother, I called in at church to spend a few moments in silent prayer. Sometimes moments could spread into half an hour. One day, the vicar asked if I was all right. I told him I mourned the loss my infant. I took comfort from the kindness of this relative stranger.

I asked for God's forgiveness – to forgive us. For, as parents, I knew we jointly had caused his death.

I could not even contemplate another child. And yet I knew that to survive, I should put the past behind me. Could I do that? My mother, on the other hand, suggested it might be good for me to bear another child to help forget my tragic circumstances. However, I was resolute. I would have none of it. I was sure that God had sent me a signal, a sign that I was not a fit and rightful person to bear a child.

As time went by, Zerah focused increasingly on work. The dinner parties became more frequent, contenting Peggy with the added attention, while I had my reading and needlework.

I would visit my mother at least once a week, sometimes twice. I enjoyed the days we spent together. Much preoccupied with my thoughts, I found it comforting to talk over with her. I did not see much of father, on the other hand. I knew he did not agree with our marriage.

Our first wedding anniversary passed without any mention of it. Just another day for the angel in the house. Did I expect too much?

The following year, 1862, proved equally difficult. In June, I suffered a miscarriage. I least expected another infant. The pain of losing that second child made the loss of my first baby even more intense. Both Peggy and Dr. Graham were kindness itself. Zerah was unaware of my miscarriage until it came to meeting Dr. Graham's statement. He afterwards expressed his concern.

One day, we had a surprise visitor. Zerah arrived in the evening with Mr. Alexander Holley, who joined us for dinner. Zerah described how Mr. Holley had turned up unannounced at *The Engineer*'s offices at No. 163 Strand; he planned to meet Mr. Henry Bessemer. That name had cropped up again. Mr. Holley timed his arrival in London to witness British Government experiments connected with armaments. It seemed Mr. Holley had received a handsome commission from a Mr. Edwin Stevens in America to study British warship design and armour. Mr.

Stevens's brother, Robert, had designed an American warship called the Battery.

Mr. Holley spoke openly about the war in America. His search in England for details of ordnance works was part of his contribution to assist his country's government.

I heard Zerah inform Mr. Holley that Mr. James McConnell had resigned only a few months previously as locomotive superintendent of the London & North Western Railway. He told Mr. Holley he had written to Mr. McConnell in a private capacity seeking an interview to "get to the bottom of what has happened to cause that" as he was such a clever man. The two men met Mr. McConnell on their first visit to England in 1857.

Following Mr. Holley's departure, Zerah explained that he would take Mr. Holley with him to see Mr. McConnell if there was time. He also told me that Stevens Battery was a revolutionary design of fast, semi-submersible Ironclad, or warship, with all its machinery positioned below the waterline. Stevens intended the ship as the first to be fitted with gun turrets. By the time of Mr. Holley's visit, two designs had been completed; a third followed later. Each design failed for one reason or another. The Battery was never completed. Despite this, Mr. Holley exuded all praise for the ship, certain that if the Battery ever put to sea, it would have set new standards in naval design.

Shortly afterwards, Mr. Holley paid a repeat visit to No. 7 Gloucester-road. He arrived alone one evening, at about 6 pm; Zerah had not yet returned from *The Engineer*. On my instructions, Rose invited Mr. Holley into the parlour, where I joined him.

I suggested that more than likely Mr. Holley would find Zerah at The Engineer public house, just a few doors further along Gloucester-road. Mr. Holley burst out laughing. He had such a charming laugh. He could not believe Mr. Zerah Colburn resided in the same road as The Engineer public house. He thought it most comical, but I told him it was true. Mr. Holley went off in search of my husband.

The two men arrived an hour later, somewhat merry to say the least. Mr. Holley found my husband holding forth with fellow drinkers, all enginemen.

I joined them for their evening meal, which Peggy had prepared. I participated little in the discussions which I recall mostly concerned the subject of iron and steel. One item of conversation did interest me. Mr. Holley, working a year earlier in New York, produced a revised edition of *Webster's Unabridged Dictionary*. I considered Mr. Holley indeed must be intelligent to undertake such important work as updating a dictionary. I enjoyed his company immensely, a refreshing change from my husband.

A more serious topic concerned Mr. Holley's remarks about the war in America. He suggested Zerah might consider returning to assist with the war effort, perhaps working for the US Military Railroad. It pleased me to hear Zerah retort it would best serve his interests to remain in London.

The two men also spoke excitedly about a new invention, the electric telegraph which, according to Mr. Holley, would be a great asset in fighting the war as it would hasten communications. I remembered hearing the word telegraph but could not at that moment place when.

As if in a further attempt to attract Zerah back to America, Mr. Holley explained how the railroads played an important role in the war. They brought large numbers of soldiers to battlefields; trains also transported ammunition and were faster and more reliable than carts and horses. Mr. Holley added that they assisted battles in remote areas; the trains brought food for men and horses. Zerah remained unconvinced.

Even so, Zerah kept abreast of the war, mainly through the pages of the *Illustrated London News* and its copious reports, maps and illustrations. I read some items, and more than once observed the name of Mr. Baldwin and the battery he built for the Federal Government.

One of the highlights for Mr. Holley of his visit occurred through his meeting again with Mr. John Scott Russell at Westwood Lodge. He told us of their children: Louise, 24, Rachel, 20, Alice May, 18 and of course Norman, 22, who had travelled on *Great Eastern*. It impressed Mr. Holley that all four children could hold serious conversations, unafraid to express their opinions.

I noticed Mr. Holley always carried a huge notebook. He informed us it contained material for his next book. He already had developed the title: *A treatise on Ordnance and Armor*. It sounded an important work, even though I could not hope to understand what it might contain. He completed it three years later.

Following dinner, I left the men to their discussions. Later, as I walked past the door of the parlour I overheard Zerah remark: 'I enjoy the company of women you understand, and the taste of a good wine; when the two go together, so much the better.'

Mr. Holley stayed the night but departed early next morning, no doubt feeling somewhat bad after over-indulgence the night before. During the evening, both men partook of gin punch, a drink I was told of which they experimented during their first visit to London. They had heard from someone it was the most wonderful beverage in the whole world. When Zerah left for work at his usual hour, Peggy explained how she and Rose were required to dispose of many empty wine bottles from the parlour.

We had another visitor in 1862 with an important message. Mr. Clark arrived early for his dinner appointment with Zerah. I had not been invited to join them on that occasion. Mr. Clark, always polite, apologised for his early arrival and, after further formalities, proclaimed that he had some exciting news for us.

We had moved by that time to the parlour where, after the door closed, Mr. Clark whispered he had a secret to discharge: he would shortly be marrying a lady with a name like mine – Elizabeth – and they would be inviting Mr. Colburn and myself to the wedding that would take place in St George's church,

Hanover Square.

I knew of the church – its parish included some of the most fashionable areas of London including Belgravia and Mayfair. But I knew it principally as George Frederick Handel, the composer, ranked amongst its most famous parishioners.

And then he admitted to something quite extraordinary. His tone changed; almost to a hushed whisper. He told me he had another Elizabeth of his own, then added: "But please tell no one – not even your husband. But I believe I can trust you to keep the information just between ourselves. It is something about which I will not speak again. I think you will understand."

I assured Mr. Clark of my agreement to his wish. I wondered what would emerge next.

"I have a daughter by the name of Elizabeth Ann. She is eight years old," he told me. "Her mother, someone I knew very well some years ago and much admired, passed away after the infant's arrival. I have assumed responsibility for the child's welfare. I see to it she is well cared for and we meet regularly. When the time comes for her to marry I intend to be present to sign as a witness on her marriage record."

There was silence. I knew not what to say. What he said was a complete surprise. I saw no reason why he should include me, of all people, into his secret.

"I am sure you take good care of her," I replied, lamely.

"She was born under another surname but gradually over the years she has assumed the name of Clark. It is a private matter. But I thought you should know; you may meet her one day. Please keep this most private to yourself. Let us say no more of it."

I assured him I would remain discrete.

The following year, in May 1863, we again saw much more of Mr. Holley who, I discovered, spent much time travelling between London and Sheffield where Mr. Bessemer had a steel-making foundry in operation. Later, Sheffield became the city of steel.

One day, Mr. Holley presented himself at the house unannounced. Although he was about 30 years of age, he looked younger. Our housemaid directed him to the parlour where I greeted him. We exchanged pleasantries. Mr. Holley appeared very happy. He told me his wife, Mary, who had been expecting their first child, had given birth to a baby girl. She was to be baptised Gertrude Meredith. I expressed my joy for them; they were both delightful names.

He asked if we planned any children. A lump immediately came to my throat and I could not reply for some minutes. To cover my embarrassment, I turned my head away and reached for a handkerchief.

'I hope so,' I said and quickly changed the subject. Years later, I heard the couple had two further children – both girls, Lucy and Alice. I thought how lucky they were to have children.

During this period, Mr. Holley spent much time negotiating with Mr. Bessemer for the rights to the Bessemer process. Many years later, Zerah told me Mr. Holley had been responsible for introducing steel-making into America. At the time, I thought what a clever man he must be.

Meanwhile, two unrelated events occurred in 1863. One day, Zerah returned from *The Engineer* saying that he had some interesting news. He discovered Mr. Healey, the owner of the paper, led a double life adding that during a 'man-to-man' talk over a glass of wine after work, Mr. Healey admitted he frequently spent time in Paris where he enjoyed the pleasures of an easy life with his mistress. He routinely crossed the English Channel in secret between his mistress in Paris and his residence near London. Zerah spoke lasciviously of Mr. Healey's mistress, hinting that he found this aspect of English middle-class life intriguing. He said he knew of many men who had mistresses, but I attached no importance to it at the time. Did he seek my approval?

The second event took the form of a request by my mother; she asked if we had discussed a second wedding, in London. I

175

had to confess that I had not. I was sure Zerah had not even considered the matter.

I asked mother why she raised the subject. The initial request had come from father, though mother assured me, it was something about which they had both talked.

My father, who had none of the sullen lethargy of the old, nevertheless appeared concerned as to the validity of his dearest daughter's New York wedding in September 1860. He was worried that it might not be valid in an English court of law, should anything untoward ever happen to Zerah and I be left a widow, possibly with children.

I told mother that I had no reason to think it was not valid, but she suggested that if it was not valid, then I might not be entitled to any benefits that might accrue from his estate.

My parents' doubts caused dark thoughts to creep into my mind. Was everything as it seemed?

Several events coincided with the spring of 1864. On Saturday, 23rd April, a special event on Primrose Hill marked the tercentenary of William Shakespeare's birthday. As the celebrations took place not far away, we joined others to witness the planting of the Shakespeare Oak.

About that time, Zerah made a visit to Paris to undertake some research. He did this with Mr. Healey's approval but I was not informed as to the nature of the work. It prove to be the first of many visits he made to the French capital. The railway lines in northern France, both from Boulogne and Dunkirk, had been extended in 1861 to make good connections between the coast and Paris. On this journey Zerah perchance had the opportunity meet Mr. Dickens travelling on the same train taking passengers for the cross-Channel boat to France. Zerah introduced himself as an admirer of the author's works.

More significantly from my standpoint, mother once again raised the subject of our remarriage in England. She explained that as Zerah embarked on so much travelling, it was possible he could experience a serious accident and I might not be entitled to any benefits as his next of kin. She also stressed the importance of Zerah making a will. Clearly, Father had spoken with her.

I understood mother's concern. It would indeed be delightful to have a family wedding in London. Perhaps a re-stating of our vows could mark a turning point in our marriage; perhaps it might provide the impetus for a 'fresh start'.

For me the idea, whilst attractive, raised the spectre of how to broach the subject to Zerah in such a way as to win his approval. Why would Zerah want to undergo a second marriage ceremony, this time in London?

One evening, when Zerah returned home in a particularly good frame of mind (something must have happened to his benefit at work), I mentioned how disappointed my parents had been not to be present at the wedding in New York of their eldest daughter. I felt very bold in asking if he had any objection to a simple ceremony at a London registry office, to which they could attend.

Much to my surprise, he willingly accepted my request, his only comment being that he hoped it would be a quiet affair; he saw no good reason to attract attention to a couple already wed.

I discovered later that day exactly what had happened to put Zerah in such good humour. On 9th May 1864, the Institution of Mechanical Engineers enrolled Zerah as a member. It made him feel proud and important to be a leading member of England's engineering fraternity.

Zerah saw himself as part of the young generation of engineers who were introducing modern scientific methods and processes destined to replace the outdated practices of older generations, bound up as they were with their traditional ways. Remarkably, in a period of three years, he had become part of London's engineering elite. He said it was an exciting time to be a young man. At 25, he had already become a published author.

At about that time, July, the newspapers carried items relating to what was then known as the 'railway murder', for which a man – an obscure German tailor, Franz Müller – later that year

(November) was hanged outside Newgate Prison for killing Thomas Briggs on the North London Railway at Hackney. A prostitute, Mary Ann Eldred, claimed as an alibi that Müller had been with her. I asked Zerah if it remained safe to travel on any railway, but he dismissed any fears I had as 'childlike'.

Some months later, in its 6th August edition, *The Times* reported that the owners of *Great Eastern* had moored the great vessel off Sheerness. Visitors could reach the ship using the South Eastern Railway (Kent Line). Public admission was 1s or 2s 6d on Saturday. Zerah asked if I would like to visit 'the old ship', but I declined. It seemed a long journey to take.

The following month, preparations marked our second wedding ceremony. It took place on 3rd September 1864, at the registry office in the district of Pancras. It was a quiet ceremony with only a dozen people present. They included mother and father, my two sisters Harriet, who was then 25, and Maria, 17, my 15-year old twin brothers Thomas John and Henry Charles, and 12 year-old Edward. Present of course also were two witnesses – my friends Miss Anna Maria Wilson and Miss Emma Farley.

Later, when able to examine father's own precious notebook, I found the following words in his flowing handwriting: "Saturday 3rd September 1864, my daughter Elizabeth Susanna's marriage with Zerah Colburn was registered at the registrar's Office, Ampthill-square, Parish of Saint Pancras. Anna Maria Wilson present."

The ceremony, in the presence of my immediate family, proved short. At its conclusion, I had a marriage certificate, my marriage line; proof that I was married – unlike our wedding in New York. I never knew what happened to that document; possibly Zerah had hidden it amongst his personal possessions, if so he never mentioned or displayed it to me.

I noticed, when it came to the occasion of signing the register, my father, already deeply suspicious of Zerah because he originated in America, a land he assumed full of gangsters, made a particular point of examining the completed certificate. He peered intently and noted, with a certain sense of relief that Zerah declared himself 'widower'. It was there in black and white. However, I had been so busy signing that I did not notice. Rather strangely, the form certified me as 'spinster'.

Afterwards, father drew me to one side and whispered: 'By agreeing to marry in a register office, was your Mr. Colburn hoping that news of the wedding would not reach the eyes and ears of friends and employer?'

'I cannot tell, father,' I replied quietly. 'I do not know.'

On the certificate also, Zerah proclaimed his profession as civil engineer. I had expected him to sign as Editor, or journalist. I did not know he was a civil engineer. Once again, in my heart, I longed to question this, but grim experience taught me to hold my tongue.

After the ceremony, we returned by cab to No. 7 Gloucester-road. My family and close friends followed in two cabs to the house where Peggy had laid out a special tea for everyone. She had even baked and iced a wonderful wedding cake. Father pledged a toast to the happy couple.

We did indeed have a honeymoon – of sorts. It was Zerah's idea. On Monday, we travelled to Paris. We made the journey by train, boat and train again. It was nothing like the arduous journey from Philadelphia to New York, but the Channel crossing proved unduly rough. We spent three nights at the Grand Hotel in the French capital.

It proved a very grand hotel; the most expensive I had stayed in and one of the attractions of the city. Zerah was in a particularly good mood for our entire period in Paris. We devoted two days to exploring the city's magnificent buildings and broad avenues. We had been married just four years and while there was a sense of connection between us, it did not extend as deeply as with some married couples. I hoped we could put all the troubles of the past behind us.

The honeymoon passed off uneventfully. There was intimacy,

of course; Zerah still liked to caress and stroke my naked skin, causing his arousal. For me, this was a strange 'honeymoon'. There were times when I contemplated whether my feelings for the man could ever deepen again, for I had to shoulder the unresolved internal conflict with the past. Certainly, Zerah could be passionate towards me; perhaps that was so for all men, irrespective of any injury they caused. The 'now' was more important to him than the 'then'. However, I carried painful memories of his beatings, and they dampened my ardour.

I was now much more careful when we were intimate; I was determined at all costs never again to give birth to another baby. A stillbirth and a miscarriage were just too much for me. I told Zerah so, but he declared I had a duty to please him. In that sense, I only half-fulfilled my wifely duties. Zerah continued to be both controlling and enveloping. I tried to confine intimacy only to those days when, as Dr. Graham had suggested, I knew it might be safe to do so. I know Zerah found my froideur and general 'distance' at times frustrating and irritating.

It seemed bizarre. In Paris we celebrated our second wedding and it was somehow faintly romantic, but it did not change my underlying attitude to Zerah. I could not dispatch from my mind the occasions he had hit me; each blow was a nail in his coffin. While that thought offered some satisfaction, I did not wish him dead.

I was in much need of a fantasy into which I could escape and through which I could shed memories of the past. However, none came.

I assumed Zerah found Paris romantic. The warm and sunny climate, even though it was September with the first hint of autumn, added to the glamour of the French capital.

Zerah's proficiency in French made our 'holiday' easier. When speaking to someone, he focused intently on the person, quite ignoring me. I was pleased as I had no wish to engage in conversation; I would not have known what to say as, by comparison, I understood few words of French conversation.

Occasionally I heard the word 'madam', which I understood. I just wished that I could speak fluent French, like Zerah. For all that, I enjoyed the 'city of love', as Zerah called Paris. I could understand why some chose to live there. However, we did not visit any area where anyone lived in misery.

Returning to London, a pleasant surprise awaited Zerah. A publisher, in a letter which Zerah found flattering, sought entries for the next edition of *Boyle's Fashionable Court and County Guide*, due to appear the following year. The letter promised the *Guide* would contain the 'names and places of abode' of the 'nobility and gentry'.

When finally published, Zerah was overjoyed; the *Guide* listed him as a resident of Gloucester-road, alongside the gentry of London. The guide, he believed, confirmed him as a very important person.

However, shortly after our return to London from Paris, our lives began to unravel in a most strange manner when, in months to come, his enthusiasm for me turned sour. Once again, I felt myself partially to blame and therefore responsible.

Chapter Seven
Problems in Paris

O NE evening, not many weeks following our 'wedding', Zerah returned to the house and pronounced his departure from *The Engineer* to start a consultancy business.

He confessed of 'boredom' with his editorial position; he wanted to practice as an engineer. He planned to become a member of the leading engineering institution in London, the Institution of Civil Engineers – the 'civils'.

He appeared flushed and I could judge by his manner he was somewhat dispirited, despite professing his new venture. He told me he would begin work immediately on the consultancy, and not return to *The Engineer*. He would conduct his new work from the house.

He added that he had a commission to write several detailed articles for the newspaper. I assumed this would to provide a bridge until his business gathered momentum.

Zerah's news came as a shock. He had not previously expressed any desire to form a consultancy. I thought his decision strange, though I knew how erratic and impulsive he could be. I might expect he would briefly discuss his plans with me, but he did not. Something must have had happened to cause this abrupt change of direction.

What mystified me further was whether there would be sufficient work to keep Zerah fully occupied. His strange combination of maturity and youthful impetuosity however made it impossible for him to remain idle. He was ceaselessly active with reading, writing and, of course, nationwide visits to see manufacturers at work.

As if reading my thoughts, Zerah explained that as a result of the various soirées held at the house during preceding years, he now had a substantial list of men, he them called 'contacts', who could provide work. Most work would be in London and would pay handsomely. He said his contacts were most anxious to engage his services.

It was only many years later I discovered the true cause of Zerah's swift departure from *The Engineer*, as I shall disclose.

To replace Zerah, *The Engineer* engaged a young Irish engineer by the name of Mr. Vaughan Pendred. Although born in Barraderry, Co. Wicklow, Mr. Pendred and his family could trace their line to the sixteenth century to a Mr. John Pendred of Northampton. Mr. Pendred, who had six brothers and sisters, came to England in 1862 and subsequently wrote many letters to Zerah at *The Engineer*.

When Mr. Pendred arrived in England in search of work, it was Zerah who found him employment at John Smith in Coven, Staffordshire, makers of ploughing machines and traction engines. Within months, the Irishman had moved to London and found himself editing a journal.

For Mr. Pendred's letters on engineering subjects had also attracted the attention of Mr. Passmore Edwards, proprietor of *Mechanics Magazine*. The *Mechanics Magazine* first appeared on Saturday, 30th August 1823 and, according to Zerah, was the first mechanical engineering paper to be published in Great Britain worthy of the title. It continued to be published for many years until purchased by a firm of patent agents.

Zerah told me that Mr. Passmore Edwards, whom on one occasion Zerah had been to visit, purchased a seven-year lease of the title. Under his stewardship, the journal flourished, due to the appointment as editor in 1863 of Mr. Pendred who became highly regarded.

Mr. Passmore Edwards later returned *Mechanics Magazine* to its owners, who then sold it to the proprietor of *The Engineer* and he in turn sold it to the publishers of a new paper called *Iron*. Mr. Passmore Edwards meanwhile purchased a new paper, *English Mechanics*, which first appeared on 31st March 1865.

Zerah observed all this activity with much interest and some amusement. As time went by however, following Mr. Pendred's appointment at *The Engineer*, friction intensified between the two men. Zerah judged himself a far more superior editor and publisher than Mr. Pendred, and their relationship deteriorated.

Life took on a new meaning as Zerah worked from the house. Previously, I was alone, apart from those in service. However, with Zerah present most weekdays, the building seemed noisier.

Zerah came and went, sometimes disappearing for half a day before returning for luncheon. Our daily routine began to change as invariably we now had a mid-day meal together. This caused Peggy also to adapt her routine.

By the middle of 1864, I began to notice that Zerah consumed at least half a bottle of wine during mid-day meals, often much more. I drank mostly water. I did not enjoy wine; I found alcohol all too quickly went to my head and I became dizzy. Especially was this so if the wine was strong.

As before, Zerah was never motionless. He remained active all day. He would come or go, meeting people or writing reports. No one could say he was idle; indeed, it was the reverse. He remained obsessed with work. In addition, many men visited the house. They would retire to Zerah's study and sometimes remain all day, not even stopping to eat.

Were they to venture out, it would to a coffee-house. Then, in the evening, the men would take a cab to one of Zerah's two clubs where they would dine and drink – I supposed. His clubs were St. Stephens, and the writers' club, the Athenaeum with its palatial clubhouse and library. Peggy was unhappy when this happened – on several occasions, food was wasted and she asked me what to do.

To assist, I suggested that at the beginning of each day I could ask Zerah for his plans. Sometimes he would co-operate; at other times, he would not. It was clear he had no wish to be committed to any other kind of scrutiny or discipline except that which he himself laid down.

I could see from his behaviour that he must have been a law

unto himself while working at *The Engineer*. As editor, I imagined he would have been 'king'; respected and feared alike by everyone. And, with someone of Zerah's presence and attitude, not to mention also his temper, few would dare challenge him. Working from the house, he expected similar treatment.

However, I could tell that he was preoccupied with a topic he chose not discuss.

Zerah wrote articles for *The Engineer*, but I understand the number to be small and only on subjects of his special interest.

He widened his horizons by becoming a director of the London Engineering and Iron Shipbuilding Co. Ltd of London-yard, Isle of Dogs, in Poplar. According to a notice he showed me, published in *The Times* of 6th August 1864, the company had capital of £500,000. The advertisement named one director as Zerah Colburn.

The notice gave his address, with a misspelling, as No. 7 Glocester-road. That would irritate Zerah. Another director shown was that of Mr. William Austin of No. 137, Adelaide-road, Hampstead. He was a director of the Metropolitan Railway. Another was Rear-Admiral George G. Wellesley C.E., late Commander-in-Chief of the Indian Navy. Then there was Mr. Robert Baillie of Messrs. Westwood, Baillie and Company, shipbuilders and engineers of London-yard, Millwall, on the Isle of Dogs. The majority of other directors were directors of banks, credit and finance companies.

The 1850s and 1860s bore witness to a huge increase in the production of warships for governments at home and abroad. Zerah believed Britain's wealth depended on the quality of its merchant ships and fighting vessels. However, times were changing and London, as a centre of shipbuilding, began to decline. In the light of this, it surprised me Zerah took up a shipyard directorship.

A reflection of this change was evident in an advertisement in the same newspaper two months later. On 16th October 1864 *The Times* declared Zerah's company 'prepared to tender for wrought and cast iron bridge work'. A third advertisement appeared in *The Times* of 26th October1864. Zerah's name appeared in all three.

Zerah took little interest in ballooning, or aerial locomotion as he called it. He was, however, fascinated by the endeavours of Mr. Felix Nadar, a well-known French photographer and balloonist, who constructed a balloon 20 times larger than any previous balloon. In 1864, on its second flight it crashed on a journey from Paris, injuring all 20 passengers. Zerah expressed relief for all concerned; it could have been worse.

Early the following year, 1865, war in America ended with the surrender on 9th April of the Confederate army. For Zerah the news was welcome; he hated his country to be at war. The war lasted four years and killed over 600,000 Americans.

He explained that England had played a hand in the war – Confederate soldiers fired the first shot of the war using a gun made in Liverpool by Fawcett, Preston & Co. Iron Works, known locally as Fossetts. With the war now over, would Zerah entertain crossing the Atlantic in search of engineering news – or indeed for some other purpose? Whether the question ever arose in his mind, he chose not to disclose it.

Meanwhile, further welcome news for Zerah came in the form of a letter from the Institution of Civil Engineers. The Institution's council had elected him a member. He regarded this as one of the highest accolades awarded to any engineer; further proof that he was part of Britain's engineering establishment.

To celebrate, Zerah invited some of the engineers who had sponsored him to join him at the Langham Hotel, in Langham-place. This hotel, opened a year previously and furnished in an extravagant manner in gold, scarlet and white, quickly established a reputation as an exclusive meeting place for members of society. Zerah revelled in its atmosphere.

Zerah could now rightfully declare himself a civil engineer. One of the first to be invited to Zerah's latest round of dinner parties at No. 7 Gloucester-road was none other than Mr. Joseph

Bazelgette. He much admired the man as one being so one closely involved with railways in London, one of Zerah's interests, and not only from a journalistic viewpoint.

Zerah explained that of over 50 different railway proposals for London, Mr. Bazelgette had rejected all save that which ran beside the River Thames, later the District Line. Construction started on 29th June 1865, but completion took 20 years. Ironically, that same month, a train carrying Mr. Dickens and his entourage to Charing Cross, London, hit a bridge with loosened plates and partially fell into the river below at Staplehurst, Kent. Mr. Dickens and his party escaped the worst of the damage, being in First Class at the front. Zerah, needless to say, took great interest in the accident.

Zerah regarded the 'civils' as the epitome of engineering excellence. Many famous engineers were members of the institution and it made Zerah proud to be numbered among them. He devoted much time to his new-found membership, both in attending lectures and writing papers.

No similar body existed in America and indeed, this feature of English life appealed particularly to Zerah. As a member, he maintained he was part of England, the great powerhouse of wealth. More especially, he had become a qualified engineer. He deemed engineering as one of the most important professions to which any man could ascribe.

The 'civils' was more than a gentleman's club – it was a meeting place for engineering minds where topics of national importance could be discussed. In Zerah's eyes, England's engineers had made the country great. He now judged himself one of the country's elite.

Amongst his endeavours, he produced *The Gas-Works of London*, a book of which he was extremely proud principally because it marked the first time in public he used the letters CE after his name, signifying his position as a civil engineer.

He also delivered several lectures, spreading his net as far as possible. However, his articles on steel-making in *The Engineer* drew acclaim, and wide attention, most notably that of Mr. Henry Bessemer, Mr. Alexander Holley's friend.

Zerah told me at the time that Mr. Bessemer, an inventor of some prominence, had obtained by 1851 no less than a dozen important patents; some led to very useful machines. Three years later, he developed an improved metal for the manufacture of guns and, as a result, had a meeting in Paris with Napoleon 111. However, Mr. Bessemer's most notable work was his invention of steel – an engineering material, more useful than iron.

Ironically, it was Mr. Holley, who while editing *Railroad Advocate* in New York, had read an item about Mr. Bessemer's work in *The Times* of 14th August 1856. Mr. Bessemer's lecture at the British Association meeting in Cheltenham revealed details of his new steel making process. According to Zerah, Mr. Holley immediately reported the lecture. A week later, he likewise published a similar claim by American inventor, Joseph Gilbert Martien of Newark, New Jersey; he lodged his patent on 23rd August 1855.

Zerah told me that between the first announcement of his process and its successful application, Mr. Bessemer had encountered stiff opposition from sceptics. However, both he and Mr. Holley recognised the value of Mr. Bessemer's process for making steel rails for railways.

Zerah explained that Mr. Bessemer had wanted to produce a superior quality iron; his new metal had the characteristics of wrought iron or steel, but could flow into a mould or ingot in a fluid state instead of being forged.

Eventually, after overcoming many difficulties, Mr. Bessemer was successful and Zerah wrote many articles supporting Mr. Bessemer's work, including his major treatise published in *The Engineer* of 30th December 1864. The newspaper published the article, *The Origin and Principles of the Bessemer Process*, shortly after Zerah's sudden departure. Two years earlier, in May, Zerah described the inventor's exhibit of Bessemer steel at the London Exhibition in *The Engineer*.

Among his many activities, Zerah prepared a notable paper he delivered to the Institution of Civil Engineers on 3rd April 1865 in his position as vice-president. The subject of the lecture was one of his favourites: *Methods of treating cast iron in the foundry*. This was an important lecture Zerah told me at the time.

He showed me hand-written notes he had prepared. As I turned the pages, I saw numerous references to Mr. Bessemer. From what Zerah said later, there were many engineers present who held him in high regard.

That same year witnessed the death of Mr. Abraham Lincoln. Zerah showed little concern however for his president's passing; of more interest was an American newspaper report showing a photograph of The Old Nashville locomotive; it had drawn Lincoln's funeral train from Washington to Springfield.

Meanwhile, newspapers reported that 'our ship', *Great Eastern*, which the owners had put up for sale the previous year, had been chartered to lay the first Transatlantic telegraph cable. The first such voyage took place in July 1865; a month later the Queen sent the first official telegraph to the new American president, Mr. James Buchanan. 'Our ship' laid a second cable a year later.

Strangely, the president's death caused Zerah to take a sudden but quickly passing interest in death, and in particular cemetery railways, the most notable of which was the London Necropolis and National Mausoleum Company.

Zerah even undertook a journey on the 'black line' – the London & South Western Railway from Waterloo to Brookwood Cemetery, described as the largest in England and the 'most beautiful cemetery in Europe'.

So taken was he with the 'City of the Dead' that he declared a wish to be interred there in a family plot, among the green fields of Surrey in 'God's acre' – but not in a 'pauper's burial'. There was another cemetery railway, the Great Northern London Cemetery, but surprisingly Zerah showed no interest in that line.

However, as a result of Zerah's articles on steel making Mr. Bessemer began to regard my husband as an important ally and, during 1865, the two men spent much time together. Mr. Bessemer visited the house on several occasions, mostly during evenings; the two men would talk long into the night. I think Zerah even engaged in consultancy work for Mr. Bessemer.

By the middle of 1865 however, I noticed another change in Zerah. He gave greater focus to his work – if that were possible. I was aware of this because he would talk to me about his plans for the future. He said he had put behind him all that happened at *The Engineer*, details of which he did not disclose. He had grown tired of working as a consulting engineer; he became impatient with men who always changed their minds.

He told me he had decided that he would make a return to journalism and publishing. Acting as an engineering consultant did not fulfil his needs; the only activity that gave satisfaction was that of journalism.

'I am a writer, and a writer I shall remain,' he told me, but did not explain further.

Zerah had an unwavering sense of his own destiny and took the alchemy of success as his birth right. He was, if nothing else, extremely confident. Indeed, some envious rivals categorised his immense self-belief as that of arrogance; maybe it was so.

It was as though we lived on a switchback. One minute he was editing a journal, then he was an engineering consultant, and then he had reverted to being a journalist and an editor again. He changed his occupations so many times.

As to our own personal relationship, it was not my position to question what he might choose to do. He and I were more like brother and sister than husband and wife. I put that down to my own attitude to Zerah; I could not trust him. He could be so erratic; one day he would be kindness itself and the next he would be moody and loathsome. Sometimes, he would refuse to speak to me for two or three days in an attempt to secure his own way, which more often than not he did.

When I lost my babies – our babies – I became determined that I would never go through that again. He seemed to share my

191

view, though I did not know if he was genuine. He once told me he did not want me to have to go through the heartache of losing another infant, which might happen were I to fall pregnant again. Was he being sincere and genuine?

We spoke to one another of course, but there remained a divide between us. After everything I had been through, I did not feel comfortable in Zerah's presence. Our relationship had become loveless. I lived on a knife edge – as if expecting something to happen at any moment. His temper could explode like an unpredictable volcano erupting. Its ferocity terrified me.

Following the loss of each of my babies the intensity and frequency of Zerah's demand for intimacy waned somewhat, but only for a short time. Perhaps he thought I was to blame for their deaths as I had carried them. Increasingly, I blamed him, especially for the stillborn; a further reason to have less to do with him.

So, while we remained on speaking terms, I lost any real love I ever had for him. I respected him as a writer and as an engineer, but as a husband and a close friend whom I might trust, I held him in low regard. I had to be friendly with Zerah but, as I was to discover, there were different levels of friendship. At that time, I had no real friends.

I was unloved. There was no longer any real affection; that he might seek to protect me or make me feel loved or wanted.

Life was difficult. There were times when I despaired of my low self-esteem. I had no one in whom I could confide. I had mother of course but there were subjects we could not discuss.

I had Harriet, my younger sister. We used to share 'secrets', but even so, there were some matters I could not disclose. I did not want my personal life revealed to Harriet's friends. So I felt lonely and miserable. Maria was not only far too young to understand the cause of my unhappiness, but from time to time she could lapse into mawkish sentimentality.

As to finding a means of escape, I was no closer to resolving the matter, so I decided to remain resolute; convinced God would find a way out of my dilemma. I felt unable to take charge of my destiny and make my own decisions in the way that Zerah did with his own life. I did not have enough experience of the world to live on my own. I would have to watch and wait for something to happen.

I was afraid to leave Zerah, however unhappy my life at No. 7 Gloucester-road. There were too many unknowns to face. It would have been all too easy to retreat to my parents, but that would be to admit defeat. I had to find my own salvation, but I hoped desperately that God would find it for me.

On Sunday, I usually went to church for morning service; on some Sundays I would rise early and attend communion. I had been confirmed at 14, and I enjoyed being back in the fold of the Church of England and its 1662 Book of Common Prayer. I enjoyed the services. While I was at church, Zerah would remain at the house working. The Sunday morning service took place at 11 a.m. A similar service took place at the same time on Wednesdays; on such occasions it would be mostly women who attended. There were further services on Fridays at 11 a.m. and 7 p.m.

The church was so convenient. St. Mark's Church in St. Mark's-square required but a short walk over Grafton-bridge and along Regent's Park-road. The vicar was the Rev. Edward Kendall; I found his sermons comforting and reassuring.

One advantage of attending church was the opportunity to meet those outside my limited circle. When I started, I was obviously alone but gradually, through the offices of the vicar, I met other women and occasionally, as the vicar learned from what I had told him, I went to meetings of the Mothers' Union. Once this happened I began to feel more at ease again.

I occasionally attended the Baptist church in Berkeley-road, some distance away, but there I did not feel quite so comfortable. The churchgoers were very religious, urging me to become a Baptist. However, I preferred to remain where I was.

I loved the Baptist hymns and prayers but the sermons could

be deep and thought-provoking; sometimes, the sermons left me with the impression I was not a Christian at all, but merely masquerading as one until I had made a full commitment in front of the congregation.

Once, Zerah asked me if I believed in God. I told him I did. Sometimes he accused me of religious fervour.

'How can you believe in God when you have not seen him?' he asked. 'We are born and we die. There is nothing else.'

'I just have to look around to see what God has created. God is everywhere, even though He remains at the far end of our knowing,' I told him, fiercely standing up for my faith in God.

The last sentence was something I once heard a preacher say and it has remained with me ever since.

Zerah was a man who could, and did, take charge of his destiny, exercising changes that affected the direction of his life. At that moment, I was part of that life and had to remain so until something happened – as I had confidence it would. I depended on him for a roof over my head, food and clothing.

One day, there was another surprise. Zerah told me that he had finally made up his mind. He would create a new newspaper. It would be a competitor to *The Engineer*, as engineering was the only subject close to his heart. He was widely knowledgeable on the subject; he believed he could bring his influence to bear.

Zerah had a desire to influence people and events. As a journalist, he believed that he had such power through the written word. I admired someone so convinced of his brilliance and singularity that he could behave with such confidence.

As *The Engineer* no longer published any of Zerah's ideas or opinions on engineering matters, he considered the time had come to launch his own weekly newspaper. In that way, Zerah could publish his own opinions, and he would be in control; just as I was being controlled.

I asked him who would provide the money to support a new weekly newspaper. Would not the amount be substantial? I had no idea how much money we had as man and wife. Zerah kept our financial details closely to himself. That was not my business. At the back of my mind loomed images of our life in Philadelphia where Zerah's newspaper survived barely four months. What was so different about the newspaper he planned to create in London that separated it from the newspaper in Philadelphia? I dare not ask. As it was, Zerah told me without prompting, so full was he of his new 'baby'.

The difference was, according to Zerah, that he had found a benefactor who would, as he said, 'bank-roll' the newspaper until it became successful. I was intrigued, but I had to wait some time until he unfolded all his plans.

In Philadelphia, he had used his own capital to start *The Engineer*, relying heavily on new annual subscriptions to finance each issue. He said he would not repeat that error of judgement. Not that it was his error; he claimed the financial crash caused the paper's demise. But why would someone be prepared to 'bank-roll' one of Zerah's ideas, I wondered?

Zerah remained in confident mood and we continued to reside at No. 7 Gloucester-road; there was no indication that we were undergoing any kind of financial hardship.

As I have mentioned, some distance away on Gloucester-road from where we lived was located The Engineer public house. I was aware of the public house almost from the first day that I moved into No. 7. What I found amusing, from my own perspective, was in deciding which came first.

Did Zerah choose to live in Gloucester-road because of the presence of The Engineer public house? Or did he choose the road because he was working at *The Engineer* newspaper? Was it all pure chance? It certainly seemed more than a coincidence.

I dare not put the questions to Zerah; I supposed it to be chance, rather than any deliberate action. The publican was Mr. James Kitchen or Mr. Jim to his friends; Zerah spent much of his time and money in his company.

Meanwhile, we continued to employ the same servants and I had sufficient faith in Zerah's business acumen to believe he would take care of our needs.

One day, in early July 1865, some six months before he started his new weekly newspaper, Zerah instructed me to expect more dinner guests than usual. He would be inviting men who could assist with the new journal, he told me. These meals would require Peggy and Rose to undertake additional work.

At the same time, Zerah revealed he had invited a young man to the house that evening for dinner; he would remain for the weekend. He said I should inform Peggy to prepare a bedroom. Zerah suggested I might like to join the two of them for dinner. He named the man as Mr. William Maw; he changed my life.

I wondered what Mr. Maw would be like. I did not have long to wait. That evening, he arrived half an hour before Zerah.

The doorbell rang.

'Is this the residence of Mr. Zerah Colburn?' he asked Rose as she opened the door.

'Yes it is, and who shall I say is visiting?'

'I am Mr. William Henry Maw. Mr. Colburn expects me.'

Rose came and I instructed her to show Mr. Maw to the parlour where I was seated.

He must have been a few years younger than Zerah; he had a friendly face and an eager personality. I found him easy to engage in conversation. We discussed items in the news. He told me that Mr. Colburn had some ideas about a new newspaper.

'It is extremely confidential,' he said. 'I am not supposed to mention it to anyone, but I expect you already know.'

'I know a little,' I replied, cautiously. 'But I am sure Mr. Colburn will discuss it with you. It will not be long before he arrives. We have newspapers and journals you can read while I arrange dinner. Here are copies of *The Times*, and we have French newspapers.'

From that moment, in my own mind I decided to call him William. He was handsome and good humoured.

That evening we sat around one end of the huge solid mahogany dining room table. Zerah was at the head, of course, while William and I faced one another. It was not often I was included in such discussions, and I wondered what made this event so different – and so special.

During the meal, at which we consumed one large bottle of red wine – I say 'we' because I consumed not even one quarter-glassful and I noticed that William declined to have his glass replenished halfway through the meal – much of the discussion was about Zerah's plans for his new publication. It was clear to me that Zerah was hoping he could engage the young man to work for him once publication began.

I remained silent for most of the meal. As I sat opposite William, I could study his features and mannerisms. He gave the impression of a deeply conscientious young man with a strong sense of attention to detail; a man bounding with energy. I judged that, like Zerah, he had a deep interest in engineering matters, especially railways and locomotives.

He told us of his background. As an only child, he had lost both parents by the age of 16 – his mother and father died within 21 months of one another. From an early age he relied on his own resources.

His father, Mr. William Mintoft Maw, had been a ship's captain in the Merchant Navy, while his grandfather, Mr. Robert Maw, was a former captain in the Royal Navy. His mother was the daughter of a ship's captain too, Captain Lewis Maxey, the son of the Reverend Lewis Maxey.

William's father spent much of his time at sea, travelling to Australia, India and China. Following his father's death, William's mother brought him up and they became close friends. Mrs. Minna Maw was, according to William, a woman of strong personality. She was also clever, and taught her son to read and write. She also brought him up as a Christian. Even from an early age, his parents assumed he would become an engineer.

Following the death of her husband, Mrs. Maw moved to London where she opened a shop in the Mile End Road to sell fancy goods. However, she suffered poor health and, missing her husband's support, died on 4th December 1854, aged 40.

Three months later, William began work at the Stratford Works of the Eastern Counties Railway under the supervision of Mr. John Viret Gooch who, until 1850, had been locomotive superintendent of the London & South Western Railway. In 1856, Mr. Robert Sinclair replaced Mr. Gooch as the new locomotive superintendent; Mr. Gooch was elder brother to Mr. Daniel Gooch – a passenger on *Great Eastern*'s maiden voyage.

William made good progress at the works, and it was there some two years later, that he first met Zerah, then in the company of Mr. Alexander Holley. William had the responsibility for taking the men on an inspection tour of the Stratford Works as part of their fact-finding mission of locomotive manufacture in England and France. Zerah remembered William from that day.

In 1859, William became head draughtsman in the locomotive and engineering department, and a year later Mr. Sinclair appointed him his personal assistant.

Three years later, in 1862, during an amalgamation of several smaller railways, such as the Norfolk Railway and the Eastern Union Railway, the Eastern Counties Railway Company became the *Great Eastern* Railway.

Among William's particular contributions were the designs of rolling stock for the Great Luxembourg Railway and locomotives for the East Indian Railway. Both employed Mr. Sinclair as their consulting engineer.

On their first meeting, Zerah immediately recognised William's potential, and the two men met many times, including at the 1862 International Exhibition. From that point, William collaborated with Zerah on his book *Locomotive Engineering*. It was at that exhibition Mr. Bessemer demonstrated steel, his new material.

During that weekend, to our surprise, William told us about his beau, Emily. They had met two years earlier, in September 1863, when he visited a friend. He was 24 and Emily a year younger.

Emily was the eldest daughter of Mr. Thomas Chappell, a civil servant in the customs department. By all accounts, her father held an important position, which perhaps clarified how they came to live in an area like Canonbury. When Emily first met William, her mother had only recently died.

To William, Emily was not only beautiful, with dark eyes and a fine complexion, but she was someone who much valued innocence as a virtue. He described her long golden hair which, he thought, was quite remarkable with a coil over one shoulder. He added that Emily enjoyed a striking personality and an elegant figure. I mused how long it would be before we met her.

Apparently, Emily was as much attracted to William as he to her; they met often when she was out walking with her younger sister, Katherine.

Some 18 months later, he explained, the couple came to what he called 'a mutual understanding' and walked out more frequently. However, Emily had not told her father about William. Only when Emily's father called to collect her from a friend's house did William formally introduce himself. The meeting passed off so well, that Mr. Chappell asked William to accompany them on their return to Canonbury. Afterwards, William walked to Stratford to work off 'the exuberance of his feelings'.

It seems the following day, William called again at the house, whereupon he was openly welcomed; from then onwards he became a regular visitor.

Thereafter, William met Emily practically every day, enjoying long walks in the evening, sometimes accompanied by Katherine, but more often alone. He would then walk back to Stratford ready to start work the following day. On most evenings and Sundays, William spent time either with Emily or with Emily and Katherine.

Sometimes, when the couple passed their evenings at the Chappells' home, Emily and William would play chess, or discuss poetry. At other times, he would bring work to the house. On one occasion, he wrote his address to the Civil and Mechanical Engineers' Society, (which he had helped to establish) as well as other literary work, including his chapters on locomotive engineering for Zerah's book. From this, I assumed William to be extremely knowledgeable on the subject.

It was at that point in our conversation that the discussion returned to Zerah's new weekly newspaper.

'Swear to me that you will keep details to yourself of what I am about to unveil,' said Zerah.

'Certainly, Sir,' replied William dutifully.

'I plan to launch this newspaper in the first week of January next year – 1866. I am doing so because I feel a great sense of duty to dispel the fog of ignorance and fear that surrounds the subject of engineering and its many related subjects. I also wish to broaden the knowledge of engineers in many industries and widen their outlook,' he said.

'We have only a few months in which to prepare for this great undertaking and I am looking to you, Mr. Maw, with your background in railway matters and writing, to act as my assistant. You have risen by merit from modest beginnings – as indeed so have I. There will be much work for us. My own appetite for work is voracious,' he told the young man.

'You and I will have complete responsibility to write for this newspaper in its early days. I may use some contributors, but at the end of the day, we will be responsible. I plan to make it a great newspaper. It will far eclipse *The Engineer*, of which no doubt you have heard. That is our foremost task.'

William said nothing, as if waiting for Zerah to continue.

'I have edited weekly newspapers before and know how much work is required. It is a huge task,' added Zerah. 'Maintaining great attention to detail on a weekly basis is demanding for anyone, and the more so for someone as young as you. You have never undertaken such responsibilities before, to my knowledge. There will be many stresses and strains, just as in a structural joint under complex loading. Do you think you will cope, Maw?'

'Sir, Mr. Sinclair, my superior at the Great Eastern Railway, has placed much responsibility on my shoulders in months past and I have never let him down. He will provide a reference that will, I am sure, provide every satisfaction,' replied William.

At the conclusion, the two men retired to Zerah's study, where I suspect Zerah might have had another drink.

The following morning, Saturday, at breakfast, before William joined us, Zerah asked me 'Well, what of the young fellow? Do you think I will be able to rely on him? Can I trust him? What does a woman's intuition tell you about him?'

I was flattered; it was most unusual for Zerah to seek my opinion. Indeed, I may even use the word 'unique'. I could only say that Mr. Maw seemed an honest and conscientious individual. I liked the young engineer's manner and decided, from my limited association, on his trustworthiness.

Following breakfast, the two men embarked on a spirited walk. Zerah declared they intended to head in the direction of Hampstead Heath, and would endeavour to reach the Suburban & Hampstead Heath Hotel (later renamed Heath Tavern). They expected to be absent for most of the day.

By their return, they had clearly become firm friends. Their journey took them via Rosslyn Park, Haverstock Hill and High-street, Hampstead with its own Golden Square. They explained how they passed several public houses on the way, and they did indeed find their way to the relatively new hotel owned by the Suburban Hotel Co. Ltd. and overlooking Hampstead Pond.

That part of London had undergone continual development from the sixteenth century as lawyers, merchants and bankers moved into the vicinity. Later, in the 1850s, large houses were built for gentry. By 1866, clerks and others moved out from central London to occupy other newly-built red brick villas. The construction of Hampstead Heath station at South End Green in 1860 made journeys to London by railway more convenient.

I did contemplate if perhaps Zerah had considered a move

into that desirable area; I knew of his grand ideas as to where he might live next. However, our house in Gloucester-road was so convenient for Westminster and the Institutions.

I had a feeling too the two men, on their return journey, called in for liquid refreshment at The Engineer. Zerah would have delighted in introducing William to Mr. Jim, the landlord.

I can imagine, even now after all these years, Zerah poked fun at *The Engineer* newspaper as they walked into The Engineer public house. They possibly smiled to one another as they looked up to see the face on the signboard peering down at them. The irony of such a visit was not lost on Zerah as he planned his competitor to *The Engineer.*

'Maw has agreed to work for me starting next year,' pronounced Zerah. 'He and I will produce a steady stream of words to fill our columns. But first we have to settle our differences as to how I am to reward him.'

The matter of William's salary proved protracted. Zerah declared an unwillingness to pay more than 200 pounds a year but finally, in the face of William's persistence in seeking a higher figure, had to agree to a figure of 250 pounds. William immediately sensed his value to my husband.

Afterwards, Zerah told me that the average weekly wage for a man in industry was just one pound, or 52 pounds a year.

'Of the 20 million or so people in England and Wales, there are no more than 500,000 in England and Wales whose yearly income is as much as 100 pounds,' he said, by way of explanation. 'I am paying Maw well for his services.'

'What concerns me more is the penalty of social degradation at which the industrial greatness of England is maintained. For make no mistake, labour in England is cheap. Nineteen twentieths of the population is poor. Many live in the wilderness of the mean hovels of manufacturing towns. My instinct against injustice and oppression are deep-rooted. You are indeed fortunate to live here,' he told me.

William's acceptance letter arrived on 18th July 1865. As

Zerah ripped open the letter and scrutinised its contents, a grin spread across his face; another piece of the jigsaw was in place.

After that, William paid several return visits to the house, usually during evening after work. Zerah was always present when William presented himself and they spent much time closeted in Zerah's study. Between those various meetings, Zerah worked almost continuously on plans for his new newspaper.

However, Zerah had yet to name the identity of his 'benefactor', and the location of the paper's offices. I did not have long to wait.

Some short time after appointing William, Zerah announced that Mr. Bessemer would be 'our guest' for dinner one evening; his first attendance for a meal, suggesting the importance of the occasion. Zerah requested no expense should be spared, and that I join them. It was my first and only meeting with Mr. Bessemer.

On his arrival, I estimated Mr. Bessemer was some 20 years older than Zerah and an inch or so taller. With his greying hair he gave every appearance of an amiable father figure.

Zerah had informed me beforehand that Mr. Bessemer was extremely wealthy and lived at Charlton House, a large house in Highgate. Mr. Bessemer pioneered the manufacture of bronze powders, gold paint and sugar; he had devised also a continuous sheet glass furnace, and taken out a patent for optical glass.

Zerah told me the grounds of Charlton House adjoined the beautifully wooded domain of Lady Burdett-Coutts, known as The Holley Lodge. Although Zerah did not say so, I assumed that he had visited Mr. Bessemer's house.

Mr. Bessemer explained that he had named his house after his birth village of Charlton in Hertfordshire. In the quiet walks round his own meadows at Charlton, he said he could imagine being at his 'dear old birth place'.

It seemed Mr. Bessemer's parents moved to Charlton following their escape from Paris during the French Revolution. In Paris, his father was a member of the Academy of Sciences and for a time engaged by the Paris Mint, where he invented the portrait lathe. By such means, artists could engrave medallion dies in metal of any desired size using an enlarged model. His father was born at No. 6, Old Broad-street in the City of London.

Aged 13, Mr. Bessemer and his parents went to live in Holland; later as an apprentice, he helped build the country's first steam engine.

He explained that Charlton House enjoyed extensive grounds where he kept cows and Shetland ponies; he also grew tulips. It sounded idyllic. His father grew tulips in Charlton village and created a type foundry in which Mr. Bessemer worked for a time. Mr. Bessemer's eldest sister, an artist, specialised in water colours.

Following the meal, the two men retired for drinks to my husband's study. Of course, I do not know what they discussed, but to while away the time, and out of curiosity, I went to the library in search of Zerah's copy of *Who's Who*.

I found that Lady Burdett-Coutts was the 1st Baroness Burdett-Coutts. As Angela Georgina Burdett-Coutts, she was the daughter of Sir Francis Burdett, Member of Parliament, and the former Sophia Coutts, who was the daughter of Thomas Coutts, the wealthy banker who founded Coutts & Company. Some 20 years earlier, she was the wealthiest woman in England when she inherited her grandfather's fortune.

She appeared ever ready to donate large sums of money to the causes she took up, and she was also deeply religious. As one of her many endowments, she established, with the author Mr. Charles Dickens, Urania Cottage, a home that assisted young women to escape immorality, particularly prostitution.

Set down a lane in Shepherd's Bush, then in the country and surrounded by fields, Urania Cottage provided a haven for young women who led forbidden lives and were prepared to make amends. She provided money for schools in Devon, and in 1869, in another philanthropic gesture, founded Columbia Market, a covered food market for the East End with 400 stalls for which she was called the Queen of the Costermongers. Zerah later explained that a planned railway for the delivery of fish was never built.

Lady Burdett-Coutts also established public parks and built clean apartment blocks all over London for working people. Although the Prime Minister William Gladstone later bestowed on her a peerage, she was not allowed to sit in the House of Lords. Living so close to Lady Burdett-Coutts I concluded Mr. Bessemer must be wealthy also.

Following his meeting with Mr. Bessemer, Zerah decided his office should be at No. 37 Bedford-street, just off the Strand where many other publishers could be found. On the corner of Bedford-street and the Strand, *The Lancet*, a journal for doctors, occupied an office and, ironically, across the road *The Engineer* occupied No. 163, Strand, adjacent to Norfolk-street. Later *The Engineer* occupied 33 Norfolk-street.

At the time, I was minded to ask myself if Zerah planned to have an engraving completed of the facade of his new office in Bedford-street in the same manner in which Mr. Healey had engravings made of *The Engineer*'s offices, first in The Strand and then in Norfolk-street. Zerah placed copies of both in frames; they hung on the wall in his study at the house. He was proud of his years at *The Engineer*, even if they finished in disharmony.

During the early part of the century, the Strand and adjacent streets were popular sites for newspaper and magazine production. However, by the 1850s Fleet-street became the preferred location for most new titles, as well as the centre of London's printing industry. Fleet-street was close to city intelligence and world news from Reuters, established in 1851.

Fleet-street and the Temple linked literacy with law; together they injected into the English language the precision normally associated with the legal profession.

Located also in the Strand was G. H. Harris, where Zerah purchased his boots and shoes, as well as Simpson's where later, once a month, the editorial staff of Zerah's newspaper would congregate for luncheon. Simpson's specialised in traditional English cooking, and was famous for its saddle of mutton.

Zerah, while explaining briefly about his new office, also informed that Mr. Bessemer had offered his support to the new publishing venture on the understanding Zerah would do all he could to 'further the development and understanding of steel'.

It seemed that Messrs. Sands, Hunter and Company, photographic dealers, were the previous occupants of No. 37 Bedford-street. Before that, it traded as a wine and spirit merchants under the patronage of Mrs. Ann Fanny Drake.

Looking back to those days, I now reflect it rather ironic that Mrs. Drake had dispensed wines and spirits in premises where later journalists, like Zerah, would fuel themselves with liquor.

I assumed the choice of No. 37 Bedford-street was a deliberate action by Zerah, being close to their requirements for typesetting and printing.

Zerah later located a printer, Charles Whiting at Beaufort House Printing Works in nearby Beaufort-street, Strand. These works printed Zerah's newspaper for many years, but much later, Mr. Maw designed the newspaper's own print works in Bedfordbury.

Zerah described it as a 'swell' office; but never extended an invitation for me to confirm this. Zerah must have recounted it as 'swell' also to Mr. Maw, who used the word several times to me when he visited our house, although when he did so he could not have actually seen it for himself.

Bedford-street could be found two streets to the west of Exeter-street and Hexel's Exeter Hall Hotel. Mr. Edward Hexel was the proprietor of the hotel. This hotel offered another curious link with Zerah's past, especially as Mr. Hexel became one of Zerah's friends. For it had been at the Exeter Hall Hotel that Zerah, Mr. Alexander Holley and Mr. George May stayed when they first visited London in late 1857.

Clergymen widely indulged in Exeter Hall as a place to attend for sermons on temperance; a subject on which Zerah held his own quite specific views.

Much later, William revealed that, in the early days of Zerah's newspaper, on a Friday, editorial staff would sometimes retire to the Windsor Hotel and Restaurant at No. 427 Strand (close to Bedford-street) where they would enjoy luncheon and drinks, before returning to the office, late in the afternoon. It became a weekly tradition. William once quoted one of the many sayings Zerah gave at such luncheons: 'Better to be with others when celebrating; better not to be alone when drowning one's sorrows.'

Meanwhile, Zerah worked on plans to advertise the arrival of his new newspaper. I gleaned morsels of information from time to time when I noticed papers lying on tables, which I read when no one was present. So much activity took place in the house between September and December 1865 that I could not escape an insight into Zerah's plans.

I had no idea what the title of the new publication might be until I observed a piece of paper in the hall. Marked 'Private and Confidential' and written in Zerah's characteristic scrawl, I could not resist reading it. The last page went as follows:

I will not indeed be in a position until early January next to honourably enter into any apparent competition with it (*The Engineer*), by publishing and conducting a journal of my own. In January 1866, I will commence the publication of a large, first-class, illustrated weekly newspaper, entitled *Engineering*.

So there it was, bold as brass. The new paper, described as a 'first-class illustrated weekly', would carry the title *Engineering*.

To my simple mind, the paper's name appeared not dissimilar to that of *The Engineer*. I was not aware at the time of the subtle significance of the words Engineering and The Engineer; only later was the difference fully explained. Would Zerah's choice of title cause confusion? Zerah must have put great thought into the matter.

Two other men visited No. 7 Gloucester-road before the end of that year. One young man, by the name of Mr. James Dredge, came only once; he too attended in the evening and stayed for dinner, though I was not present at table.

Zerah later told me that he had engaged Mr. Dredge to draw the illustrations. Employed as a draughtsman in the offices of Mr. John Fowler, Mr. Dredge worked on the Metropolitan Underground Railway. Zerah and Mr. Holley met Mr. Dredge on their first visit to London in 1857.

The other man to visit the house was Mr. Charles Gilbert who, Zerah told me, would act as publisher, or commercial manager. Likewise, he visited only once; I never saw him again.

In November, Zerah referred me to an item in *The Times*. It reported the British-built Confederate raiding ship Shenandoah had sailed into the River Mersey and docked at Liverpool. The captain, who had refused to surrender to the Northern states, instead did so to the mayor of that friendly city. Zerah gave a wry smile and said that the British had had a hand in the beginning and the end of the war in America. For not only had Liverpool exported guns, but Confederate President, Jefferson Davis had sent delegates to Liverpool to oversee warship building and to obtain arms.

Later that month however, returning from work one day, Zerah was much less happy. More than that, he was exceedingly angry. He threw *The Times* to the floor and shouted: 'Something must be done.'

Seemingly, the word *'Engineering'* had appeared in the columns of *The Times* and he told me he would place an advertisement in the paper to 'put a stop to it'.

Zerah's advertisement appeared in the issue of *The Times* on 9th December 1865, and read:

Mr. Zerah Colburn finds it necessary to state, that an ADVERTISEMENT, which has once or twice appeared in *The Times*, and headed "Engineering" has no REFERENCE to his NEW WORK, which has never been advertised. Offices No. 37 Bedford-street, Strand, WC, near Messrs. Coutts and Co's.

Possibly Zerah thought someone was playing a joke, or

copying his idea. Perhaps it was a clever contrivance on Zerah's part to advertise his new journal prematurely. He said no more about it.

And so on Friday, 5th January 1866 the first issue of *Engineering* appeared. Zerah told me the printer had produced 65,000 copies. This seemed to be a very large number indeed.

Zerah could not contain his excitement. He reminded me that exactly 20 years previously – 21st January – Mr. Charles Dickens had been instrumental in the formation of the *Daily News* newspaper, a paper he considered would rival *The Times*, adding 'I hope that fate does not befall me. Mr. Dickens relinquished his position as editor after several months because of his objections to the paper's business management.'

But Mr. Dickens admitted to a friend that the editorship 'proved beyond his powers' and that 'I have no doubt made a mistake.'

It seems that in the *Daily News* Mr. Dickens promised financial news, foreign coverage, scientific and business information on every topic connected with railways, as well as criticism of books and art. It was perhaps Mr. Dickens's interest in railways that sparked Zerah's particular following of the paper.

For the first edition of his own newspaper, Zerah worked at the printers all the previous day, from 6 a.m. until midnight, meticulously checking every minute detail. Also present were William and Mr. Dredge – each engaged in proofreading to avert mistakes.

Of course, I was not invited to attend but Zerah informed me of a festive party held at the office to celebrate the first issue; a common practice for newspapers and magazines. The party lasted long into the night, as confirmed by Zerah's return to the house early next morning.

So began the life of *Engineering*, which completely consumed Zerah's attention throughout 1866. I could tell from his conversation that he had surrounded himself with clever young men; young men who were as eager to learn from him as they were to flatter and fawn. I suspected Mr. Maw to be one such person; studious and always busy, concerning himself with the detail of all he touched.

The following evening in bed, he whispered, jokingly, I assumed: "You are a fallen lady. You are the only woman to have slept with the editor of *The Engineer and* the editor of *Engineering*."

Zerah devoted the entire year to establishing the journal in the eyes of the engineering fraternity. Distribution was not confined to this country, where it was avidly read. Copies found their way to subscribers in Belgium, France and Germany. But he did not neglect other matters; his energy appeared undiminished by the enthusiasm he directed towards launching *Engineering* on its journey.

For example, three weeks after the start of *Engineering*, on 22nd January 1866, he gave his inaugural address to the Society of Engineers, of which he had just become president, having duly paid his subscription of ten guineas. The Society, just 11 years old, claimed a large number of members. In this lecture, Zerah drew attention to Mr. Bessemer's steel-making process and its benefits, thus fulfilling his promise to the inventor – and no doubt mentioned his new newspaper.

As to his own journal, Zerah was determined to eclipse the performance of *The Engineer* in every way possible. And he refused to let pass any opportunity to, as he said, 'assassinate' *The Engineer*. The word 'assassinate' sent a shiver down my spine – what a strange word to use, I thought. On the other hand, he knew from experience not to irritate readers but to educate them as far as he was able.

Such was the case in April 1866, when *The Engineer* reported that construction of the new District Line would be in open cut behind the new Thames Embankment. 'Pure invention', reported Zerah in his paper, as he continued his invective with ferocity.

There was so much competition between *The Engineer* and *Engineering* that it spilled over into the house. Especially was this manifest in *The Times* newspaper, which arrived every morning before Zerah's departure. The newspaper carried advertisements from both journals.

For example, page three of *The Times* for 2nd June 1866 carried six items advertising *The Engineer*. In the same newspaper, there were four advertisements for *Engineering*. The length in column inches was two-to-one in favour of *Engineering*. That pleased Zerah; such was his desire to dominate.

And whereas that week *The Engineer* gave much space to gun carriages, *Engineering* favoured "*A Trip to America*" and "*The Severn Valley Railway*" as well as "*Two Full Page Engravings, in the highest style of Art, of the Albert Edward Bridge of 200-feet span on the Coalbrookdale Railway.*"

The advertisement in *The Times* described *Engineering* as "the New Illustrated Journal, conducted by ZERAH COLBURN". He boasted that the first half-yearly volume of *Engineering* as containing "a far greater amount of matter of permanent value than ever appeared in any professional journal within twice the same period of time."

Zerah had complete recall when it came to technical information. He could remember every precise detail whereas others, William declared, had to resort to reference books.

I saw little of Zerah that year – again, we could be as ships that passed in the night.

However, the following year events began to unravel alarmingly. They began, innocently, when they renumbered the houses in Gloucester-road. Instead of No. 7, our house overnight became No. 13. I asked myself 'Was this to be unlucky 13?'

For some time, this renumbering rightly caused some consternation, especially for those who delivered the post. Quite frequently, we received misdirected mail; post destined for Zerah went to the 'new' No. 7, the residence the Rev. Edward Hayes Plumptre, M.A. Such incompetence, of course made Zerah angry.

Much more significantly, Zerah decided that *Engineering* should participate at the great 1867 Paris World Exhibition. Not

211

content that an agent should represent the journal Zerah, backed by unshakeable self-belief, embarked on his next mission. He committed *Engineering* to exhibit at the Paris World Exhibition *and* carry weekly reports.

It was early that year that I again read of 'our' ship, the *Great Eastern*, which had been commissioned to sail from New York to take 191 passengers to the Paris World Exhibition. Among the passengers was the French author Jules Verne who ironically, some two years later, wrote a novel *Une Ville Flottante*, a tale of marital infidelity played out on the *Great Eastern* as it navigated it way across the Atlantic. The first edition of that, I recall, contained a set of illustrations by Jules Férat.

Zerah made his first visit to Paris in late February to prepare for the journal's participation in the exhibition, sometimes named the Second World Exhibition, or Exposition Universelle. He began collecting 'copy' to publish in *Engineering*. He said he looked forward to renewing his friendship with Mr. McConnell of Wolverton Works. They had met at the exhibition and he sat on various juries judging exhibits. He told me that Mr. McConnell had been selected to represent the British Government in the interests of English railways at the exhibition.

That evening, on his return from the opening ceremony, he could not contain his excitement as he opened the door to greet me. Had he missed me? I never knew as he had other things on his mind. For example, for the first time he had tried absinthe.

He described it as a green-coloured, highly alcoholic spirit much favoured by Parisian artistes and writers, known colloquially as *la fée verte* – the green fairy. He said many writers became addicted to it. I wondered at the time if he was still recovering from drinking it. And how long would it take before we had some in the house? I did not look forward to that. Later, I pondered if *la fée verte* sparked Zerah's descent into alcoholism.

More seriously for me, he heard some French men speak of *soixant-neuf*. I had no idea to what he referred. Only later, after he led me upstairs, did I find out, much to my utter disgust and repulsion. Nothing like it had ever happened to me. And I had no desire for a repeat, but I was powerless against Zerah's overwhelming strength.

His lovemaking reached new levels of depravity; it was at the same time savage and delivered with ferocious energy. At times, I considered he verged on the indecent. It was a side of Zerah I had not seen before. I did not like it, but I had no choice but to accept.

He could be so immensely self-absorbed, self-centred, abusive and threating, that I questioned why I had ever enjoyed any romantic attraction for him or agreed to marry him. Could it be that at first I had fallen under the same magnetic power that caught the attention of others?

The following morning, quite ignoring events of the previous night, Zerah explained how the sheer size of the exhibition had driven him to new levels of inspiration. He informed me the exhibition, held in the Champ de Mars, contained nearly 52,000 exhibitors from 41 countries. By far the biggest proportion came from France, some 16,000. Zerah said the theme was The History of Labour, and the organisers awarded 20,000 prizes to those who participated.

The exhibition, which he described as breath-taking, extended from 1st April to 3rd November 1867. Zerah joined thousands who attended the official opening ceremony performed by Emperor Napoleon 111. He told me the exhibition reflected the brilliance of the emperor's 'Second Empire', something that made Zerah smile. When the exhibition concluded, I recall Zerah said there had been between 11 million and 15 million visitors. I could not even begin to visualise so many people.

Zerah described how visitors had arrived by train or boat. He was enthralled by the steam-driven buses as they plied their trade within the grounds. He caught sight too of the first French-made velocipedes in the exhibition. Zerah viewed them as just another French idiosyncrasy. He did not envisage velocipedes as engines of social change or even as a means of personal liberation.

'For that reason we shall not allude to them in the columns of *Engineering*,' he told me firmly. 'However, they will probably be manufactured at a lower cost in England if they ever come into extensive use, as is not unlikely, considering that they afford opportunities for vigorous exercise.'

Some velocipedes were already available in England. However, the sight in the French capital of a large number of the machines proceeding back and forth, especially during evening, was enough to cause heads to turn. Indeed, the number in the Champs Elysées was large enough for police to demand that each rider affix a lamp in consequence of the many accidents.

Zerah was particularly impressed with the Café de la Paix, opened five years previously on 30th June 1862. The café proved an attraction to visitors to the great exhibition. Zerah used it frequently, especially as subsequently he paid many regular visits to Paris to produce 'copy' to publish in *Engineering*.

Chapter Eight
A mysterious encounter

ONE DAY in March 1867, I received a surprise letter marked 'Personal. Private and Confidential'. Zerah was absent on the day of its arrival, which, I thought at the time, perhaps was just as well.

On the same day (13th March) an item appeared in *The Times* – I had meant later to draw it to Zerah's attention. It declared the *Great Eastern* 'Having received new screw boilers and a thorough refit. Accommodation was to be in the staterooms'. The news item made me feel honoured. Every day *The Times* was delivered I would search for an item on *Great Eastern*, almost as though drawn to it by a mystic strand. I had sailed on that ship seven years previously.

The letter, from William Maw, suggested that perhaps, one week when Mr. Colburn was absent on business at the forthcoming Paris Exhibition, I might join his sweetheart Emily and himself to hear one of Mr. Charles Dickens's readings that had proved so popular over the preceding years.

William informed me later that Mr. Dickens had delivered 36 such readings alone between 15 January and the end of March that year. So popular were they that it was even referred to in newspapers that Mr. Dickens's readings might prove more profitable to the author than his book sales, numerous as they were. Being a journalist, and aware of tittle-tattle rife amongst scandal mongers, William hinted that perhaps the readings were made more popular as Mr. Dickens might be in a deep relationship with a woman other than his wife, Catherine. Later, it transpired, Mr. Dickens consummated an affair with actress Ellen Ternan.

I wondered too if William had an ulterior motive for attending the readings as, like Zerah, he much admired the gentleman for his fine contributions to the *Daily News* newspaper. Zerah once even admitted to me he envied Mr. Dickens's journalistic skills of describing what he saw and in some case alerting others as to what they might do about it. In this respect, Zerah tried to emulate the author. On the other hand, perhaps Zerah initiated the invitation. Maybe he had wanted to provide me with some entertainment while absent on business.

I had not attended any of these readings, though I had seen reference to them in *The Times*. The readings took place at St James's-hall in Piccadilly.

An alternative, William suggested, might be to join a concert at the Albert Hall, or visit the popular Madam Tussaud's Exhibition in Baker-street. I had read that the Albert Hall could easily reach its capacity for performances of Haydn's Creation, or Handel's Messiah.

I replied at once to say I would give me much pleasure to join them at any venue of his choosing. Almost by return, a letter from William recommended we hear Mr. Dickens read 'Doctor Marigold' and 'Trial from Pickwick', which would take place 'on Tuesday evening, 26th March' and would commence at 8 precisely'. I knew not to be late.

William enquired whether we should be extravagant and sit in the 'sofa stalls' at the princely sum of five shillings, or the balcony at three shillings. As it was the first occasion I had accompanied the couple, I wrote that the balcony would be quite adequate and that, as a matter of course, I would reimburse him for the cost of my seat.

William replied that he would obtain tickets from the offices of Keith Prowse & Co at No. 48 Cheapside; he and his wife would travel by cab to collect me. There would be no need for me to pay.

As it turned out, the week of 25th March 1867 coincided with a visit by Zerah to Manchester to various locomotive builders. He would be absent for a week, so I welcomed an evening's entertainment. By coincidence, shortly after, in the cellar I came across an old copy of *The Times* of Saturday, April 10, 1858 and there on the front page I found an advertisement for Mr. Charles Dickens to read his Christmas Carol for the benefit of the Hospital for Sick Children on Thursday April 15th at 8 o'clock. On the same page I read it was possible to steam to Australia with the Black Ball Line for 14 pounds in less than 60 days.

The outing passed off pleasantly; I would go further and admit it was an evening of enormous fun and light relief. I much enjoyed the atmosphere of St. James's-hall, and I found the couple's generosity touching. Perhaps they felt a sense of duty to entertain the editor's wife. Rarely did I go out in the evening – except to church on Sundays. However, seeing London lit by gas lamps and people in their finery sitting in the sofa stalls gave me a tremendous thrill.

More than anything, it enabled me to meet in a relaxed atmosphere two young people who dearly loved one another and had a wide understanding of the arts and politics. I envied them. I needed so much for someone to love and cherish me. I wanted nothing more than that human emotion of living with someone who would care for me tenderly.

The evening reinforced my opinions of William. More than ever, I felt that I could trust him.

He did mention quietly, while we were waiting for the readings to commence, that he had first asked Mr. Colburn's permission for himself and Emily to invite me to hear Mr. Dickens. Zerah in reply had simply stated 'Excellent. What a good idea. Put it down to expenses, Maw.'

Many years later I was to read that over 2,000 were present at St James's-hall when Mr. Dickens gave his last reading on 15th March 1870. Such was their popularity.

The visit to St James's-hall marked the turning point in my relationship with William and Emily, who I would describe as somewhat mousy. William and I were to become good friends, though I did not know it at the time. Indeed, I was surprised months later when William, then Zerah's senior editorial partner, came to the house alone. It occurred six weeks after the opening of the Paris Exhibition; Wednesday, 15th May 1867.

Zerah had said previously that 'Maw' planned to marry his sweetheart, Emily Chappell, in three months' time – on 24th August 1867. That same year, I recall, when parliamentary reform was under debate, John Stuart Mill proposed an amendment in the House of Commons that would have given a vote to women on the same terms as men. It was heavily defeated. The event reminded me of Doris who held sympathy for the suffragette movement, then in its infancy when I worked in Golden-square.

The purpose of William's visit, it turned out, was to deliver an invitation to their wedding.

Rose answered a knock at the door. She came to tell me that Mr. Maw requested permission to hand deliver an envelope personally. She asked if I would see him. I told Rose to bring Mr. Maw into the parlour.

Rose took Mr. Maw's hat and coat and showed him in.

'Mr. Maw, ma'am,' said Rose.

'Thank you Rose,' I said. 'You can leave now.'

'Please take a seat, William,' I told him, shaking his hand. He had such a genial smile and a friendly handclasp. It was the first time I called him William to his face and in doing so my heart gave a little flutter. He was such a nice man. By then, I had known William for two years, from the day in July 1865 that he spent a weekend at the house.

Seated opposite, William withdrew an envelope secreted in a folded copy of *The Times* he carried. He said he and Emily much hoped my husband and I would attend their wedding. In doing so, he leaned across and handed me the large envelope. Opening it, I found the invitation.

Removing it slowly I read the words.

'Thank you so much, William,' I said. 'That is most kind of you and Emily. I will talk to Mr. Colburn. I am sure we will be able to join your celebrations. We will send a formal reply.'

Reading their names on the invitation conjured further thoughts of this delightful couple. Emily was such a nice, sweet young woman and I considered, for what it was worth, she to be ideally suited to William. She came from good parents in Canonbury, a pleasant residential district north of Highgate, almost in the country. I considered she would make an ideal wife.

I believed Emily was fortunate to have met and fallen in love with William, a solid, dependable, intelligent and hard-working young man. He was also considerate and thoughtful, and offered Emily security. As far as I knew William had a strong faith, upholding Christian values of honesty, compassion and forgiveness. In other words, William was a good man.

Above all, from Zerah's point of view, William was conscientious, diligent and reliable. Zerah would have been much impoverished without him. I knew that while Zerah was intelligent, he could also be erratic in his habits and he required a reliable assistant like William to ensure they published the paper each week on time. He called 'Maw' his anchor.

I knew also that Zerah was impulsive, but decisive. This feature could be attractive. I recalled how all those years ago, he handed me that note: 'I have great plans. Marry me.' Was it an attraction of opposites? He was also uncompromising and tenacious; and he could be impetuous and a fearsome opponent. I imagined Zerah's opponents would shrivel under the weight of persuasive arguments. No one openly quarrelled with him.

I understood too from what Zerah had told me that he relied on William to put the newspaper 'to bed' every Thursday; to 'sign off' the pages before printing. Zerah had complete faith in William's ability, even though he had no training in newspaper publishing – like Zerah, he was a locomotive engineer.

Zerah had made a sound choice in selecting William as his second-in-command, even though five years' Zerah's junior.

William's capacity for work appeared unlimited. Calm and not easily ruffled, he frequently remained behind at the printers on Thursdays until the small hours. Often he would stay up until 2 or even 3 a.m. on other nights writing articles, and sometimes even later, especially when the paper occasionally got much behindhand.

He had told us, when he first visited the house, that he was meticulous in maintaining a diary. That encouraged me to continue with my own journal to record various events; that journal travelled with me everywhere. I had found a safe place to keep it secure from Zerah's prying eyes.

Our conversation strayed from the subject of the wedding invitation as William spoke more of his early years. It seems, when employed at the Stratford Works, William contemplated a life in India working for Mr. Sinclair. Zerah opposed this idea. He even admonished William, advising that his talents would earn him something more worthwhile in England than ever he could find in India.

Mr. Sinclair had told William the railways in India were the engine of social change; that they would launch a new industrial revolution in the country. Mr. Sinclair even claimed there would be more railway activity in India than in the whole of Britain – for example, they had built and opened a line from Calcutta to Benares, a distance of 541 miles. He added there was much, much more to come. The British government had encouraged private investors to set up railways in India by guaranteeing an annual interest of five per cent.

To this day, I do not know how Zerah acquired his knowledge of railway development in India – he never visited the country – yet he rebuked William so sternly and convincingly that he was able to deflect the young man.

'I should point out, the railways also aided and abetted the '57 Indian mutiny,' Zerah had told William crossly. 'If you must go abroad, try America; but only for a time. Trade is generally bad in America and it is not easy to obtain employment. Also, the cost of living is greatly beyond anything to which the lower and middle classes have ever been accustomed to in England. There is no place in the world like old England, and no one prizes its advantages better than I do. Mr. Dickens had his own view; he described it as impossible for any Englishman to live in America and be happy. I mean to stick here, and you should also. I have just renewed my sever-year lease on this house.'

Those words have remained with me ever since. Seven-year leases allowed families to move as their circumstances changed.

Zerah even offered to give William 'a push in the States' whenever he cared to visit the country but then warned 'Do not go to stay. And never, ever go anywhere else.'

William had asked my husband why he loved England so much. He replied 'Because it is so compact, unlike America.' I could see what he meant, not that I had travelled much.

William then went on to explain more about Emily. Their holiday in 1865 turned out to be William's last, because in the autumn of that year he had to inform Mr. Sinclair of his plans to leave the Great Eastern Railway, even though the Stratford Works kept William fully employed until the end of that year.

Before William's final departure from the Stratford Works, both Emily and Katherine had paid him a visit and taken tea. Later, their father also spent the evening there. It was clear Emily's father, Mr. Chappell, began to think of William as one of the family, as William and Emily spent so much time together in becoming acquainted.

William told me he had spent Christmas Day with the Chappells, and immediately after Christmas, he took up new lodgings at No. 8 Duncan-terrace, Islington, to be within walking distance of Engineering's office in Bedford-street.

In addition to their long walks, William spoke of various jaunts to the River Thames at Richmond and Greenwich and other places of resort, and especially to the Royal Academy and Crystal Palace, for which later, in 1866 and subsequent years, they purchased season tickets. Other favourites were Albion Hall in Hammersmith, and the Academy in Stoke Newington, where they attended dances. They also attended Madam Tussaud's. Zerah never visited any such place.

Among their favourite theatres were the Princess's and Drury Lane. One evening at the Princess's they saw *Arrah na Pogue* and

Reade's *It's Never too Late to Mend.* The couple enjoyed Shakespeare and saw Henry V111 at Drury Lane. On another occasion, they went to hear Charles Dickens give one of his readings at St James's-hall. This was after William joined *Engineering*, because following the performance he returned to his lodgings and worked for the paper until 2.30 in the morning.

I was mindful, as William spoke, just how much he and Emily knew about one another, even before their wedding. In contrast, even at that time, with William in the room, I knew so very little of the real Zerah Colburn.

Zerah, it seemed, had been most helpful towards William, even before joining *Engineering*. He introduced him to editors of *The Engineer* and *Mechanics Magazine* for whom he also wrote articles. I detected already there was complete absorption and mutual loyalty.

William proved conscientious even before joining *Engineering*. He told me that one day, after seeing Emily briefly in the evening, he returned to Stratford Works, and starting about 8 p.m., he worked through the night until 8 o'clock the following morning undertaking special tracing work.

He also explained how, in the early days of *Engineering*, after seeing his fiancée in the evening, he would often return to his lodgings, working night after night until the early hours.

I listened intently to William but wondered if perhaps it was time he should leave. I used that as an appropriate moment to re-read the wedding invitation, and adopting it as a hint.

'This is card is beautiful, William.' I told him. 'Thank you. I am unsure of our engagements but I will discuss it with Mr. Colburn. And thank you too for our conversation.'

I reflected that he and I had had a pleasant encounter. On previous occasions, Zerah had been present, exerting, as he always did, a magnetic influence over proceedings. It was the first time William and I had been alone together.

William however gave no hint of wanting to leave. We talked of everyday matters, but I sensed William's unease. Was he uncomfortable to be alone with me? Was he perhaps nervous that my husband might stride through the door? I knew this most unlikely, as Zerah was at the Paris Exhibition preparing material for the next issue.

Perhaps William had brought the invitation as a pretext for something else. He was the kind of person who would think of others, and offer sympathy and support.

Suddenly, he summoned his courage. Impulsively, he blurted out that what he had to say was 'most private'. He wished to express his concern about my husband.

William's demeanour was so serious that I wondered what he was about to reveal. Indeed, he wanted me to swear on the Bible I would not repeat what he was about to reveal. Should I do so, William would doubtless incur Zerah's wrath and that could compromise the entire office at No. 37 Bedford-street.

I told William it was unnecessary for me to swear on the Bible. I would be most discreet. Anything he said would be safe.

There was a long silence, after which William said: 'I am not sure I should tell you this.'

William was clearly agitated.

'Tell me what, William?' I replied. 'You have not told me anything.'

'I do not know where to begin,' he said.

I suggested the beginning might be a suitable place.

William's concern rested with his editor's visits to the Paris Exhibition where Zerah met Thomé de Gamond; it was his ideas for a stone-vaulted Channel Tunnel that sparked Zerah's interest. In Paris also the Frenchman met Mr. William Low with his designs. Mr. Low was an associate of Mr. James Brunlees, who proposed Zerah's membership of the Institution of Civil Engineers in 1865, and Mr. John Hawkshaw who seconded Mr. Brunlees's proposal from 'personal knowledge'. No, there was much more to William's disquiet than that.

During their first visit to the exhibition, Zerah and William stayed at the Grand Hotel. Zerah had already published an article in *Engineering* describing the hotel's laundry, one of the largest laundries in Paris. The manager expressed such pleasure on reading the article that he allowed Zerah and William to stay free of charge whenever they visited Paris.

The manager, however, did not appreciate Zerah's plans to visit Paris every other week and remain four nights. When he discovered this, the manager revised his concession to half the normal daily rate.

During the exhibition, the two men frequently took breakfast at the British and American Restaurant, operated by Mr. Donald Cameron, licensee of the Wellington Restaurant at Nos. 53-54, St James's-street, London. The Wellington Restaurant was situated adjacent to Bentley-street (I remember that name for reasons that will become obvious), and a few doors from White's, a place I heard Zerah describe several times as a very exclusive club. The restaurant served breakfasts, luncheons and dinners and was located in the exhibition precincts on the banks of the River Seine, adjacent to Pont de Jena.

William attended Paris only infrequently. His duties at *Engineering* confined him to remain in London. However, on occasions when he attended the French capital, William noticed Zerah's heavy alcohol consumption, not only in the evening but during the day too.

'I am aware he consumes much wine in the evening when he is here,' I said. 'But I believe it is associated with the start-up of the newspaper.'

'But he drinks heavily during the day as well as at night,' insisted William. 'I speak out of turn, but it is not good for his health to drink so heavily. We require your husband to be in charge of the newspaper. The atmosphere at work is becoming increasingly corrosive. Employees are fearful of what might happen. No one is in a position to control him. He is the editor – the conductor. He is a law unto himself. We are all concerned. I am fearful too. Do you think you could request him to consume less alcohol? They say it is the enemy within.'

This was a very unusual request; even outrageous. I had long realised that trying to guide Zerah away from a bottle of wine, especially red wine, in the evening after his day's work was the worst action I could take. I had tried it once; he became angry and violent.

On occasions, when Zerah travelled to meet important people at their works, I have no doubt he was polite and courteous. He had much less consideration for those around him with whom he associated daily.

'If I may say so, I think you are speaking out of turn, William. However, I will see what I can do,' I replied lamely. Did William know how powerless I was, even in my own house? Not that it was 'our house'; Zerah paid rent for the property.

Without doubt, ever since Zerah's departure from *The Engineer*, he drank more heavily. At first, it was just a little extra, but gradually it gathered momentum, especially with the start of *Engineering*.

Even so, he appeared able to control himself. It seemed that at work he would drink from noon until three o'clock in the afternoon, and then resume in the evening at dinner. Strangely, it did not appear to inhibit his writing. Indeed, having imbibed alcohol, he would write even more lucidly and furiously than ever. The drink appeared to fire his brain to new levels.

On Saturday and Sunday, when he was at the house, he could easily drink two bottles of wine a day. For my part, I did not drink alcohol, except perhaps a little with dinner. Sometimes, he would order me to drink. With stinging remarks from Zerah ringing in my ears, it was difficult to disobey. From this, I understood the problem to which William referred.

William remained hesitant. I sensed he had more concerns than the issue of Zerah's use of alcohol. He rose from the chair and walked to the window, staring into Gloucester-road. Another silence ensued.

'Mrs. Colburn. I do not quite know how to say this. I am not even sure I should discuss it with you,' he said.

225

What was to come? I knew that Zerah, since his visits to Paris, had become fascinated by Les Diableries – a series of stereoscopic images published in the city in the 1860s, but they surely were of little consequence here in this context. Was William just a silly busybody or was something much more serious about to emerge? Was it my intuition or the tone of William's voice? Did I know what he was about to reveal even before the words fell from his lips?

'Please continue William,' I said, trying to encourage him.

He turned from the window to face me.

'Well, one evening when we were in the Grand Hotel, I had retired to my room, quite tired from walking the length and breadth of the exhibition, goodness knows how many times. Though I am well used to walking long distances, there is something heavy about the atmosphere in a large international exhibition that makes one feel quite fatigued.'

Still no further forward, I wondered what would be coming. I had already gained an image of William as Zerah's disciple, trailing after his editor whom he regarded as an artist; William would hang on every word he uttered.

'I instantly realised I had left my notebook at the hotel desk. There is nothing worse than leaving a private notebook in public gaze. In my anxiety, I ran down the stairs two at a time to retrieve it,' said William. 'While I waited at the desk to make my enquiry, I noticed your husband descend by another stairs and hurry to the door. It was half an hour to midnight. I wondered where he could be going. I judged it late to be going on an exploratory walk through the streets of Paris.'

'I know I should not have done it, Mrs. Colburn, but I was intrigued,' went on William. 'Immediately Mr. Colburn disappeared through the door, I begged the receptionist to guard my notebook and I followed the editor at a respectable distance. We negotiated numerous gloomily lit streets and past various shadowy figures huddled in doorways. It was silly of me. I should not have done it, but I was in the grip of a strange compulsion that pulled me ever forwards. Perhaps it was the inquisitive journalist within me.'

'Mr. Colburn appeared familiar as to his destination, for he quickly weaved down one side-street and then the next. Eventually, he reached a large wooden door set in a building. I stopped. He pulled a cord, and I heard a bell clang in the distance. The door opened and Mr. Colburn disappeared. The door closed quietly behind him.'

'Well, probably there was nothing mysterious. Perhaps it was to meet an engineer or a professor he had engaged with during the day,' I replied.

'At midnight?' countered William.

Next morning, as they enjoyed croissants and coffee for breakfast, William asked my husband if he had slept well. Zerah replied that he had, although he admitted to a midnight walk 'to clear his head'.

'Mr. Dickens walks the streets of London at night to see sights that others miss. So why should not I examine a strange city such as Paris at night?' was all he would say to me.

William noticed that even though Zerah drank heavily at night, he was always punctual for breakfast, apparently unaffected.

William continued: 'The next evening, out of curiosity, I returned to the reception area at about the same hour and, seated in a chair, I read a French newspaper. As before, Mr. Colburn came downstairs and walked out of the hotel into the street. Again, I was drawn to shadow him, but at a discreet distance. We retraced the steps of the previous night, and the same happened. With the editor inside the building, I wondered what to do. I waited a short time and in a while, two men approached in my direction. As they drew level, I pointed to the door through which Mr. Colburn had entered. One of the men shrugged his shoulders and said with a half-smile, or was it a sneer?

"*Des horizontaux, monsieur. Frappez à la porte. Vous rencontrez une fille horizontal – très délicieuse.*"

'"Merci," I replied, in not-very-good French.'

The man, recognizing my mother tongue, replied in perfect English: "I am sure the madam of the bordel will entrust you to the experienced hands of a young woman, most likely Paulette."'

'Deeply embarrassed, I hurriedly returned to the hotel and my bed,' said William. 'I knew prostitution was but a byword for unwholesomeness.'

'I think something strange is happening, Mrs. Colburn,' William continued, torn between remaining silent and speaking his mind out of turn. 'I thought you should know. But then again, I do not know if I am doing right.'

'What do you mean, William, doing right?'

'Well, was it Mr. Colburn's planned intention that I should follow him to observe his activities and subsequently pass the information on to you? Was that a deliberate act on his part? Or was it an absolute coincidence that I just happened to be in the hotel foyer as he emerged; and on two separate occasions? In other words, Mrs. Colburn, am I doing Mr. Colburn's business by informing you of his behaviour or....'

William's voice trailed off into a hung silence. He looked guilty at having revealed the information. Perhaps he regretted doing so.

'Well, thank you, William,' I replied, not knowing how best to respond. I did not know to what he could be referring. 'Let us assume it was a coincidence.'

'You are kind to inform me, but it probably has nothing to do with me,' I said. 'I have to assume Mr. Colburn visited a work associate.'

'What will you do?' asked William.

'Well, nothing at the moment, William,' I said. 'But thank you all the same.'

What was Zerah up to, I wondered? Was something mysterious taking place, or was William just being nosey – a busybody? I thought, whatever the nature of Zerah's activity, it was more than my life was worth to interfere.

William was much relieved at having discharged his concerns and brought them into the open. However, he had not finished.

'Perhaps I should warn you too of something else that Mr. Colburn is contemplating.'

'Oh, what is that?' I replied, half in surprise and half in annoyance.

'Well, he has discussed a new idea with me,' added William. 'It is to start an engineering newspaper in Paris.'

'Goodness me,' I replied. 'Is it not enough that we have two engineering newspapers here in London? Why another in Paris?'

'Mr. Colburn's idea, as he described it, is to have a weekly newspaper devoted to French engineering matters. The title of the publication would be *L'Ingenierie*. It would be a French-language version of *Engineering*, but published in Paris and focused on French engineering matters. Your husband would the 'conductor' and editor, and would live partly in Paris.'

'But where would my husband find resources to support such a venture?' I asked.

'Mr. Colburn did not explain. Clearly the idea is in his head and, as you know, his ideas can quickly become realities.'

'Please do not inform Mr. Colburn of my presence here, nor of what I have detailed,' William pleaded. 'Please keep my information to yourself.'

'Do not worry, William, I will not tell a soul.'

I rang the bell and Rose appeared.

'Mr. Maw is leaving. Please bring his coat,' I said.

'Thank you for listening, Mrs. Colburn. I do hope you and Mr. Colburn will be able to attend our wedding,' said William.

'Goodbye, William,' I said. 'I hope so too.'

When the door had closed, I sat down and wondered what to make of the events William had described. I had more to concern me than the possibility of a new journal in France. It was his other news that worried me. What did he mean? I was innocent. I had some little knowledge of French, for I presumed that was what they were speaking. I remembered the French/English dictionary in the bookcase in the parlour. I looked for the word *fille*. A young girl. It then dawned on me. *Fille horizontale*.

A shiver passed through me. Then I had another thought. The news that Mr. Healey had a mistress in Paris had fascinated Zerah. Had that given rise to a similar idea in Zerah's head? I had read in a book, possibly one of Mr. Dickens's, of the willing acceptance of the French of vices of the flesh. Had someone, a woman perhaps, propositioned him? Was that the moment Zerah first sowed the seeds of self-destruction?

As I replaced the dictionary, I noticed another book close by: *Confessions of an English Opium-Eater* by Thomas De Quincy. I had seen references to the author in *The Times*; I left it untouched.

Not many days after, on his return from Paris, Zerah greeted me with kisses to both cheeks. That was a novelty. In addition, there were also some small unexpected gifts. Life with Zerah was constantly like living on a knife-edge; one did not know quite what would happen next. Within minutes of his arrival he bundled me upstairs to the bedroom whereupon, on pushing me down onto the bed immediately began removing sufficient of my clothes to engage in intercourse. Despite my protests I was powerless against his force and could do no more than yield to the ordeal. And, as he forced his tongue into my mouth, I could detect alcohol.

That night, again he acted unduly roughly. Sometimes he treated me as if I was no more than his rag doll. He subjected me to the most unusual physical positions and actions that even today I am ashamed to commit to paper. Zerah had no understanding as to what I might need. No doubt he intended that I should feel grateful. I went to sleep exhausted; I had no energy for any argument.

I had been married seven years and relieved to have no sign of another baby, yet it was not uncommon of a dropped baby being found in the street, the outcome of some illicit relationship. I carried terrible memories of the two unsuccessful births; I was anxious for these not to be repeated. There were days when part of me longed for a child. However, waves of guilt quickly overwhelmed me – two infants had died at my hands and I could not face another. Anxiety, remorse and guilt are all spoilers of joy.

Zerah had already fathered a daughter, but he wanted a boy to continue the Colburn line. Possibly something might be amiss with me to cause the infants' deaths. Of course, I had been careful not to conceive. I had also seen the doctor several times; he assured me I remained healthy.

Each time thereafter he returned from Paris, Zerah became more ardent, zealous and demanding. He was ever more licentious in what he sought from me. He would kiss fiercely, brutally even as he stroked my body and grasped my bosoms in his hands. When finished, he would lay limp beside me.

On one particular occasion, Zerah unexpectedly unleashed into a rage; there appeared no justifiable reason for his change in attitude. He had returned late from Paris and entered our bedchamber. With only light from gas lamps in the street to illuminate the room, I saw he was naked.

He threw back the bedclothes and climbed on top, straddling me. Then, using two short silk ropes, seemingly produced from nowhere, he tied each of my wrists tightly to the brass bedposts. He then tore away my nightclothes with both hands, and proceeded to explore my flesh in every way. I had no possibility of protecting myself. His long fingernails probed and dug deep into my skin, drawing blood.

As his face came close to mine, I inhaled his stale breath. I wanted to reach and turn my head away. With one hand, he opened my mouth and thrust his tongue deep into my throat. However much I struggled and kicked it was futile; he was too strong and heavy for my light frame. His ravish was short and brutal.

'You are no good, even for that,' he declared afterwards, cruelly.

His deeply hurtful words caused me to feel miserable and

humiliated; convinced that he was depraved.

'Untie my wrists you beast or I will scream for Peggy,' I said fiercely.

I writhed to free myself; it was useless. He reached for his clothes and, taking a handkerchief, rolled it into a ball and thrust it into my mouth.

'Not with that in your mouth, you won't,' he replied, throwing the bedclothes back over me. 'I have a good mind to leave you there.'

Believing I would suffocate, I began to reach. How long would he keep me like this? My struggles made no difference. I shook my head from side to side in an attempt to rid myself of the handkerchief but it remained firmly in place. It grew wet from my saliva. In the end, I gave up. I was more determined than ever to leave that house.

In a few minutes he returned. Throwing back the sheets, he untied my wrists and removed the handkerchief from my mouth. I was desperate for breath. I spat out the saliva, but before I had finished he ravished me again with a barely concealed expression of disdain.

It was in the first week of July that I first noticed the appearance of some sores. I applied cream but without success. The sores were on the lower part of my body. A week or so later, they were accompanied with other local swellings. As the enlarged areas were not painful, I endeavoured to ignore them. Nevertheless, I remained deeply concerned, as I had not seen their like before. Later, I treated the rash with glycerin, but this too had no effect. Little did I know that this was the first signs of a tragic disease; a cruel disease that heralded the onset of an illness that would affect me for the remainder of my life.

Tempted to seek advice from my mother the next time I saw her, I found I could not bring myself to raise the matter.

As the day of William and Emily's wedding approached, I became increasingly worried. Not only had I experienced a loss of appetite, but I had become tired and listless. I had regular headaches and aching limbs.

Causing far greater anxiety, however, were the distinctive rashes that appeared on my skin. These rashes developed into conspicuous circular pink spots. I was very self-conscious. As their wedding day approached, I contemplated not attending. That would have been unthinkable. My clothes concealed most of the spots. I spread cold cream on others.

Zerah must have been aware of the rash, but said nothing. Eventually, I told him of my concern and he instructed me to see Dr. Graham, suggesting it might be measles or chicken pox.

The day of William and Emily's wedding finally arrived. I recall the day for many reasons – mostly the wrong reasons. The weather on 24th August was warm and beautiful, with not a cloud in the deep blue sky. However, in contrast, the mood between Zerah and me, as we travelled by cab was chilly. Preying on my mind were various rashes and scars I longed to keep hidden, not to mention the deep unease they caused. Just prior to the Maw's wedding, I had made an appointment for Dr. Graham to visit on 2nd September.

At the wedding, I hoped desperately no one would notice my ailment.

The service took place in the parish church of St Mary, in Church-row, Islington. Among those present were relatives from Emily's side and guests from *Engineering*, as well as a few of William's colleagues from the Stratford Works. The curate, the Rev. George Hills, conducted a beautiful service – much different from our bare ceremony at Notting Hill registry office three years earlier.

From his comments, the curate clearly regarded William and Emily as friends; he had read their banns in church as, for some time, both had attended church services there. At the time, Emily lived at No. 22 St. John-street, Islington. She had moved to be near her beau, and to allow the couple to marry at St Mary's.

Following the service, we remained in church with everyone as William and Emily signed the register. William had no family, as neither parent was alive. Emily's sister Katherine and Emily's father acted as witnesses.

When I look back, I think it must have been the last occasion Zerah and I were seen in public together – though we did not know it at the time. We both had to be on our best behaviour for the sake of the Maws. However, it did not last for long.

I would rather forget the Maws' wedding, not for their sake of course, but from our point of view. After the service, Zerah behaved disgracefully at the reception. He drank far too much for his own good and made a fool of himself. I feared he might make outrageous statements concerning my appearance. We had to leave early and took a cab to Gloucester-road. We were unable to witness the couple's departure for their honeymoon. This omission on our part irritated me, but I refrained from passing comment; it would only have caused more trouble. My irritability was as much due to my poor health, as to Zerah's foolish behaviour.

Following a short honeymoon, William and Emily moved their possessions into a new residence, a small house in Westbourne-villas, close to Royal Oak station. The station, adjacent to the railway line to Paddington, was convenient for reaching Bedford-street. However, William seldom used local trains – he preferred walking.

With an income of 250 pounds a year, William could afford to employ a housemaid to undertake the house work. The couple enjoyed quiet respectability, far removed, in spirit if not in space, from the life of the teeming poor who lived in London's squalid housing. With twice that income, they could employ three servants.

In later years, as their family increased – Emily eventually bore 11 children, of whom, sadly, three died – the Maws moved to Elgin-crescent, then to Russell-road and finally to Addison-road. By that time, William also enjoyed a country house in Outwood, Surrey.

Dr. Graham duly arrived on Monday 2nd September as,

following the Maw's wedding, I continued to feel poorly. It pleased me to see him. Rose brought Dr. Graham into the parlour. After she closed the door behind her, I said 'Thank you for coming, doctor.'

'How can I help?' he asked. 'Does something trouble you?'

'Well, I have not been feeling well. In fact, I have not been like this before. At first, I dismissed my concerns but now I have aches and pains throughout my body. I also feel feverish and I have a sore throat,' I replied. 'And I have some strange spots on my body.'

'Would you like me to examine you?' asked Dr. Graham.

'Yes, please, doctor.'

By now, I knew Dr. Graham well. I had visited him at his surgery on many occasions, so I felt confident of taking his advice. He was about 10 years older than me. He felt around my neck and asked me to open my mouth wide and cough.

'What is wrong, doctor?' I asked.

'I think we might need a more detailed examination. Would you please attend surgery first thing tomorrow morning? Nurse Gilbert, whom you know, will be present. However, first I must talk to you in private, Mrs. Colburn,' Dr. Graham said.

'Dr. Graham, what is wrong?' I asked.

'Mrs. Colburn, please sit down.'

Chapter Nine
An unseemly illness

I COULD NOT, at first, believe Dr. Graham. There must be a mistake. I had heard talk of syphilis; people spoke in hushed tones of the disease normally associated with those living in poor conditions, or, even more likely, people of loose morals and sexual deviances. Confronted with it face to face, Dr. Graham's words were like a physical blow to the head.

'There must be a mistake, doctor,' I exclaimed, fearing immediately I could be permanently scarred.

'Well, I cannot be absolutely certain, which explains why I must examine you more thoroughly,' said Dr. Graham.

My head started to spin and I felt light-headed. Within seconds I had fainted. I could not to prevent it.

Then I heard Dr. Graham talking; his voice came to me from out of my oblivion. It appeared he left the room to attract Rose's attention, for he held a glass of water in his hand, which he pressed to my lips.

'It is all right, Mrs. Colburn. Everything is all right. There is nothing to fear. Thank you, Rose. I will attend to Mrs. Colburn,' he said.

I must have collapsed on the floor, for I found myself seated with my back against a chair. Rose and Peggy would be aware of the 'goings on' between Zerah and me. It was impossible for them to ignore Zerah's erratic behavior; my present predicament would further fuel their gossip.

What happened behind the closed doors of married couples should remain private, but my dilemma at that moment was that my life had unravelled, in danger of becoming public knowledge.

'Everything is all right, Rose,' I said, feebly. 'You can go, I am sure Dr. Graham can manage.'

Following Rose's departure, Dr. Graham closed the door deliberately. Returning, he said, 'Please try to rest, Mrs. Colburn.

You have suffered a terrible shock. My news has upset you.'

My head continued to swim, but I sipped the water and struggled to compose myself. I rose slowly, still confused, and sat in the nearby chair.

'Thank you, doctor. It is remiss of me. I will be all right now.'

'I suggest you sit quietly until you improve,' said Dr. Graham.

He waited until I moved to a more comfortable chair before continuing.

'I should tell you, Mrs. Colburn, the certainty of diagnosis of syphilis is not nearly so well made out in women as it is in men. That explains why I must examine you. Do you think you will be all right?'

'I shall sit here for a while until I feel better,' I replied. 'Rose will show you out. Please ring the bell. Thank you for coming, Dr. Graham. Thank you for your patience.'

Rose appeared almost immediately. Had listened at the door?

'Dr. Graham is leaving, Rose,' I said. 'Please bring his hat and coat.'

'Goodbye, Mrs. Colburn. I will see you in the morning.'

As the door closed behind him in the hall, I wondered what I should do now. There was but one person from whom I could have caught this disease – Zerah. Had he been with another woman? If so, Zerah in particular and society in general, would expect me to remain the dutiful wife in the face of an adulterous liaison. This was the repulsive side of marriage.

If I mentioned this to Zerah, violence would erupt. Yet the facts appeared irrefutable. He must be guilty. There was no one else. Not only did I suffer from syphilis, a disease about which no one spoke, but I would have to confront my husband and his wrath.

That night I did not sleep. There were many questions and no answers. No longer could I turn a blind eye to adultery. Adultery was for law courts and a subject unmentionable in decent society; the shame of it.

The following morning, as I arrived at Dr. Graham's surgery, a nurse ushered me immediately to his surgery.

'Good morning, Mrs. Colburn,' said Dr. Graham. 'Thank you for coming. Nurse Gilbert will help you remove some of your clothing. And she will be present when I examine you. Please do not feel distressed. It will not take long and will not be painful.'

Within seconds, another nurse appeared at the door and took a seat by the window. She smiled. She must be Nurse Gilbert. I became embarrassed. I felt my face turn pink. Dr. Graham left the room.

Dr. Graham returned after five minutes or so and immediately requested I lay on the examination table. I wore just chemise and stockings. He looked into my eyes, and then down my throat, as he had done yesterday. He felt my glands, and then, to my further embarrassment, lifted my chemise slightly and examined private regions. Worse was to follow. Unsatisfied with his examination, Dr. Graham asked that I sit up and raise my chemise. He looked intently at the sores before carefully feeling my breasts. His hands were cold. I jumped.

When he told me to replace my clothing, I could not have felt more ill at ease. I became further embarrassed when Nurse Gilbert watched intently as I dressed. I could not bring myself to meet her gaze.

Dr. Graham went over to the nurse; they spoke in hushed tones, whereupon she left the room. In a moment, she returned with a glass of water covered with a small linen cloth.

'Please sit down, Mrs. Colburn,' said Dr. Graham, as soon as the nurse had left the room and closed the door.

'Diagnosis of syphilis can be difficult. I have to say it is a cruel disease. Physicians call it the 'great imitator'. To me your symptoms are clear. However, you may wish to seek further advice. I have made some study of the subject matter but I am aware of a consultant in Harley-street who is even more familiar with these matters.'

'Generally speaking, not much is known about syphilis,' Dr. Graham explained. 'You have some small sores; most are hidden from sight. They are symptomatic of the disease, which accounts for the headaches, fever and general malaise you have experienced.'

'Do you know anything about syphilis?' asked Dr. Graham. 'How do you think the disease might have been transmitted?'

I shook my head. I sensed myself blushing as blood rushed to my face. I knew little about syphilis except that it carried strong social stigmas of deviance.

'The disease is communicated sexually between a man and a woman,' explained Dr. Graham. 'Has your husband referred to any unusual symptoms?'

The conversation had moved into uncharted waters for which I was completely unprepared. I remained in partial shock from the doctor's diagnosis.

'No,' I replied. 'He has mentioned nothing.'

There was another silence.

'I must warn you that what I have to say is not pleasant,' said Dr. Graham. 'There is much that I could tell you, but suffice to say that because female organs are more secreted they can be less easily explored as with the male. In the circumstances, women are not aware of the gravity of the lesions because they cause no suffering. It is only later when the tissue has disappeared that problems arise.'

'I have to say that I think you are in the early stages of the disease,' Dr. Graham added. 'That would explain your sickly look. You have some soft sores in the *labia majora* and later these could become hard. Some of these sores can become ulcerous. They are already contagious. You also have some enlarged lymph nodes.'

'You have what we call mammary chancres; now these are only slightly eroded. But again these could become eroded papules.'

My head had begun to reel from the medical terms.

Dr. Graham continued: 'Perhaps I should explain that syphilis is known as the 'French disease'. It is a disease common amongst the French elite. It is said that one-tenth of men in Europe carry the disease. There are three stages: primary, secondary and tertiary. You have passed the primary stage. The secondary stage is contagious. The disease may not be communicable during the tertiary period. Some physicians report that a good secondary eruption protects against the tertiary stage.'

As I sat listening, I found it difficult to absorb, but I persevered. The words 'French disease' set my mind racing.

'The secondary phase is temporary,' Dr. Graham explained. 'The secondary lesions secrete a fluid and, as I said, are contagious; that is how syphilis spreads. These lesions, which can appear in the groin or neck, can be eruptive and may appear at various other places on your body, for example on your ribs, or on the head. You may also suffer headaches, jaundice, insomnia and nervous weakness. There have been reports of eczema too from physicians, and the disease may awaken consumption.'

He said that I might experience a loss of appetite, as well as pains in my joints – in my knees, ankles and elbows. I explained my bones already ached and I experienced other symptoms.

He warned too that there could be 'extreme coldness' on the surface of my skin. He said some of the 'indurations' could persist for the rest of my life, and that I could lose some hair, although it would grow again.

'It is unlikely that you will have all of these symptoms,' added Dr. Graham. 'If you undertake my instructions and follow my treatment carefully, then I hope you will pass through the secondary stage well.'

'As to the tertiary or third stage, I have to warn that this is most unpredictable. It could appear within three years, or 10 years. It could even be as late as 25 years.'

I had become further confused. There was too much to absorb. Some of what Dr. Graham told me I might have not remembered correctly. My face reflected despair; despair that walked like a dog at my heels. Would I ever emerge from this abyss?

'The third stage can be most debilitating,' Dr. Graham continued. 'The disease, if it behaves as with most sufferers, is likely to affect bones, possibly permanently deforming them and causing you some pain. The ravages of syphilis will not stop there. Syphilis affects internal organs, including liver and kidneys. Both could become impaired. It could affect your heart and possibly your brain.'

'I have been deliberately pessimistic, Mrs. Colburn,' said Dr. Graham. 'I hope we can minimise its effects with your help.'

'It is possible to use a treatment of potassium of iodine. Some physicians suggest this is of inestimable value in helping to prevent or limit the effects of the third stage.'

'Are you all right, Mrs. Colburn?' Dr. Graham had continued to talk seemingly unaware of my plight. 'Would you like a drink of water?'

Dr. Graham handed me the glass, first removing the covering. I took a sip and looked at him. He looked grave.

'Can I be cured, Dr. Graham?'

There was a long silence.

'It may take months,' he replied. 'It could even take years. However, you must remain hopeful. Hope is essential.'

His words horrified me. I took another sip of water.

'Youth is on your side, Mrs. Colburn. One physician suggested that it is better to have syphilis in youth rather than make its acquaintance in old age. I believe that to be a wise statement.'

Dr. Graham became serious.

'In 1605, Cataneus called syphilis a monstrous disease. He declared that it so attacked the human race that any other form of death was more to be chosen.'

I became frightened. Was that Dr. Graham's intention? Why did he try to frighten me? Was I about to die? How had I come by this terrible disease? My husband was my only contact with the outside world. He was the one man who used me. What terrible thing had he wrought upon me?

Dr. Graham could see that his words caused concern.

'Please try to be at ease, Mrs. Colburn,' he said. 'What I have described is the worst that could happen. With hope, it will not. I have great sympathy and, as we are neighbours, I will do my utmost to help.'

'As you may be aware, Mrs. Colburn, mercury is used by physicians in the control of all kinds of diseases, and syphilis is no different. Some physicians report that it is a cure and recommend nothing else. Others suggest the treatment is rarely successful. It can be unpleasant. Mercury is poisonous. It can loosen teeth and cause hair to fall out. However, some other physicians treat all their cases with iodine of potassium combined with tincture of iodine. They do not use any form of mercury because it can be painful. Some physicians also use small doses of turpentine in an almond solution together with an internal administration of opium. Opium is for those who strenuously prefer non-mercurial treatment.'

Mention of the word opium caused me to feel dizzy again.

I took yet another sip of water and gripped the arm of the chair with my left hand. My knuckles were white.

'I have said too much,' said Dr. Graham. 'But I want you to be aware that this is a serious matter, not one to be treated lightly.'

'If we are to cure this terrible disease you will need regular treatment. M. Ricord in Paris, an eminent and distinguished physician with much experience of syphilis, has recommended treatment of lesions with a daily dose of mercury for six months followed by three months of iodine of potassium. He gave that advice when he visited the British Medical Association. And I shall follow his practice.'

My hands began to shake. I put the glass of water down on the table. I gripped the arms of my chair again tightly, so tightly the bones again showed through the skin.

'Tell me this, Mrs. Colburn, and I will endeavour to help.' The serious look deepened on Dr. Graham's face. 'Answer me truthfully, now. You can trust me to maintain this conversation as private between ourselves.'

There was another pause.

'Have you had sexual interaction with anyone other than your husband?'

His question cut like a knife. I was shocked; the man's impudence.

'Of course not,' I replied, infuriated Dr. Graham should even consider such a thought. 'How dare you ask?'

'If what you say is true then your husband requires help. Your husband could be a carrier. I must consult him urgently. Syphilis can affect your husband in the same way. As I have said, your disease is contagious.'

'Please do not talk to my husband. I implore you not to say anything about this to him,' I pleaded.

'But Mrs. Colburn, your husband might be in serious danger. You must reveal your ailment at some time. It is better to speak now than wait until it is too late. I can treat you both.'

There was another silence.

'I have one last important matter to raise, Mrs. Colburn, and it is this. You would be most unwise to have another child. It could be seriously impaired. The child might be very sickly; on the other hand, it could be unaffected. That is something you and your husband must discuss seriously. I would advise you strongly not be intimate with your husband until you are cured. You have endured a miscarriage and a stillbirth.'

'It is too late. It has already happened,' I muttered. 'I believe I am pregnant.'

Had I but known the full explanation for my symptoms, I would not have been so ready to call on Dr. Graham's services. But I was in complete ignorance. I felt my face blushing at the thought. Had Dr. Graham not lived in Gloucester-road he would, quite rightly, have had good reason to label me a common prostitute.

Syphilis. I would have to nurse my shame in silence – and

alone. I could not, and dare not breathe a word to anyone, not even to my mother with whom I was close. What would become of me?

Which was uppermost in my mind: anger or despair? It was anger surely. Was it a reflection of my damaged pride? Was it perhaps that I knew deep within me that only one person was responsible for this terrible contagious infection. That person was – my husband.

He had infected and maimed me, a healthy woman. Now I feared I might be pregnant. I could be carrying Zerah's infant. What monster would I bring into the world?

The man whom I had trusted implicitly had caused me such disgrace, such humiliation; he had brought nothing but betrayal and indiscretion. Above all, he had brought profligacy. All I had wanted was love and physical affection, both of which I was deprived.

How could I face my family, especially my father? Could I tell them? Dare I tell them? If so, who would I inform first – my mother or my father? How would they react? My father would be horrified, even outraged. He had not trusted Zerah. I hoped he would treat me gently. My mother, of course, would be furious. Would they disown me? To my knowledge, nothing like this had happened within our family. And my sister; what would she think?

How could Zerah do this? What had I done to deserve such ill treatment? I was and would remain for the rest of my life, a victim of this dreadful disease. Zerah had inflicted a life sentence.

Two words instantly entered my head, as if from nowhere: *Fille horizontale.* That was it. That was how and where Zerah had contracted the disease – in Paris.

That was what William Maw tried to tell me weeks ago when he arrived with his wedding invitation. His purpose had been to warn of Zerah as a sexual predator. So that was where Zerah had gone in Paris: a house for women of the street. What a fool I had been! It was there that he broke our marriage vows.

I heard Dr. Graham's voice in the background as my mind slipped away with its own thoughts. I tried to pay attention. I had become angry. What had Zerah done? I shook my head.

'Mrs. Colburn.' I heard the doctor call my name. It was as if he spoke from far away.

'I am sorry, doctor, what was that?'

'I asked again about your husband,' repeated Dr. Graham. 'I urge him to see me.'

Dr. Graham was obviously concerned about Zerah's health.

'What about my husband?' I replied.

'He should be examined. Your own predicament could be hereditary, but I think that unlikely.'

'I will discuss this with my husband, Dr. Graham.'

I was surprised at the sound of my voice. It was firm, determined and resolute. In an instant I knew the truth of it, and I had become a different woman; transformed even.

'I shall inform him immediately on his return from Paris,' I said.

'As you wish, Mrs. Colburn,' the doctor replied. 'But should you or your husband require further advice, then I am at your disposal. Should I make an appointment with the consultant in Harley-street?'

'Thank you, Dr. Graham, but no,' I said. 'I would like to keep this matter entirely private.'

'As you wish, Mrs. Colburn; I do understand. Meanwhile I will arrange your treatment. I will visit in the morning with instructions. And I will need to examine you in a month's time with regard to your pregnancy.'

That was the first time he had mentioned the word.

'Thank you, doctor.'

'Please remain in the waiting room until you have recovered sufficiently to make your way home,' said Dr. Graham. 'If necessary, I can arrange that nurse accompanies you.'

'That will not be necessary, doctor,' I replied stoically.

I walked gingerly to the waiting room; empty, thankfully. I sat in a deep, comfortable chair. Journals lay on the table; I ignored them.

To whom could I talk? I had no close friends. I was isolated in that house. Outside in Gloucester-road life continued as normal, everyone unaware of my plight.

Clearly, I had to face Zerah with the truth. I would need to take medication so there was every chance he would be aware of my condition. Was it possible I could take the medication and no one notice? Could I heal myself? Dr. Graham might call upon Zerah or ask him to attend his surgery. He would not like that.

I was tempted to visit mother. Could I convince her to tell no one, absolutely no one? It would break father's heart – he was about 76 – for my mother to inform him of my despicable illness. He would regard it as a family disgrace for a child of his to have syphilis – as indeed it was. The entire matter would be outside his experience. Father was a proud man.

Father would probably instruct me to leave my husband at once. I was terrified; I feared making the wrong decision.

Even now, as I pen these words so many years later, I can hear what father would command: 'You have a duty to do what I ask of you. You are my daughter and I am your father. Leave that man immediately. Have nothing more to do with him.'

As I sat in the waiting room, I began to come to terms with Dr. Graham's news, but how would the shock affect my parents? They would have to know, and have every reason to hate Zerah.

After half an hour or so, I made my way slowly to No. 7 Gloucester-road. I knocked. It was Peggy, not Rose, who came to the door.

'Would you like a cup of tea, ma'am?' she asked. 'Are you alright? You look most unwell, ma'am.'

'There is nothing to worry about, Peggy.'

'That's good. We cannot have anything happening to you. You are always so kind to us.'

She brought tea into the parlour. I sat and drank it slowly. It was exceptionally sweet. I remained idle for what seemed hours. I

247

just sat in the chair and stared out of the window; figures passing by the window meant nothing to me. So many thoughts swirled through my head.

I started to cry. I searched again for an explanation as to how and why this tragedy had happened.

This was the second time Zerah had pitched me headlong into disaster through his actions. How many more times would it happen?

What angered me most was from where the disease had come. So far, I had only surmised from William Maw's comments regarding Paris that its source must be Zerah. The doctor had suggested it could be hereditary, but that was unlikely as it would have reared its head before and I remained certain of my parents' utterly moral lives.

The only other conceivable possibility was that it must have come from Zerah. I could not drive this recurring thought from my head.

It was all Zerah's fault. Had he been with other French women, apart from the mysterious *fille horizontale* – FH as I called her? How long had this been going on? Was FH the first? Were there others? And what did these French women possess he found so alluring?

Were these prostitutes – for that is what they were – better looking than me? Were they dressed more prettily? Were they younger? Did he find them exciting? Did these women add some strange luster to his life? And did he physically penetrate them? The more I gave thought to what might have happened, the more disgusted I became. His attitude appeared outrageous to my naive nature. Surely, he understood the element of danger; did that heighten his excitement? Did he not have any sense of shame? Had he no conscience – no sense of right or wrong?

These were women of the street; drawn for some reason to a wretched fate, though some no doubt were willing partners of the men they met. Although, as I have mentioned, Mr. Dickens had established his Home for Homeless Women through the generous Lady Burdett-Coutts but this would barely scratch the surface of the problems of these poor defenceless women. Oh, the hypocrisy of men; as one or two may attempt to rescue some of these poor women from the gutter, many more continue to prey on them and enjoy the pleasures they offered.

I had been available for Zerah whenever he required. I know that since the loss of my two infants, I was less and less inclined for intimate relationships with him. Only very infrequently did I deny his sexual pleasures through illness, yet he continually forced his entry. However, in terms of physical closeness, he made it impossible for me to feel affection.

Had Zerah become tired of me, just as he had grown tired of his first newspaper, the *Railroad Advocate*; his land warrants in Iowa, his steam saw mill all those years ago, and his consultancy? All too often in his life, there were recurrent examples of enthusiasm for new ventures that died quickly after birth. His business ventures were stillborn too.

Here surely was tangible testimony that he had grown tired of me. Mrs. Baldwin had told me that the necessity of a good marriage was to remain 'friends'. Since the loss of my babies, there had been a strained atmosphere between us. I had been so frightened of Zerah's moods that I would do anything to keep the peace.

Another thought occurred to me: had the whole of our life together been an act? Had there been any meaning to our marriage? Even as I pondered such questions, they bewildered me. According to my upbringing, even to consider them was an act of Christian betrayal.

Zerah had described some of his work to me and I had tried to understand. Perhaps I had not shown enough interest in him or his work. Should I have done more to indulge in his work? I had an intellect which I used to educate myself as much as I could under the circumstances, reading various newspapers and journals to bring myself to a point where I thought I could begin to understand. Of course, I failed. Zerah worked in a man's

249

world of engineering – a world without place for women. Or so I thought.

Clearly, however, women were accessible. William Maw had told me how on occasions finely dressed women had stepped onto the *Engineering* exhibition stand. Why did they come, if it was not at some point to sell their services? The Paris Exhibition drew in men from all over the world; wealthy men. They could easily fall prey to these women and their forbidden enjoyments.

I wondered how many other men there were like Zerah. William Maw was such a devoted man that I could not imagine him straying far from Emily; they had been almost lifelong friends and loved each other passionately. I was so innocent, so child-like. I was ignorant of what happened in the world.

I had made a dreadful mistake in agreeing so quickly to marry Zerah. The attraction of opposites had melted away before my eyes.

The more I turned matters over in my head the more confused I became; and angry. I had no one to whom I could turn; no one I could trust with my thoughts.

The vicar was a kind, family man who had spent his working life in the Church, but my dilemma was so humiliating for a woman of my standing – the wife of a London newspaper editor. I could not approach him.

And my mother? Could I go to her? Dare I completely unburden myself to her? Perhaps I would have to work out my own salvation.

I needed desperately to talk to another woman. The only person I could think of was Emily Maw with her milky-white skin. However, I did not know her sufficiently well, I thought, to confide my problems.

In addition, if I did reveal all to Emily, would she be compromised? She and her husband were close. If I unburdened myself, would she pass everything to her husband? Naturally, she would. Would the information find its way to Zerah? And if it did – would that make him even angrier?

Whichever way I turned, I found no solution.

Peggy asked if she should prepare luncheon; I declined. I could not eat. I felt hollow inside.

'Would you like a nice sandwich, ma'am?' she asked. 'You must eat something.'

I declined again.

That afternoon, I went out into the fresh air and made my way to church. The door was open as usual and I walked to the front, knelt down at the altar rail and prayed. I prayed for forgiveness; and I prayed that God would help me in my hour of need. I had social stigma to overcome, and I would have to endure much personal pain. The future was bleak. And now possibly there was a baby to consider.

I then sat in one of the pews near the front of the church. I stared out of the east window, confused, angry and tormented.

I had been a loyal and dutiful wife, yet Zerah had deceived me; betrayed me. He had cast me aside for another woman. The appeal of an illicit relationship with another woman must have overwhelmed him. This French woman must have offered him something he found satisfying and lacking in our marriage.

She would not be terrified of him as I was. She had no fear of a beating for revealing the name of the first Mrs. Colburn. Zerah had no cause to tell her about Mrs. Adelaide Colburn and his daughter, Sarah Pearl. Even the thought of their names made me shiver.

And were there others of whom I knew nothing?

My life had become unmanageable; so too the thoughts that welled up in my mind, continuously. However, there were little luxuries. When Zerah was in Paris, I enjoyed being alone in bed. I took great delight in stretching my limbs between clean, cool sheets. Sometimes, despite my illness, I would pull the bedcovers over my head to create a tiny, private cocoon to escape the world. It gave me a sense of freedom, albeit short-lived. There I had time to think; time to pray.

My mind had wandered. I knelt down to pray, putting my

hands together. I prayed to God that should I be pregnant, my child would be another stillborn; that I would not have to answer in years to come for any disfigurement or disability.

After a short while, I left church and made my way to No. 7 Gloucester-road. Eventually I would have to confront Zerah.

Then, I decided to visit mother. I knew even though I had been rebellious in longing to leave home and make my own way in the world, my mother was the most important person in my life. I was sure that however angry she might be, she would give her support and offer courage and strength.

On arrival, I said I had something serious to tell her. We went into the kitchen and sat down. I outlined what Dr. Graham had told me. I expected to feel her anger. I had brought shame upon the family. What she had to say surprised me.

'It is not your fault, Elizabeth,' she said. 'You were innocent. You were not to know. Why do you stay with him? Is it love or duty?'

As my mother talked, I could see she had watched my life unfold with great sadness. And I soon understood she knew of illnesses such as mine. Yet I could tell her only half my story. I dare not tell her I could be expecting another baby.

'Soldiers and sailors are the usual sources of such infections,' said mother. 'But so too are other men who, driven by unspeakable obsessions, make frequent visits to prostitutes and women of easy virtue who then pass on the disease.'

Her advice to me was clear. I should attend the consultant in Harley-street for a second opinion to Dr. Graham's diagnosis. She also implored me to tell Zerah what the doctor had said, whatever the consequences. She said that, for his own sake, my husband should seek medical help.

I did not stay long. Heartened by some of what she said, I returned to No. 7 Gloucester-road, confident of her support. I knew however it would not be easy to engage with Zerah.

I will not forget the day I visited mother. It was Wednesday, 4th September 1867. I had the remainder of the week to myself.

Zerah implied before his departure for Paris that he would not return before late Thursday at the earliest, more likely it would be Friday.

Wednesday was a strange day. After seeing my mother, I remained restless for the remainder of the day, worried lest my fears of pregnancy were realised. In *The Times* earlier in the month, I had noticed French poet Charles Baudlaire had died the previous month, aged 46, damaged from his way of life. Zerah had read some of his poems, including *Les Fleurs du mai*. The poet had a mistress.

Thursday evening arrived and Zerah did not appear. I had more time to turn events over in my mind. During the long night in bed, I stared up into the darkness of the room, waiting for sleep that never came. From outside in Gloucester-road, I heard the clatter of the occasional horse and cab as each edged along the street; a late-night reveller returning to bed perhaps, or a straying husband heading home to his wife. I examined every possible alternative. I had had little to eat. I felt quite weak.

Friday arrived and I was not sure when Zerah would return, but I guessed that it would be in the evening.

Before his arrival, I went to the dining room where there were bottles of wine, sherry and port. I noticed a bottle of Madeira wine; the label described it as a fortified wine made in the Madeira Islands. I had not seen it before. I poured a glass of port, and returned to the parlour and sat down. I took occasional sips, each time feeling more relaxed and assured. The port offered a warming glow; a new confidence swept through me.

I heard Zerah's key in the door. I went to meet him.

'Come to the parlour, Zerah, I have something to say,' I said boldly.

'What is that, my dear?' he replied, as he pecked me on each cheek. I pulled my face away.

'Dr. Graham informed me I have syphilis,' I blurted. 'He said you also should visit a doctor for examination.'

A long silence followed. I remained quiet and still, believing I held all the cards in my hand.

I recognised the sign. His top lip quivered and then curled into a snarl as his teeth bit into his lower lip.

'Do not tell me what to do, woman,' he retorted. 'Is Dr. Graham certain? That is a serious contagious disease. Doctors often make mistakes.'

Zerah was angry, but the evasive look in his eyes revealed the truth; it made him more like a stranger than a husband.

'Dr. Graham is certain but suggests I visit a consultant in Harley-street whom he knows will confirm his diagnosis,' I retorted.

'Have you been intimate with another man?' Zerah asked.

I could not credit his affront.

'How dare you? How dare you make that suggestion to me when you know that I am completely faithful? You are the culprit. You have infected me with syphilis and now I am damaged for life. The doctor wants to examine you.'

'How dare you meddle in my private affairs? In any case, I am sure there is a simple answer to this problem.'

There was not for a single moment any hint of confession or guilt nor any wish for repentance.

'There is a simple answer. It is your irresponsibility; your shameless infidelity. You carry this filthy disease and have infected me. It is worse for me; I could be pregnant with a sickly child that could carry your syphilis and likewise be maimed for life. I want nothing more with you. You are weak-willed with your filthy habits.'

With my outburst I seethed with anger, sure in the knowledge that he had shattered my self-esteem. I could not forgive him for what he had done. To forgive would be to condone.

I could not believe his affront. His evasiveness and betrayal compounded my anger. How did I come to say such a thing without first deliberating the implications or the consequences? For a moment, I had forgotten the magnitude of Zerah's wrath when roused.

Like a lightning's strike, he slapped me across the face,

knocking me backwards into a chair, my body already frail. I lost grip of the glass of wine and it fell to the ground, shattering.

'Whore,' he screamed out at me with such venom. 'Well, if that is what you want then I can get my pleasure elsewhere. We will now have separate rooms; as it is, our life together has become aimless and limpid. I will enjoy morning glory alone. I am retiring to bed. I do not know why I bother to speak to you.'

'If you dislike me so much then it might be better if we separate completely,' I blurted. 'You once said you found me irresistible.'

'You will not escape as lightly as that,' he retorted ignoring my last remark. 'You are mine and will remain here. Now, I am tired. I have endured a frantic week in Paris. It has been exhausting.'

'I am sure it has,' I fired back angrily, still smarting from the slap. 'Are you not already weak to want to satisfy your desires elsewhere?'

He moved towards me, bending over me.

'Weak am I? Then take that, and that.'

And with those words he hit me violently across the face with the palm of his hand, once in each direction; his face gripped with a sarcastic smile. Abruptly he left the room, slamming the door behind him.

His violent behaviour, though terrifying, confirmed his guilt. Had he been innocent, he would surely have been more concerned for my well-being. He had not realised the enormity of his actions.

What had just happened deepened the divide; our relationship would grow more distant. Did he hope to drive me out, or that I kill myself? From then onwards, I was his target for reproach, a subject for ridicule.

Peggy hurried in to assess the commotion.

'Clear up the mess, Peggy. I have had an accident with a glass of port,'

'Yes, ma'am. Is that all ma'am?

'Yes, Peggy that is all, thank you.'

And with that I went to bed, locking the door and barricading a chair against the handle. I was determined that somehow I must begin a new life. But how? And when? In the meantime, I would have to pretend to the world that Zerah and I had just grown apart.

First, I had to learn how to deal with the shock and humiliation of what had happened. The dreadful possibility of another child obsessed me. I had my fears, but I needed confirmation and soon.

So many storm clouds had accumulated suddenly. Other women turned to drink to cope with rejection. I would not. Yet the memory of rejection and simmering resentment long outlive any memory of desire. Would the resentment I held against him ever come to the boil? And what would be the effects?

It occurred to me that should I develop more of the symptoms of syphilis, then so too would my husband. Dr. Graham had painted a depressing picture of my future; a similar future surely awaited my husband. Had it already started to take effect, including perhaps the degeneration of his nervous system?

I did not discover whether Zerah ever visited a doctor. He did not discuss it. I dare not ask for fear of reprisal. I had to assume that he did; if the disease went untreated then it could ruin his life.

Dr. Graham stressed the necessity for me to apply treatment regularly for any chance of limiting the disease's effects. I was too frightened to do otherwise, as he had warned that the side effects of the mercury could be stomach ills, nausea and aches in my body.

I knew that Zerah had no reason to feel proud. His devious activities in Paris and their effect, cancelled out for me all his achievements. Without doubt, I would be the fractured half of what had previously appeared to be a conventional but successful couple.

The following day I wrote to William and marked the envelope 'Most private'. I judged it would arrive just after their return from honeymoon. I asked if he and Emily would visit one evening, if they could spare the time. I offered several dates when I knew of Zerah's absence.

I grew concerned about my appearance. The effects of syphilis must be obvious to all. I had also begun to have doubts about my own attractiveness. Zerah must have found me attractive at one point in time. Did he not call me his English rose? Did I now have so many thorns as to be untouchable? Was the fragrance I used not attractive enough? I understood how naïve I had been.

Although I wanted nothing more to do with my husband, I questioned whether I had done enough previously to make myself attractive. Should I have spent more time and effort on my hair and clothes? Would he have provided money to do so? And did I now wish to make myself attractive to him if he had been with other women? Of course not.

I looked in the mirror. All I could see was a subjugated and downtrodden woman; a woman bound like a slave. My complexion was poor and my skin spotty. Zerah knew I would not, could not leave him. Yet how could I be a worthwhile woman if my husband looked for relationships with other women? I had no future.

I resolved to put on a stoic front for the few people I knew. I reasoned this was for the best, though inside I experienced nothing but desperation. There appeared no solution to my ills, yet what was to come would test my reserves of patience, self-discipline and forbearance to the limit.

A reply from the Maws informed me of their delight in accepting my invitation. I asked Peggy to make special cakes.

When William and Emily arrived, I was grateful for their company; two people close in age. Although 32, I felt older, especially in the light of events. I weighed up whether to inform them of my disease – or was it so obvious. And would they be too polite to mention it? I decided on silence. We talked of various matters but discussion inevitably turned to *Engineering*, which continued on its upward path, both popularity and, presumably, financial success.

As if without prompting, Emily said:

'Mrs. Colburn. There is something you should know.'

I wondered what Emily could be about to reveal. Would it be concerning my illness?

'Mrs. Colburn, you must be most careful.' Emily emphasised the word 'must'. 'Your husband has been seen brandishing a gun at work. I am sure one day he will kill someone. William referred to the gun some weeks ago and I believe you should hear of it.'

Throughout, William sat quietly, meekly clasping his hands. He looked nervous, fearful of speaking. He said nothing. I had been wrong in classifying Emily as 'mousy'. Like a cat with claws, she could strike.

'We must not keep Mrs. Colburn in the dark, William,' declared Emily. 'Mrs. Colburn has a right to know such things.'

I knew from experience that Emily could be a determined talker.

'Is that true, William?' I asked.

'Yes, Mrs. Colburn. Please do not say we told you.'

'That is all right,' I replied. 'I know about a gun.'

I felt it necessary to explain on Zerah's behalf. Goodness knows why I should be loyal to him.

'It is quite simple. Mr. Colburn informed me of his requirement for a Colt revolver for house protection; as well as for his travels in the event of thieves accosting him. He acquired the weapon specifically for those occasions when he collected subscriptions from businesses by the river, many in the East End of London where thieves are common. Mr. Colburn visits the offices of Colt's Fire-Arms Company at No. 14 Pall-mall to inspect their latest firearms. He has one of theirs.'

On rare occasions, I had caught sight of him polishing the weapon, almost caressing it, admiring the precision of its construction. I mused at the time: had he ever used a pistol? Did he know how to discharge it? Would he ever aim it at me? Would he use it to prevent me beginning a new life with someone else?

'Yes, Mrs. Colburn, but William told me your husband has been seen waving what he described as a Derringer in the offices of *Engineering*. This was not a Colt pistol. One day, Mrs. Colburn, your husband will kill someone with that gun, you mark my words. I do not want him to slaughter my William.'

'And I am worried about your own safety, Mrs. Colburn,' Emily added somewhat lamely as an afterthought. She was most concerned.

I did not know what to say. I knew nothing about a Derringer. What was that? I was not aware Zerah had two weapons – guns, pistols or whatever they were. It was news to me, but it did not surprise me.

I told Emily that Americans were accustomed to owning pistols; possibly he had brought the Derringer with him from Philadelphia. News of two pistols made me more frightened as to what might happen to me. He had not held a gun to my head, though I would not put it past him.

'Please do not worry, Emily. It is kind of you to think of me. You are very sweet.'

'And thank you,' I added. 'I will take care. I can think of no reason Mr. Colburn would want to kill me – or your husband.'

'I was not thinking of any deliberate action, Mrs. Colburn, God forbid,' said Emily. 'It was just that I thought there might be a terrible accident in the house. It has been known for guns to be fired accidentally.'

'I will be careful, Emily. Please rest assured. But thank you for the warning.'

I rang the bell for Rose to bring more tea, before moving the conversation to other matters. Then Emily spoke out again.

'Tell Mrs. Colburn what else you know, William,' she said.

If William had been sheepish before, he was even more so now.

It surprised me how forceful Emily had become. I used to like her mouse-like nature, but at that moment she appeared more outspoken and strident than her husband. What lay behind it?

'It is a rumour in the office, Mrs. Colburn,' said William, as if trying to defuse the matter. 'There may be nothing to it. Best to ignore it.'

'Perhaps I had better be the judge of that,' I said. 'What is it?'

There was a long silence. Determined not to speak first, I thanked Rose for the tea and asked her to pour.

'As I say it is just a rumour,' said William when Rose had left. 'Please, please keep this to yourself.'

There was another long silence.

'Speak up, William,' said Emily. 'Tell Mrs. Colburn what you know.'

I looked William in the eyes; he looked away immediately. I could judge he felt shy and very, very uncomfortable. Indeed, I had not seen him in such a state before. Perhaps during our previous engagements he had said too much. Had Emily put him under some pressure? Was she even more of a busybody than her husband?

'There is gossip that your husband is seeing one of the kitchen hands,' he blurted. 'I know nothing more. I speak completely out of turn. Please, do not reveal this to anyone else. Keep it private.'

The news completely surprised me. I wanted to know more.

'It is really not for me to tell you this,' added William, after another long silence. 'Emily thought you should be informed, your husband being such a good-looking man. I cannot tell you any more, even if I knew it. It is more than my life is worth. Your husband is bad tempered – a curmudgeon, someone once described him. You must not speak about it to anyone. Please keep this information to yourself.'

William refused to say more. Shortly afterwards the couple departed. The atmosphere in the room at the end had become stilted; the spell of friendship momentarily broken.

Following their departure, William's remarks left me hanging in the air, as if suspended by a rope from the heavens.

Chapter Ten
Time for a detective

I REALISED for the first time I had to learn what, if anything, had taken place behind my back. William's remarks caused concern. As a quiet, passive and tolerant Christian, I had, and still have, a desire for justice.

The following month, in October, when making a planned visit to my mother, I found father at home. Perhaps mother had arranged his presence to coincide with my arrival.

Mother must have informed father of my husband and events in Paris. I had pleaded with her not to reveal too much, but I suppose she felt matters were getting out of hand. Much as she did not want to interfere in my affairs, she concluded I needed help. I had no desire to act out of spite, more in self-defence.

On greeting father, I expected unbridled criticism. Instead, his eyes gleamed with steely determination. I had not seen him like that before. As well as meeting women in Paris, he said, Zerah could be 'up to no good' in London. If we could obtain proof and this information, together with his prolonged ill-treatment, would provide enough evidence to seek divorce.

Divorce – the word struck like a knife thrust through my heart. Beyond the means of most people in the land, divorce was a word rarely mentioned in conversation. It happened but only to rich people. For me and my family it would mean nothing less than social stigma and hardship.

Father held firm views. I considered him wise and that I should pay attention. If I did not act, he would take matters into his own hands. He did not beat about the bush, but spoke openly and repeatedly of divorce, a subject quite clearly at the forefront of his mind even though it could bring stigma to the family as well as myself. He and mother must have discussed it many times. He was plainly worried.

He told me that when a man and woman marry, the rights of

the woman are legally given over to her husband. Under the law of England, the married couple become an entity; the husband alone represents this entity, placing him in control of all property, earnings and money.

He told me in no uncertain terms, and in a language I had not heard before, that marriage gives a husband ownership over his wife's body; that their mutual matrimonial consent is a contract in which she gives herself completely as her husband desires.

'Many women do endure their husband's control, cruelty, violence, abuse and deprivation,' he said. 'They have no way of escape. But for you, Elizabeth, we must find a way for you to leave this man.'

I remained silent. He seldom used my Christian name; this implied concern. I had no wish then to light a fire I could not extinguish but I knew enough from father's tone to understand I had to fight for my freedom.

'It is the only way I can see open to you,' father told me more than once. 'However, it could be costly. Women are seldom successful without firm evidence of adultery and brutality – there is brutality in many marriages; man against woman.'

'Divorce is for wealthy people,' he told me once. It was obvious from his remarks he had studied the subject carefully on my behalf. I noticed how frequently he would repeat himself, a sure sign of his fatherly concern.

'Following the Matrimonial Causes Act of 1857, a new Court for Divorce and Matrimonial Causes was established to hear all matrimonial cases which came within reach of people with moderate incomes,' he told me. 'However, while men can claim adultery as a reason for divorce, a woman must prove her husband's adultery, along with another offence, such as cruelty, bestiality or rape, in order to petition for divorce. That your husband is a newspaper editor should not be allowed to conceal the issue that he has conducted these atrocities against you.'

Father explained that a wife could obtain a divorce on grounds of incestuous adultery, where her husband committed adultery with a woman whom he could not legally have married.

And, as if to add some words of comfort, he implied divorced wives no longer forfeited all their property and they might be able retain any income they had managed to earn. However, such matters would not affect me – I had no money.

Father said newspapers could, and did, report proceedings of the Court with chilling intensity, usually much to the delight of the prurient Press, ever keen to add the spice of triviality, and of which my husband might be duly frightened.

Father added that the attention of the Press would be frenzied and uncontrollable, and while scandal surrounding royalty might quickly pass unheeded by deferential newspaper editors, the same could not be expected by a miscreant journalist, indulging in marital infidelity.

Zerah would fear such proceedings would heap shame on his career, exposing his secret passions, his secret history. London journalists would gleefully ridicule his eagerness for prostitution; street sellers would broadcast the lurid headlines of newspapers.

'Your unscrupulous husband would dislike such exposure,' father said. 'I suggest you engage a private enquiry agent to follow that husband of yours and find out exactly what he is doing behind your back. If you want rid of him, and I recommend you do, you will require evidence both of adultery *and* a crime against you to secure divorce.'

My father instructed me to keep a diary: he promised to obtain one with a locking clasp to ensure what I recorded would remain hidden from prying eyes.

'Conceal the diary. Make sure no one observes you,' he ordered.

I told him of my journal in which I maintained a diary of events.

'Keep that beside you, and use this new one to record evidence for divorce. But keep it safe,' he said. 'I am with you; do not feel unsettled or alone. You made a mistake marrying a cruel and disloyal man. But we must pull together to find the best way out.'

Heartened that father had not been as harsh as I expected, I turned again to *The Times*. Feeling my reputation completely unsullied, I resolved not to remain a powerless bystander, indifferent to Zerah's infidelities.

Zerah's daily copy of *The Times* arrived alongside various other newspapers, some foreign. Often the following day I read those news items that interested me.

And there, the very day I made up my mind to discover more about Zerah's secret life, I found near the bottom of column two, just the advertisements I required. Ironically, they were situated between items relating to the Paris Exhibition, as well as one for the sale of locomotives, which read:

LOCOMOTIVE ENGINES, immediate delivery. Apply to G. England and Co. New-cross-road, London.

The advertisement of particular interest to me read as follows:

PRIVATE ENQUIRY OFFICE, 2 Southampton-buildings, Holborn – Mr. BENTLEY, late sheriff's officer, having had 20 years' experience, undertakes ENQUIRIES of all kinds, requiring secrecy and despatch. All matters connected with the Divorce and other Law Courts attended to. Rents collected.

Another, directly above it, read:

POLLAKY'S PRIVATE ENQUIRY OFFICE Confidential enquiries in England and on the Continent instituted with secrecy and despatch by Mr. Pollaky, 13 Paddington-green, London, W.

I had a choice and selected Mr. Bentley, if for no other reason than his name sounded friendly, and obviously more English than Mr. Pollaky. Should I need enquiries made on the Continent, then Mr. Pollaky might be more appropriate.

I had become more confident, brave even. At last I had a focus for my attention; a new quest offered new determination.

Rather than write to Mr. Bentley, I decided a personal visit might be more effective. It was 13th November 1867 and that morning, in London's winter air, there hung a brown fog, the product of the universal use of coal fires in houses and offices. The air was thick and I covered my nose and mouth. It was my mistake to venture out but, having made up my mind I was determined not to withdraw.

Unfamiliar with omnibuses, and to give myself more confidence, I hailed a cab in Gloucester-road. I gave the driver my destination. During the lengthy journey I witnessed some of the vices and wretchedness of life, as well as many other sights including London's courts and alleys squalid with poverty and overcrowding. Eventually we arrived whereupon I paid the driver and surveyed the scene.

Southampton-buildings in Chancery-lane looked imposing as it emerged from the foggy gloom, the domain of law stationers, barristers, solicitors, shorthand writers and patent agents. Mounted on the wall outside, brass plates signified the building's various occupants. Mr. Bentley's Private Enquiry Office was on the top floor. When I had climbed all the stairs, I felt exhausted. A wooden chair had been conveniently placed outside a door marked 'Private Enquiry Office'. I sat for a few minutes to collect my breath.

By then I knew I was pregnant; Dr. Graham had earlier confirmed my worst fears. Each day, I would imagine the baby inside me; its presence reawakening past miseries. I had become conscious too of the spots on my skin. Would Mr. Bentley notice them? If so, would he understand their significance? I feared he would.

I knocked at the door, my hand shaking; this was the first time I had undertaken anything so clandestine. I was not sure what might transpire.

'Come,' said a gruff voice.

I opened the door to find a dingy, brown office with one grimy window. Brown wallpaper and brown furniture predominated. The man, seated behind a large desk, wore a brown suit. It was as if he was seated waiting for something to happen. Brown wooden cabinets lined the wall behind him. The top of the desk was empty but for two trays, one marked 'In' and the other 'Out'. Both were empty. The office had a smell of stale, smoky air. The man stood up.

I had entered a world far different from anything I had ever encountered. I felt out of place, like a fish out of water. I was nervous and insecure in a room with a complete unknown.

'Shut the door, please. Come and sit down, young woman,' he said. There was but one chair, identical to that outside.

I closed the door and sat to face him. I had no idea what a private enquiry agent should look like; I half expected a tall, thin man of nondescript appearance; a shadowy figure who could merge into the background.

Instead, the man took on a rather rotund stature; a somewhat sorry figure with sagging shoulders. A cigarette lay in an ashtray on the desk, the smoke from it curling to the ceiling. Behind him, standing on shelves, I noticed several bottles of spirits. It was clear the man enjoyed either his food or a drink or two – or even both. Nicotine stained fingers on his right hand.

'How can I help?' he asked, extinguishing the cigarette. 'My name is Bentley.'

'Well, Sir,' I started hesitatingly, 'I am in need of help. I require enquiries made concerning my adulterous suspicions of my husband. Do you undertake such work?'

'Would you like a cup of tea?' asked Mr. Bentley in a softer, kindlier voice. 'I just happen to have a freshly made pot brewing. I suspect we could both do with one.'

'Yes, please,' I replied, gratefully.

I adjusted my coat somewhat. He stood up and went to another room. I heard the clink of crockery and, in a few minutes, he returned with two cups of tea, milk and sugar, all on a tray.

Mr. Bentley had every appearance of a friendly if somewhat shabbily-dressed, middle-aged man. I knew nothing of him, yet I was about to reveal private family details. Could I trust him? It seemed as though he read my mind.

'Young lady, if we are to make progress, you and I must trust one another,' he said in a sympathetic voice. 'Tell me about yourself. As the notice on the door says, I act as a private enquiry agent, and I endeavour to uncover information as unobtrusively as possible. Please help yourself to milk and sugar.'

I took a cup and poured in some milk and a spoonful of sugar. I did not usually take sugar in tea but I considered it might help.

'But first, you mentioned adultery. I should say that evidence of adultery collected by private detectives is cited in about one-third of divorce cases in Britain, so we can be regarded as making an important contribution,' he added somewhat pompously. 'I have been in this business a long time and I can assure you I am completely trustworthy.'

'I must have your assurance, Sir, that what I reveal remains within these walls,' I insisted with more confidence than I had mustered for a while.

'You have my word. I know from experience that what happens between a man and his wife is both mysterious and private,' he replied. 'Now tell me what troubles you.'

I began by giving him my name, where I lived, my husband's name and the nature of his business.

At that point Mr. Bentley stiffened.

'So, your Mr. Colburn is a journalist?' he interjected.

'Indeed so, Sir,' I replied. 'Does that make a difference?'

'No. But it means we will need to be particularly vigilant – and diligent. Members of the Press have a habit of causing trouble when they choose. They can be cunning as foxes. I never trust them myself. Please continue, Mrs. Colburn.'

As I confided details, Mr. Bentley began to make notes. He used a scratchy quill pen recovered from a drawer in his desk, and several sheets of paper retrieved from another drawer. He repeatedly dipped the pen into an inkwell set into the desk.

I explained my need of a divorce from my husband, adding that my father had said that any man seeking a divorce could simply claim adultery, whereas women had to prove adultery and cruelty.

Mr. Bentley interrupted: 'Quite so, quite so, Mrs. Colburn. I am well aware of that. Your father is correct. But first, we must prove adultery. Cruelty is a quite separate issue.'

He added 'I should perhaps point out that while divorce is no longer the exclusive province of the wealthy, it can involve considerable expense. It effectively excludes those who are poor. However, if you were to be very poor then you could sue without payment of fees *in forma pauperis*, but you would have to prove your lack of means. I assume, Mrs. Colburn, that you do have the means to meet costs?'

I replied that I had a little by way of private income; whether this would be sufficient remained to be seen. However, I told him that my parents had pledged their support to meet some of my expenses. This was extremely kind of them bearing in mind the trouble I caused. I found it embarrassing to discuss financial matters – something of which I was unfamiliar.

'Perhaps you should continue, Mrs. Colburn,' said Mr. Bentley. 'By the way, will you be able to prove cruelty?'

I told him of the journal I had maintained for several years and in which I noted occasions when Zerah ill-treated me, even brutally.

'Good. Because your solicitor, if and when you instruct one, will require this as evidence,' said Mr. Bentley. 'Please continue.'

There was a long silence.

'Come, come, Mrs. Colburn. Please continue.'

I felt myself blush. I averted my eyes, looking down at the cup and saucer in my hand. The cup rattled slightly, breaking the silence.

'My husband has infected me with syphilis,' I whispered.

There was a short silence. I looked at the floor.

'I have no wish to be insensitive, Mrs. Colburn, but are you certain?'

'I am. My doctor has instructed me.'

I sipped the tea. What kind was it?

I moved on quickly. I told Mr. Bentley there were good

reasons to believe that my husband might be meeting a woman in London with whom he was having extra-marital intercourse.

'Does that have any connection with your present predicament?' Mr. Bentley asked.

'I think most likely not,' I replied, explaining that my husband had worked also in Paris, where I suspected he had met at least one woman.

I told Mr. Bentley I did not expect his enquiries to take him to Paris.

'Just as well; that could be expensive. Do you have proof of your husband meeting a woman here in London, Mrs. Colburn? And who is this woman? This meeting with a woman, if it is taking place at all, of course, could be one of all innocence. There has to be more evidence than just 'a meeting'.'

'That is what brought me here, Mr. Bentley,' I replied boldly.

'But Mrs. Colburn, you must have some idea, some indication of these misdeeds, if there are any,' he countered. If I may suggest, Mrs. Colburn, desire and deceit invariably sneak hand in hand. And deceit breeds suspicion, but we need proof of infidelity, if any.'

Mr. Bentley's remarks suggested he doubted my suspicions. As a man, would he favour my husband's side already? I had no wish to reveal William Maw as my source.

'A wife has good indications when something is amiss,' I said lamely. 'You could also call it intuition.'

Of course, that was not so in my case. But by then, I began to lose confidence of Mr. Bentley's willingness to give assistance. My flimsy evidence was based on hearsay.

'Hmm', said Mr. Bentley. 'A solicitor would require much more substance than that to go on.'

'My husband despises me, but for what reason I know not. I have not taken a lover, neither am I slovenly, yet he has rejected me. I was hoping you could follow him and find where he goes, who he meets and what he does; even compile a description of what is happening outside his home life.'

'That could prove expensive, Mrs. Colburn. For that I would need to shadow him day and night for several weeks. Being a journalist, he could prove elusive. We must not forget the devious nature of the Press, and other members of the street of ink, as Fleet-street is sometimes known. Perhaps you might know some of his evening movements, so that perhaps we can eliminate those first.'

'I am no longer permitted in his study without his presence; that is where he records his engagements,' I told him. 'But I do know that he regularly attends meetings at the Institution of Mechanical Engineers and the Institution of Civil Engineers. He also spends evenings at the Society of Arts.'

'And where does he work? Perhaps I could have his address?' asked Mr. Bentley. 'And his appearance? Please give me a description.'

I gave the address of *Engineering* – No. 37 Bedford-street – and described Zerah as tall, erect and with a heavy beard.

'Would it assist if I accompanied you?' I asked. 'I could single him out.'

'Most certainly not, Mrs. Colburn if I may say so. I think you might be a hindrance. Mr. Colburn would recognise you, which would never do. He could become angry. When anger and bitter resentment against you are woven together there is danger for all concerned.'

'Does Mr. Colburn belong to a club?' enquired Mr. Bentley. 'That might be a useful starting point. Can you recall any particular nights of the week when your husband does not return home? Can you give me dates of meetings he is likely to attend at the two Institutions you mentioned? If my geography of London serves me well, I think the Institutions are close together in Great George-street, near the Houses of Parliament and Westminster Bridge.'

I told him that I would make enquiries and send details.

'Please keep records of anything you send, but also keep them secure from prying eyes,' said Mr. Bentley. 'Is your diary safe?'

'It is safe. It has a lock, and I keep it in a secure place, together with my journal,' I told him. 'I keep the key on a string round my neck.'

'Is that wise, Mrs. Colburn? Should he see it, your husband might enquire as to its purpose. Perhaps you should find an alternative place, somewhere very private.'

'As soon as I receive times and dates of the meetings I will commence my work. In the meantime, I will conduct a few discrete enquiries and make an examination of No. 37 Bedford-street. On the matter of expenses, Mrs. Colburn, could I ask for an advance of five pounds? And I would suggest I do not write to you, but that you visit me in one month's time. Shall we say 11th December at 11a.m.? I will endeavour to have something for you.'

'I should warn you, Mrs. Colburn, that this investigation could take some time. Courts require evidence of repeated sexual activity – and cruelty – to have any chance of success in divorce action.'

'I have already been warned of that,' I told him. 'But I do ask you to be meticulous while making your best endeavour to minimise expense. Can I pay you next time we meet?'

Mr. Bentley nodded, adding: 'You can rely on me, Mrs. Colburn. I can provide excellent references and, hopefully, if my work proves satisfactory you will be prepared to give me a reference.'

Without further ado, I had set in motion the wheels that would lead towards a successful divorce. I felt much better, though deep down I was extremely worried, even frightened, lest Zerah should discover what I was doing. Had I bitten off more than I could chew?

Clearly, with Mr. Bentley I had begun a journey to establish the truth. After my meeting, I posted him as many details as I could gather.

Time dragged but eventually Wednesday, 11th December 1867 arrived, just one month after my visit to Mr. Bentley's office. I took the cab as before, but unlike my previous journey I noticed other sights and sounds of London, such as the carts, horses and even pigs that formed part of the scene, as well as men on horseback. We drove past gritty churchyards and I saw crowded streets, noisy and dirty with rubbish heaps, old bones and tiles. Piles of dust lay at the side of the road. Smoke filled the air and filth lay on the ground. In contrast to the naïve watercress girls, tramps and vagrants lurked at street corners while in alleyways I glimpsed the pinched faces of undernourished children. Somewhere in these alleyways someone would be dying. Each journey I made to see Mr. Bentley proved an education in itself.

Again, I climbed the stairs to the top floor of Southampton-buildings and knocked on the door.

'Come,' said the voice I recognised as that of Mr. Bentley. I opened the door.

'Mrs. Colburn, come and be seated,' he said. 'I have something interesting for you.'

I sat down and waited expectantly. There was no offer of a cup of tea this time; he entered directly into business. Mr. Bentley bent down, took some papers from the bottom right-hand drawer of his desk and placed them facing him.

'Well, Mrs. Colburn, it seems you were correct,' he said, shuffling the papers until he found the one appropriate for his message. 'The actions of your husband do merit more than mere suspicion. I followed your instructions and focused my attention on No. 37 Bedford-street. Mr. Colburn is a gentleman of distinctive appearance; he is quite easy to observe at distance, even in streets thronged with activity.'

'He has been seen entering and leaving the building at various dates and times; mostly these have been in the morning and towards evening. However, some intrigue does surround his whereabouts at certain times of the day. On one occasion he did not turn up at the office, and I took the opportunity to make a few enquiries myself, posing as a deliveryman seeking to leave a private parcel.'

'As I waited in the lobby, quite by chance I heard two employees in quiet discussion. I managed to overhear them. It was one of those lucky coincidences. I do not have many.'

'It seems that your Mr. Colburn is the gossip of the building. He has established a close relationship with a Miss Lucy Taylor and there is evidence of misbehaviour. Now I understand there are several businesses at No. 37 Bedford-street, as a result of which there is a resident housekeeper and his wife; he is also the general handyman to the building.'

'I took the trouble to make his acquaintance. I do not at this stage need to trouble you with his name. I told him that any information he provided would be appreciated and well rewarded. I have already passed him a few coins with the promise of more to come should the information prove correct.'

'Now, it seems that your husband has an assignation for Miss Taylor,' revealed Mr. Bentley. 'My informant added that Mr. Colburn appeared quite smitten with Miss Taylor – and she with him. She, blonde and cherubically pretty, was taken aback when he appeared before her in the kitchen, tall, elegant and statuesque.'

'Whatever her charms, he yielded to the temptations of the flesh to the extent that sexual interaction would appear to have taken place in Mr. Colburn's office. I am told it has occurred on several occasions, late in the evening, long after everyone else's departure,' he added.

'According to my informant, who was making his rounds, gaslights in Mr. Colburn's office, burned late into the night,' explained Mr. Bentley. 'My informant moved quietly to the door of the office, not wishing to disturb Mr. Colburn who he believed to be working late. He saw exactly what was taking place and departed as quickly and as silently as he could. I do not need to enter into precise details, but you can imagine as to what I am alluding. Suffice to say, the two were in a state of undress; sexual proclivities and marital indiscretions did occur. That tells you something about this man, Mrs. Colburn. Mr. Colburn appears to be a most unsatisfactory husband, if I may be permitted to suggest. He would seem to enjoy the company of other women.'

Although I had had my suspicions, I could hardly believe my ears. Was this Lucy Taylor the same Lucy Taylor of whose name I had heard? Surely not? The prospect of Zerah suffused with desire for another woman I found overwhelming. I sat wide-eyed as one piece of information after another tumbled from Mr. Bentley's lips. Why would Zerah need to look elsewhere for a woman companion when he had me at home?

'Has he been seeing anyone else?' I asked.

'Now be careful, Mrs. Colburn. All we have is hearsay. This is someone else's word, but it supports your suspicions. We need to establish time and place. We must tread with care. It would seem there is definitely a liaison between these two people. There may be other instances. My informant is unsure when this relationship began. He said it could have been in the first week of November, or even much earlier. My informant went even further; he suggested Mr. Colburn might possess a contiguousness to yet more promiscuity.'

I was horrified; stunned into silence. Some words I did not understand, but I knew enough. I sat staring ahead into space. My father's suspicions were correct. And so too were those of William Maw.

'Who is Lucy Taylor?' I asked. 'And what does she look like?'

'Well, Lucy Taylor works in the kitchens, helping prepare food for some who work in the offices of *Engineering*, your husband's newspaper. The employees seem to want for nothing by the way of food; there is plenty to eat. At this point, I do not know precisely what else she does, but I gather she assists cook with her duties. I have seen her only once as she entered the building. She is tall and slim, with blond hair. As to whether she is a bonny young woman – I would imagine she is about 25 years of age – I am not in a position to judge. Beauty is in the eye of the beholder, as they say.'

'Now I gather that because of the presence of Miss Taylor, a sexual opportunity of some kind beckoned Mr. Colburn. So this relationship could be in its early stages, or it might be well established. We may have to observe carefully events as they unfold,' said Mr. Bentley. 'I am at your service to pursue matters, if you so wish, Mrs. Colburn.'

'Certainly,' I muttered, my head not fully engaged on matters in hand. As I had no yearning to be a lamb sacrificed on the altar of Zerah's waywardness, I had no alternative but to continue.

What an untrustworthy rogue! Men could not be trusted to be loyal and true. How could he behave in that lecherous and opportunistic manner? I felt raw and ravaged. Why did he treat me in that way? I began to feel faint. I gripped the seat of the chair.

'I will try to establish where Miss Taylor lives and make further enquiries,' said Mr. Bentley. 'Now, Mrs. Colburn, I would implore you not to disturb the *status quo* by embarking on any untoward actions. However angry you may feel, I implore you to restrain yourself, and remain long-suffering and outwardly loyal. Tell no one. I will maintain the utmost discretion. I shall record events as they develop. Should Mr. Colburn become aware of what is taking place, it might anger him and hinder our enquiries. Do you understand the implications?'

I nodded.

'Incidentally, Mrs. Colburn, we have also seen your husband entering and leaving Coutts & Company, a well-known bank nearby in the Strand. He may have an account there.'

'Are you alright, Mrs. Colburn? You look pale.'

I nodded again.

'Now, please remain seated as long as you like and compose yourself. I can prepare a cup of tea or, if you so wish, I do have something a little stronger, like whisky or brandy.'

'Thank you, but no,' I replied. 'You are kind. I will however remain outside for a while before retracing my steps.'

'I know this is hard for you Mrs. Colburn. I have seen this

275

happen time and time again. You are not the first woman to be let down by her husband – nor will you be the last. However, I ask you to remain resolute. If I may, I would suggest that you return here in about four or five weeks, by which time I am sure we will have gathered more information.'

'As you might know, it would appear your Mr. Colburn consumes large quantities of alcohol in taverns during the day, joining those who likewise imbibe and take one more step to a dark and dangerous place,' commented Mr. Bentley, somewhat disapprovingly. 'Some might regard him as part of the Bohemia of the Press. However, there are those who argue that any self-respecting writer is certain, even allowed to be a wastrel in his private hours, but it is not to for me to judge, merely to observe.'

I remained seated for a few minutes. How was I to face Zerah? How would it be possible for us to continue our usual existence? Without doubt, life would never be normal again. Not that it had been completely 'normal' for years. Zerah had overstepped the boundary.

I thanked Mr. Bentley and presented him with a £5 note.

'Thank you, Mrs. Colburn,' said Mr. Bentley.

I took my leave. Once outside his door, I sat on the chair and composed myself. Then I grabbed the handrail of the spiral staircase leading down to the front door, gingerly placing one foot in front of the other. Outside in the pale December sunlight, people hurried about their business. I made my way to the cab rank and prepared for the journey to Gloucester-road.

Once inside the house, and having removed outer clothing, I withdrew to the parlour and sank into a chair, deep in thought. I remember thinking that some people were fortunate if they had found someone they loved affectionately, so affectionately they held hands, kissed and embraced as often as they met. How often was it that this someone also stayed true and honest? How often did it happen the other way?

Had it not been for Mr. Bentley's intervention I would not have known of Zerah's devious activities in London. Although I lived with him, I clearly did not know him at all. I imagined that all families had secrets, but Zerah held his darkest, most intimate secrets from me; his sordid actions infected me with that dreadful disease.

I prepared for Zerah's return. My tranquility surprised me. I was now in possession of ammunition. I smiled to myself and thought of Mr. Holley and his book on armour. What would he think if he knew? No doubt I would obtain further details of Zerah's antics. I was in a strong position; Mr. Bentley's information offered me new-found confidence, although I was uncertain how long such confidence would last.

However, behind my veneer of coolness and composure I had mixed feelings of low self-esteem and anger. I would be unable to express my anger for fear of reprisals. I was angry that through Zerah's duplicity, lechery and thoughtlessness he had infected me, an innocent party. I experienced a deep sense of betrayal and the shock of it went like a hammer blow to my stomach. Zerah was as cunning as a fox – and wantonly wayward. I had an image of Zerah and this other woman. Was she attractive or ugly? What did she wear? Did he ill-treat her?

There had been times when I wanted to hold Zerah's hand, but he would have none of it. I yearned to feel close to someone, but always everything had to be on his terms.

By then my emotional attachment to him had ebbed away. If I wanted to divorce him, I needed grounds to support this. I experienced no urge at the time to punish Zerah or vent my vengeance; I wanted only to find a means of escape from him.

Repeatedly, I returned to the same question: was she exciting? If she was exciting, what did Zerah constitute as excitement? Was the excitement born out of the fact that their relationship was illicit?

Did she have experience of other men? Or was Zerah her first experience? Zerah was, at the time of our marriage, the only man I had ever known. In that sense, I was the inexperienced person. Perhaps this woman had been a virgin too; maybe not.

Was I to blame for his behaviour? Was I not always available? He was intimate with me more or less on demand. I admit to pretending an interest in his work, but mostly it was to promote conversation. Zerah had no outside interests apart from work, unlike other men of whom I have heard and read. Work was Zerah's all-consuming interest. How selfish can men be when work is their only interest?

When Zerah returned, I decided to say nothing, in spite of my earlier feelings of confidence. I trusted my instinct. I preferred to heed Mr. Bentley and wait for the appropriate moment.

Some two weeks after I had seen Mr. Bentley, Zerah returned late in the evening. As he came towards me, I detected a very strong smell of perfume. My suspicions began to deepen.

'That perfume smells unusual,' I remarked. 'Did you meet someone special today? Are you meeting another woman?'

'And what if I have?' he replied. 'It is none of your business. We enjoyed a Christmas party today at *Engineering*. I invited our most influential advertisers to share our hospitality at a nearby hotel. Some brought their wives; their perfume would not have been cheap.'

I thought that excuse unusual, because I assumed *Engineering* and publishing as entirely a man's world. I thought it unlikely their wives would accompany them. Of course, I did not know.

'I merely enquired,' I countered.

'Well, do not bother,' he replied curtly. Many were the times he cut me down to size and spoke sharply, even harshly or dismissively.

The following day a letter arrived addressed to Mr. & Mrs. Colburn. Tempted to open it, I deferred until Zerah returned that evening from the office. It was not my place to open joint correspondence.

Christmas Day that year fell on a Wednesday and *Engineering* took Christmas Day and Boxing Day as holidays.

'This invitation from the Maws; he and his wife have invited us to luncheon on Boxing Day. I will write and inform him of our acceptance,' announced Zerah.

It had crossed my mind as to whether we should invite William and Emily during the holiday, but the matter was taken out of my hands.

It proved pleasant for me to visit another couple's house. The Maws' residence, Westbourne-villas in Westbourne Park Grove, was modest but homely. Emily was clearly house-proud, fastidious; I detected not a speck of dust in every place I looked. Even the clock on the mantle was under glass to protect it from invading dust or smoke. If Emily ever employed a housekeeper or maid I would vouch that however devoted to her work the woman would not be able to maintain the house's cleanliness to the level of Emily's satisfaction.

Caring for her house clearly made Emily feel better in every way, both mentally and morally. Once, I caught her eye, and minutely shook my head from side to side. I had no wish of her speaking her mind, whatever she thought.

Emily had indulged much effort in preparing the meal. It was delicious. She was an excellent cook. We had choice of white and red wine. Emily and I indulged in minute sips of white wine; the men drank full-bodied red, offering an opportunity to be sociable after putting in so much effort that year.

Emily whispered how she had read that, in society circles, alcohol was viewed by some as a poison that could help fill the void, distracting men from loveless marriages. Her comment made me think: how much did Emily know – or suspect?

The meal culminated with a flaming Christmas pudding, expertly orchestrated by William but Zerah was unamused.

'Christmas is a sham,' he declared, followed by a dreadful silence.

Then, despite this, and when we had completed our meal, William raised a toast: 'God bless us every one'. I thought what good-hearted, Christian people were the Maws.

Also hovering at the back of my mind was the information that Mr. Bentley had imparted. That information gave me a sense of power.

After lunch, and before retiring to the sitting room, Emily and William were anxious to show us their home, the product of a frenzy of house-building. Even so, their attractive, tastefully-appointed home gave every sign of high respectability. At one point, upstairs, while Zerah and Emily examined one bedroom, William gently steered me into the small bedroom, half closing the door.

I wondered what was to happen, especially as William, unusually for him, had had a little too much to drink and thus was a little merry.

Impulsively, his face turned serious; he pulled me close to whisper.

'Mrs. Colburn, I must confide in you. Those rumours about your husband and one of the kitchen staff; they are true. I thought you should know. I thought I must warn you.'

The door swung open and in strode Zerah with Emily.

'I was just showing Mrs. Colburn the view from the window, dear,' said William lamely, looking slightly flustered.

'I am sure Mrs. Colburn knows what Westbourne Park Grove looks like, William,' said Emily laughingly.

'It is a lovely room,' I countered. 'It will make an excellent room for children.'

When we arrived home and were alone, Zerah immediately asked what William and I had discussed in the small bedroom.

'Did you embrace and kiss?' he asked.

'How dare you? No. Not at all,' I replied. 'He pointed out the view from the window, as he said.'

'Do not tell lies, woman,' shouted Zerah, now more than ever dedicated to confrontation. He struck me hard on the face with the back of his hand. Caught off guard, I fell to the ground, whereupon he kicked me brutally on the shins.

'Keep away from Maw! He is a married man. I have had my suspicions about the pair of you. Is there a simmering attraction between you? Have you, my cheating wife, taken advantage of your privileged life here to seek solace in the arms of a lover to counter your loneliness, your anxiety? Personally, I find you a boring wench,' he blurted in my face, striding out of the room.

I retired to my room before Peggy or Rose could see the red blotches on my face. It was not the first time Zerah had hit me so hard. Nor the first time had I suffered his kicks. I was deeply upset. What upset me more were his last words: that he found me a bore. I supposed it to be the alcohol doing the talking but, because of what I had learned and had confirmed by William, I knew that I was on dangerous ground. In future, mindful of his volatility, I would have to keep Zerah at arm's length when he was out of control.

I went to the bathe my face. When I looked in the mirror, I could see my right eye already swelling from the attack. There were the beginnings of a black eye and other evidence of a damaged face. I used my face towel soaked in cold water as a compress. Then I applied it to my ankle. Later, when I went to bed, there was already a large violent purple bruise on my shin. I counted myself fortunate; he could have broken bones.

Early in January, I paid a visit to Mr. Bentley. I wanted to show him evidence of my plight. I had to borrow coins from Peggy for the cab fare. I felt humiliated, but I was desperate. I promised to repay her as soon as I could.

That journey was a further occasion when I refused to travel by omnibus and subject myself to staring passengers.

As I mounted the stairs at Southampton-buildings, I tried to shield my face, to conceal the bruising. Mr. Bentley came to the door. As soon as he saw me, he ushered me inside.

'Mrs. Colburn, I am so sorry. I cannot spare you time at the moment,' he said hurriedly. 'But what has happened?'

I told him briefly my husband had struck and kicked me during Christmas.

'I am very sorry to hear what you have to tell me,' he said. 'Unfortunately, I am very, very busy at the moment with another client. If you can wait a while, I will see you. If not, please can you please come back next Tuesday at 11 o'clock when I will have information?'

To say that I was dismayed understated the obvious. I was crestfallen. More than that, the ecstasy of frustration seethed within me. My heart sank. I had journeyed across London and to no avail. I could ill afford to wait as Mr. Bentley requested; I had no alternative but to return empty-handed. But at least he had a vision of my plight.

For the next few weeks, a subdued atmosphere fell over the house made worse by the winter weather outside. The frosty relationship between Zerah and me continued well into 1868, a year that saw November's general election bring about the resignation of Mr. Disraeli and the return of Mr. Gladstone as Prime Minister.

In March, I journeyed across London to see Mr. Bentley. It proved a long wait; I was impatient to hear his news. I had borrowed money from my father to repay Peggy, and pay Mr. Bentley's retainer and fees, but I consoled myself that this could not continue much longer. Father granted me a further small loan. I relied heavily on him as I could not tolerate an interrogation from Zerah as to how I spent my small allowance.

Mr. Bentley had a surprise.

'Ah, Mrs. Colburn,' he said, offering me a seat. 'If I may say so, you look much improved compared with the last time we met. There have been two developments.'

'Really, what have you found?'

'Well, first of all we now have material evidence that your husband did conduct an adulterous relationship with Miss Lucy Taylor, at least from early October 1867 until recently,' said Mr. Bentley. 'We can with certainty say that this affair lasted until this month.'

'You say first of all,' I replied. 'What else have you uncovered?'

'Well. While Mr. Colburn conducted his adulterous relationship with Miss Taylor he has also been visiting another lady'.

Mr. Bentley coughed and paused, as if to dramatise his news.

'We are able to name her as Miss Mary Ann Jennery.'

My mouth gaped; I could not conceal my astonishment.

'You may well look amazed, Mrs. Colburn,' said Mr. Bentley.

'You must have used all your skills,' I said. 'How did you discover this? And can you be certain of your facts?'

'Well, shall we say at this juncture, Mrs. Colburn, that we have ways and means,' he said, glossing over details but looking at his notebook.

'However, we know little at this point about Miss Jennery; suffice to say that Huntley-street, close to Tottenhamcourt-road is where Miss Jennery appears to, shall we say, 'operate'. Various tradesmen occupy the street. There is, for example, a pianoforte van proprietor at No. 1, a tailor at No. 4 and a builder at No. 7. A pianoforte action maker resides at No. 12, a builder at No. 16 and a cabinetmaker at No. 22. Mrs. Harriet Laxen, who describes herself as a ships' chandler's merchant lives at No. 23, and then there is Thomas D. Bretnall & Co. at No. 24. The latter company makes tracing paper. I have every reason to understand from my sources that Mrs. Laxen is who she says she is, however, the comings and goings at No. 11 suggest that it is a boarding house of sorts.'

'Now your Mr. Colburn has been seen entering and leaving No. 11 at various times of the day and night,' went on Mr. Bentley. 'He began, shall we say, attending No. 11 Huntley-street in February of this year and we are now in March and the activity shows no sign of abating.'

'Just in case you think Mr. Colburn might be conducting serious publishing or engineering business at No. 11, I can assure you that a number of 'conveniences' operate from the house and none has the least interest in either publishing or engineering. They are, in common parlance, 'ladies of the night' or 'conveniences': prostitutes, in other words. I can tell you these women operate from nunneries or brothels, often having male protectors who provide comfortable rooms. Some call these men bawds or what we, in the trade, call pimps. They also hire out fine clothes. Some are high-class bordellos. We have reason to be certain these particular women are controlled by a pimp.'

'Some men see these women 'dashers' – a dasher is someone who cuts a dash, a fast young woman, a flashy prostitute,' explained Mr. Bentley.

Then, as an afterthought, he said 'There are also demi-reps – married women who are in need of fun or money, or both.'

'Perhaps I need hardly inform you that these 'ladies' provide sexual services for their clients. Sexual interactions, shall we call them? Men pay the women who in turn pretend to enjoy themselves. With your husband, no doubt they were willing victims of his manly exterior.'

Did I detect a slight sneer at this point? Was he in favour of such women – or against them?

'I am not familiar with such practices, Mr. Bentley,' I replied primly, quickly blushing. For the first time Zerah's actions made me feel deeply soiled.

'Of course not, Mrs. Colburn, no one suggests you are; but men who engage in this practice do so for various reasons, not the least of which is the obvious one, but there are those who enjoy the element of danger; to be caught red-handed in the act, so to speak. Your husband is a man of dark energy. These women openly ply their trade – it would not difficult for him to find them.'

'Of course, they are useful to private enquiry agents like myself; in exchange for a coin or two, they can provide valuable information, so we tend to treat them with kid gloves,' he added.

'The Strand, Haymarket and nearby streets are often crowded with women from East End homes; they join girls housed in brothels there or nearby. They are there for one purpose only. Indeed, Haymarket at night is one of the sights of London. Then, again there are the *grandes horizontales* of the West End, the conveniences of the rich.'

There was that word again. *Horizontales.*

'All of this no doubt is a great shock for you,' he went on. 'I may have said this before, but I will say it again: if it is any consolation, you are not the first and you will not be the last.'

'Meanwhile, we shall continue our surveillance,' he said. 'But I must stress that to be successful we must let matters continue until Mr. Colburn has enough rope to hang.'

I was dumbfounded. I stared at Mr. Bentley. His revelations numbed me into disbelief. Not content with a liaison with one woman at the offices of *Engineering*, it was clear that at the same time my husband was conducting illicit activities with a second woman, a prostitute, no less. He was truly devious, a cheat. Why pay for such soulless encounters?

I walked slowly down the staircase at No. 2 Southampton-buildings. Outside, I adjourned to the nearby Bedford Hotel in Southampton-court where they served coffee. I ordered a cup and sat at a table, my mind in a whirl. Several men stared.

Seated there, it dawned on me that Zerah had redrawn the boundaries of our relationship. The undercurrent of uncertainty and mistrust now dominated everything between us.

When he departed from the house every morning, he donned a mask to conduct his daily life – he became a new person. Just when I thought he was working, he could be with other women, engaged in a secret 'second' life beyond my knowledge; a life that was as pleasant for him as it was destructive to me. From now on, when he was absent I would not only wonder where he was, but with whom he was conducting business. No wonder he called himself 'the conductor'.

I was as far as ever from engineering my escape. I allowed myself a brief smile at that small joke; but my life was anything but funny. Added to which, had Mr. Bentley been completely forthcoming? Had he told me everything he knew? Or did he spare some lurid details?

Without doubt, Zerah's life was spiralling away from mine and had been doing so ever since the Paris Exhibition. That exhibition had opened his eyes to a new way of life – a life that had rebounded in my face. The ruination of both our lives began with that event. Or had it started earlier?

In his ever-relentless search for excitement, had Zerah found his perfect alternative to marriage? If so, he could have his cake and eat it.

Zerah deflowered me in New York. That was the moment when, timidly and innocently, I peeped at a vision of a future together; one of united admiration. Then, our relationship quickly became difficult – thanks to Zerah's temper – and even then, I tried to remain loyal. How could my love prevail in the face of such a fowl temper and now his waywardness?

He had changed the rules and plainly enjoyed life without me, philandering as he was with a prostitute. Would more to follow?

The coffee arrived but proved too hot to consume. I waited for it to cool.

People would judge me. They would see me at fault. I was not ready at that moment to answer anyone's questions – except perhaps those of my mother – about the demise of our relationship. I was certain I carried no blame.

I had no knowledge of the lives of prostitutes. Why would I? I led a life shielded from such unsavoury activities. If I had imagined them at all, it was as sad burlesques of women, presenting themselves as objects of lust instead of as partners in honourable relationships. They were a source of base gratification, seeking to arouse desire in return for money. I despised them. They made me angry for it was through contact with them that he infected me with their syphilis.

By their very nature, prostitutes solicited and tempted men from the straight and narrow. Thousands of contaminated men yielded to their temptations. Zerah was no different from the commoner; he had no wish to please them, instead to energetically possess them completely for a short time.

It was in Paris that he went seeking lewd women who had taken his eye and who debased Zerah's mind and hardened his heart, each act of gratification stimulating fresh lust and indulgence. Zerah had become obsessed with these women; they were after all, nothing more than women of the street. Were they in any way attracted to him?

I must have sat there for half an hour, gradually sipping my coffee. One question went round and round in my head: Could I ever trust a man again? I did not finish the coffee. Then, much as I hated it, I took an omnibus that delivered me almost to my parents' house in Brewer-street where I spilled out everything to mother.

I told her how, on Boxing Day, Zerah struck my head and kicked me. I did not tell her that he spat in my face or how badly he had bruised me and reduced me to tears.

Up to that time, I had tried to remain loyal to Zerah: even when he shouted. Should I question in future where he was going? He was, after all said and done, my husband; we were married and betrothed to one another. Mother warned that illicit sexual malpractice threatened family and home; it was best I held my tongue for the time being.

'That is how syphilis spreads, by malpractice,' she said.

She made a pot of tea and we both shed tears. I felt much better.

'Father will support you for as long as necessary. I will see to that,' she said, comfortingly but firmly and defiantly.

With mother's moral support reassured, I made my way back to No. 7 Gloucester-road. I now had complete loathing for Zerah. I despised him. Some women would seek revenge; for revenge, some say, is very good eaten cold. I was not that way inclined. My instinct had been first to blame myself. My Christian upbringing had taught me that I should turn the other cheek.

While I could be in some way at fault, I also experienced some guilt. Was I not tall enough? Was I ugly? Not forceful enough? Was I not amusing? Had I not yielded enough? Was I not intelligent enough? Had it been a loveless marriage from the beginning?

If I consoled myself at all, it was that the first Mrs. Colburn and her daughter retraced their steps to America for some reason. What could that reason have been? Why did she leave her husband? Was she deeply unhappy? Did she regard him a tyrant? Was he evil to both? Did he beat them? Did Zerah instruct them to leave? I doubted it; Mrs. Colburn was strong-willed and assertive.

Zerah told me his wife was unhappy in England, but was there another reason to leave? That decision to return to America cost Mrs. Colburn and her daughter their lives. They escaped from Zerah, yet paid the price with death.

Zerah's actions frightened me. I had begun to arm myself with powerful and destructive ammunition. If he became aware of how much I knew of his private life, he would surely kill me. He had at least one gun, and more likely two. Perhaps he would think nothing of shooting me and disposing of my body in Regent's Canal only a short distance away.

I began to conjure up all manner of terrible events that could befall me. Might he push me 'accidentally' under a horse and dray? He might suggest we travel on the new 'underground', and then jostle me onto the rails ahead of an oncoming locomotive. Might he administer poison without anyone knowing, or strangle me as I slept? Father had warned that poison was not unknown as the favoured method of dispatch by husbands anxious to be rid of their wives.

Might he arrange with an unscrupulous doctor to have me, his 'inconvenient' relative, confined as a lunatic to an asylum – or even engage a stranger, accompanied by a policeman to have me bundled into a waiting carriage, with a shawl wrapped around my head to stifle my screams, never to be heard or seen again? By that point, I had developed an extreme sense of paranoia.

My life was one of continual fear. I was fearful most of what Zerah might do if I voiced publicly any personal matter; I was also fearful of an unprovoked attack. Mother urged me to live at home, but I refused. I had to remain at No. 7 Gloucester-road.

Something else concerned me, quite apart from my own well-being. Had Zerah infected his latest women with syphilis? Or were they already infected? I knew he had not visited the doctor. It was grossly unfair of Zerah to be in such a state of disease and yet have regular intimate contact with other women. Did I have a moral obligation to warn them?

Perhaps such women were undeterred. Surely, they would be concerned to be carriers of damaging diseases. Perhaps it was all part of earning a living; a living that was no living.

Whenever possible, I avoided Zerah. Fewer and fewer were the reasons for us to have much to do with one another. Clearly, I had no wish to have Zerah close when he could find gratification elsewhere.

Increasingly I would eat food on my own in the evening. I found taking tea alone could carry me through until morning. I was aware that I had put on weight since Christmas. Clothes that I had worn previously no longer fitted. The shadow of impending birth loomed ever darker. Whenever I went to church, sitting inconspicuously at the back, I would pray for a safe deliverance but, most of all, a stillborn.

In February, God miraculously answered my prayers. I gave birth to another stillborn. Dr. Graham attended, with Nurse Gilbert giving assistance and, as before, he administered chloroform. I experienced immense relief yet at the same time I was full of grief for the infant. I had been spared pain during the ordeal, but not so baby. Following the delivery, I could do nothing to prevent another uncontrollable outburst of tears.

Nor could I prevent myself feeling deeply morose, helped no doubt by my desire again to dress in black. Three times had I given birth to sickly babies who died; I had blood on my hands. These tiny infants, who would have grown up as Colburns, had paid the price of Zerah's intolerable behaviour. God had given me a sign that we were unsuitable parents. Now, it was up to me to start afresh.

Zerah appeared completely unconcerned by events, or the

plight of the infant. From his viewpoint, No. 13 Gloucester-road could not be viewed as a 'house of mourning' as it would draw attention to his household.

However, I was mortified; my grief and guilt were unbearable. Thankfully, as before, Dr. Graham arranged the infant's burial. I could not bring myself to be involved, while Zerah remained indifferent as ever on the subject. Had the child lived, he might have acted quite differently.

As for Peggy, she again brought me a small posy of flowers, and curtseyed briefly as a token, before placing them in my hand. She had not curtseyed before.

I visited my parents and immediately burst into tears. Father did not understand at first, but mother knew; she had suffered her own stillbirth.

The issue of infant mortality is much written about in Dickens's works. Dickens used fiction to chronicle the sad fact that many children did not live to become adults, yet in my own family all but one had survived. However, in *Dombey and Son*, Paul demonstrates all too plainly that wealth does not guarantee longevity.

As for myself, I took the measure to dispose of all the clothing I had set aside for baby and myself. I could not bear to know they were close by, acting as a constant reminder of all that which had happened. I also took the precaution to spend some time in bed during the day, as I had on previous occasions, following Dr. Graham's strict instructions that I should take of myself, first and foremost.

As spring turned to summer, I spent more time outside. Regent's Park acted as the closest of London's parks; I could almost step out of No. 7 and walk into the park. It was beautiful and I spent many hours there. I knew almost every tree. One or two trees were so beautiful I put my arms round their reassuring trunks and hugged them tight. I felt better having discharged anxious energy into the tree.

At occasional moments I found myself looking back. I was

horrified by some of the silly measures I had taken to secure my freedom. It was foolish of me to use a cab to travel to secure Mr. Bentley's services. I had no understanding of the time required to make the journey into Holborn, itself a notoriously congested region of London. As Zerah had pointed out in his fit of anger, I could have travelled from London Bridge to Brighton – a journey of some 55 minutes – in the same time it took me to reach Holburn, a distance maybe of some five miles. Not that I had ever been to Brighton.

Omnibuses, carriages and carts that were subject to the vagaries of the horse pulling them, and all manner of people thronged the thoroughfares, added to the general confusion along the journey.

And yet I continued, as you will see, primarily the cab was the most comfortable means of transport, especially if rain was likely; and I had time at my disposal. Also I felt secure. The thought of travelling alone by omnibus horrified me and to take the train was out of the question. I was left with but one alternative to secure my freedom, the proviso being that I had to take more care with my journey times.

This reminded me of Mr. Dickens' *Dombey and Son* in which Mr. Dombey, the head of a large shipping company, finds himself unable to leave his business activities behind when he returns home; his only thoughts being of 'Dombey and Son'. By allowing his work to contaminate his family life, he destroyed the latter, and by extension the former. As an admirer of Mr. Dickens, Zerah would be aware of this.

Chapter Eleven
Drops of poison

B Y JULY 1868, three months had passed since I last visited Mr. Bentley, and it was time to retrace my steps to Holborn. A beautiful day with the weather bright, I almost felt enchanted with the world. However, such joy soon evaporated with my visit to his office.

A brass visitors' bell now lodged on a small table outside the door. When I rang, a young man opened the door. I had not seen him before. I noticed his spotty face. I gave him my name and he led me to an ante-office; there had been changes since my last visit.

'Mr. Bentley will see you in a moment,' he said. 'Please wait.'

In a short while, Mr. Bentley emerged.

'Ah, Mrs. Colburn,' he said. 'Are you able to return in half an hour? I have some very interesting developments to tell you.'

This was completely unexpected, but I had no choice. I walked slowly down the stairs and across to a coffeehouse. The minute hand on the clock behind the counter inched forward slowly as sipped coffee.

When I returned, Mr. Bentley stood waiting outside the door.

'I am so sorry to put you to such trouble, Mrs. Colburn, but I had to arrange additional time to explain matters to you.'

He bid me sit down. He closed the door and shot the bolt.

'I do not wish for us to be disturbed,' he explained, as I looked round in a somewhat agitated manner.

'It is all right, Mrs. Colburn,' he added. 'You are quite safe.'

Zerah once locked me in a room and the outcome then proved nothing short of violent.

'Mrs. Colburn, your husband has kept my colleagues extremely busy; so busy that I may have to request an increase in my retainer,' said Mr. Bentley, but added positively. 'But I think you could say we are closing in on him.'

293

'Oh dear, I have already relied heavily on my father.'

'Well, we will see how we progress,' he said. 'You see, as a result of quite extensive enquiries, we have discovered that Miss Jennery, according to the 1861 Census, was born in 1846. That makes her about 22 years of age. As a servant, she lived at No. 3, Fern Villas, Albion-grove, Stoke Newington. There she worked in the household of a Mr. George Neave. However, since then she has turned to a more lucrative trade, as young women do.'

'Now I must prepare you for a shock, Mrs. Colburn,' went on Mr. Bentley. 'Your husband appears to have an eye for the ladies, particularly the younger ones; indeed I would go so far as to say he has developed an unrelenting passion for the pursuit of women. He has uncovered yet another young woman in addition to Miss Jennery, spreading his net even wider. His latest conquest lives – and works – from No. 265 Vauxhall Bridge-road, in Pimlico.'

'We have observed that particular address for several days and such trysts as I have mentioned were a regular occurrence. I think we can be certain that Mr. Colburn is committing adultery with these two ladies concurrently. That libidinous gentleman who is your husband knows how to pleasure a woman, I'll be bound,' he added with what I once again interpreted as an admiring sneer.

'Who lives at that address in Pimlico?' I asked, ignoring Mr. Bentley's last comment. I could think of nothing else sensible to say.

'The lady is known as Fanny Porter to her clientele. Not a particularly glamorous name, if I may say so, Mrs. Colburn. But that is only a personal observation.'

'What does she look like?'

I wondered if I should pay one of these women a visit to satisfy my curiosity.

'She is tall and slim,' replied Mr. Bentley, 'and quite good looking, by all accounts. It is best not to think about these things, Mrs. Colburn. You can dwell too much on the particular.'

That may be so, but every wife wants to know something of the women who, for whatever reason, have stolen her husband. In this case, they were welcome to him.

'Are you certain that sexual intercourse has taken place?' I asked, already aware of the reply I would be about to hear. Even as the two words left my mouth, I became embarrassed, aware again of my shyness. No self-respecting woman should have to utter such words in everyday conversation.

'Without entering into detail, Mrs. Colburn, you can rest assured that is so. I will not elaborate, but we have enough evidence to stand up in court. Any excuse your husband might offer will sound threadbare when the evidence of his tottering behaviour is presented to the court.'

I could visualise my husband in court, head drooped low, as prosecution revealed lurid detail after lurid detail. Reporters in the gallery would hang on every detail, while the Press would delight in revealing Zerah's philandering, and worse. Did he imagine his status would lend him protection from the Press? Far from it – just the opposite, no doubt. And would I be required in court to bear witness?

'Now, can I turn to other matters? Has your husband been married before, Mrs. Colburn?' asked Mr. Bentley, bluntly.

I was shocked by the question. It seemed a strange one. I told him that he had, and that his wife had fallen victim to a shipping disaster in the North Atlantic during her return to New York. Mrs. Colburn and her daughter both lost their lives through drowning, I explained.

'What date was that, Mrs. Colburn, and what was the name of the vessel?'

I told Mr. Bentley I did not know the precise date, nor did I know the name of the ship.

'If you have the opportunity, please try to retrieve that information for the next occasion we meet. It could prove useful.'

'As to fees, Mrs. Colburn, I am prepared to continue to work for you until the end of the year under our existing terms,' said Mr. Bentley. 'That will give you the opportunity to contemplate whether you wish to continue, and to what extent. In the meantime, we will resume our surveillance.'

I thanked him and expressed my gratitude. I left shortly afterwards deciding to take a cab. I walked to the rank. I wondered what she was like, this woman with whom Zerah had most recently consorted. On impulse, I instructed the driver to take me to No. 265 Vauxhall Bridge-road, Pimlico.

'It is some distance from here, ma'am,' he said.

'Yes. I am aware of that,' I replied.

'Very good, ma'am.'

And with that the cab lurched forward. As the journey unfolded, I grew more than a little concerned as to its extent, but I was determined to see where, according to Mr. Bennett, this woman lived. Did she in reality live there at all? Perhaps it was simply where she 'worked?'

As I reclined in the cab, I realised London's enormity. We passed all manner of large buildings I had not seen before. I wondered how my husband had discovered his new source of pleasure. I felt a sense of relief. Was I now closer to being free of him? Not satisfied with one streetwalker, my husband required the services of two. And at the same time! Could there be more?

After a while, the cab drew to a halt. The driver stepped down and, looking through the window, opened the door.

'Number 265 Vauxhall Bridge-road, ma'am,' he said.

I alighted and looked at the property.

'One minute, please. Wait and I will return,' I told the driver.

The house looked quite nondescript in a quite respectable road. However, I noticed street urchins and beggars in the vicinity; both were to be avoided, as in many parts of London. Next door, at No. 267, a sign outside the door read Robert Webb, Esq. I walked some short distance in the opposite direction past a few houses and found at No. 251, a sign showing: B. V. Hutchinson, Solicitor. Could it be that in such a district as this that Mr. Hutchinson was a pettifogger?

I retraced my steps back to No. 265. The house had a blue door making it appear quite fashionable. And could it be here too, that behind this innocent-looking blue door, much mischief took place, namely that the naked instincts of men were unfurled, like flags atop a mast? Was it here that a woman became a man's plaything, an animated doll, an item to use and fling away? Did he abuse and beat her, or was he kind and loving?

I longed to sweep away my timidity and reach out for the strength and confidence to knock on the door, to speak with whoever appeared on the other side of the blue door. Would she even answer the door? What would I say? How would I introduce myself? Should I announce myself as Mrs. Zerah Colburn? Could I look her in the eye?

I was nothing but a coward. I could not do it. I retraced my steps to the cab and gave the driver directions.

'No. 7 Gloucester-road, driver,' I told him.

'Yes, ma'am, now that *will* take some time. I will take the quickest route but traffic is congested as I am sure you are aware.'

'Do your best,' I said.

It did indeed take a long time and this time my concern deepened considerably. I noticed a passing clock; its hands approached 6.00 p.m. Shortly after, the cab pulled into Gloucester-road. Would I have enough money to pay the driver?

'There you are, ma'am,' said the driver, opening the door.

I opened my purse and found I had just enough fare. I walked to the house and knocked on the door. Peggy greeted me.

'Thank goodness you are home, ma'am,' said Peggy in an agitated voice I had not heard before. 'Master arrived early for a change of clothes before attending a lecture. He is most angry you were not here to greet him. I told him I did not know where you were. Master is in the parlour, ma'am.'

My heart sank. I had grossly underestimated how long it would take to cross London. The streets were busy with all manner of vehicles – broughams, cabriolets, gigs, growlers, hansoms, landaus and phaetons as well as omnibuses, not to mention carts and wagons carrying produce. I immediately regretted my stupidity.

Peggy took my hat and coat, and I went into the parlour.

Zerah bit deep into his quivering lower lip. I knew what was coming. He always bit into his lip when angry.

'Where have you been? No one knew your whereabouts. I was about to seek a constable. You could have made me look foolish.'

He banged the parlour door shut with such force the frame almost shook. He grabbed hold of my arm and pulled me closer. I could smell alcohol on his breath.

'I have been to inspect some clothes,' I replied. 'But the streets were so crowded. We were delayed.'

'You are lying.'

'I am not lying, Sir. I went to High Holborn to look at some shops,' I replied, struggling to free my arm.

'You are lying. Shops in High Holborn are not worth a candle. They are trifling. High Holborn is full of solicitors and lawyers. You cannot fool me. What are you planning?'

'I went in search of small dressmakers, Sir. They are situated along side streets,' I said, trying my best to remain assertive, even though deeply conscious I had told a lie – for which even now I am ashamed.

'Did you buy anything?' asked Zerah.

'No, I did not.'

'There. I knew you were lying.'

And with that he struck me forcefully on side of the face.

'And for good measure, here is another,' as he slapped hard the other side of my face.

'That will teach to go on a wild goose chase. No one will wish to examine your face now, particularly those fancy dressmakers you like so much. Go to your room and remain till breakfast. We will talk again about this, but if you ever repeat that journey worse will follow.'

With that, he left the parlour and slammed the front door, presumably taking his hat, coat and umbrella. Once again, through his brutality he wanted to humiliate and dominate.

Peggy heard the commotion and came running once the front door slammed shut.

'I am sorry if I said anything amiss to the master, ma'am. I did not know what to say,' said Peggy. 'Are you all right?'

'I am going to my room, Peggy. Please bring a cup of tea and smelling salts,' I said, trying not to sob. I wiped a tear away with the corner of my handkerchief. I knew before long my face would carry visible evidence of bruising.

'I will make you a nice sandwich,' said Peggy, obviously concerned.

I had no wish to eat anything, but I had to be brave.

'You must take care of yourself, m'dear,' said Peggy, putting a sheltering arm round me, quite out of keeping with her station. It was the first time she had shown warmth to me since I lost my last baby, yet there had been many times after my last infant death when I had been distraught at my failed attempts to have a family of my own.

Housekeeper and housemaid now knew something was 'going on' between Zerah and me. It was impossible for anyone in the house not to be aware of Zerah's sudden fits of temper.

'Sit yourself down while I get something for your face. It is bleeding by the corner of your eye,' Peggy said comfortingly.

As she left, I became more determined than ever to rid myself of Zerah Colburn who had no understanding of how miserable he had made me feel. If he did, there was no demonstration of it. Now there was nothing between us – no vestige of love or loyalty remained.

For the remainder of 1868 I navigated a narrow tightrope. On the one hand, I did my utmost to avoid making Zerah angry; yet I had to remain resolute until I found an answer.

I told myself to hold on and all would be resolved; that I had to develop a core of iron. This was difficult, however much I tried, as the striking, kicking and beating doled out by my husband continued until the end of the year.

On one occasion, he had gripped my wrist, twisted it behind my back and then rotated my whole body until our lips met. He pushed his tongue into my mouth, all the while bringing me closer and closer, until I could feel every movement of his body. What happened next amounted to rape.

His sexual needs were more than vile. Deep emotions of one kind or another fired the intensity of his performance. Did they stem from the feverishness of his mental and physical illness? In marriage, could it be rape if a husband molested his wife without her consent? He claimed his entitlement to treat me as he wished; I was his wife. He owned me; I had no worth. He showed no respect.

Apart from the sexual indignity, physical beatings and other unwanted attention, I was also the target for reproach and the subject of ridicule. He criticised me for the slightest 'error'. I frequently held my tongue, lest I received verbal chastisement almost as bad as anything physical. He enjoyed beating, dominating and intimidating me. He took any opportunity to belittle me.

The assaults varied in frequency. I recorded them in my private diary, but they had no rhythm. I hid the diary beneath my mattress, but later I placed it in a drawer beneath underclothing. My journal I kept separate.

As time went on, I became increasingly wary, anxious to preserve the secret whereabouts of my diary; even to the point of being obsessive as information contained therein became ever more damning. For security, I varied its position day to day.

He declared once, with a sneer, 'diaries are for people who have not grown up'. Was he aware that I kept one of his misdemeanors? I prayed not.

Meanwhile, the atmosphere between us remained frigid; I tried where possible to keep my distance.

In the Christmas period, I noticed a change in Zerah's general demeanour. He became increasingly moody and irritable. Even so, *Engineering* held its second Christmas party for workers; Zerah congratulated everyone for their effort.

Just before Christmas, however, Emily Maw and I had agreed to meet; I travelled to their house in Westbourne Park Grove where she kindly offered to provide luncheon. I told Zerah my destination. On that occasion I had nothing to conceal.

On meeting, I embraced Emily tenderly. I much enjoyed conversations with her; in the time we had known one another, a bond of friendship developed – albeit not quite on level terms because I still remained the wife of her husband's employer.

Emily availed me of events at *Engineering*. Her husband never failed to inform her daily of his work, where he had been and how well the newspaper progressed under his stewardship. She was eloquent in her praise. It seemed that Zerah spent less time managing affairs at the journal; most day-to-day activities, it seemed, were in the hands of Emily's capable husband.

I spent an unsettled Christmas in the face of uncertainty. However, as for Christmas day itself, my parents invited Zerah and me for luncheon, which my mother cooked. I could sense father's deep discomfort. I hoped he would maintain a dignified silence; he already knew too much.

Were my father to speak out it could result in further punishment for me. There were occasions when both he and Zerah retreated into long silences as each weighed up the other's thoughts. However, the day passed without mishap.

In the New Year, we continued to experience the misdirection of mail following the earlier renumbering of houses in Gloucester-road. One day, a very important item of Zerah's mail was delivered to No. 7 and it took some days before it finally arrived. This infuriated Zerah.

Peggy, like Zerah, grumbled when the numbers were first changed. She saw no good reason for it, as she regaled me on numerous occasions. I told her simply 'Ours is not to ask the reason why, Peggy.'

As time went on, Zerah's mood swings – for that is what they were – became more pronounced, and more frequent. The New Year marked the start of *Engineering*'s third year and thus far, everything had progressed well. With the newspaper now even more successful than its competitor, *The Engineer*, Zerah had no obvious reason to be morose, as week by week readers looked forward to the content with what Zerah called 'undiluted enthusiasm'.

Often, Zerah would poke fun at *The Engineer*'s editorial content. For example, *The Engineer* devoted three whole pages spread across several issues, in March and April that year, to velocipedes, which he claimed would soon be irrelevant and disappear.

However, I had read in *The Times* only a few weeks' previously, that Mr. Rowley Turner, the son of a Coventry textile machinery manufacture, had ridden his velocipede (together with a Mr. John Mayall, a photographer friend of his, and a Mr. Charles Spencer) from Trafalgar-square to Brighton to publicise their machines. They arrived, the article declared, 'all in good condition for dinner and the second part of Kuhe's concert at the Grand Hall. Mr. Turner had purchased his velocipede in Paris in November 1868 and brought it back to London.' I record this only because Zerah was so dismissive of the 'contraption'.

Mr. Turner, it turned out, had persuaded his father's company to make parts to supply to France, later to make and sell velocipedes, sales of which 'took off' as many new makers appeared.

While Zerah continued to dismiss velocipedes, he nevertheless informed me that two years previously, machines had arrived from an American company, Pickering and Davis of New York, while the local gymnasium in Liverpool had changed its name to the Liverpool Velocipede Club as they had become so popular.

Despite such activities, Zerah remained unconvinced, even when that same year *English Mechanics* carried full-page advertisements on the subject. Zerah continued to belittle velocipedes as having 'no engineering content', and dismissed them as irrelevant.

Mention of velocipedes is but a digression, but the subject reinforced my image of Zerah's dogged, almost ruthless determination. Should he dislike something, or somebody, he could become deeply entrenched.

In spite of what I assumed 'his illness', Zerah appeared to write prolifically. Though I had no exact measure of his true contribution to the paper, he spent much time at the house with engaged in writing. I have no doubt that William Maw produced 'copy' in abundance.

Although he never discussed the matter, I sensed Zerah suffered the effects of syphilis. These effects seemed to cause him to sink to even lower depths of depression than previously; it was on those occasions that he was particularly moody and violently unpredictable, and when I felt most vulnerable. For myself, my condition appeared to improve slightly.

Increasingly, Zerah would wander off in the evening air to The Engineer public house, to meet friends, old and new. Zerah and Mr. Jim, the publican, remained good friends. I would hear Zerah return to the house late at night. Sometimes, he lurched in long after normal closing time.

He did much of his writing in the house, sometimes early in the morning or late at night. It was a life dictated by writing. Seemingly, he never wasted a moment. Zerah would declare he was 'born to write', however, when he wrote, even in the morning, he had a glass of wine on the desk beside him. He said it improved the flow of words. It would be more than my life's worth to venture that he should reduce his consumption or to suggest it not good for his health and could lead to poisoning.

'Good wines give sparkle to good writing,' he opined.

However, I found on more than one occasion that he could

turn nasty when he had drunk more than a few glasses of wine. He could be a monster; other times he could be most pleasant.

One day he confessed, 'Maw always double-checks my work. He is so fastidious. He reads all the copy I write to ensure it is without error; which of course it is. His presence is vital, nosy busybody that he is.'

Whatever happened inside Zerah's body, his outstanding memory seemed unimpaired. Nor did he experience a shortage of motivation. I found this difficult to comprehend as Dr. Graham had told me that syphilis might affect Zerah's brain. He always found new engineering subjects on which to express opinions, though iron and steel, and locomotives remained his forte.

By this time, there was no diminution in the size of *Engineering*. The post brought a copy every Saturday morning. The paper continued with 16 pages of editorial matter, which I know from Zerah's countless exhortations, required over 30,000 words a week. This did not include 'cuts' as he called them – woodcuts or illustrations – as well as a page of patents.

In addition to written contributions from Zerah and William Maw, Mr. James Dredge created all the drawings; he produced some written work too. Even so, there was much for three men to create weekly. I imagined that with time, the burden on Mr. Maw and Mr. Dredge would become greater.

Zerah was ever restless for change. He discussed moving to larger house. Would it make him any more cheerful? He said it would be a joy to own a house overlooking Hyde Park, to see children playing and couples strolling beneath the trees. It sounded idyllic; too me, however, we would simply have a more imposing house to which he could invite his guests. It would require more work, but would it be within our means? Of course, I was not allowed to express an opinion. As people became wealthier, they moved to larger houses and Zerah had every wish to follow suit. Nevertheless, for whatever reason, he chose to remain in Gloucester-road, situated close to *Engineering* and

Bedford-street.

I would muse to myself: What was it that motivated Zerah? His life had been a succession of 'new excitements', including his women of the street. He experienced a hunger for all things new. It reinforced my view that life for him was like a giant book of which Zerah constantly turned the pages to experience a new thrill. His life had been littered with 'new thrills' of which I had been but one. Mrs. Colburn and Sarah Pearl had been others.

Apart from anything else, as time went on, I noticed he drank even more heavily, if that were possible. As a household, we consumed much alcohol – yet I drank little wine and certainly no spirits. I hated spirits as they made me feel light-headed and out of control. I said nothing.

Then, one day, Peggy brought a small empty bottle, labelled laudanum, she found discarded with household rubbish.

'I found this the other day, ma'am. I have not seen its likes here before. I cannot think where it came from. Unless it belongs to the master,' she told me, with a knowing look.

Peggy was a woman who took notice of minute details yet remained silent, like a heron standing motionless on the side of a lake, waiting to strike. I knew Peggy had brought me the bottle for a purpose.

'I think you must be right, Peggy,' I replied. 'But it would be wise to leave it where you found it.'

Peggy informed me also of a new decanter that recently appeared on the sideboard in the dining room. I had not noticed it. She took me to see it. It appeared to contain sherry.

'Is that sherry, Peggy, do you think?' I asked her. It was as though we were conspiratorial, mistress and housekeeper.

She poured a little into a sherry glass and sipped it.

'That is laudanum too, ma'am. 'You try it. It is opium dissolved in alcohol. I recognise the taste. That may have come from the apothecary.'

'The Shadwell opium dens are notorious for the easy access they give to sailors and whoever else,' Peggy added knowingly.

I tasted it; I found it most awful.

'Do you know what that is for, Mrs. Colburn?' asked Peggy. Without waiting for a reply she declared: 'We have no small children here who need to be ushered to sleep.'

I nodded. I wished she had not said that, suddenly feeling sad at the thought of a house without children. My mother had had so many children; I had none.

'And some says it causes awful constipation, ma'am,' added Peggy.

It was then I knew the reason for Zerah's mood changes – laudanum. On some occasional days he could be effusive and even warm; more frequently, on others he would be distant, argumentative and stormy. I tried to maintain a quiet acceptance, hoping that one day I would find peace.

In addition to alcohol, and in particular mulled port, he was lacing his body with opium and laudanum. I debated with myself whether he might be taking larger doses for medicinal purposes. Artisans took laudanum for recreational use, while several well-known writers were frequent users of opium. I concluded Zerah took it for another reason – to dull his syphilis, of which he said nothing at all. I did not take opium – Dr. Graham had warned against it.

As to my own battle, due to the diligence and persistent work of Dr. Graham, I began to overcome the secondary stage. I no longer displayed some obvious signs. Dr. Graham said the disease had not attacked as viciously as with some people he had treated.

Ulcers and papules remained visible on my skin, but I had no patches of baldness on my scalp, and no mouth ulcerations. My skin, although no longer discoloured from mercury treatments, still exhibited an ashen tint. Anyone with knowledge of the disease would understand my suffering.

I was not as tired as previously and it seemed as though I had discovered some fresh energy to tackle my mission: to find an exit from beneath Zerah's roof and end my downfall of despair.

Countless times, at night in bed when I was alone, my thoughts turned to Zerah and the other women in his life; I knew of but three, but were there more? How did he behave? Was he naked with them? What happened between them? I was so innocent.

Many months passed since I last visited Mr. Bentley at his inquiry agency. After my last beating, I had no desire to retrace my steps. However, I had written, using my parent's address, to inform that father was prepared to engage Mr. Bentley's services for another year, though it might be some time before I could see him. I also gave him the approximate date when I thought the first Mrs. Colburn was lost at sea.

Indeed, it was not until June 1869 that I wrote to make a firm appointment to visit No. 2 Southampton-buildings. This time, I made certain I embarked on the journey when Zerah was in Manchester for several nights. I had no wish to make the same mistake twice.

On one occasion, I caught myself thinking: had Zerah paid Peggy to spy on my activities. I hoped not.

I did not discover the name of the ship that sank in the Atlantic and caused the loss of life of Mrs. Colburn and Sarah Pearl, but as to the date, I could not be certain only that the tragedy took place before we embarked on the maiden voyage of *Great Eastern*.

This time I did not have to wait to be ushered directly into Mr. Bentley's office.

'Mrs. Colburn, please be seated. I must say how fortunate of you to come at this time. Once again, we have important developments to report; but perhaps not as you might expect. Please convey my appreciation to your father for settling my account so promptly. I hope you will judge it money well spent.'

As I sat down, I wondered what Mr. Bentley was about to reveal.

'We now know, Mrs. Colburn, that your husband is no longer visiting Miss Fanny Porter; you remember she was the young woman at No. 265 Vauxhall Bridge-road, Pimlico. That relationship ceased just after Christmas.'

'Since then your husband has proved even more elusive. His movements are most erratic, to say the least. He may now be aware we are following him. Eventually, in May of this year, we discovered him visiting on a regular basis a house in another part of London, namely Manchester-street. Several young women operate from No. 22, but we ascertained that he attended one female in particular. Her name is Louisa Rose.'

'We are not confident as to her proper name; we suspect Louisa Rose could be her working name. Rose is certainly not her surname. I can tell you she is not a tuppenny upright, as we call them; they perform the act itself against a wall and are regarded the lowest form of streetwalker.'

I blushed at Mr. Bentley's description; thankfully, he was too engrossed to notice.

'Just who she really is we do not know. We will discover that. The house may be operated by a bawd, or by 'hags of hell', as they are sometimes known.' continued Mr. Bentley, seemingly delighted with his expressive descriptions. 'These are prostitutes who have lost their looks and take in novices. They live short, miserable lives. Occasionally, they gather at street corners, wicked looking and coldly calculating, haggard and wretched in their worn beauty. They hire fine clothes from the bawd. This one may be a novice. The house could be a brothel, or nunnery, and she might be working under the protection of a madam. There could even be a male protector.'

Mr. Bentley seemed exceedingly knowledgeable on the subject. He continued with enthusiasm.

'That brings to at least four women with whom Mr. Colburn has committed adultery,' he said emphatically. 'There could be more. And he has attended at least one hedonistic party, of which we are aware. There could be others.'

I suppose by that time Mr. Bentley's revelations no longer shocked. What came next however did cause surprise.

'We have conducted a search of passenger liners missing at sea,' said Mr. Bentley. 'You said earlier that in 1860 your husband received a report notifying him of his wife's death.'

I nodded.

'Our investigations reveal only one tragedy in the North Atlantic close to the date you mentioned. *S. S. Austria*, a steamship of the Hamburg America Line went down on 13th September 1858. She sailed from Hamburg on her third voyage destined for New York City. In the disaster, one of the worst in the North Atlantic, the liner was destroyed by fire. Of the 538 passengers and crew, all but 65 lost their lives. As I say, she sailed from Hamburg to New York City; in 1858.'

At this point Mr. Bentley stopped dramatically.

'Now here is the interesting part, Mrs. Colburn. There is no mention of Mrs. Zerah Colburn or Miss Sarah Pearl Colburn on the passenger list.'

In the silence that followed, Mr. Bentley stared, holding my eye.

'Now then, this raises a number of possibilities. One is that Mrs. Colburn and Miss Sarah Pearl were on the *S.S. Austria* but for some reason their names went unrecorded on the passenger list. Again, we might have our dates wrong; 1858 or 1859? Another possibility is that Mrs. Colburn and her daughter might still be alive.' He said pointedly.

'Alternatively, and this seems unlikely, Mrs. Colburn and her daughter sailed on a vessel whose loss was not recorded. I think we will reserve judgement on that.'

I told Mr. Bentley of my uncertainty of the precise month the incident took place. I knew it to be either June or July of 1859 – a full year before Zerah and I sailed to New York. We were married in September 1860, a year I could not forget.

'Very well, Mrs. Colburn, I believe you,' said Mr. Bentley. 'I should say in passing that we have retrieved a copy of your marriage certificate; it does disclose Mr. Colburn as widower. That seems to be in order. But I will make more enquiries.'

'Now then, Mrs. Colburn, what do you wish me to do? Shall I continue my surveillance? Or have you enough information to proceed? I can compile my report for you.'

I did not know what to do. Mr. Bentley's work had been of considerable expense to father, even to reach this point. I did not know how much more he was prepared to release on my behalf. I made up my mind.

'Please continue until the end of this year, and then my father and I will review our next steps,' I told him boldly.

'Very good, Mrs. Colburn, I will keep the file open and anticipate seeing you before the year end.'

I slowly made my way down the long flight of steps. I went to my usual café and ordered coffee.

Mr. Bentley had raised the prospect of Mrs. Colburn and Sarah Pearl not being 'lost at sea'. I did not know what to make of it. One certainty remained, Zerah continued to philander with women; clearly his way of life.

Some months elapsed before I returned to Mr. Bentley's office. My diary showed it as Tuesday, 2nd November 1869. I did not visit him on the previous day as I thought this might be a busy day.

I had to wait some15 minutes before Mr. Bentley received me into his now familiar, but still untidy office.

'Ah, Mrs. Colburn,' said Mr. Bentley in a bright tone of voice. 'Do sit down.'

'I am sorry to say that I have no more information as to the matter of souls lost at sea. We will put that to one side for a while,' he said. 'I did not think it relevant just now, as I have more important developments relating to your husband. We are now certain Mr. Colburn has established a tryst with yet another woman, this time by the name of Miss Lillian Claire Loveaux. She too resides at No. 22 Manchester-street. That seems to be a popular rendezvous for your husband. We understand he has committed adultery with her too.'

'Just who she is we do not know,' declared Mr. Bentley.

'However,
we are certain Miss Loveaux is a French lady recently arrived in London from Paris. As you might expect, she speaks the French language fluently and with a French accent. Many French women work in London; their remunerations are more beneficial, shall we say, than in Paris, the so-called city of love.'

'A French woman?' I asked. My blood ran cold.

'Yes, a French woman. She is aged about 25 years. She too is tall, slender and smartly attired, according to my colleague,' said Mr. Bentley. 'My source reveals she moved only recently onto the street. It is safe to say, Mrs. Colburn, the two women residing at No. 22 Manchester-street are prostitutes. My source has spoken to one. It is a house of ill repute. I am sorry to inform you, but in substance they differ little from Mary Ann Jennery, Fanny Porter or Louisa Rose. Your husband is duplicitous in the extreme, Mrs. Colburn. Duplicitous.'

I thought about the French woman. Could she be one of the women Zerah met in Paris at the exhibition? That would be most unlikely, but stranger coincidences do happen.

I stared out of the window. There was little to see through the grime-laden window, save for the sooty brick wall of the building adjoining some three feet distant; the window had not been cleaned for years.

The women I heard about in that room could be the tip of a giant iceberg. Each one, as her name emerged, morphed into a drop of poison. The detective may have identified but a few. There may be many more. In addition, perhaps Zerah had a mistress hidden away somewhere – or even two, each might be unaware of the other, and one could be in Paris. Each, or both, might have a higher claim than me on his affections. The thought filled me with compelling horror.

As to the prostitutes, how much time did Zerah spend with each? Did he hand over money at the beginning or the end of their meeting? How much did it cost? Did he undress fully? How clean were they? Did he infect them, or vice versa? A myriad of other questions streamed through my head. I had asked myself before, yet they continued to flood back.

How could a man who was so meticulous as to his dress and cleanliness, and who minutely examined every word he wrote on paper as to its accuracy and appropriateness, spend time with filthy, diseased women, and then return to the house with goodness knows what? Who else did these women sleep with; men from the gutter? Or were they 'high class' prostitutes? It made no difference to me.

What was Zerah's attitude to these women? I knew from experience, he could be brutish and selfish yet indulgent and charmingly assertive, judgmental yet again always serenely confident. On the worst of days, he could be acidic and venomous. At times the quarrels could be so fierce that he insisted on being alone in his study.

There was a long silence. I knew of Zerah's addiction to concealment; it had become the essence of his life. Eventually I said:

'Thank you Mr. Bentley for your work. My father will write, as we have probably exhausted our savings. You have been most helpful, but now we must decide as to the future direction.'

I knew from my parents' remarks, the cost to them of my 'misfortune' had proved expensive, and something I could not repay. I was so grateful to them. The price of my freedom, should I ever be free, would be great.

'I do understand, Mrs. Colburn,' said Mr. Bentley. 'I should tell you that I am frequently called upon to give evidence in the Divorce Court, so it is of no discomfort to assist the petition on your behalf. It has been a satisfaction to work for you. Your husband clearly objectified women; he treated women as his inferiors. There could be many more hidden, like Miss Loveaux. I wish you have a successful outcome.'

He then adopted a more sympathetic and caring tone.

'I hope your health improves,' he said. 'As to other matters, I shall send your father my final statement of account. Once settled, I will provide a full record of our work, including dates, times, and appropriate names and addresses. Good day, Mrs. Colburn and thank you.'

He led me to the door. I made my way downstairs to the café opposite, and sat at my usual table.

As I waited for coffee, my thoughts focused on what to do next. I had enough information to take divorce action against my husband. He had infected me with syphilis; conducted, and was still conducting, adulterous sexual relationships with various women and had carried out vicious assaults against me. He had been brutally cruel, and repeatedly delivered a miscellany of kicks and beatings.

From what father had said, this was surely sufficient to force a successful action for divorce. The question would be, could we afford it? I had to discuss that with father.

I took a cab to my parents' house. They had moved recently to No. 11 Cambridge-terrace. The house was slightly smaller than the previous one in Brewer-street, and located in an area subjected to rapid development since 1865. The house lacked the elegance of the terraced houses in that other Cambridge-terrace, namely the one adjacent to Regent's Park; but that was only to be expected

A variety of trades occupied Cambridge-terrace. Two doors from my parents was Mrs. Jean Horby's Ladies' School, while several doors further on could be found the Lord Clyde public house, and at No. 32 resided Samuel Joseph Cole, an undertaker. At the top of Cambridge-terrace, the Cornwall-road Baptist chapel occupied a prominent position.

Cambridge-terrace itself abutted Cornwall-road and was situated about three-quarters of a mile west of Westbourne-villas, where Emily and William Maw lived. It would be a simple matter, whenever I visited my parents, to call on Emily, which I did occasionally.

At the time, father was about 79 years of age; although elderly, he continued with a little of his work as an accountant. Mother would be some 20 years younger. Twin brothers Thomas and Henry were then 19. Thomas worked as a clerk but Henry had yet to find work. My parents' domestic servant, Louise Gould, was about 33; she came from Kent.

Mother appeared pleased to see me, but when I revealed my news, she was fearfully angry and said she would not hesitate to tell father everything as soon as she saw him.

I returned to No. 13 Gloucester-road. On arrival, I wrote a letter to Emily Maw. I much wished to meet her for conversation. I invited her to luncheon the following week.

On the day of Emily's arrival, Peggy cooked a delicious meal of fish; it drew an appreciative smile from my guest. I knew it to be a favourite of Emily's. It was a pleasure to exchange views with someone close in age.

I did not reveal any personal problems; they were between Mr. Bentley, my parents, and me. I hoped, however, in my search for more information, that her husband had raised the subject of office gossip. And indeed, during our conversation, Emily disclosed that her husband required a private meeting with me. He did not know what to do for the best, as he had no wish to visit our house alone.

Chapter twelve
Contra mundum

W HAT NEWS could William possibly possess to cause him such anxiety? I assured Emily I could arrange to meet her husband discretely. I found it most mysterious and almost clandestine. As we continued to talk, I had an idea.

As my husband frequently informed, he published *Engineering* every Friday; I knew it to be the quietest weekday. All work for that week's issue would be complete. I suggested to Emily that I meet her husband in the entrance hall of the British Museum, Great Russell-street, not far from *Engineering*'s offices, the following week at 11a.m. That would be Friday, 26th November 1869. I would wait no longer than 11.30a.m.

That particular month, November, London had witnessed much activity. On 6th November, Queen Victoria opened Blackfriars Bridge over the River Thames. On the same day, the queen celebrated the opening of the Holborn Viaduct, which crossed the bed of the River Fleet. Construction work on that began in 1863. Something else I noticed in *The Times* that month: the launch of the magnificent tea clipper, *The Cutty Sark*, in Dumbarton on 22nd November. The event drew much attention.

The following week I journeyed to the British Museum as arranged; even though I arrived too early, I found William waiting. He appeared ill at ease, looking anxiously from side to side, as if expecting to be recognised. We quickly retired upstairs to find a place we could talk privately. The Reading Room was ideal; two women only occupied the room, which surprised me. We found a corner distant from them. It might at first sight appear that we were conspirators, yet I was aware a personal friendship had developed between us. But it was no more than that. As soon as we sat down, William began to unburden

315

himself.

'Mrs. Colburn,' he whispered. 'I remain most concerned about your husband. It is perhaps not for me to mention this, but I think you should be aware of repeated gossip regarding your husband's association with some unwelcome ladies. I have urged him that he conducts himself with insufficient discretion.'

'I am all too aware of such rumours, William,' I replied, also whispering, but perhaps a trifle too testily. 'You have raised the matter before. Do you have anything new?'

Of course, I knew much, much more about my husband's movements than William could possibly imagine. Or so I thought.

'Well, Mr. Dredge and I now have to undertake a great amount of work at *Engineering* because of Mr. Colburn's heavy drinking. Your husband is self-obsessed and tortured; a man of many hidden problems. When drink and demons take hold, he can disappear for entire afternoons, days even. We have to decide which items to include, and then he will appear on press days and invariably disagree with our selection. There are bitter arguments, even harsh words exchanged. I wish he would be a little less immoderate in his language, Mrs. Colburn. I know I should not repeat this, but your husband is a very difficult man. We think also he consumes large quantities of opium in the form of laudanum. Combined with alcohol, this makes life extremely difficult for everyone at *Engineering*.'

'Your husband appears to find it easy to procure opium,' William continued. 'You may have read that a recent Act of Parliament has restricted opium sales to professional pharmacists; prior to that, anyone could trade opium potions, pills and patent medicines. Even so, your husband continues unabated to obtain the drug. Much entangled with the practice of opium taking, is deviance and sexual licentiousness. I deem he has become dangerously addictive. On one occasion, when he had consumed too much drink, he confessed to us that opium made his problems smaller and lighter. Opium, he told us, drained away anxieties and his self-loathing.'

I was unable to halt William, then in full flow.

'There are times when your husband's idea for an article is one of pure genius; at such times, seemingly his powers are not impaired or diminished in any way. We, poor mortals, cannot produce anything of near equal. There are times when he becomes preoccupied with facts, figures and events; yet he has no feelings for those who work alongside. As he sinks into lassitude, he is the dead weight we all carry.'

William's comments gushed forth as a reservoir bursting its banks. Unnoticed, a librarian joined us. 'Please be quiet, or you will be instructed to leave,' he ordered William in a fierce whisper.

In much subdued tones William continued: 'We endeavour to discover, as best we can every Monday, his plans for the next issue. He retorts by informing us he is too busy. Too busy with what? *Engineering* is his business; it was his idea and it is his livelihood – and ours. He has a habit of putting everyone on their metal with his distinctive, cutting voice with its hint of American. What can be on his mind?'

'William, I am unable to help,' I whispered. 'I know nothing of newspapers and publishing. I cannot intervene. My husband is far too strong-willed for me to intercede. I too am fearful to say anything that might assist. But I know he is preparing an important lecture for the Royal Society of Arts next month. He will discuss the Channel Tunnel, a subject about which he is passionate. This subject, together with its tunnelling requirements, has exercised his interest since meeting Mr. Hawkshaw. You will recall Mr. Brunel and Mr. Stephenson both favoured a rail tunnel and French engineer, M. Thomé de Gamond issued a tunnel proposal some years ago. Keep all this to yourself.'

'Then why does he not inform us? Why does he keep it secret?

William was relieved to share information with me. He

paraded it as a problem halved and we then agreed to go our separate ways.

The Society of Arts lecture was the second paper Zerah delivered that year. He intended both to enhance his stature. And for these he acquired frilled shirts and diamond studs to reinforce his importance.

Earlier, in March, he presented a lecture to the Institution of Civil Engineers with the title *American locomotives and their rolling stock*. Those in attendance, including William, remained in no doubt my husband held a coveted position; one that commanded both admiration and respect among engineers. The lecture drew such acclaim, according to William, that the Institution later awarded Zerah a James Watt Medal and a Telford premium in books – this was in addition to the Telford Medal he received in 1863. He was proud to receive them all.

'Everyone in the audience was impressed both with delivery and content,' William had explained earlier. 'I could see how the audience nourished his spirit, while contact with those who came to hear his delivery was clearly most precious. It was as though he could exercise power over them.'

William added that Mr. Colburn 'with his worldliness and familiar displays of self-regard, commanded everyone's attention', and had collected a strong following among the membership who saw him as a young, vibrant and ambitious engineer. 'The work of a genius,' someone declared of Zerah's paper.

How was it that a genius could cavort with prostitutes?

Such was the interest in Zerah's subject that the Institution had to continue his lectures on two further dates, namely 6th March and 23rd March 1869, 'to the exclusion of any other subject'.

William had told me many in the audience expressed their reverence for Mr. Colburn's literary gifts; it was through this lecture that my husband 'reaffirmed his credentials as a locomotive man of some repute'. William then still held my husband in awe.

I could vouch that Zerah had spent many hours working on his paper, which he titled *Anglo-French Communications* and contained his proposals for the Channel Tunnel, including laying a tube on the bed of the English Channel. Later, I was told the lecture proved most popular – so many members wished to speak – that the chairman closed the meeting with the hope members could meet after Christmas to hear further discussions on the subject. The chairman told members he could 'not omit a tribute of praise to that gentleman (Zerah) for the very excellent and practical character of his paper'. My husband, who craved public fame, was greatly pleased by the chairman's comments.

Months later, in a letter to me, William expressed his praise of Zerah's excellent paper – a masterpiece, he described – with its 'bewitching interest in speculating upon the mere possibility' of a tunnel. He sensed Zerah recognised the power of his presence and ability to enthrall; he used this to good effect. According to William, the audience was full of praise for Mr. Colburn and his contribution as well as his great powers. I should be proud of him, William wrote.

Daringly, I thought, William added that while my husband had his 'enemies' who loathed his boastful, selfishness and occasional drunkenness, there were many others who were enchanted by his handsome presence, his undoubted intelligence, his brilliant conversation and a certain charm.

The audience was plainly unaware of anything that might be afflicting Zerah, or his deviances. I knew otherwise, of course as I had recognised the slow but steady and relentless change that had worked over him for the past year or more.

Contradiction ran through Zerah like a dark seam. On the one hand, he declared public speaking as his greatest pleasure, to bring understanding to engineers; on the other hand, he performed in secrecy, taking pleasures from complete strangers – filthy street women.

I knew from what I had seen, Zerah could write long and detailed articles on specialised subjects of engineering. These reflected the immense spread of his knowledge. However, why would he ruin his career on the altar of fornication and prostitution, when he could, by all accounts, secure even greater fame in England? Why embark on scandals when the door to his success was wide open? Such questions I was unable to place before him to answer. Even so, his career bore the scars of self-inflicted wounds which were visible for some to see.

Yet if Zerah was the recipient of praise from outside the rooms of *Engineering*, within them he remained a thorn in almost everyone's side. William's comments suggested to me that Zerah faced a serious situation. His unbalanced habits caused deep schisms, as he no longer confined his cantankerous nature or bouts of anger to his home where we faced many personal differences.

I knew, without any words from William, Zerah most likely had to endure one or more effects, like nausea, vomiting, alternating chills and sweats, as well as irritability and depression. Collectively, if he had them, they must have had a debilitating effect.

Zerah's career faced serious risks as his editorship faltered. Far from reporting news of engineering interest, he would be the subject of news following his spiral into a vortex of sin. He would be the focus of unpleasant gossip; life for him would become difficult.

Long since disappeared were house parties of the early 1860s with their charm and conviviality, and which he so excellently stage-managed. Then the centre of attention; now he had retreated into an almost permanent gloom.

Zerah returned from his lecture on the Channel Tunnel in a foul mood, even though all those present fell upon his words with fascination. Ironically, it was to be his last public appearance – but no one knew it at the time. Something had not been to his satisfaction. He was depressed, withdrawn and moody. It was not long before he went out into the evening air. I did not see him for several days.

Until his return, I spent most of the time on my own or with my parents. Following that, Zerah would go out on numerous occasions but I did not know where or what he was doing. I began to experience feelings of abandonment. Unlike William and Emily, Zerah and I were not seen together in public. I did not know which was worse: to be the subject of ill-treatment and ridicule, or to be abandoned and left to my own devices.

One day, while enjoying a brief stay with my parents, father told me the time had come for action.

'You now have enough evidence to file for divorce,' he said. 'Make 1870 the year for a fresh start. Begin a new life.'

It was not quite so simple. It was as if I had created a huge snowball and was about to dispatch it from the top of Primrose Hill; no one could predict the damage it might inflict or where it would come to rest. I understood what father was trying to tell me; it was just a question of whether I had courage to take the first step.

My father, however, made the first move.

'I shall find a solicitor,' he said. 'But you will make the appointment to see him. We will try to meet costs as we proceed.'

I knew of no alternative; not revenge, as I have mentioned, but to obtain justice for myself. My first thoughts were to let my husband rot in his own obscurity, but increasingly I became determined to expose his intrigue, secrets and treachery. To retract would be admit defeat

I had read somewhere that my husband's 'hero' Mr. Dickens, had some years earlier rid himself of his wife, Catherine, in favour of his mistress. I had no wish for such indignity to befall me.

And so it was on 20th December 1869 I wrote a letter to a Mr. John Holmes using my parent's address and seeking an appointment. His office was located at No. 34 Clements-lane in the City of London. A reply arrived the same day. Mr. Holmes would make himself available next day. I did not have long to wait. It was now a matter of *contra mundum* – against the world.

Mr. Holmes took pride in his appearance. A short, dapper man he wore morning suit with a black tie. Everything about him was black, with the exception of his white shirt. A greater contrast to Mr. Bentley I doubt one could find.

While his personal neatness no doubt reflected his standing in society, his office did not. It had the appearance of extreme untidiness. Piled everywhere were papers; on the floor, and in bookshelves around the room where they battled for space with heavy law books. Perhaps there was order to it but to me they were but pile upon pile of papers.

Piles of papers jostled for space on each side of the heavy table that divided Mr. Holmes from me. Any moment I expected a pile of papers to fall. The table itself was in dire need of a thorough cleaning. Behind Mr. Holmes, a glass-paned wooden cabinet contained yet more books.

On the day of my visit, many of the encrusted ulcers and papules on my body had begun to disappear, though some remained on my face and scalp. My head still itched from time to time. My hair had continued its growth where I had lost it, though of course I always wore my bonnet when I went out.

If Mr. Holmes was aware of my ailment, he gave no hint. He appeared kind and sympathetic, clearly familiar with the law as it concerned divorce. As soon as he saw the extent of my carefully prepared notes, with dates, names and details of cruelty, he could judge the serious nature of my quest.

I assumed father, having communicated with Mr. Holmes, explained the outline of my case. I wished to have father at my side but this task I had to face alone. Private thoughts suddenly became public reality. I spent an hour in Mr. Holmes's chambers, carefully explaining every detail. Mr. Homes spoke well, precisely, slowly and clearly. There was no mistaking his voice which reflected a good education. When I reached the subject of syphilis, I blushed visibly, but he appeared unconcerned.

'Please do not distress, Mrs. Colburn,' he said. 'I have heard –

and seen – far worse as husbands attempt to normalize sadistic behaviour for their own benefit. Domestic abuse remains a dirty secret, a shame that has to be borne in private by a violated wife. However, I am confident you have an excellent chance of success, unless your husband can submit an even better counter defence. The evidence is firmly in your favour. However, I must stress that any social stigma born by your husband will be shared by you also. Any shunning that may follow the revelations in a public court of household secrets is certain to have its impact on you too. Alas for you at this moment Mrs. Colburn, with all your vulnerabilities and transparencies, I fear loneliness and indignity are your principal grim outriders.'

I had not heard that phrase before.

Mr. Holmes further asked if I could strengthen my case with additional details. I found this upsetting and declared emphatically: 'I have given you the truth; the whole truth.'

'I am sure you have, Mrs. Colburn. Your husband would appear to be a misogynist; a serial philanderer. I would even judge he suffers from narcissism,' said Mr. Holmes in a tone of voice that suggested our meeting closed. 'I shall prepare papers and later lodge them with Mr. Colburn. See me at the end of this week to confirm details.'

When I left that City of London office, I knew nothing could stop the ensuing snowball. My principal concern: would I be further damaged in the process?

I returned to Mr. Holmes's chambers on Friday, 24th December as instructed, and when I saw the full extent of the details, carefully written on parchment, a shiver swept my entire body. As my body shook, so my heart raced. What had I done? Yet in my heart I knew there was no possibility of a rapprochement. The die had been cast. Life had to proceed despite my husband's betrayal.

A cold day, I had wrapped myself against the winter winds, yet still I shivered. Mr. Holmes handed over the documents. The shock of seeing the words on paper caused my hands to tremble further. The first page read: Petition No. 1433: Colburn vs Colburn, Petition for the Dissolution of Marriage.

The brutality of the wording brought home the full measure of my action. Without warning, my action had become serious. The Petition contained 10 items, including names and addresses of women with whom Zerah had committed adultery. One item stood out above the rest.

Item 4 read 'That in the months of June or July 1867 the said Zerah Colburn knowingly and wilfully infected your petitioner with a venereal disease called syphilis.'

It was there as bold as brass; in black and white. Everyone would know the blatant truth of my private disgrace. I could no longer hide the truth. By inference, Zerah carried the disease.

I observed the document carefully word by word. It read:

1. That on the 24th day of September 1860 I, then Elizabeth Susanna Browning, spinster, was married to Zerah Colburn, the above named Respondent at New York in the United States of America and also again on the 3rd day of September 1864 at the office of the Superintendent Registrar for the District of St Pancras in the county of Middlesex according to the forms required by the laws of England.

2. After my said marriage I lived and cohabited with the said Zerah Colburn at No. 13 Gloucester Road, Regents Park in the said County of Middlesex and there is no issue of the said marriage.

3. That for two years past the said Zerah Colburn has been guilty of divers acts of cruelty to your petitioner hereinafter referred to.

4. That in the months of June or July 1867 the said Zerah Colburn knowingly and wilfully infected your Petitioner with a venereal disease called syphilis.

5. That repeatedly between the month of January 1868 and the month of January 1870 the said Zerah Colburn was guilty of cruelty to your Petitioner by striking, kicking, beating and otherwise assaulting her.

6. That between the month of December 1867 and the month of March 1868 the said Zerah Colburn frequently at No. 37 Bedford Street, Strand committed adultery with a female named Lucy Taylor.

7. That from the month of February 1868 to the month of October 1868 the said Zerah Colburn at No. 11 Huntley Street, Bedford Square committed adultery with a female named Mary Ann Jennery.

8. That from the month of June to the month of December 1868 the said Zerah Colburn frequently visited a female of the name of Fanny Porter at No,

265 Vauxhall Bridge Road, Pimlico and on diverse of such occasions committed adultery with her.

9. That for four months in or about the months of June and July 1869 the said Zerah Colburn frequently visited Louisa Rose at No. 22 Manchester Street, Argyle Square London and on diverse of such occasions committed adultery with her.

10. That on two occasions in or about the months of August and September 1869 the said Zerah Colburn at No. 22 Manchester Street, Argyle Square aforesaid committed adultery with Lilian Claire Loveaux.

Wherefore your Petitioner humbly prays that their honourable Court will be pleased to decree her a dissolution of the said marriage by reason of the cruelty and adultery of the said Zerah Colburn.

Petition in Dissolution of Marriage

Filed................ 1870

I must have appeared perturbed by the severity of the wording; wording which exposed the hypocrisy of my marriage.

'Do not worry, Mrs. Colburn. Everything will be all right,' assured Mr. Holmes. 'Try not to upset yourself. Principle and justice are more important than self-interest. Please be seated quietly and study the document again. Please inform of any errors.'

The petition required but one minor change, so Mr. Holmes suggested I return to Chambers immediately following Christmas to review the final document.

I spent the entire Christmas period in a state of nervous tension. I went to midnight communion on Christmas Eve; it proved a moving service. I walked back in the cold night air accompanied by a neighbour. I had prayed for a happy outcome to my dilemma.

That night in bed, thoughts raced through my mind. I pulled the bedding over my face to exclude the world and hide myself in a cocoon. In my dream, I had become lost in a dark wood; I could find no escape. I was friendless and alone. In life, I had no real friends apart from my parents. Where had I gone wrong?

I returned to church twice on Christmas Day. I attended as much to pray for myself as to escape from the house.

I could tell from the atmosphere in the house that Zerah was deeply unhappy within himself; but I knew his predicament was entirely of his own making. I dreaded his long sulks and silences. I prayed that he would find a happy outcome – but not involving me.

Behind that façade, that veneer, was a man suffering deep bouts of depression, brought on by his various addictions. I knew too of how Zerah's depression alternated with a restless desire for carnal pleasure.

Our marriage stumbled on, but for how much longer. In reality, it was not a marriage at all that I had to endure. We were aliens; not even brother and sister. In my loneliness I longed to embrace a man I could admire and whose company I could enjoy; to be able to pull him tightly close. I had almost forgotten how to laugh. Nothing could now rescue our relationship, a marriage fractured by Zerah's abominable behaviour. He had entrapped me in the maelstrom of his despair and regarded me with such derision.

Peggy prepared Christmas luncheon but, as Zerah and I stared at one another across the table, the meal was far from joyous. We merely re-enacted a ritual played out in countless other homes across the country, except there was neither conversation nor children to lighten the atmosphere. As to any laughter, that had long since disappeared. Zerah was unaware of what was about to strike him.

My parents invited us to join them for Boxing Day and, with my family, we created quite a gathering. My mother cooked as she usually did; father ensured we had something to drink.

As for me, I was acutely aware of the strained atmosphere. I understood what I had set in motion. I knew what could befall me. Father knew too. How did he feel? I never asked him.

Zerah was in an emotional state over the holiday period. The long-running combined effects of syphilis – I assumed he had done nothing about trying to cure it, as he did not discuss the matter with me – the effects of his long-standing abuse of opium and his unchallenged drinking habits, made him a difficult living companion. Possibly he suffered from the effects of mercury poisoning, if my assumption had been incorrect and he had been receiving treatment.

Zerah's mood swings were obvious to all, especially Peggy. He offered no words of praise, as before, for the high standard of her cooking; indeed the reverse was most often the case. Increasingly, he would criticise her food, which I deemed excellent. I tried to placate Peggy: I did not want her to leave; she was my only source of daily comfort.

Early in January, I returned to Mr. Holmes. I made certain Zerah would be absent for the entire day. The meeting lasted but a short time. I was anxious to know when the next move would to take place.

'When will you deliver the divorce petition?' I asked. For, while the lack of progress frustrated me, I was desperately afraid of the consequences.

'I will arrange to have Petition delivered by hand to the offices of *Engineering* late this month, or possibly early in February. There are still matters to resolve, but it should be possible towards the end of the month. I will ensure it is delivered into Mr. Colburn's hands personally to avoid any doubt or confusion.'

I suggested to Mr. Holmes that a Friday might be suitable; it was when copies of *Engineering* arrived from the printers. Zerah was always present in the office to examine the newspaper when it came up.

I remained tense for the next few weeks. As the end of the month loomed, I became more nervous by the day. I did not have long to wait for the storm to burst. It was Saturday, 29th January 1870.

It was just before midday when the house filled with a frightful noise. Zerah burst thunderously through the front door. He had not returned the previous night and I began to speculate where he might be. I had not seen him with such an evil temper. Had he spent hours drinking with Mr. Jim at The Engineer prior to his return?

His violent alcoholic rage, explosive and volcanic as ever, caused this mouth to foam. His opening remarks said it all.

'Vixen. You are my ruin. You seek divorce. Is that true?'

So, the divorce papers had been served.

I told him in a faltering voice that I found him difficult to live with.

'Difficult to live with? Preposterous,' he blustered.

'You have been with other women,' I countered. 'And you have been extremely cruel to me. You are a bully. It is in my petition.'

'I shall fiercely dispute everything your esteemed solicitor has compiled. Do you think I have time or inclination for the countless women detailed in your petition? His document is a tissue of lies from beginning to end.' Zerah retorted. 'You will never win. And what you claim to have suffered is but a fraction of what else is destined for you now.'

He grabbed my forelock and dragged me into the parlour, slamming the door behind. My face turned red and tears welled in my eyes. Zerah's face contorted with hatred and his right arm thrust upwards with a clenched fist, what came next was unexpected.

He hurled a fusillade of blows to my face and body. His attack came with a frequency and ferocity I had never witnessed. He almost knocked me senseless. I feared a fractured cheekbone, so severely did he hit me. Then, with a blow to the stomach, he dispatched me to the floor. As I lay there, he strode over and kicked mercilessly.

'Take a look at yourself. Who would want you?' he demanded.

I had no wish to hear any more.

What followed I know not, even to this day. I must have fainted from pain. The next thing, I found Peggy bending over me. Gently raising my head, she pushed a glass of cold water to my lips.

'There now, m'dear,' she said in a comforting voice. 'Take a sip of this. We must get you to a hospital or to Dr. Graham.'

'No, no. Please not that. I shall recover,' I replied weakly.

'But you are in a terrible way, m'dear. Shall I find a police constable?'

'No, Peggy. Please not that either,' I said, fearful of the outcome.

I tried to sit up but my head ached; so did every part of my body from the bruising. Peggy placed a cushion under my head.

'Leave me be for a few minutes,' I said, trying to gather my thoughts. I had known, once Zerah had read my petition, he would subject me to an ordeal. It was inevitable, but I had not expected such a vicious tirade of wrath and vengeance.

I laid there for some time. I heard the tick of the clock. As Peggy spoke, I drifted in and out of consciousness. I made little sense of the conversation.

Then I heard Peggy speak: 'Take your time, m'dear. I will stay here with you. What have you done to deserve this?'

I held my tongue. Truth would emerge in due course, but for the moment, I had to gather my thoughts.

After what seemed a very long time I was able to move my limbs, but they ached so badly it required a huge effort.

'I will retire to my room. Please help me, Peggy,' I said. 'I will feel better there. Please warm the bed.'

'At once Mrs. Colburn,' replied Peggy much formally. She drew closer a chair to support my back and then disappeared from the room.

I was glad to be alone. Was the worst over? Or was there yet more to come? I will never forget that day, 29th January. I carry the vision in my mind; it will remain always.

I could only expect that further ordeals would follow, unless I could escape to my parents. If I lived with them, would I be safe from that monster of a husband?

Peggy gave assistance as I limped painfully upstairs to my room. I looked in the mirror. I looked like a tramp; completely dishevelled. I was hardly recognisable as a woman. My hair was awry and my face and body marked with deep violet bruises.

Zerah was vile and reprehensible. I wished I could lay my hands on his gun. It was in the top drawer of his chest of drawers. Would I be able to use it? But that would be murder.

'Help me into bed, please, Peggy. I want to rest now and try to recover,' I said.

Peggy drew back the bedclothes and gradually, without undressing, I eased my body between the sheets.

'Leave, Peggy, please leave' I muttered, with relief.

Peggy pulled the bedding over me, drew the curtains and closed the door.

I was alone and isolated with no one to help. I knew I must contact my parents but I was in no fit state to do anything. As I lay there, staring at the ceiling, thoughts came and went, as spasms of pain pierced my body every time I moved.

It was a joyless marriage; a loveless marriage. Zerah had sacrificed my life to sustain his lifestyle – a lifestyle of obsession with street women. He was like a moth to a candle. Sexual intercourse without love and affection were grotesque.

Through his selfishness, he subjected me to a life sentence. Some of what he did was too horrible to commit to paper. I needed someone to love; to hold me close, to care for me.

Zerah had not strayed, like some lost dog. Instead, quite deliberately he pursued excitement. Once a superior individual, now, in my eyes, he was inferior. I was not jealous of new lovers he found in his life; on the contrary his actions disgusted me, for he had imposed on me almost 10 tempestuous years. I could never forgive him.

Not for the first time in my life, I drew myself deeper and deeper within, as if to isolate myself from that terrible man. I fell into a fitful slumber. All of a sudden, I woke in the night and sat upright, covered in sweat yet shivering with cold. I shook my head and lay down again. I no longer knew the man who lived in the same house.

Next morning I awoke, having experienced the most vivid dreams; they were almost lifelike. I woke with a voice in my head.

It said 'Depart'. It was an hour or more before the voice disappeared, only to leave me in a strange cloud of despair. There appeared no future. The memory of Zerah and his actions filled my mind. Whatever he did, he could no longer edit the past to suit the present. He was a wife beater. All I had wanted was a husband, a home and a child; not a tyrant. Was that too much to ask?

It took several days to recover, even partially. During that time, I ate little and drank mostly water. I went in search of a hammer, which I found in the cellar, later secreting it under my pillow for use in self-defence.

I wrote to mother to inform her of what had happened. I did not enter into details. My handwriting was a scrawl. I had little movement in my fingers. I could not control them sufficiently to write legibly.

The following week, Zerah returned on at least three occasions. Each time, he made straight for me, shouted and hit me about the face and body, and kicked me whenever the opportunity presented. His last visit was on Sunday morning, 6th February when, without speaking, and without reason, he beat me again.

He had metered out far worse treatment four days earlier, on 2nd February. I had been upstairs in my bedchamber when I heard some of the stairs creak under his weight. He burst in with a length of rope in his hand. Although I struggled, he was so strong that I had to yield. I had no time to resort to the hammer. He tied my wrists behind my back. I wondered what he was about to do. I feared another rape; even death.

He slapped my face repeatedly, and knocked me to the floor where I hit my head. Finally, he hurled a kick at my buttocks before leaving me sobbing.

Immediately after completing the attack, he strode out of the house and slammed the front door. I could hardly move. Following his departure, I heard Peggy's footsteps on the stairs, and she quickly released my wrists and rubbed them with her hands. As I faced her, Peggy's lips pursed deeply at what she witnessed. We looked at one another, eye to eye. Without a word, she bathed my wounds and helped me to bed to recover. I dreaded to think what passed through her mind.

I could continue no longer. I had to do something. Resorting to spirits offered one alternative; their numbing effect would blank out what had happened. I resisted the temptation.

On Monday, 7th February, matters moved out of my hands. I received a letter marked Private and Confidential. I recognised Zerah's scribble.

I tore open the envelope and removed a single, folded sheet. The terse letter proved difficult to decipher.

Thanks to the disgrace you have wrought, I am compelled to settle my debts with Mr. Bessemer. I am no longer part owner of *Engineering*. The future for me is bleak. I will now close 13 Gloucester-road.

Remove ALL your belongings by the end of tomorrow, Tuesday 8 Feb'y or I will destroy them.

ZC. 6 Feb'y 1870

The instructions were clear: 'Remove ALL your belongings.' It gave no hint as to what would happen to me. I must leave immediately. What would become of Peggy and housemaid Emma? Emma had replaced Rose who left our service on the last day of 1869, to pursue alternative employment.

My parents were most unhappy that I should remain alone in the house, not knowing when Zerah might return, or in what state he might be. I remained resolute. I could not give in so easily.

The next eruption, however, was only hours away. It happened midway through the same morning. I expected no one and Zerah's letter lay open on the table.

With the weather bitterly cold outside, we enjoyed fires burning brightly in the downstairs rooms. I heard the front door bang. It was as though a prison door had clanged shut. It could only be Zerah.

He came straight to the parlour where I sat. He lunged forward and grabbed what hair remained, twisting it round in his hand.

'You are hurting again,' I cried.

'You have spied on me, you vixen; paying nasty, greasy little detectives to snoop behind my back to garner evidence for your silly plot; a plot to belittle and ridicule me. You are a deceitful wife. No one will want you after this; not even my not-so-faithful assistant, Maw. I know you two have been seen together. You are lovers, I'll be bound. I am not blind.'

What absurd thoughts coursed through that head of my vicious, quarrelsome, controlling husband? His accusations could be quite wounding; shocking even. Was he consumed by jealousy? If so, it was completely unfounded; nothing could be farther from the truth that William Maw and I had eyes for each other. I had not given it thought.

I knew from his breath he had been drinking heavily. He not only took in alcohol by the day but, as Peggy informed me, there were empty bottles of all varieties at his bedside, and others secreted about the house.

To which she had warned: 'If I may say, ma'am, they do say that anyone seeking relief in alcoholic libation can expect gout, which can be painful and lead to swelling in the legs. I have seen it before.'

His appetite for liquor had multiplied to extravagant proportions, further fuelling his anger. His voice was slurred and he looked as though he needed a good wash. Normally immaculate, that morning he carried the unkempt appearance of a tramp.

'It is you, Sir. You are deceitful behind my back. Spending time with other women instead of with me,' I said bravely.

I became angry, able for once to meet his gaze and make contact with his steel grey eyes.

'What were they like?' I screamed at him. 'Did you beat them like you beat me? Did you tie them to the bed? Or were they too strong for you? What about Lucy Taylor? Did you find her exciting? Did you infect her as you did me?'

I could not help myself. I could not trust myself. All the frozen emotion and anger of the past years spilled out.

'You have no proof. You are an up-start relying on the idle tittle-tattle of a grubby private enquiry agent. Who paid for his services?'

'My father paid, Sir,' I replied with fury, quite forgetting my need for self-control. 'And he will vouch for every detail.'

'My father paid,' he said, mimicking me, rocking his head from side to side. 'You have ruined me with your deceitful plan. It is your fault. Now I have no money. I will be ridiculed should you proceed with your scandalous case. I shall look a public fool. Everyone I have worked with will laugh behind my back – as well as to my face; they will point fingers and smirk. And for what purpose? If all of this breaks out in the Press, it will be the end of me, and the end of you. I will make sure of that.'

'You have but yourself to blame, Sir,' I said with courage. 'You created the scandal. I know what happened in Paris. Do you not admit the sins you committed? I hate you and your kind.'

I had taken a step too far. His eyes blazed with a furious intensity to be followed by a sinister flash that lasted just a moment; his entire face cadaverous and his meaning naked. (I had learned the word cadaverous from Zerah when he described a fellow engineer at one of the Institutions.) He grasped my hair and, with his other hand pushed my head in the direction of the fire, moving it ever closer to the leaping flames, until I could stand the heat no more.

I screamed 'Stop! Stop! Help! Help!'

'You have been nothing but a hindrance; not even a comfort. There is no one to help you. Peggy and Emma have been dispatched on errands. They will not return for an hour and when they do they will find you a sorry sight. I will then dismiss them and you and I will alone. And I shall eat elsewhere of course – I have no wish that you secrete arsenic in my lunchtime dumplings, if that be your plan.'

In a moment of well-directed fury, with my heart pulsing to

bursting point, I aimed a kick at his ankle with all the force I could muster. I missed but then in my confusion I saw his left hand resting on his knee as he bent down to push me closer to the fire. This was my last opportunity. I summoned all courage, jerked my head sideways and bit as hard as I could into his wrist.

My reprisal took him off guard, causing him to release me. I darted away. Fortunately, he had not locked the parlour door, and I escaped down the hall, through the kitchen and scullery, and out of the back door. I ran as hard as I could out into Gloucester-road. With no time for a backward glance, I gratefully hailed a passing cab. I gave directions to my parents' house.

'No. 11 Cambridge-terrace, and quickly,' I said.

'Quickly, quickly,' I repeated with a sense of urgency.

'That's just round the corner, Miss,' retorted the driver.

'No. No. Cambridge-terrace near Cornwall-road, Notting Hill, and make haste. Quickly. My father will pay handsomely.'

And with that we were off. As I glanced through the oval rear window, I saw Zerah at the front door, gesticulating and shouting.

When we arrived at No. 11 Cambridge-terrace, the cab driver said on opening the door 'My goodness, that was close, Miss.'

'Closer than you think,' I replied. 'Wait. I will retrieve your fare.'

'Right-oh, Miss,' he said.

I burst into the house, on the verge of tears. My scorched face caused mother deep concern, ever anxious to learn details. She hurried outside with her purse and paid the cab driver, then returned to attend my wounds.

'You are not returning to that house. Do you hear me?' scolded mother, reminding me of childhood days. 'You will remain here; later we will collect your possessions.'

On the spur of the moment, I remembered.

'My journal, my diary,' I wailed. 'And my clothes and letters.'

I could not wait a moment longer, rushing away in search of father before she had finish treating me. I found him upstairs.

'Please, please,' I implored him. 'Retrieve my journal and my diary. My letters are there too. They are on top of my wardrobe. They must not fall into my husband's hands. Bring as many clothes as you can.'

'Your father is frail; he cannot travel alone into that lion's den,' ordered mother. 'Your brother Henry will accompany him.'

Father and Henry immediately took a cab to No. 13 Gloucester-road where Peggy assisted in forcing as many of my clothes as they could into two cases; they also retrieved the journal, my precious diary and my letters. The letters came from my sisters; no letters of endearment ever arrived for me from Zerah as none were ever sent.

Peggy by then had begun to pack her own possessions. Only later did I hear of Zerah's dismissal of both Peggy and Emma, and the house's closure.

However, that was not the end of the matter. On Wednesday, 9th February, feeling slightly improved, I braved a short walk in the frosty air. As I turned the corner from Cambridge-terrace, someone came behind me and, grabbing an arm, held me by the throat and pushed me against the wall. From nowhere the man produced a gun. I felt the cold steel of the muzzle held menacingly on the side of my head.

'Do not think you will get away with this, Elizabeth Colburn.'

It was my husband, his face strangely grey and menacing in the wintery air. Barely an inch separated his face from mine.

'I will haunt you for the rest of your days until I finally put an end to your life,' he said.

Once more, fate stepped in. At that instant, two women emerged from the corner. They stopped and stared at the commotion, their looks enough to let me jerk free. Zerah put away his gun and ran away.

From that moment, I never again felt safe; that is, until I met Christopher, of whom I shall explain later.

The following Sunday I went to the church where I had spent so much of my time. As I waited for the service to commence I reflected on the immensity of the schism that had opened up between Zerah and me due to his philandering. And how there had been a time when he celebrated me as virtuous and beautiful, only now, years later, for me to be defamed as scheming and ugly. I lapsed into silent prayer.

After service, I remained in prayer, only dimly aware of the chatter of choirboys as they exchanged their robes for hats and coats. There was much for which I had to be so grateful.

No. 13 Gloucester-road was, for me, a house of horrors. I had to get as far away as possible. Even today, I would not venture past it.

I wrote to Mr. Holmes, requesting an urgent appointment. A few days later, I visited his office and related my husband's latest actions. He took copious notes and asked me to return the following day when I could read the amended petition.

'What you have told me manifestly strengthens your petition, Mrs. Colburn,' said Mr. Holmes. 'Even so, I should warn that the collapse of your marriage *could* be played out in a courtroom.'

The following day, when I arrived, he placed the final petition in front of me.

'Is that now correct? I am aware your husband's relationship with you has been fraught with truly violent and demeaning behaviour; I hope this petition reflects that.'

I read the text. Items six and seven referred to my latest maltreatments. They read:

6. That on a certain occasion on the second day of February 1870 the said Zerah Colburn struck and otherwise assaulted your Petitioner.

7. That between the twenty ninth day of January and the sixth day of February 1870 the said Zerah Colburn on several occasions struck and kicked your Petitioner and threatened her with violence.

Only when I had read the entire text again, including the additions and agreed the facts, could I regard my task as complete. I made my way to my parents' home.

Before leaving, Mr. Holmes issued a warning.

'I should perhaps point out Mrs. Colburn, that should proceedings be seized upon by the Press and published in newspapers you might find they make hurtful reading. I would advise you to do your best to ignore them. For, the more prurient among their readership might infer that you perhaps either did not satisfy your husband or you took a lover and in doing so drove your husband into the arms of other women. But we know the truth, Mrs. Colburn. You have told me of your husband's indifference to you. Indeed, there is no worse poison than indifference in a marriage. And, in a great city like London, prostitutes will be somewhere to be found; men will seek them out wherever they exist. The prurient might suggest it is normal for men, through their incontinence, to make use of them.'

I departed Mr. Holmes's office feeling deeply disconsolate, perplexed even as to what the future might bring. For a split second I experienced a desire to be no longer part of this world. The prospects for the future were frightening. If Mr. Holmes had intended to console me, his words had the opposite effect.

I had not long to wait for the results of my visit to his office. Solicitors filed the petition for my Divorce – Colburn, Elizabeth Susanna vs Colburn, Zerah – on Wednesday, 16th February 1870, a date I shall not forget.

A week earlier, on Saturday, 12th February, I took up lodgings with a Miss Wilson at No. 40 Woburn-place, Russell-square. Even for a few more days, I could no longer be a burden to my parents who had done so much to help. However, while I believed no one, especially Zerah, would ever conduct a search for me in Russell-square, I continued to live in fear of his sudden appearance. I had to find a place of safety where nothing bad could happen to me. And I had to find employment.

Miss Wilson, a kind, elderly woman, ran a quiet and discrete lodging house for gentlemen and gentlewomen. She offered me a room on the top floor. I took a few essential clothes and, of course, my journal and diary. My remaining clothes hung in a wardrobe at my parents' house. I hoped to collect them one day.

In Russell-square, sometimes I woke early following a nightmare as thoughts returned to those terrible days at

Gloucester-road, surely the worst of my life. No wonder I hated that house – and the man inside.

Outside, just as February's air was cold, inside the warmth of Miss Wilson's house met me as I walked through the door; she supplied a plentiful supply of coal for the fire.

Chapter Thirteen
Little kisses

THE LETTER from William Maw arrived on 21st February, two weeks after my last encounter with Zerah. Suffice to say, after my husband's attacks and threats I hardly dare venture outside my lodgings, save for necessities, and even then I took great precautions.

By taking lodgings with Miss Wilson, should make life difficult for Zerah to find me, I considered. I had no wish for him to discover where I lived, and to ever threaten me again.

At No. 13 Gloucester-road I had learned to live with the consequences of his rasping observations and brutal attacks; but as I had no wish for a repeat of such behaviour, I chose a life of obscurity until I could collect my thoughts. Even so, various aches and pains continued unabated.

My lodgings, however, proved somewhat expensive. I could not continue indefinitely living with Miss Wilson, homely though her house was, but I decided to stay there as long as possible. I could have found cheaper accommodation, or even receive a small payment as a companion. But Russell-square offered such pleasant surroundings that I found it difficult to move: I could lie in my bed in the mornings without interruption. Life with Zerah had instilled ideas above my station. But move I must. I had to find the courage.

I searched once more in the Personal Columns of *The Times* under COMPANIONS and found one from Selina D. Pressland seeking a companion: "A lady, well-mannered, cheerful and domestic. Willing to read aloud in return for remuneration." The address given was 92 Upper Tulse Hill Road, Lambeth. I replied to the advertisement and on meeting Mrs. Pressland, she accepted me and I started immediately. Mrs. Pressland, a widow, appeared to be a lady of independent means. Another lady of my age, Elizabeth Baughton, acted as cook. No one would find me in Lambeth. The accommodation, very comfortable, suited me well.

William's letter came as a great surprise. I recognised his handwriting instantly. He had addressed his envelope in the first instance to No. 11 Cambridge-Terrace, but mother redirected it to 92 Upper Tulse Hill Road.

What I found inside proved most disturbing. William perhaps intended to set my mind at rest. Instead, he raised many uncertainties that served only to concern me. His letter had the formality of a business letter.

I still have it:

Dear Mrs. Colburn,

Please consider the contents of this letter as Private and Confidential. I thought you ought to be aware of your husband's latest movements.

Following disagreement with Mr. Henry Bessemer, Mr. Colburn stood down as editor of *Engineering* and relinquished control over editorial content and management.

Mr. Colburn departed the offices of *Engineering* without as much as a backward glance or farewell. For him it had been an oasis; a refuge from the regrets and complications of his life. He did not clear his desk, as Mr. Bessemer requested. There are several small personal effects. If you require them, we can hold them until collected; failing that, we can dispose of them.

Both Mr. James Dredge and I wish to express our deep regret at your husband's departure. It has been our great pleasure to work with him from the beginning of publication. Readers of *Engineering* will miss his writing. He had great acuity. As a writer on engineering matters, he was surely without equal. His intellect and fluency of writing were undoubted; his understanding of the subject wide and penetrating. His scientific judgements too were perceptive and he displayed an energetic initiative in writing about important engineering developments. He never, for one moment, demonstrated any lack of confidence; his leadership always flinty. He much believed he had every entitlement to comment on any development, large or small. He often said that scepticism should be the natural instinct of any journalist. We have both learnt much from him.

He intended the columns of his new paper should, without exception, take special care to give America, and Americans, ample space for fair hearings. And so it was, for he considered his roots were in America, the place of his birth. And it was through his long established friend, Mr. Alexander Holley, that its circulation in that country was properly established

As you may be aware, he enjoyed a 'magic circle' of fellow followers within the engineering fraternity; we equated it to the shared activity of small iron filings that are drawn to a magnetic presence.

However, the last months of his tenure were not without their problems. Increasingly, his life revolved around excesses of various kinds. His character carried many flaws; in particular he could be unpleasant and arrogant. His personal discipline also has endured severe strain, to the point that an atmosphere of sustained rancour developed within the office. Indeed, he issued some instructions with such severity as to cause many to quail. In the light of such disharmony, and Mr. Colburn's tarnished personal reputation which seemingly he made no attempt to protect, Mr. Bessemer informed he could not allow matters to fester further. Mr. Colburn's position had become untenable.

I can tell you that as to Mr. Colburn's financial interests in *Engineering*, Mr. Bessemer has transferred those to Mr. Alexander Hollingsworth, who will manage the business. Mr. Dredge and I continue with joint editorial responsibility.

Increasingly a tormented writer, your husband also accrued substantial debts. He made a considerable and, at times, exhausting effort to remain ahead of his creditors, but eventually he failed. Many pursued him through writs and bailiffs; all caused him – and Mr. Bessemer – much distraction. Mr. Bessemer has arranged with Lamb's of Conduit-street for sale by auction of your husband's furniture and personal effects from his house as part of selling up. His clothes also will be taken and sold in a further attempt to reduce his indebtedness.

You may not be aware, but Mr. Colburn has now departed this country. We understand he travelled to Paris, though of this we cannot be certain. If I obtain further information of your husband's whereabouts, I will write.

Should you believe I can be of help, please write to me in confidence at *Engineering*. Perhaps we could meet at your convenience.

Yours, in the strictest confidence,
William Maw.

William displayed much courage in writing. Reading between the lines, Zerah was in no fit state to continue his position at the helm of *Engineering*, the journal he founded only four years previously. However, his addiction to alcohol and opium surely caused his downfall, as much as any moral misbehaviour. Fear of the courts and the Press, and the humiliation were he to lose, no doubt caused him to flee. The news much pleased me.

The contents of the letter were at best sketchy, and my

inquisitive nature yearned for more. I wondered what personal items William had discovered in Zerah's desk. I was intrigued.

And so Zerah had fled England, the country he claimed to love so much. Why did this apparently most British figure leave behind so many of the things he cherished: his London clubs, the engineering gossip, the circle of friends – and women of the street? I knew of course: he could not accept what fate had in store. He had ruined my life, dragging me down; and ruined his own too.

If Zerah travelled to Paris, did he have plans to remain? Or would he return to England, and London? Would he seek me out? If he planned a return, my life could be in danger. Zerah Colburn was a violent and dangerous man. Should he be 'on the loose' in London he could be a menace, not only to me but possibly to the staff of *Engineering*, were he to pursue revenge.

Shortly after the arrival of William's letter, I received a visitor. Peggy, our housekeeper had sought out my parents who, after introductions, redirected her to my lodgings. Pleased to see her, I prepared cups of tea. I had no cakes to offer.

If both William and Peggy were able to find me, then so too could my husband, should he return to London. This was of serious concern. I later told my parents to be careful to whom they revealed my address.

Peggy told me that she and Emma had been 'paid off' by Mr. Colburn. She said it took place without warning. One morning Mr. Colburn arrived and instructed them to collect their belongings and leave immediately. Then he closed the house.

'He no longer required our services,' said Peggy.

I was sorry for both women. Emma had burst in tears, Peggy told me. I could do nothing to help. I thanked Peggy for everything she had done to assist me in my plight. I hoped one day I could repay her kindness.

Meanwhile, I decided to take up William's suggestion. The following day, I wrote a short note to him at *Engineering*. Writing from Woburn-place, I suggested our previous venue in the

Reading Room of the British Museum, at 11 a.m. that Friday. I added that I would be grateful to see Mr. Colburn's personal possessions.

I received a reply almost by return agreeing arrangements; the location was convenient for William, although tedious for me.

We arrived coincidently at the museum's entrance, but William then suggested a secluded coffee house nearby where we could talk in confidence. We walked in silence; I felt no discomfort. It seemed perfectly natural; in contrast, our earlier meeting at the museum proved most surreptitious.

Having ordered coffee and muffins, William asked what I wished to know.

'But first,' he said, 'the departure of your husband from *Engineering* changes our relationship somewhat. I have a feeling we may see more of one another in the months ahead. I hope we remain friends. Please address me as William, as you have been doing.'

'In that case,' I replied, 'please call me Elizabeth.'

He reiterated how Zerah's behaviour had become completely irrational, inexplicable even; made worse by his obsessions for alcohol and drugs. I knew Zerah drank far too much alcohol, liquor as he called it. Did he use it to ease the pain of his sickness? I hated those occasions when he returned to the house smelling of drink. I avoided him where I could; unashamed to admit my fear. His behaviour endangered his own life as well as others. Emily Maw had been rightly concerned for the well-being of her husband. Zerah's mercury treatment, if indeed he received treatment and the combined effects of opium and alcohol together formed a dangerous cocktail. He had no discipline to help himself.

'Your husband was an unhealthy man, Mrs. Colburn,' said William, forgetting the agreement he made a few minutes earlier. 'His urge for drink and his craving for opium lit an explosive charge within his head from which there was no escape. On occasions, he was delirious. We could continue no longer. Mr.

Bessemer was aware of your husband's state of mind and would have taken matters into his own hands had Mr. Colburn not pre-empted matters by handing in a letter of resignation following verbal disagreements with Mr. Bessemer. Previously, both men were great friends. Now, alas, Mr. Bessemer is one of your husband's unforgiving friends – an enemy even.'

'I have no wish to pry, but can you think of anything that might throw light on these personal matters?' asked William. 'For example, would you know why he took the train to Paris?'

I thought for a moment. Surely, William would know the reason. Again, I suspected that William, in keeping with his character, was much too inquisitive. I could have told him about Zerah's syphilis. This disease, together with the poisonous effects of any mercury treatment, as well as the alcohol and drugs, could have caused Zerah to collapse into depression and act irrationally. In the event, I broached the subject only obliquely. I did not know how much William really knew about Zerah's physical state, given they spent so much time together.

'He may have been physically unwell and this may have contributed to his problems,' I said rather lamely. I knew no cause to explain his visit to Paris, but I could imagine one.

'In that case, what I have to tell you will prove hurtful,' said William. 'And for this I apologise in advance.'

'Please proceed,' I replied nervously, wondering what to expect.

'Mr. Colburn told us with some obvious pride, yet in a somewhat delirious and rambling voice, of plans to visit to Paris to see his muse. He hoped they could live together in that city. Should that fail, he said, he would return to America, to meet a former lady friend.'

I was shocked, and stared at William in silence. For the first time, did I detect a malicious streak in the man I regarded as a friend? William could have maintained his silence. What he said was hurtful. A muse? Was she his mistress? I knew not of her existence. And why did he ask me about Paris when he already knew the answer? And who did Zerah mean by 'a former lady friend'?

I hoped my face displayed displeasure; however, William continued, seemingly unaware of my feelings.

'I have yet more upsetting information, Mrs. Colburn. Much has happened behind your back. I have to tell you that some of us knew that Mr. Colburn had, for some time, engaged in an *affaire du coeur* with Lucy Taylor, a kitchen hand at No. 37 Bedford-street,' he said. 'It was common knowledge in the building. She had a room in the attic; it was a simple matter for the two to spend time together. Some people gossiped she was his mistress. They gave her a nickname – Juicy Lucy. There was gossip too of Mr. Colburn's liaisons with other women during the day. Life must have been difficult for you. Remain assured that Emily and I offer you our deepest sympathies and condolences.'

William knew almost as much about Zerah as I, but not quite. Thanks to Mr. Bentley, what I knew could and would incriminate Zerah. However, in my view, to have mistresses in London *and* Paris plunged Zerah to new depths; but Juicy Lucy; that *was* a new name.

I began to feel more confident, though I remained concerned about future physical assaults Zerah might inflict. For the first time I was in control. Zerah was powerless – providing he did not find me.

There were fleeting moments when I longed to be his closest and indeed only friend; I had sought reassurance and affection in his arms. However, this was not to be. No one, not even I, could peer through the blocked keyhole to the secret chamber in Zerah's head that defined his other world. He had no wish for me to be close, except for one reason, and one reason only.

Zerah's actions were in complete opposition to the Christian attitudes towards honour, love and marriage I had grown up with and which remained dear in spite of a ruined life. Here was a man whose actions mocked family life. Was he not weighed down by an inner guilt from illicit love or wanton lust – guilt that left indelible stains?

That Zerah was a serial adulterer offered only half the story; there were his paroxysms of anger too. Such anger would carry no boundaries, given the exposure and humiliation that publication of his shameful malpractices would bring were I to pursue him through the courts. There would be public disgrace, ignominy and shame.

Every detail of my abused body would be widely reported for public scrutiny in the Press. Journalists would have a field day; seen as one of their own they would expose him for his hypocrisy; surely the last accusation Zerah would desire. Colleagues and important acquaintances would then recognise the true nature of the man they regarded as their engineering figurehead; the man who praised Samuel Smiles for *Self Help*.

That might explain his escape to Paris. Had he decided to begin a new life in the French capital? He spoke fluent French and would feel secure in the city. And did he have mistress waiting for him? Was she the muse? I had seen no correspondence from France arriving at the house.

Had I remained a timid and dutiful wife, Zerah would have pursued unhindered his flamboyant lifestyle. That I intended to seek divorce through the courts to expose his behaviour was surely one spark that ignited his departure from his beloved England. His future was bleak.

'You are very quiet, Elizabeth,' said William, suddenly remembering our agreement.

'I am thinking,' I replied. 'I have said enough for the moment. I am sure you will understand how careful I must be.'

'Well, I can shed further light on his visit to Paris,' said William.

William's right hand moved to an inside pocket to withdraw a small bundle of envelopes. He handed them to me. Someone had tied them with string. I scrutinised the writing before placing the envelopes to my nostrils. A hint of expensive perfume lingered.

'All were posted in Paris,' he said. 'The letters are in French. They are love letters.'

I looked again at the handwriting; neat, small and rounded it reflected a young person. In the top left-hand corner were the words: '*Petit bisous*'.

'I understand only a little of the French language,' I said, handing William the letters. 'I would not understand them. Destroy them.'

The feel and sight of the envelopes unsettled me further. On the contrary, I knew the meaning of the two French words: 'Little kisses'. I would never know what endearments this woman had extended to my husband; this mistress in Paris who ensnared Zerah and lured him from me. Was ignorance bliss?

'What is her name?' I asked, curiously.

'Louise,' he replied.

There was silence. I had no clutch of love letters from Zerah to treasure and preserve as evidence that he once loved me. I had just a tiny scrap of paper with 'I have great plans. Marry me' written on it. I was to be part of his 'plan'. It did not carry an ounce of emotional tenderness or closeness, such as: 'I love you so much and long to spend the rest of my life with you. Marry me.'

I changed the subject and turned to another matter.

William said 'You asked for Mr. Colburn's personal items. Alas, there were not many, apart from the letters. He used several paper knives and they are here. There were also several quill pens; I viewed them as of no consequence.'

'Thank you, William,' I said, as he handed me the knives. 'I have no attachment or even need of them. Destroy them also.'

Taking them, William pronounced: 'You must come and take tea with Emily and me – or even come for Sunday luncheon. I know Emily would enjoy seeing you again. Please write when you feel able. And in the meantime I will inform you of any developments that affect you with respect to your husband.'

'Thank you William, I would much enjoy paying you both a

visit,' I said. We then went our separate ways.

OOOOOOOOOOOOOOOOOOOOO

BASED on William's information, and my own understanding of Zerah's condition, I surmised how my first husband's visit to Paris might have taken place:

Crossing a choppy English Channel, from which no doubt he would be attacked continuously by spray as he stood exposed to the elements on deck of the paddle steamer as it forged its way to France, Zerah would have arrived in Calais and caught the first train to Paris. He would cut a remote figure as he took his seat in the carriage.

No longer interested in locomotives or rolling stock, as was his usual habit, his sole intent would be to reach the French capital as quickly as possible. Calais to Paris was his quickest route by far and I am sure he would have had a flask of whisky in his pocket and enough opium to take him through the journey.

On arrival in the city, he would have made his way to No. 6 rue Tournon, the home of Dr. Philippe Ricord, one of Paris's most celebrated surgeons who specialised in venereal diseases. The doctor had become famous for establishing syphilis (the pox) and gonorrhea (the clap) were quite different infections. In his researches he had even categorised the different stages of syphilis.

Dr. Ricord had retired from practice some 10 years previously but remained partially active having been 'honoured', the previous October, as consulting surgeon to Napoleon III.

Like Zerah, Dr. Ricord was American by birth, though he chose to make France his residence. Dr. Ricord, born in Baltimore in 1800, studied medicine in Philadelphia before settling in Paris in 1820; he graduated in medicine six years later. In 1831, he became surgeon-in-chief at the Hôpital des Vénériens, later renamed Hôpital du Midi. There, he quickly established a reputation as the country's leading syphilis physician. Following this, he earned worldwide repute in his speciality of venereal diseases. As Americans both, Zerah would reckon the two men had at least one factor in common.

Zerah pulled the bell at No. 6. An elderly woman appeared.

"Oui," said the housekeeper.

Believing it best to speak in English, Zerah said: "Can I see Monsieur Dr. Ricord? I am an American in Paris and urgently require his advice."

"Un moment," she replied.

Within minutes, a man of 70 shuffled out of the gloomy interior to confront Zerah at the door.

"What do you want?" he asked, with a slight but still noticeable American drawl.

"I request a consultation, please," replied Zerah. "I have travelled from England for your most esteemed advice."

"I do not see patients," responded Dr. Ricord, curtly. "My work with the public is finished."

"Please, can we talk for one minute," pleaded Zerah. "You are the only man I can turn to. If I may say so, you are the master; the specialist in these matters. Also, I detect a fellow American."

"Many people tell me that. Eh bien, un moment. Come in."

Dr. Ricord's Paris house, befitting someone reputedly the wealthiest doctor in France, contained five magnificently furnished rooms; they were once used for patients. Men had their own waiting room downstairs, while women reached their upstairs waiting room using a separate staircase. Another salon catered for friends and fellow doctors. It was to this room that Dr. Ricord led Zerah.

"Be seated," said Dr. Ricord.

"Thank you," said Zerah, who had not seen so many books in one room. They stretched on every wall from floor to high ceiling.

Dr. Ricord retreated behind a large desk and slumped into his chair.

"I will not beat about the bush. I do not need to tell you what is wrong with me," Zerah declared. "You are the acknowledged authority. Is there anything, I repeat, anything you can do to help? I have tried everything that I know. I am desperate."

"Yes, I know what ails you," replied Dr. Ricord with a shrug of his shoulders. "I can tell just by looking at you. I have seen many like you in my time. Speaking frankly, you are seriously afflicted. I can examine you, but I suspect there is nothing I can do. You have left it far too late."

Dr. Ricord shrugged his shoulders again in a dismissive manner.

"I also do not need to tell you that treatments are toxic with unpleasant side effects. They have limited effectiveness. Nevertheless, I know of instances where poisons like mercury have cured some nasty cases of syphilis."

"Please examine me. Perhaps, for once, you might be wrong," replied Zerah.

"I am not wrong. I do not make mistakes. Tell me about yourself; where are you from?" asked Dr. Ricord. "From your voice, I hazard you are from New York.'

Zerah's manner became irritable and impatient. He was close to vomiting. He regarded the surgeon's tactics as nothing short of time wasting, yet Zerah knew he must humour the doctor.

"I am a journalist and publisher," Zerah told the doctor. "I was born in Saratoga, New York. I became a locomotive engineer before moving to New York City in the 'fifties. There I published a weekly newspaper for railroad presidents and their managers. In 1858, I travelled to England and worked for an English engineering newspaper in London. Two years later, I created my own weekly newspaper in Philadelphia, but after three months, the financial crash hit the paper. I closed it."

At this point Dr. Ricord's eyes lit up.

"Philadelphia? I studied medicine in Philadelphia," he said. "I was born in Baltimore. They have railroads there too, you know. I left America when I was 20 and came to the French capital, where I graduated in medicine. So, we have one thing in common – we both left America to seek our fortunes."

Zerah was becoming increasingly agitated; he was getting nowhere.

"What happened after your newspaper closed?"

Zerah sat impatiently on the edge of his chair.

"I returned to London, where I have been ever since," he replied. "Six years ago I established my own newspaper, called *Engineering*, but in the last year I have found it difficult to concentrate. I departed the paper a few days ago. I could continue no longer with the work."

"I see. So the pox badly affects your way of life."

"Of course it does," snapped Zerah.

"Now, now, that will not help," replied Dr. Ricord. "Let us see what we can do. I do not hold out much hope for you. It looks to me as though the disease has progressed too far. Let us go to the next room and I will briefly examine you."

Dr. Ricord led the way. In the corner was a large screen; in the opposite corner another very large desk. It was completely empty.

"Remove your clothes and I will return in five minutes," said Dr. Ricord.

When the doctor returned he proceeded with his examination. It was over in a few minutes.

"Replace your clothing and return to my study," said the doctor, leaving the room.

It was not long before the doctor returned to his study with two glasses in one hand and a bottle of brandy in the other. He set the glasses on the table and half-filled them.

He handed a glass to Zerah, before grasping the other.

"To us both," he declared. "The Lord be with us."

"I am very sorry, but it is as I thought," he continued slowly, nodding his head. "The disease is too far advanced. I can do nothing for you. Yes, I can offer mercury ointment. I warn you it is very toxic – but maybe you have tried it already. We do not yet fully understand this disease. Many people are working on it including M. Fournier, who was perhaps the best student I ever had at the Hôpital du Midi. Even for him, progress is slow. I hope he will soon have success."

"As for you, mon ami, I very sorry, but I cannot help you," said Dr. Ricord. "You will not be pleased to hear that, but if I may say so, you have wrought your own destruction."

Zerah was crestfallen. The brandy quickly had a warming effect.

It had been a long journey – all for nothing. He had half expected the result, but now there was no alternative. He had made up his mind. There was only one thing to do.

"Thank you, at the very least I have tried," replied Zerah, shaking hands with the doctor. "Thank you for the brandy."

"Bon chance," said Dr. Ricord, raising his right hand. 'Adieu.'

As he too raised his hand, Zerah was not so much waving goodbye as drowning in despair – despair that would have tragic consequences.

Before leaving the city, however, Zerah made his way to some memorable haunts. He went to the Grand Hotel where he and William stayed for the 1867 Paris Exhibition. He recognised no one; even the manager he knew so well was no longer in residence. In a period as short as three years, the city and the people had changed so much. Wide, fashionable avenues had materialised as if from nowhere.

Even Louise, the irresistible *femme fatale* with whom he had rendezvoused on many occasions for their *cinq à sept* interludes together in bed all those years ago, he could find no trace. She was not at her address. Was she with another lover, or married with child? For Zerah this was possibly an unrequited love that managed to slip from his noose. But was even she a lover he could not bear living with permanently?

Memories of the exhibition rekindled his ideas for a French engineering newspaper, *L'Ingenierie*, but those thoughts faded as quickly as they arrived. He would require finance from many quarters and he knew no one in France who would support him as had Mr. Bessemer.

During the first few months of 1870, the mood in Paris had been buoyant, confident and expansionist. Building took place on a large scale as the country embarked on reconstruction and architectural revolution. At the same time, others were preoccupied with how to deal with the ever-threatening Prussians. With the benefit of hindsight, it would not have been an ideal time to commence a new journal as the Franco-Prussian war began on 19th July 1870; it ended on 10th May 1871 having put paid to ideas of a Channel Tunnel, although Mr. Low, Mr. Brunlees and Mr. Hawkshaw did submit new ideas in April 1871.

Meanwhile, Zerah took the train to Le Havre where, with barely sufficient money, he calmly boarded a Boston-bound passenger ship to face his destiny.

OOOOOOOOOOOOOOOOOOOOOOO

I ACCEPTED William's offer and the following weekend joined them at their house. In her letter, Emily wrote to say she would expect me in time for luncheon on Saturday, 5th March and bring overnight clothes, as they wished me to stay the weekend.

That was a most welcome suggestion as I continued my lonely residence at No. 40 Woburn-place. Despite William's news of Zerah's departure for Paris, I experienced continual feelings of fear and insecurity. On the one hand, his news brought some relief; relief that Zerah no longer posed an immediate threat. On the other hand, there remained that element of hidden danger as to the exact certainty of his whereabouts, and his future plans.

Zerah could return at any moment and I had no desire for him to confront me with his huge frame. Previous encounters would remain in my mind for a long time to come.

I wanted to give myself as much distance as possible from the vicissitudes of scandal and sexual intrigue that hung like dark clouds around Zerah Colburn's name. I presumed that in the tightly knit world of publishing, rumours of his misdeeds could leak out to fellow journalists, and the name Zerah Colburn would conjure elements of multifarious seedy and disgraceful behaviour. I no longer had the desire to be seen as the wife of Zerah Colburn. Indeed, that moment marked the hatred I had for my husband. I had no wish to be known as Mrs. Colburn.

I much enjoyed my time with the Maws. We played card games and dominoes, talked and read books.

Emily and William were becoming my firm friends; indeed my only friends outside family. I appreciated their kindness. On Sunday morning, we attended the nearby Baptist church where the minister delivered a thought-provoking sermon on the subject of sanctification. He based this on Paul's Epistle to Titus, chapter 2, verses 11 and 12:

'For the grace of God that bringeth salvation hath appeared to all men, teaching us that, denying ungodliness and worldly lusts, we should live soberly, righteously, and godly, in this present world'.

I found the verse most appropriate for someone in my predicament. The minister impressed everyone with his powerful, if somewhat fiery words and references to temptations of the flesh. Zerah should have been present in the congregation to meditate on the implications of the sermon. The minister preached that if we loved God, we would not want to do anything that was against His will.

After church, we returned to the house, where William poured out a small sherry each. This was followed by cold luncheon and a delicious pudding. Afterwards I left the Maws to themselves and retraced my steps to Woburn-place, furtively looking behind from time to time to see if I was being followed.

The couple had been kind and did not pry into my private life; though I presumed they would have wished to know more about 'life at the Colburns', especially William. However, I maintained a dignified silence, not knowing what the future might bring. Had Zerah raised the matter of my petition for divorce with Mr. Bessemer? If he did, then I might assume William would know 'something'. However, I did not know.

One fact was undeniable. My status had changed. I was no longer the wife of the 'conductor.' Zerah had used that word to describe himself; he even put the word 'conductor' on the front page of *Engineering*: 'Conducted by Zerah Colburn'. His was the opinion that such words gave him and his journal an air of authority.

Zerah achieved fame at an early age as a locomotive engineer, but when he became an editor he exploited the romantic opportunities it brought; and much worse than romantic opportunities.

Whereas previously I enjoyed some status as the editor's wife, that no longer existed; I had become a woman without husband, though still addressed as Mrs. Colburn. I hated that. Much more to the point, I was concerned about my finances as I no longer benefitted from any income. All I had was that which I had saved from my weekly allowance from Zerah, which was small. I was, and am to this day, prudent in my spending habits. Father taught us all to save, and this has remained part of my daily life.

'Save your pennies and the pounds will take care of themselves,' father would say. I was not entirely without money, but I had to be particularly prudent. I would have to find work. My parents were content for me to stay at home with them for as long as I chose, but I knew that before long I would have to enter the world again.

Before I left the Maws' house, William repeated his promise to keep me abreast of any developments. He assured me that if he and Mr. Dredge received any news of Zerah, they would inform me.

Meanwhile, my solicitor having delivered the petition for divorce, failed to bring Zerah to court. Indeed, Mr. Holmes had had the reverse effect. He and I had driven Zerah out of the country he loved.

On 9th March 1870, a letter from Mr. Holmes declared that on the preceding day, the "Judge Ordinary had read a statement filed on behalf of the petitioner (myself), and having heard counsel thereon in default of appearance of respondent to the Citation issued against him (Zerah Colburn), in the Cause directed, that the Cause be heard by oral evidence before the Court itself."

Chapter Fourteen
Death in an orchard

I HEARD first of Zerah's death from William. He came with the news to my parents' house, No. 11 Cambridge-terrace. The housemaid, Louise, led William into the front room. I soon joined him. It was Tuesday, 3rd May 1870.

We exchanged pleasantries and I offered him a seat. We had not spoken since our last meeting when we attended church.

'Will you take tea, William?' I asked. 'How did you find me?'

'I went first to your lodgings in Woburn-place, but Mrs. Wilson explained your return to your parents,' he replied.

I had lodged in Woburn-place for some six weeks or so, until the end of March, when no longer could I afford to remain. I judged it safe to join my parents, anxious as ever for my return. Also, by then I had little money remaining.

William declined my offer of tea and instead launched into the purpose of his visit; so typical was it of him to concentrate on matters in hand.

'I am sorry to have to inform you, Mrs. Colburn, but I have distressing news.'

William had reverted to calling me Mrs. Colburn. I wondered what could be so important; his voice carried the tone of someone on official business. William looked so serious.

'You can call me Elizabeth, William,' I told him.

'We heard by the new electric telegraph today from Mr. Alexander Holley, you may remember him. He informed us of the death of your husband,' said William, ignoring my interjection. 'Apparently Mr. Colburn committed suicide in a pear orchard in Belmont, not far distant from Boston in the United States of America.'

I could hardly trust my hearing.

William's news carried a significance far beyond the word 'suicide'. In that moment I experienced relief; not the usual

359

release of anguished tears associated with death. Suddenly, I had emerged into bright sunlight and freedom; released at last from an abusive husband and the chains that bound me to him. Should I remove the two rings he gave me nearly 10 years previously? Life's pendulum had finally swung in my favour.

Feelings of joy turned to bewilderment. I would be alone for the first time in 10 years; completely alone with only myself for company. I had my parents, but they could not care for me. Who would care for me? Who would feed and clothe me? What work could I undertake? Could I return to domestic service?

William had paused, perhaps expecting the usual outpouring of tears. I could not experience grief's rolling depths at his passing; just relief. Without a word from me, he continued:

'Boys walking a dog found Mr. Colburn lying on the ground with a gunshot wound to the head. The boys went in search of a policeman. Later, constables came and arranged your husband's removal to Boston General Hospital where he died next day. I am sorry to bear such bad news, Mrs. Colburn.'

What an extraordinary series of events. Ordinarily, William's news would have been distressing in the extreme; to lose one's husband in such a manner would be awful. But I experienced no feeling of sadness in the knowledge of his death. Rather, I did not know whether I should laugh or cry. Zerah dead; it could not be true, surely. I could not think straight.

I said to William: 'Goodness me.'

We looked at each other. We could not decide who should first break the silence. Did William expect me to burst into tears, or demonstrate grief? I resented the manner of my treatment at Zerah's hands, and the wretchedness he created. For this reason, it pleased me – unchristian like - to learn of his death.

The silence continued as, quite suddenly, I put myself in Zerah's position. He had decided never to see the inside of a court of law, or to look his victim – me – in the eye again.

Then I heard William's voice.

'Mr. Dredge and I have tried to perceive a reason why your

husband should kill himself. Mr. Dredge, ever observant – he described your husband as 'the spirit of darkness' following their first meeting – likened him to Narcissus, the youth in Greek mythology who, you may remember, was so handsome everyone fell in love with him, which hardened his heart. He became indifferent to others and the gods, who grew tired of the human wreckage he left in his wake, and placed a curse on him so he would know the pain of unrequited love. Shortly after, Narcissus happened to pass a pond and, on catching sight of his own reflection, fell in love with himself. So drawn was he to the reflection that he dived into the water to be with it and drowned.'

I nodded. I wanted to change the subject. I kept counsel. I had my own view about Zerah's suicide; he had reached the edge of the precipice and, realising the futility of his existence, fell into oblivion.

Towards the end of his life in London, Zerah appeared to lack power over himself. The once enthusiastic advocate of self-help could not finally help himself. He had returned to his roots where, filled with self-doubt, he barely had enough strength to pull the trigger; even then not very effectively. Zerah left this world without saying 'Goodbye'. Our last exchanges were acrimonious.

William's news, if anything, served as an antidote to sorrow. Here at last, to my immense relief, the news heralded an end to my turbulent years.

'I am very sorry,' said William again. 'If there is anything I can – that we can do, because I include Emily – then please do not hesitate to write to me at *Engineering* or to Emily at our house. Emily said she would much like to see you and personally offer condolences. You can stay with us should you wish. As before, you can remain for the weekend, or even longer, should you so desire.'

'That is indeed kind of you, William,' I replied. 'Please inform Emily that I shall write, and I am sure we can meet soon.'

I owed William an explanation as to why I lived with my

parents. I had no wish to enter into details, but saw no reason either to be ashamed of anything I had done.

'As you may be aware, before Mr. Colburn left for Paris, relations between us became exceedingly strained. Mr. Colburn closed the house at No. 13 Gloucester-road, and I had no alternative but to seek immediate accommodation. It pleased me to leave and I quickly found lodgings in Woburn-place, but after a time I assessed it safe to return to my parents until I more permanently find my feet,' I said. 'They wished me home again.'

'You may not be aware of it, William, but I planned to divorce Mr. Colburn. But, from your news, that will no longer be necessary.'

'I am sorry to hear that, Mrs. Colburn, but in the circumstances I am not surprised. I imagine your husband was not easy man to endure, nevertheless while he enjoyed a gilded life he continued to possess unfulfilled talent as a writer.

William, as disciple, felt obliged to remain faithful to his former editor.

'He could be difficult,' I replied, suddenly experiencing a release of emotion. 'I do not like to speak ill of the dead, but he made life very difficult, though now I am free to it say his conduct was one of pride, obstinacy and cruelty. I never knew where I was with him. One minute he could be kind, and the next he would embark on a tirade about the most trivial. However, his moments of kindness were few and transitory. Arguments and sulks lasted for weeks, resulting in, for me, sleepless and tearful nights. He could start an argument and quickly thereafter lose his temper. He became violent and angry and beat me. He inflicted regular bruising. Such were the consequences for me of an intensely fractured relationship. He subjected me to humiliations of all kinds. I had no alternative but to seek divorce.'

I wondered afterwards if I had exaggerated Zerah's brutality. However, what he imposed was evil beyond comprehension.

'If I may say so, Mrs. Colburn,' said William. 'You have been very brave – and tolerant. Your decision to divorce may have acted as the catalyst for his last visit to Paris. I say 'may', for it required only the slightest challenge to his authority to cause him to fly off the rails. He was an unbalanced man, a sick man, I maintain. Mr. Colburn could not live facing rejection. He looked ill; his face and hands were grey.'

'Did Mr. Holley offer other references to my husband?' I asked, never once daring to challenge Zerah's authority myself.

'He suggested that should we carry an obituary in *Engineering* – which we will – then he would be privileged to contribute. I responded that we would be delighted,' replied William. 'As editor, I will prepare one myself, but I am not familiar enough with Mr. Colburn's early years in locomotive engineering and publishing. I may combine my own tribute with some of Mr. Holley's words.'

'Mr. Holley promised to dispatch copies of obituaries that appear in Boston and Lowell newspapers,' added William. 'It seems the suicide has attracted reports in some papers and yet more will follow in the wake of the inquest. I have no knowledge as to how Americans deal with suicides, but I imagine it is similar to that which is adopted here.'

'When did the suicide attempt occur?' I asked.

'Well, in his second telegraph in response to our questions, Mr. Holley informed us the attempt took place on Monday, 25th. April. Mr. Colburn died next day, three days after William Shakespeare's birthday. Had he planned to die on the Baird's birthday but become confused?'

'According to Mr. Holley, the Certificate of Death gave his age as 40, and his occupation as draughtsman,' added William.

I thought for a moment.

'That is strange,' I replied. 'Mr. Colburn was 37, not 40 – he was born 13th. January 1833 – and he was not a draughtsman. I well recall his birth day. I always wondered if 13 would prove unlucky.'

'At the inquest on Friday, 29th April, the coroner stated Mr.

Colburn's body was identified by Mr. John Winslow, superintendent of the Boston & Lowell Railroad and an old friend of your husband,' disclosed William. 'Possibly he suggested Mr. Colburn's age and gave the only occupation of which he was aware.'

'When will they hold the funeral? And where?' I asked.

'Mr. Holley's telegraph informed that it will be held tomorrow, Wednesday, 4th May,' said William. 'Mr. Holley offered to attend on behalf of *Engineering*, and I accepted.'

'Mr. Colburn will be interred in Lawrence-street Cemetery, Lowell, in a charity 'lot' of the Hospital Association. It is a special lot – a pauper's lot – for poor people, former workers at the Lowell Machine Shop,' William continued

'Is it to be a pauper's funeral? Are they not able to afford a more appropriate burial?' I asked.

'It seems not,' William told me. 'All that was discovered on his person was a pocket watch, a magnifying glass and 27 dollars and 51 cents, according to Mr. Holley, who had read reports in newspapers.'

'Are they likely to bury my husband in an unconsecrated portion of the burial ground?'

'I do not know, Mrs. Colburn.' William then changed the subject. 'Would you like to see the newspaper reports when they arrive? It seems Mr. Holley has already written one obituary for *The New York Times*. The newspaper published it yesterday.'

'Do please call me Elizabeth,' I said. 'We have known each other many years now. And, yes please, I would like to read these reports, if only to understand more fully what happened.'

'I will ask Mr. Holley to collect all available reports and dispatch them. It will of course take many weeks before they arrive.'

And with those remarks William departed, swallowed up in the sun-blessed streets of London.

I could not quite absorb the enormity of Zerah's death. There was finality in William's news. Would I miss him? Hardly. It was as though someone had extracted an aching tooth. I felt relief, yet his death introduced a gap. How would that gap be filled? I could show no remorse whatsoever for what had happened. He caused all my troubles, and it was he who ended his life. Fortunately, I had no cause to write, as a token of respect as some did on the death of a loved one, any letters on black-bordered notepaper informing recipients of Zerah's death.

Following William's departure, my mother naturally displayed curiosity as to his purpose.

I repeated what William told me. While I did so, my mind moved ahead. No longer married, I had become a widow.

I could sense my parents' relief to hear of Zerah's death. Father hinted 'that man Colburn' had 'chickened' and 'run away' from problems he caused in England. Seething, he knew the solicitor would require payment; and Mr. Bentley's account had to be settled. Mother was more sympathetic.

'Life has a way of healing itself,' she told me. 'You will meet a good man one day and marry.'

I felt obliged to dress in black, wear a widow's bonnet and enter into mourning, as the custom. On this I consulted mother; she advised that as I was no longer a resident of Gloucester-road and among its neighbours, I had no requirement to demonstrate the more usual mourning, the more so as I did not mourn his loss. Certainly, women could be expected to spend at least two-and-a-half years mourning a lost husband; some confined it to a year. Mother directed that it would be a 'waste of money' to mourn, however slim and youthful I might look in black. I considered myself sensible enough to grieve for no more than three months, and that discretely. For rather than grieve, I recall his death as a beautiful moment – though perhaps I did not realise the complete extent of it at the time. All I could feel was an overwhelming sense of peace and relief that together flooded through my whole body.

And, as I had cause to send so few letters of correspondence, I resisted as before, the purchase of black-bordered stationary and cards.

Free at last; Zerah's death triggered my release. In a heart-wrenching twist of fate, he delivered the freedom I yearned and deserved for so long. God had delivered me out of prison.

In the preceding year, I had been desperate. Misused as a person, it seemed not to matter what I did to try to improve our relationship: he could be violent in his passion or hard and cold in his conversation. He killed any sensitivity and loving emotions I had at one time held towards him.

Had Zerah killed himself out of kindness to me? Or was he close to madness – the madness of a genius – as evident from his temper and tantrums? I guessed neither caused his death. He surely committed suicide because of the damage our divorce would inflict on his pride. If I had not intended to pursue divorce, would he still be alive? Had I, inadvertently and remotely, killed Zerah Colburn? Was I the catalyst of his death, as William inferred?

For me, it was now a matter of what to do next.

A few weeks later, the death of another writer was announced – that of Mr. Charles Dickens whom my husband so admired; a man who lived life at a furious pace. Could it be just a coincidence that two literary Catherine wheels should expire almost simultaneously?

On 20th May, as if by some unwritten mutual agreement, *Engineering* and *The Engineer* published obituaries to Zerah Colburn. William brought copies of both. As promised, he had written the obituary in *Engineering*. It was long and deserving.

William did not stay on that occasion – he had passed by on his way to the newspaper's office; he could not delay. William suggested I read *The Engineer's* obituary very carefully.

Following William's departure, I sat down and studied both newspapers. I read first the short text in *The Engineer*. The kindly obituary in *Engineering* understandably was longer – it ran to over two columns. *The Engineer's* obituary began harmlessly but later contained harsh comments:

"It seldom falls to the lot of the journalist to discharge a sadder day than that which we have to perform to-day in announcing the death of an engineer for several years connected with this paper, and whose name will be familiar to each one of our readers."

It went on, after reporting his suicide:

"In this way has passed from amongst us an engineer whose abilities were sufficient, had they been but wisely directed, to raise him to any position that a member of the profession can reasonably hope to attain. Of the causes that led him to commit suicide it is not our place to speak."

It then added:

"To tell the tale of Mr. Colburn's life would be to place on record the biography of a man blessed with enormous mental powers; but, alas! too little permitted to be governed by those influences which tend to make a man not only great, but good."

It concluded, with more than a suggestion the writer knew more than he was willing to reveal:

"That in this country he has left few friends and many foes, as the result of a peculiar temperament which would not brook a moment's contradiction, is, we fear, but too certain. We trust the good angel Charity will efface with tender hand, the record of poor Colburn's faults, and leave for another generation the memory only of his virtues, his talents, and his good deeds."

The obituary in *Engineering* contained more details of Zerah's early life, drawing on information from Mr. Holley. Even that was factually incorrect, stating that Zerah was born in 1832. I knew he was born in 1833. The obituary itemised all Zerah's published books and technical papers. Only towards the end of the article did the author reveal any personal feelings:

"In January 1866, Mr. Colburn started as his own property this journal, and he continued its active management, and gave it the full benefit of his journalistic experience and of his talents as a writer until its success was firmly established. This done, however, his editorship became a nominal one, and at length at the end of February last he ceased to be connected with the paper in any way. On the events of the last few months of his life, we have no desire to dwell here, and in fact, the subject is such a painful one, that we would willingly, if it were possible, omit all reference to it. The story, however, sad as it is, must be told. Naturally restless and exceedingly impulsive, Mr. Colburn went to greater extremes both in work and relaxation than most men, and his irregularities were attended with melancholy results. On giving up his proprietorship of *Engineering*, he proceeded to Paris and subsequently to America where it appears that he avoided all his old friends; and last week the sad news reached us of his death by his own hand, at Belmont, Massachusetts, on the day we have already mentioned."

The obituary concluded:

"Writing was to him a pleasure – in fact more, a necessity, and those who have been intimately associated with him well know the rapidity with which he acquired and generalised information, and the tenacity with which he retained it. As an engineering journalist he was unrivalled, and we are certain that, besides his extensive circle of friends, there are hundreds in our profession who, although knowing him only by his writings, will deeply and sincerely regret his untimely end."

Staring back at the page for a while I realised just how generous William had been in his tribute to Zerah, and how skillfully he avoided Zerah Colburn's ugly weaknesses – of which I was only too aware.

For me worse was to come. By strange coincidence, that same day also I received two letters; both addressed to the Editorial Department of *Engineering* and both forwarded to me. I did not recognise the handwriting on either envelope. One came from Mr. Vaughan Pendred, the editor of *The Engineer*. In it he extended his sincere sympathies and expressed sadness at the tragic and untimely death of my husband. Whilst he did not agree with some of Zerah's views, he wrote that he was nevertheless a fearless and forthright editor who had shown appreciable initiative and foresight is starting his own paper, *Engineering*, which was no mean competitor to his own journal.

In conclusion, he added that by way of a compliment, he had it in his mind to follow in my husband's footsteps and write a book on locomotives that he would title *The Railway Locomotive*.

The second letter, much shorter, came from Mr. D. K. Clark, who told me that he had read in *The Engineer* of my husband's untimely death. He expressed sympathy and extolled the virtues of my husband who would be 'greatly missed' by the engineering fraternity across the world wherever engineering is pursued. He described Zerah as an aristocrat of the technical press.

The following day, 21st May, father pressed me to visit Mr. Holmes, the solicitor handling my divorce petition; father was concerned lest my husband's death held implications.

Was I not entitled, as next of kin, to any of the assets held by my husband? The news that Zerah possessed only 27 dollars and 51 cents about his person and interred in what amounted to a pauper's grave, suggested he died a poor man. Was this so?

My father was suspicious. He did not trust my husband – alive or dead. He insisted I inform Mr. Holmes of my husband's death, so that he might take out Letters of Administration for Zerah's estate.

As my father expressed such concern, I wrote immediately and surprisingly received a reply late on Monday, 23rd May. Mr. Holmes suggested we meet the following day.

Mr. Holmes appeared pleased to see me, even though he confessed at the outset there had been little progress with my divorce petition. I replied suggesting that perhaps no further action would be necessary as my husband had committed suicide close to Boston, in America.

He appeared, judging by his face and in the manner of solicitors, neither shocked nor surprised by the news of my husband's death. He simply raised one eyebrow and suggested that perhaps my husband, suffering from syphilitic despair, had no wish to die in England from such a shameful disease.

"Thankfully you and your husband have no children to imitate his life," he said before questioning if Zerah had drawn up a will. I declared unaware of one; Zerah had not mentioned a will.

'Perhaps you should take steps to make a search,' said Mr. Holmes. 'If your husband died intestate, Mrs. Colburn, then your husband's estate will be divided, after payment of debts, between his close relatives. You might be entitled, as his widow, to inherit some or all of his property. Or you could claim to administer his estate as a creditor to whom he and his estate owe money.'

'If, on the other hand, your husband has left a will disposing of his property and not appointed executors, then you would require Letters of Administration, should you be a beneficiary under the will or a creditor.'

'I am sorry Sir, I am unable to search for a will,' I told him.

'My late husband closed the house and his employer disposed of the contents. My husband immediately journeyed to Paris, thence to America. I know not what happened to his private papers. He possibly destroyed every one.'

It seemed so complicated. But if my husband died a poor man, then I would have to make my own way in the world.

I told Mr. Holmes about the small sum of money found on Zerah's person and that, according to Mr. Maw, Mr. Bessemer had written off Zerah's debts through the sale of his share of the title of *Engineering*.

'If I may say, Mrs. Colburn, that does not look hopeful,' said Mr. Holmes. 'Most likely your husband's estate is indeed small or even non-existent.'

Mr. Holmes added that he would still like to see a copy of the death certificate 'to complete my records'. He suggested it might take several months for him to obtain a copy of the certificate, lodged in Boston. However, with access to the telegraph, he said he might at least be able to establish some facts and set in train the appropriate procedures, adding that in the meantime, as a precaution, he would draw up Letters of Administration.

Many weeks later, William arrived armed with various Boston and Lowell newspaper reports of the inquest, as well as several obituary notices. Not a single reader knew the *real* Zerah Colburn. Papers with obituaries included *The New York Times* of 2nd May, and another from *Scientific American* of 14th May. The obituary in *Scientific American* was identical to that published in *The New York Times*. William pointed out several paragraphs. *The New York Times* spoke of my husband as:

"The best general writer in his profession."

A paragraph in *Scientific American* read:

"Overwork was at least a powerful agency in his early downfall, and this, together with his natural impulsiveness and his habitual irregularity in relaxation, as well as in work, drove him, within a few months into partial insanity."

Another, referring to his American journal, *The Engineer*, read:

"It was an excellent paper, and the few numbers published will have permanent value, but the time was not ripe, in America, for a publication of this kind, and Colburn, although he had learned to labor, had never learned to wait."

'The newspaper states that overwork was the principal cause of my husband's downfall,' I said. 'My husband was not one to relax certainly, but overwork was not the cause of his death.'

William did not reply, but looked at me directly. We both knew our own version of events.

Referring to his period at *The Engineer* in London, the same obituary noted:

"At this time he familiarized himself with the French language and professional literature."

William had brought another obituary. It was the longest he had seen – he estimated it at 1,500 words. Published in the *Lowell Weekly Journal* of Friday, 20th May 1870, the same day that *Engineering* and *The Engineer* published their obituaries, the obituary made me angry.

The obituary's glowing and posthumous approval implied the writer's deep and personal knowledge of Zerah. However, as I was the only person who had spent intimate time with Zerah Colburn for the past 10 years, surely I would know him better than anyone.

Yet in his obituary, the author forged a narrative depicting Zerah's life as one of triumph. I knew otherwise. To justify my anger, I have repeated the obituary's two concluding paragraphs:

"While he resided in London, he delighted to bestow great and valuable attention upon American engineers visiting England, and by his position and influence opened to them unbounded opportunities of observation and improvement, and introductions to distinguished engineers abroad.

Wherever he has paused in his varied course, he has left friends as numerous as his acquaintances, and his memory will be cherished with affectionate admiration by a whole generation of engineers and mechanics. His course, although apparently erratic, had yet a perfect symmetry of its own, in that he rose at every step to a higher degree of eminence in his profession. His life affords a lesson and a warning. He died at thirty-seven, with a clouded brain; but he accomplished more than most men in thrice as many years of active life."

I thought at the time – and still do today: Is this person writing about the man I knew so well, and with whom I lived for 10 years? Was this the same Zerah Colburn who beat and kicked me, and punched me in the face, and regularly intimately abused me during our marriage? Was this the same Zerah Colburn who committed degrading fornication with the prostitutes of Paris and London, and whose behaviour inflicted me syphilis? The same Zerah Colburn who lived life in a dark gap behind the façade of polite words of obituaries?

Clearly, the author of the obituary, JCH, had no deep-rooted knowledge of the real Zerah Colburn. He had witnessed only the outer vestiges of an evil and cruel man who revelled in dangerous living. He looked no deeper than Zerah's skin.

William later told me JCH was a friend of Zerah's – Mr. J. C. Hoadley. Mr. Hoadley knew nothing of the truth; he wrote only of Zerah's "melancholic death" and his "temporary insanity".

I do not accept Zerah was insane – partial or temporarily. Zerah could not face up to the truth, or the consequence of his actions to another human being. Such secrets were between Zerah and me.

Only I knew exactly what took place between the emotional and dangerous Mr. Colburn and me, his wife. What Zerah found clandestine and exciting forged an irrevocable wedge between us.

Zerah Colburn fully understood all the theories of combustion of coal, the mechanisms of locomotives and the composition of steel, but he knew nothing of the workings of the human mind, human relationships and the manner in which one human being should treat another.

William also brought a telegraph from Mr. Alexander Holley. According to Mr. Holley, on his arrival in America, my husband first visited New York where, "avoiding friends, he wandered the streets or spent time in cafes".

William explained that Zerah visited a town called Troy where Mr. Holley had just completed the first blow of a rebuilt steelworks that he had designed. From there, my husband travelled to Lowell, where he met more old friends who found him opaque; he then travelled to Belmont. I was grateful to William; he had brought news of Zerah's last days. However, just several days before William's visit, on 11th June 1870, a letter arrived from Mr. Holmes. It stated: "Letters of Administration had been granted of all and singular personal estate and effects of Zerah Colburn, late of No. 13 Gloucester-road, Regents Park in the County of Middlesex and granted at the Principal Registry of Her Majesty's Court of Probate to Elizabeth Susanna Colburn of No. 11 Cambridge-terrace, Cornwall-road, Notting Hill in the County of Middlesex, the lawful widow and relict."

According to the letter, the deceased "died on the 26th day of April 1870, at Belmont near Boston in America, intestate".

Mr. Holmes's letter offered reassurance that I was the 'lawful widow'. Later, when I showed the letter to father, he appeared satisfied.

Chapter Fifteen
Norwegian connection

ZERAH'S DEATH and subsequent revelations left me physically exhausted, my head in turmoil. While I experienced an immense sense of relief that life in his shadow had ended, my financial circumstances remained bleak. I possessed few clothes with the exception of those father rescued on his last visit to the house; yet I remained reluctant to live permanently in my parents' home. I had unwittingly brought shame upon them, and caused them much worry and expense.

I understood from William that it had fallen to *Engineering* to dispose of the contents of No. 13 Gloucester-road to help further settle Zerah's debts at the newspaper; the contents included his many books, furniture and pictures. I was grateful not to be involved in items for which I had no claim. Various letters and documents had also been found and destroyed.

Meanwhile, in the aftermath, Emily and William provided much help and support. Emily took me under her wing and insisted I remain with them. Many times Emily and I enjoyed an afternoon *tête-à-tête*. On occasions, I opened my heart to her letting slip how much I wanted to be loved by a man I could trust. I believe she understood; she and William loved each other very much and enjoyed a deep respect of one another. I wanted to share that experience myself.

William's formal promotion to editor of *Engineering* allowed him to purchase a larger house, this time in Kensington. This they quickly transformed into a most pleasant home. I resisted their hospitality initially, as the removal of furniture and belongings incurred them in much additional work, but Emily proved most insistent. I remained with the Maws for some time and, with Emily about to have another child, I assisted with housework and care of the children.

One day, while under the Maws' roof, an innocent event

375

changed the direction of my life. It involved a young engineer from Birmingham who travelled to London for an important evening lecture at the Institution of Mechanical Engineers, of which William was a member. The man, Mr. Christopher Abelseth, became so absorbed with the following discussion that he missed the last train to Birmingham. William, who arranged the lecture, took pity on Mr. Abelseth and, being the man he was, offered him a bed for the night.

He and William returned late so it was not until the following morning that I had the pleasure of making Mr. Abelseth's acquaintance. William introduced us and, as soon as our eyes met, I detected an immediate frisson. His smile contained genuine warmth while his entire demeanour suggested an air of friendliness. I took an immediate liking to him. We made a connection – that is a railway term! Seated at table for breakfast, the conversation became relaxed as the newcomer explained himself. His friendliness reminded me of Mr. Holley.

As everyone sat and conversed, laughter filled the air; he had an infectious charm. I realised how much normal family life I had missed; the atmosphere at No. 13 Gloucester-road had never been thus. That morning, as we sat around the table, I sampled a shared experience so friendly and full of amusement that it left a great impression.

Eventually, mid-way through the morning Mr. Abelseth departed to catch a train for Birmingham. Memories of our meeting lingered many days. I was more than a little delighted when, weeks later, William returned from *Engineering* with news that Mr. Abelseth would like the opportunity to meet again, and would I like to join him at the theatre.

And indeed, a few days later – how did he discover my address? – I received a letter. I did not recognise the handwriting but the contents of the envelope caused my heart to flutter. Mr. Abelseth had written a short note to say what pleasure it had given him to meet me and that perhaps we could arrange to share a little time together.

Subsequently, we met often and, little by little, we forged a closer relationship. I had to learn all over again to understand a man, but this time I found it much more satisfying.

During this time, William and Emily were exceptionally kind. Did they detect the onset of romance? Both insisted I remain with them until my future looked more settled. By way of recompense, I did all I could to assist Emily with her new infant.

Gradually, week-by-week, the softly spoken Mr. Abelseth and I became increasingly content in each other's company. The experience was far from that which I had had with my late husband. From the beginning, Mr. Abelseth was quiet, unassuming and understanding, with none of Zerah's callous, devious and secretive attitudes. Nor did he appear tainted by a similar erratic flamboyant and extravagant ideal, both financial and otherwise, of the kind that compromised Zerah's character. Like William, he was confident, but quietly so, and his entire nature was one of kindness, tolerance and patience.

We developed genuine affection and mutual respect, and conversed with an ease I found comforting; it was as if we had known each other for a long time. Where previously I cut a somewhat timid, lonely and pathetic figure as a result of my somewhat solitary life under Zerah's domineering thumb, I soon became more confident. I began to crave for love and attention as Zerah had paid me so little in later years, a period when I thought that while life could be short, marriage could be very, very long. I recalled what Mr. Bentley had once told me: 'Truly happy marriages, Mrs. Colburn, are very rare.' Was it ever possible to be happy in marriage, I had asked myself?

After a while, romance blossomed more deeply, and I returned to live with my parents. Christopher and I grew closer – I even discovered that he had visited Philadelphia in 1868 where, with Mr. William Tatlock of Frankfurt, Germany he had taken out a patent for the invention of "Improvements in apparatus for manufacturing gas". Of course, Zerah produced his own articles on the manufacture of gas. We enjoyed the occasional laugh about how the two of us came to live in Philadelphia, but separated by eight years or so. My memories of Philadelphia, even now, are grim.

Christopher told me he had travelled, like many Norwegians, to America in search of a better life. He described Philadelphia as a mechanics paradise – the second time I had heard that phrase – finally though, he realized he much preferred life in England and returned to Birmingham to seek his fortune there.

Within a year my 'beau' proposed marriage, presenting me with a delightful but simple engagement ring. By that time I had long removed the two rings Zerah had given me.

With much pleasure I accepted Christopher's proposal. I had grown to admire him long before I fell in love with him. I loved him because of the way he was – so different from Zerah. He was such a delightful man, so well mannered, attentive, caring, thoughtful and considerate. There was a sweetness and gentleness about him I found attractive. Repeatedly, I found his quiet kindness as appealing as his lack of neediness. I knew then that I wanted to spend the rest of my life with him. I began to call him Christopher.

I began to discover the meaning of the word love; I never imagined I would ever find such love in a person

Christopher completely understood the hostility I had had to endure at Zerah's violent hands. My ill-treatment caused him such anger, so much so that one day, Christopher offered some wise words. Speaking of my late husband, he said 'Do not let that dark and departed soul cast a long shadow over your life, Elizabeth. Walk out from beneath it and find a new life. I will help you find that new life.'

Christopher was the second man who promised freedom. Unlike Zerah, I judged Christopher could be trusted as someone who possessed ideals of decency, duty and patriotism, and took them as his governing principles. Early in our marriage, Zerah had said he would 'set me free' from the drudgery of being a housekeeper. 'We will have a fine house and servants,' he had promised. Zerah did fulfil that promise, but in reality I had to free myself from him.

Of course, I gave Christopher details of my unhappy marriage. I saw it as my duty, assuming William might already have given some information away. Fortunately, Christopher remained quite sanguine.

I explained the physical and mental pains I endured, and described my illnesses and attempts to make a recovery. I also explained that while I could conceive, years earlier Dr. Graham told me it would be unwise for any further pregnancies. Such news might be a cruel blow to any man, but Christopher insisted it was not from any sense of pity that he found me attractive.

I suggested it might be wise we remain celibate. Christopher appeared to understand, although I could sense his disappointment and sadness that we could not have children.

Nevertheless, Christopher enjoyed my attention; I was more than glad to give it, as much as I was to receive his.

When I introduced Christopher to my parents, they approved immediately and expressed great happiness. I told mother I did not stop being a woman when Zerah died.

'Of course not,' she replied. 'I think this time you have made a good choice.'

Christopher was the first man for whom I had real and lasting feelings – someone with whom I could share thoughts and emotions. Even in my dreams I had not imagined that I would find such love on earth. I believed that God had sent me an angel whose attentiveness and consideration would brighten my life.

We planned to marry from my parents' house; this pleased mother. And it made father feel proud that he could give his eldest daughter's hand away in marriage.

Christopher agreed with my wish to marry in church, particularly the one I most frequented. We arranged to meet the curate of nearby St. Mark's church, Notting Hill, the Rev. Frederick Kelly, S.S.M. to discuss the reading of banns and the ceremony. As was his custom, the curate requested some personal details.

I had a confession to make to the curate. I decided to be completely truthful even though unsure of the outcome. I explained that my late husband had killed himself in America. The curate sat in silence. Christopher held my hand, squeezing it in reassurance.

A silence followed as the curate mulled the facts.

'Thank you for your truthfulness, Mrs. Colburn,' he said. 'In such circumstances I advise you declare yourself a widow on the marriage certificate. I see no reason why, as a churchgoer, you should not marry at St. Mark's.

Mother had been particularly pleased our wedding was at St Mark's; being close to my parents' house, its location simplified the arrangements. And I was more than delighted it did not to take place in September – an unlucky month for me.

The building dated from the 1840s when extensive housing developments required a new church. A temporary church opened in 1848 with 600 sittings, of which 150 were free. Donations made by 1851 permitted the laying of the foundation stone by Dr. Thomas Dale, vicar of St. Pancras. Builders completed the nave and aisles and in 1853, Bishop Bloomfield consecrated them.

Despite the church's incomplete construction, we enjoyed a beautiful wedding with family and acquaintances. Thomas my brother, and my unmarried sister Maria, ever graceful and beautiful, acted as witnesses.

It seemed a strange coincidence to be marrying another engineer; I hoped this time I would be more successful. Christopher lived at No. 2 Fairfield-villas, Birmingham but worked also in London. The ceremony proved to be a perfect family occasion. Those attending could judge, by the looks on our faces as we exchanged vows, that we were immensely happy for one another and much in love. Some onlookers even said that Christopher and I were destined for one another.

I had never been so happy. For me, Christopher was perfect.

He said he adored me and declared unconditional love. I believed him when he said how much he loved me, and the deep affection he held. He allowed me to be myself, as much as I could be; no longer a captive.

And so it was, on 10th June 1871, Christopher and I were married, barely 18 months following Zerah's death. It had been a truly whirlwind romance, and even now quite difficult to believe. And once more, in Christopher's eyes, I became his angel in the house.

Later, I discovered in my father's notebook that he wrote: "Page 187 Parish Book Married. Saturday the 10th (tenth) of June 1871 at Saint Mark District Church, Notting Hill by Rev'd Frederic Festius Kelly, S. S. M. curate by Licence (in the presence of us John K. Watkins, Maria Browning, Henry C. Browning.) Christopher Nicolay Abelseth of No. 2 Fairfield-villas, Birmingham in the County of Warwick, to Elizabeth Susanna Colburn of the District Parish of Saint Mark, Notting Hill, County of Middlesex."

My sister Maria would then be aged 24 years – Christopher paid particular compliments to her good complexion – and my brother Henry 22 years.

It was while reading that item in father's notebook that I noticed another, earlier entry. It read: "Times, May 17th 1870. Died. On the 27th of April at Belmont, Near Boston, U.S.A., Very suddenly, Zerah Colburn M.I.C.E., late proprietor of "*Engineering*", and of 13 Gloucester Road, Regent's Park, Aged 37."

Father's bald statement did not note that Zerah Colburn was his son-in-law; nor provide any additional comments, or even convey his own thoughts. I can only imagine how he felt. The item carried two mistakes: Zerah died on the 26th of April and he was 38, not 37. He died 3 days after Shakespeare's birthday.

Of course, I had a new surname; an improvement on my previous married name which by then I despised. I considered the name Abelseth most unusual, romantic and distinguished.

Both of Christopher's parents were of Norwegian extraction; he too was born and raised in the country before sailing for England to forge a career in engineering. He told me of other Norwegians who had left their country, some even sailing to America in search of new lives. I told him I had no wish to return to America.

I decided on a further change in my attempt to begin a new life. In keeping with my new wedding ring, I chose my second Christian name, Susanna. Christopher took some time to accommodate it, but I needed a means to rid myself from the evils of the past and my loveless marriage. And this was a start.

Christopher, being some five years younger, helped me navigate through difficult days. My first marriage had been a failure – a very unhappy marriage. During that time, I experienced such low self-esteem that I regarded myself as undesirable, so undesirable that I thought no man would want me. Christopher changed that. For him, this was his first marriage - with all its excitement.

For our honeymoon, we took the train to Folkestone, a town favoured by Charles Dickens some 15 years earlier. Folkestone was Christopher's choice. We stayed in a small, family boarding house on the sea front. The proprietor, a most pleasant woman, accepted Christopher like a son. She gave us the best room.

When we were alone, a huge sense of relief engulfed me, so much so that I flung my arms round Christopher's neck, squeezing him tightly; tears flooded into my eyes. For the first time, I released the tension that held me in check for so long.

Our first night was memorable. Christopher told me his body had been waiting for that moment. Given the love between us, I trusted him, while he said that I brought stillness and gentleness to his life.

Of course, I had undressed before a man previously, but with Christopher, it was so different. As I stood there, with moonlight streaming through the window, I sensed Christopher's eyes on my pox-ridden skin. He stared at my body. As he came close, he stroked my hair and then my shoulders. There followed the touch of skin on skin, his firm physique against my slender frame. What transpired was so wonderful. I experienced physical love for the first time. I had broken my vow. I consoled myself my cure was almost complete.

The next morning, Christopher woke early and threw back the bedclothes. I lay on my back without clothes. The early morning sun streamed through the window, its light picking out my slim body, marred by the pox. Christopher returned to bed and lay alongside, stroking my skin. I loved to reach across to his body to feel a response. His stomach was flat and firm to touch. As I did so, I watched him grow in stature until he became rigid. He enjoyed my attention and I was glad to give it.

It was then that I recalled one of Doris's sayings of years ago: 'It is only in bed that a couple's deepest intimacy is forged.' I knew then the truth of Doris's words. I did so love Christopher, for he gave me much needed respect, love and affirmation.

I experienced just one cause of unhappiness. Although I had persisted with medication for syphilis, my body remained scarred. Under no circumstances would I ever bear children, as I never fully recovered from the disease. This was a great disappointment to Christopher, who so wanted a baby to grow up under our parentage.

Life on honeymoon with Christopher was idyllic. He went to great lengths to ensure my happiness; he even suggested we leave London and start again, somewhere completely different. At last, I had found someone I could not live without.

He told me how much he would like to visit America and begin a new life. I reminded him that I had already been and it no longer held any attraction for me.

Our honeymoon in Folkestone, however, gave Christopher an idea; that we should become lodging-house keepers ourselves. We chose Folkestone, a town with many happy memories for us and where many cross-Channel visitors gained their first experience of England.

Eventually we found a suitable house at No. 6 Longford-terrace and before long we moved in, devoting our lives to helping other people. While we could not view the English Channel from upstairs windows, only a few hundred paces separated our house from the sea front.

Christopher quickly became fluent in French and German, as many who lodged with us came from France and Germany. We employed Harriet, a pleasant, hardworking servant girl, and she too became familiar with the words and phrases of foreign languages. I joined a church in Folkestone and we gradually became part of the community. We did not accumulate much money but we were deliriously happy with our new way of life.

I often reflected that our present world, entwined in organizing and running a humble lodging house in Folkestone, could not be much farther removed from the constant comings and goings of well-to-do engineers in Gloucester-road and publishing in Bedford-street.

I much regretted not meeting Christopher sooner; he gave me a new experience of life. Yet it was only through Zerah that both Emily and William entered my life, and through William that I finally met Christopher. Perhaps it was God's command that I should endure evil in order to experience goodness

Unable to focus on the future, Christopher enabled me to look beyond Zerah Colburn to a world of love and serving others, albeit the humdrum world of a lodging house, with its fresh faces every day; people eager to start the next day of their lives.

When Christopher knew I should not bear a child, he suggested adoption, but I could not bring myself to agree. I deemed myself too old to carry the responsibility of a child who was not of my own flesh, and who I might not even love. Thoughts of my own dead infants continued to linger heavily. My health too was poor, and who would care for the bairn if I left this world suddenly?

However, the matter of adoption caused occasional

disagreements although Christopher refused to allow them to come between us; we loved each other so much.

With the passage of time, I gave the matter of adoption more thought. I concluded that by selfishly standing in the way, I denied Christopher the opportunity to experience the pleasures of children. One day, I happened to raise the matter with a doctor who attended me from to time. However, the idyll of life in Folkestone was not to last much longer.

Chapter Sixteen
Mr. Bentley's revelations

TOWARDS the end of September 1871 Mr. Bentley, tidying away some papers in his office, found a folder marked with my name lodged inside another. Its sudden appearance caused him both surprise and displeasure. How it came to be misplaced was a mystery.

Opening the folder, he immediately recognised a letter from an associate in New York who had investigated Zerah's family. Mr. Bentley remembered he had not communicated the letter's contents to me. For, although to all intents and purposes Mr. Bentley had closed my file – father having settled Mr. Bentley's final statement of account – several outstanding matters aroused his curiosity sufficiently to embark on further investigation.

The appearance of the 'lost' letter prompted Mr. Bentley to contact me. Unaware of my whereabouts, he wrote in the first instance to my parents. They informed him of my marriage and offered my address in Folkestone. His letter, which came as a great surprise, requested my presence and that I should travel to London to witness 'important news'.

I discussed the letter with Christopher; we were mystified.

Christopher, having no wish that I travel alone to London, suggested we visit Mr. Bentley together. Christopher asked if the news could be to our benefit. I thought this unlikely, or Mr. Bentley would have requested we attend quickly.

I replied suggesting a date the following month. I gave no mention Zerah's suicide in America.

When Christopher and I travelled to Mr. Bentley's office, I discovered little had changed in the intervening period, with one exception – there were more people. The streets appeared busier with traffic and teeming with pedestrians. On arrival, we waited a while for Mr. Bentley to see us. When we were ushered into his office, I introduced Christopher as my husband.

'Ah, Mrs. Colburn, I have some very interesting news for you,' said Mr. Bentley, so intent on his papers that he quite ignored my correct surname; he almost ignored my husband. 'I must first apologise. I misplaced some important correspondence from America that arrived a few months distant. I should have drawn it to your attention. That is remiss of me.'

I then told him that my first husband having attempted to commit suicide in Belmont, Massachusetts, had died the following day, 26th April 1870, in Boston General Hospital.

'He shot himself,' I added. 'I am sorry. I should have written to you as soon as I knew. I did not consider it important.'

Mr. Bentley said nothing for a minute. Did I detect irritation?

'I see. I do wish you had informed me earlier, Mrs. Colburn. You could have saved considerable expense on my part,' he said sternly.

'Following our marriage, my wife of course took my name and I would appreciate if you could address her accordingly,' intervened Christopher, equally severely. 'She has had much to contend with, when all things are taken into account. I think my wife is entitled to dignity and an allowance for any lapse in her concentration.'

'Quite so, quite so,' said Mr. Bentley, quickly. 'I apologise for my oversight. Please forgive me.'

As if embarrassed, he reached down and opened a drawer. He brought out another sheaf of papers, and looked at me. Once again, in that fateful office, only the tick of the clock broke the silence.

'Mrs. Abelseth,' he said, carefully pronouncing my married name. 'I have some important information for you.'

I wondered what was coming. Zerah had been dead for some 18 months – what could be more serious than that? Surely, there could be nothing else to affect my life?

'As I mentioned in my letter, I have conducted some enquiries on my own account, as I found your case most interesting.'

I waited.

'Well. You may recall I asked you to name the vessel in which Mrs. Colburn and her daughter were lost at sea,' declared Mr. Bentley, looking down at his notes.

I nodded slowly, as if in agreement. However, I recalled it only vaguely; it was some time previously. I would require my journal for a precise date.

'Well,' he said, again with deliberation in his voice, 'my colleague found a short item in *The New York Times* dated 11th July, 1859. Would you like me to read it out to you?'

I nodded slowly.

'An item on page eight of that day's newspaper reads as follows under the headline Passenger Arrivals: In the ship Southampton from London and Portsmouth – Mrs. Adelaide F. Colburn, Miss Sarah Colburn etc., etc., and 175 in the steerage,' said Mr. Bentley.

He paused, allowing time for the information to register.

There was a long silence.

'You see, Mrs. Abelseth, the arrival in New York in July 1859 of Mrs. Adelaide F. Colburn was so important to the editor of *The New York Times* that he placed her name, and that of her daughter, at the head of the list of passenger arrivals in his news story. He did not merely list the two Colburns amongst steerage. To him they were the most important new arrivals in New York that day. The newspaper editor clearly understood the importance of Mrs. Adelaide F. Colburn. She and her daughter were so noteworthy to him that he took special measures to include them. If they were ordinary passengers he would have not mentioned them. But he considered their arrival so noteworthy to inhabitants of New York that he gave them top billing, so to speak. Do you see what I am alluding to, Mrs. Abelseth?'

I could but nod in agreement. I knew why Mrs. Colburn's name featured so prominently in the newspaper. Mr. Holley told us on his visit to London that, in 1859 as a special correspondent for *The New York Times* in his quest for information about *Great*

Eastern, he had crossed the Atlantic on the *S. S. Orago*, a new steamship of the U.S. Mail Line, with the founder and editor of *The New York Times*, Mr. Henry J. Raymond. Mr. Holley and the editor were on friendly terms; their friendship spanned more than 15 years. Even before the maiden voyage of *Great Eastern*, the editor commissioned Mr. Holley to write various other articles, as well as several articles of that epic voyage for his newspaper. *The New York Times* editor knew Zerah Colburn and Alexander Holley were not only great friends, but partners in the *Railroad Advocate*. The newspaper's editor was also well aware of Mr. and Mrs. Colburn, and their daughter Sarah Pearl as residents of New York. Mr. Colburn was an important resident of the city.

'Also Mrs. Abelseth, Mrs. Adelaide F. Colburn did not sail from Liverpool, as your husband informed you.' He paused. 'Mother and daughter sailed in the *Southampton* from London and Portsmouth.'

'The only other sailing I could find with the name Colburn on a passenger list was that dated 30th January, 1858,' said Mr. Bentley. 'That was when Mr. Zerah Colburn, aged 25, an engineer and a United States citizen, arrived at the port of Boston aboard the *S. S. Canada* of Glasgow from Liverpool. That would be two years before his voyage on *Great Eastern*, and of no concern to us in this matter. However, six months later, on 3rd August 1858, the same Zerah Colburn of 119 Waverley Place, New York, applied for a passport. The documents record his birth in Saratoga, New York, on 13th January 1833. The passport declared that he would travel accompanied by his wife and child. That would be when the entire family sailed for England.'

'Do you understand the gist of my discovery, Mrs. Abelseth?' asked Mr. Bentley. 'Mrs. Adelaide Colburn and her daughter Sarah Pearl did not die through an accident at sea, as Mr. Colburn claimed. They did not drown. They arrived fit and well in New York in July 1859.'

I nodded again slowly. I knew exactly to what he referred.

At the time, all those years ago, I should have taken notice of

Zerah's absence for only a matter of weeks, following Mrs. Adelaide Colburn's 'death' at sea. He would not have had time to sail to New York and return to London. Why did that not occur to me? He was in London all the time. He must have taken me for a stupid child.

Mr. Bentley interrupted my train of thoughts.

'The document your husband claimed to receive, informing him of an accident at sea to his wife and child, was a complete fabrication – an untruth. It was dispatched by Mr. Colburn, possibly from his office, to his home address to deceive you,' he declared. 'Mr. Colburn could not have learned of his wife's death by telegraph. It was not until five years later that the Atlantic telegraph cable was laid using *S. S. Great Eastern*.'

'You must also be aware from what I have told you. Mrs. Colburn and Sarah Pearl were alive when he advertised for a housekeeper,' Mr. Bentley added.

'And I have something else.' Mr. Bentley became even more dramatic, having warmed to his subject.

'I made some additional enquiries in New York, through another colleague who moved to the city to undertake investigative work. You showed me your marriage certificate in which Mr. Colburn declared himself 'widower'. Well, my informant obtained further proof that your husband was not a widower at all. And there is more.'

Another silence followed.

'I have to tell you, Mrs. Abelseth, that Mr. Colburn's wife and child, Mrs. Adelaide Colburn and her daughter, Sarah Pearl, even now are living in New York City,' said Mr. Bentley, dramatically.

'If I remember correctly, you mentioned some time ago that you and Mr. Colburn married first in New York in 1860 and then again in London in 1864. Is that correct?'

I nodded my head.

'I should at this point add that Mr. and Mrs. Colburn did not obtain a divorce. So, until Mr. Colburn's death, he and Mrs. Colburn were still legally married and therefore man and wife.

Your 'marriages' to Mr. Colburn in 1860 and again in 1864, were bigamous.'

In the silence, I struggled to come to terms with the information. I did not even hear the rhythmic tick of the clock. My thoughts focused on the last three words: 'still legally married.'

'I assume you are aware of the implications, Mrs. Abelseth?'

Without warning, the room around me went black. Blood drained from my head and my heart began to thump. I slipped into oblivion. The next thing I knew, someone cradled my head in their arms and pressed a glass of water to my lips.

'Bring smelling salts, quickly,' urged a voice in the background. 'My wife has fainted.'

I opened my eyes to see Christopher crouched over me, kneeling on the floor. I must have collapsed.

'Are you all right, Susanna?' asked Christopher in a concerned voice. 'You fainted. I could not move quickly enough to save you from falling to the floor.'

Someone entered the room with smelling salts and passed them to Mr. Bentley. He opened the bottle and waved it beneath my nose. He called out 'Bring a softer chair, and then help me make Mrs. Abelseth more comfortable.'

Within a short while, I found myself seated in a different chair, feeling slightly improved, though my head was still spinning.

'Is that better, Mrs. Abelseth?' asked Mr. Bentley. 'I am very sorry if my news has upset you. I should have prepared you more thoroughly.'

I had yet to speak. After a while I said, 'I will be all right, shortly.'

Mr. Bentley handed the smelling salts to Christopher and returned to the chair behind the desk, where he seemed more at ease. He shuffled papers on his desk nervously before asking someone to bring a 'cup of tea for Mrs. Abelseth.'

A man returned with a cup of heavily sweetened tea, which he passed to me. I took a sip and almost immediately felt better.

At the time, I did not know which caused most upset: the indignity of fainting in an office amongst strangers, or the unpalatable news about Zerah. It was some minutes before Mr. Bentley spoke.

'If you have recovered sufficiently, Mrs. Abelseth, is it reasonable for me to continue? I must warn you the news is not pleasant.'

I nodded. I remained in a somewhat dazed condition. What more could he say?

'I should perhaps inform you that bigamy in this country is a serious and punishable offence,' said Mr. Bentley. 'If convicted, Mr. Colburn could have been sentenced to serve time in prison. The shame of that alone might have prompted his suicide.'

At that precise moment the idea occurred to me: the fearsome prospect of prison surely provoked Zerah's suicide – not his illness or the pending divorce.

'Were you aware of the presence of your husband's first wife when you married Mr. Abelseth?' he asked, gently. 'Were you aware she was alive?'

I shook my head. I could not speak.

The word 'no', although spoken, did not emerge. I had to repeat it. 'No, I did not.'

'I should perhaps say that I first became suspicious when we discovered many months ago there were no vessels lost at sea at the time you described. Any man who leaves his family has to be ruthless,' said Mr. Bentley, 'It was for that reason I made further enquiries in New York. But I will not burden you with these costs,' Mrs. Abelseth.

'Thank you,' I murmured.

'I can tell you that as a result of those searches, we have ascertained that Mrs. Colburn and her daughter Sarah Pearl now reside, as I speak, at No. 882, 8th Avenue, New York. However, they moved to that address only recently. I should add that it is not unusual for New York's residents to remain for only a relatively short period at any one lodging house as rents increase year on year. Rather than pay the increase, residents find somewhere cheaper to live. We have no idea why Mrs. Colburn moved.'

'Mother and daughter proved difficult to trace,' added Mr. Bentley. 'The population counts of the three largest cities – Indianapolis, Philadelphia and New York – were challenged as inaccurate. That required a second numeration for New York. Even so, eventually we found Mrs. Colburn and Sarah Pearl listed in both numerations.'

'Previously, Mrs. Colburn and Sarah Pearl were found to have lived in a lodging house at 33 Norfolk-street. The head of household is Mr. William Kellock and his wife, Caroline. The Kellocks have four children, Mary, 15, William, 13, Sarah, 11 and George, four. Mrs. Colburn and Sarah Pearl were the only other occupants of the house. We believe they lived there for some time.'

'My investigator has spoken with Mr. Kellock and his wife; her occupation is shown on the 1870 census return as 'keeping house'. Both were born in New York. Mr. Kellock is aged 40 and his wife is 33. Mr. Kellock confirmed that Mrs. Colburn's name had been entered on the census return; her age was given as 36 and her daughter's as 15. So, they are both alive.' said Mr. Bentley dramatically.

'Does this surprise you, Mrs. Abelseth?' asked Mr. Bentley.

'Yes,' I replied, softly. 'Yes, it does.'

'Well, there may be more than one Mrs. Colburn up and down that country married to a Mr. Z. Colburn, but as far as I can ascertain, you are the only one in England. That may be a crumb of comfort.'

Another long silence followed.

'I ought to prepare you for further bad news, Mrs. Abelseth,' said Mr. Bentley. 'If it is convenient, may I continue?'

'Please do so,' I muttered meekly, taking another sip of tea.

'To add further to your troubles Mrs. Abelseth, it seems your 'husband' dispatched valuable items and sums of money to Mrs. Colburn. My investigator friend made some discreet enquiries of Mr. Kellock. As a clerk in the post office, Mr. Kellock took more than a casual interest in the items of post arriving at the house, as you can imagine.'

'Mr. Kellock disclosed that while Mrs. Colburn remained at the lodgings, packets arrived at regular intervals over some period. The packets, addressed to Mrs. Adelaide Colburn, came from London, England. They carried the sender's name on the envelope; the name was Mr. Zerah Colburn. It seems that one day, Mrs. Adelaide Colburn casually happened to mention that some packets contained jewellery and other valuables from her editor husband in London.'

'There is reason to presume the contents of the packets may prove one day to be valuable,' Mr. Bentley said. 'Items sent may have included watches and rings. I do not of course have the exact details of the packets' contents, but on the best possible authority I can tell you that all this is true.'

'My colleague in New York spoke on separate occasions to Mrs. Caroline Kellock; she knew Mrs. Colburn well. Mrs. Colburn had told her that, over a number of years, her husband in London sent money, watches and valuable diamond rings with large stones. Mrs. Colburn showed Mrs. Kellock an 18 carat lady's watch from Thos. Russell & Sons of London.'

I was puzzled. A silly thought came to mind: A watch measured in carats. I thought carats were for diamonds only.

As if sensing my interest, Mr. Bentley added 'Thos. Russell & Son was Liverpool's finest watchmaker. Thomas Russell received a Royal Warrant from Queen Victoria. They later secured offices in London and Toronto, Canada.'

'I should say that only when Mrs. Colburn and her daughter pass away will the full value of the gifts be realised. It could amount to thousands of dollars.'

'In summary, Mrs. Abelseth, I think we can now conclude that Mrs. Colburn and Sarah Pearl did not die through the loss of a passenger steamship in the North Atlantic, as your 'husband' declared. Nor were Mrs. Colburn and Sarah Pearl by any means poor. They were quite wealthy with tangible assets. Mr. Colburn provided well for them from London. Perhaps Mrs. Colburn had some hold over her husband. Suffice to say, he decided to marry you without first undergoing divorce proceedings in America, which could be difficult and protracted. Mrs. Colburn, of course, may not have agreed to divorce him.'

'I do have yet more news for you, Mrs. Abelseth.'

I nodded, somewhat better prepared.

'The house at No. 882, 8th Avenue, where Mrs. Colburn now resides, is the responsibility of Mr. William Pritchard, 55, a saloon keeper. Mr. Pritchard appeared in the second enumeration. My friend gathers that Mr. Pritchard owns the house and rents rooms to lodgers. Several families live in the house, making 15 people in all, including children. In the enumeration, Mrs. Adelaide Colburn's age is 35 – one year younger than in the first enumeration. Daughter Sarah Pearl remains shown as aged 15. That suggests Mrs. Colburn was only 20 when Sarah Pearl was born in 1851. I think there are some errors in the census return.'

'As if to confuse matters, in the first enumeration, we found Mrs. Colburn's first name spelt as Adeline – however, I am convinced the same person appears in both enumerations,' said Mr. Bentley, who took great pride in revealing his haul of treasure.

I could not fully absorb all that he told me. It was complicated. Only later did I appreciate the full extent of Mr. Bentley's revelations when I discussed the matter with Christopher during our return journey by rail to Folkestone.

'All of this has been a shock for you, Mrs. Abelseth. I am so sorry to have been the bearer of so much bad news. I do wish I could help you more,' said Mr. Bentley. 'We may never know why Mr. Colburn made so many payments in cash and kind to his wife. It is possible, of course, she was blackmailing him.'

It was obvious Zerah's outrageous behaviour surprised even Mr. Bentley. On the one hand, Zerah openly associated with London prostitutes and infected me with syphilis, yet he showed such devotion to his wife and daughter that he sent them money and jewellery. Why did he send such gifts? Did Mrs. Adelaide Colburn, as Mr. Bentley had inferred, have some hold over Zerah? Was there a sense of guilt on his part? Did the gifts purchase Mrs. Colburn's silence; to hide her presence from those in London who might have an interest?

I had received not one single love letter from Zerah in the years we were together, yet he lavished money and jewellery on his wife.

That night, although Christopher and I retired early to bed, I could not sleep. I lay awake for hours. Too many thoughts and questions circulated through my head, accompanied by melancholic shadows from the past.

As I contemplated the day's events, two lines of thought were uppermost. I knew why Zerah was so determined, even to the point of brutality, I should never utter Mrs. Colburn's name. She was not dead at all, but very much alive.

Not only did he correspond with her through letters, he maintained his wife and daughter in some style. Why did he do that? And why did he direct his anger and bitterness at me, his English rose?

Then I contemplated Mr. Alexander Holley. He knew Zerah was married to Adelaide. The married couples met frequently in New York when the men worked for the *Railroad Advocate*, Zerah's first newspaper. Surely, Mr. Holley knew that Zerah's wife and child were still alive. Why did he not inform me? Why did he betray me?

Had Zerah sworn Mr. Holley to secrecy also? Or had Zerah spun Mr. Holley a web of deception; that he and Adelaide were divorced? Even, possibly, that Adelaide and Sarah were dead. Alternatively, had Zerah, as the elder of the two, also browbeaten Mr. Holley never, ever to mention Adelaide's name? Did Zerah have some hold over Mr. Holley?

Whatever lay behind it, God came to my rescue. I had prayed my infected infant would be stillborn. I had asked for deliverance from my husband. Later I was able to marry a new and loving husband. What more could I ask?

I had endured Zerah's bullying onslaught; he destroyed any vestige of loyalty and affection. My instinctive reaction to the news of his death had been akin to stepping into the sunshine. I was born again, instantly removed from a life of desperation.

As I look back, so much had happened. We were as two people from different backgrounds; two different worlds. I was a working class woman with parents from Bermondsey; Zerah a farmer's boy from across the huge Atlantic Ocean.

Zerah scaled the social ladder and associated with important men. He advanced from farmer's boy to prominent engineer. He powered himself with relentless energy, always chasing success; but at the same time with unpredictability. We achieved different levels of knowledge, mine the most modest.

To add to those memories, there were others, dramatic and painful: such as the wine glass that he smashed against the wall; the exciting voyage to New York with Zerah's note, 'marry me'; and that strange wedding with only Mr. and Mrs. Baldwin as witnesses – had Zerah pleaded with Mr. Baldwin to bankroll him as Mr. Bessemer did later? There was the ignominy of my first beating, the eeriness of life in Philadelphia and my relief in returning to England; our arrival in London and my second beating; and then the tragedy of my stillborn infant. From then onwards, my life became ever bleaker as Zerah's professional esteem grew in stature.

Then followed Zerah's sudden departure from *The Engineer* – what was the secret of that? There was also that damnable Paris Exhibition and the catastrophe of syphilis; the waves of persistent beatings and other cruelty, and the eventual humiliation through Zerah's dependence on prostitutes, laudanum and alcohol.

I could not say I was happily married to Zerah, or even that I was happy in my marriage. When we became married, ironically that was the end of our romance, not the beginning. Why did he marry me? Was I something initially he desired, later to discard?

Any love I had for Zerah evaporated long ago. At moments, I hated him desperately. Did Zerah ever really love me? He once said that I was his destiny. Compliments like that were few in number. Rather, I was his victim; his prisoner. For the most part, there was a detachment about him, a lack of emotional intimacy. He did not, and could not fill a domestic role with any conviction. And what was his behaviour with prostitutes? Was it purely mechanical? The secret remains with him – and them. He never displayed any hint of shame for any of his actions.

During his first year at *Engineering*, I remain convinced that Zerah enjoyed himself; he reached the pinnacle of his career. But could he have achieved more? And if so, what? To the outside world, he was the perfect English journalist and proprietor. Yet, he chose to cast that image aside. Paris reduced him to impotence.

Meanwhile, I became increasingly isolated. It ended with Zerah's death, not mine. I am still alive. Now that is a surprise. I will be eternally grateful.

Quite unexpectedly, I met Christopher. We fell in love and married. That happened in spite of my plight; and it happened to both of us. From Zerah I asked only for love, intimacy, respect and kindness; instead, he made my life one of bondage. Now I enjoy life and those past torments are a memory. God delivered me.

How can I compare all that with the money and jewellery that Mrs. Adelaide Colburn inherited?

I made a grave mistake in marrying Zerah Colburn. That marriage was not my parents' wish. Father was rightly justified to distrust Zerah from the moment the two men met. He had warned me years ago 'There is no certainty as to what does and does not constitute marriage. The means for evasion are easily available. Many people have contrived to be married in ways that defy the law, such as bigamy, or were not legally married at all.'

It was then, that I began to think about the word 'marriage'. I wondered if I was really married at all. After all, my first marriage had been a sham. I tossed and turned until eventually, I fell asleep.

Next morning I raised my concerns with Christopher and we agreed he would write to the vicar of St. Mark's church, explaining that, at the time of our marriage, I had declared myself a widow whereas in fact I was not married at all; my husband having committed bigamy prior to his suicide.

The vicar of St. Mark's, the Rev. Edward Kaye Kendall, M.A., resided at No. 20 Arundel-gardens, adjacent to Kensington-park-gardens. We soon received his reply. In his letter, the Reverend Kendall told my husband 'As regards the subsequent marriage certificate, given that your wife would have been free to marry whether she was a widow or a spinster, I cannot see that the inaccuracy in the description of her status affects the validity of the marriage. I hope you will both continue to enjoy a loving and fruitful marriage.'

I was extremely relieved when Christopher said that we were legally married after all, even though forever and a day, our marriage certificate would carry an unfortunate error.

I then wrote to Mr. Holmes with details provided by the enquiry agent, to the effect that the late Zerah Colburn had a wife and child living in the United States of America.

A week or so later, in October 1871, I received Mr. Holmes's reply. He wrote that while he entertained the utmost sympathy, he could do nothing, adding that he had long since discontinued with the divorce petition, as the respondent was no longer alive. He added that he would make enquiries of his own in New York.

A year later, in June 1872 – the same year I noted Mr. William Grove had been knighted – I received Mr. Holmes's final letter.

Correspondence received from the United States informed him that, two years' earlier, on 6th June 1870 – six weeks after

Zerah's death – Mrs. Adelaide Colburn filed Letters of Administration in respect of the 'goods, chattels and credits' of the deceased, namely Zerah Colburn. The sum total of his personal property was $750.

Mr. Holmes explained that two people signed the Petition, made in the Surrogates Court in the County of New York. They were Mrs. Adelaide Colburn of the City of New York, and Mr. Alexander Holley of the City of Brooklyn.

'You must understand from this, Mrs. Abelseth, your former husband's wife can rightly lay claim to his estate,' wrote Mr. Holmes. 'You are the bigamous wife. You have no claim.'

I was horrified; no claim. As young lovers in 1860, Zerah and I walked in New York. Yet, unknown to me, his wife and child were alive in that city. How cruel was that.

I went to the drawer in my bureau where I kept correspondence. Searching documents, I found the one stating that Mr. Holmes had taken out Letters of Administration on 10th June 1870 – just four days after Mrs. Adelaide Colburn did the same. What an extraordinary coincidence.

Mr. Holmes's last letter set my mind racing. I began to think of Zerah's funeral ceremony in Lowell cemetery. I wondered who else was present at the graveside, besides his wife.

I wrote to William Maw, wishing to set my mind at rest. Did he have a list of mourners at Zerah's funeral on 4th May 1870, in Lawrence-street Cemetery, Lowell?

A few days later I received his reply. According to William, in addition to Mrs. Adelaide F. Colburn and daughter Sarah Pearl Colburn, also present was Zerah's good friend, Mr. J. C. Hoadley. In attendance too, and no doubt giving Mrs. Colburn moral support, was Mr. Alexander Lyman Holley.

From this I became certain that Mr. Holley *did* have prior knowledge that not only was Mrs. Colburn alive, but she and Zerah remained married. Too late, I learned from bitter experience that even good-looking men, with a friendly smile and curly hair, were capable of betrayal. His sympathies clearly rested more with her than with me.

That same year, I read in *The Times* of the Great Boston Fire. Even the word Boston sent a shiver down my spine as it reminded me of Zerah. The newspaper report declared the Great Boston Fire of 1872 as Boston's largest urban fire, and one of the most costly fire-related losses of property in America's history. The conflagration began in the early evening of 9th November in the basement of a commercial warehouse in Summer Street. The fire was contained finally 12 hours later, after it had consumed 65 acres of Boston's centre, 776 buildings and much of the financial district, as well as tens of millions of dollars in damage. At least 30 people died. As I read the report I pondered how much I would hate to be engulfed by flames.

On New Year's Eve 1872, my sister Maria married her sweetheart, a man in the army, at St. Peter's church, Bayswater. Compared with my own modest wedding to Zerah, Maria's proved quite a 'grand' occasion. My youngest sister, Margaret, then aged 27, acted as witness along with my brother Thomas, to the signing of the register. The groom, Mr. Frederick Leggett, whose father George was a major general in the army, worked at H. M. Gun Wharf, Portsea. I am unaware how they first came to meet. At the time, Maria lived at 80 Talbot Road, Notting Hill, London. The Rev. Alfred Corbett, Chaplain to H. M. Forces, conducted the wedding.

It was, some 10 years later that unexpectedly I received a most compelling letter from William Maw. I recognised immediately his handwriting. His letter delivered the final twist of irony in my saga. I have that letter beside me now, dated 28th February 1882.

Dear Susanna,

For some time, I have wrestled with my conscience. Now, released at last from certain constraints, I have yielded to pressure to impart important developments in America concerning Zerah Colburn. This letter may help you reconcile past events.

It is a long story and I beg your forbearance as it concerns you personally.

You may recall one of Mr. Zerah Colburn's friends, namely Mr. Alexander Holley. Sadly, Mr. Holley died recently aged only 49.

Some two years ago, on 21st April 1880, Mr. Holley sailed on the *Gallia* headed from New York to Liverpool. He was making one of his regular tours to Europe to familiarise himself with the progress of steel-making practice in Europe.

After two weeks in London, Mr. Holley began his tour in earnest but, as he reached Cologne in Germany, doctors found him verging on collapse. Not healthy by any stretch of the imagination, he returned to London where he stayed at Morley's Hotel.

One day, my partner, Mr. James Dredge, visited Morley's Hotel and invited Mr. Holley to join him at his house on Clapham Common. I later met Mr. Holley at Mr. Dredge's house. Sadly, that was the last time I saw him alive. He returned to New York in October.

The following year Mr. Holley planned another European visit, with the exception that he intended to combine business with pleasure. He encouraged his wife and daughters to accompany him. The visit progressed as planned and all expected to be reunited in August to holiday for a month in Switzerland. However, during his travels, Mr. Holley again fell ill and had to return to New York without his family. Shortly afterwards, at 7.30pm on 29th January 1882, he died. His family – who were by then returning from Europe – could not reach their house in Joralemon Street, Brooklyn in time.

Divided loyalties can be dangerous, but now, following Mr. Holley's death, I feel released from such obligations. When Mr. Holley and I were together at Mr. Dredge's house, we recounted 'old times'. The subject of your former husband arose. Mr. Holley offered certain details of our founder's last days I thought I should make you aware.

First, I should inform you that when Mr. Colburn arrived in America for the final time, early in April 1870, he sought out former railroad colleagues, including Mr. Holley who, at the time, was commissioning a new blast furnace in Troy. Mr. Holley and Mr. Colburn were friends for many years – Mr. Holley was one of Mr. Colburn's closest confidants.

On arrival in Troy, Mr. Colburn implored Mr. Holley to journey with him to New York, there to placate his wife and daughter who were unaware of events in London. Throughout their journey, according to Mr. Holley, Mr. Colburn was full of remorse for his misdeeds. Mr. Holley, who had been aware of Mr. Colburn's wife in New York and yourself in London, was himself in a quandary as to what to do with the knowledge. He too was full of guilt.

However, as Mr. Holley declared to Mr. Colburn: 'If you lay down the tracks, that is the way the train goes.'

Mr. Holley asked Mr. Colburn how, in 1864, he came to lose his prestigious Editorship at *The Engineer*. To which your husband replied that the proprietor, Mr. Healey, had received an anonymous note. The note informed of his editor's recent wedding in London.

As Mr. Healey had met Mrs. Adelaide Colburn only some six years earlier, during her residence in London, he found the contents of the note perplexing. Mr. Healey arranged secretly to inspect Mr. Colburn's British Certificate of Marriage, only to see it describe Mr. Colburn as 'widower', and Miss Elizabeth Susanna Browning as 'spinster'.

Mr. Healey immediately dispatched a Private and Confidential letter to Mr. Holley, care of Mr. Bessemer, whom he was visiting at the time. In seeking privately after Mrs. Adelaide Colburn's health, Mr. Healey also requested her New York address, should an emergency ever arise that gave him cause to write to her. Mr. Holley replied that Mrs. Colburn and her daughter were in good health, and he provided the requested address.

Mr. Healey confronted Mr. Colburn; he accused him of bigamy and sought an explanation. The dialogue resulted in a fierce argument, with Mr. Healey brandishing Mr. Holley's hand-written note. As to Mr. Colburn's explanation, Mr. Healey declared it as 'pure masquerade'. Mr. Colburn had no alternative but to yield.

Mr. Healey, as a respected member of the engineering fraternity, held no truck with anyone guilty of bigamy, especially an employee; he wished to avoid any form of scandal. In his opinion, Mr. Colburn was not equal to the responsibilities of an editorship and immediately instructed your 'husband' to leave his premises 'forthwith'; failing that, Mr. Healey would inform police.

However, as a concession, and because Mr. Healey's newspaper could ill-afford to lose Mr. Colburn's skilfully-written work, the proprietor commissioned Mr. Colburn to write some contributed articles until a successor be appointed. Mr. Healey wanted no more to do with his disgraced editor; he also forbade Mr. Colburn from undertaking any 'competing activity' for at least 12 months.

Angered by such treatment, Mr. Colburn sought revenge. Without income to sustain the lifestyle he savoured, he employed financial assistance from Mr. Henry Bessemer, to create *Engineering* in direct competition with *The Engineer*.

In March 1870, the arrival of her husband and Mr. Holley in New York caused Mrs. Colburn great surprise; she believed Mr. Colburn to be living in London. After a short while, Mr. Holley left the couple together.

It was only later, at Mr. Colburn's funeral that Mrs. Colburn informed Mr. Holley of events following his departure. Mr. Colburn, it seemed, confessed everything and begged his wife to forgive him; and he pleaded with her to help nurse his recovery from syphilis.

Mrs. Colburn then explained to Mr. Holley that in 1858, four years into their marriage, when Mr. Colburn sailed for England to take up his position at *The Engineer*, she agreed naively to accompany him, with their daughter, even though Mrs. Colburn, well-travelled herself as a young woman, did not look forward to life in a strange capital. They even arranged to forward their furniture in New York, engaging Mr. Holley in this task on their behalf.

And it was at this point that Mrs. Colburn made a remarkable confession. It transpired that many months prior to leaving for London, Mr. Colburn might have fathered an illegitimate child with a young woman in New York. Mrs. Colburn only discovered the existence of this infant when the 19-years-old Eliza Browning appeared on the doorstep of their New York lodging house with a tiny bairn. She arrived to demand money from Mr. Colburn or the upkeep of herself and the infant. Mrs. Colburn described the young woman as an opportunist slut and sent her away with a flea in her ear.

If it was Mr. Colburn's infant, Mrs. Colburn had no time for adultery and illegitimacy, and told her husband so. Trusting her husband and anxious to maintain family harmony, she suggested they make a 'clean start' of their marriage. This coincided with Mr. Colburn's plans to live in England and well away from any possible scandal in New York. However, Mrs. Colburn hated life in London amongst foreigners and yearned for life in America amongst her family. Many arguments ensued between husband and wife over the matter, with Mr. Colburn remaining unrelenting. Mrs. Colburn braved the North Atlantic one last time and returned to New York with Sarah Pearl. She expected Mr. Colburn to follow later, as he promised. He did not.

Mrs. Colburn could not contemplate her husband had completely abandoned them, believing instead his usual quicksilver turn of mood would soon drive his return to America. But, for whatever reason, Mr. Colburn refused to return to New York; he preferred London where, as editor of *The Engineer*, he became part of the capital's elite engineering society.

When her husband failed to return, Mrs. Colburn found herself in financial straits, needing to care for herself and Sarah Pearl. Compelled to resume employment as a tailoress, she became increasingly angered by her husband's belligerence. She changed tactics.

In an attempt to force her husband's return to New York, she demanded money to support herself and Sarah Pearl; otherwise, she would inform the proprietor of *The Engineer* that Mr. Colburn had abandoned her and the child.

Ever unrepentant yet fearful of the consequences, Mr. Colburn agreed to her demands for payments; his love of England overwhelmed any immediate desire to return to America. Also, I believe by that time he had fallen in love with you, Susanna, and hence your secret marriage in New York, right under the eyes of his wife. Mr. Holley mentioned he had seen you several times on *Great Eastern* but kept the information to himself.

In 1864, while continuing to make payments to his wife in New York, Mr. Colburn came under duress from your parents for a marriage ceremony in London – the wedding that Mr. Healey later discovered and caused Mr. Colburn's dismissal.

With *Engineering* successfully launched, Mr. Colburn expanded the journal's coverage through his visit to the Paris Exhibition. As you well know, with temptations of the flesh sitting heavily on his shoulder, Mr. Colburn became subject to the syphilis that endangered his life. Gradually he drowned in the seas of alcohol and opium he used to escape the pressures of daily life.

When, for the last time, Mr. Colburn returned to New York to rebuild his life and beg forgiveness, Mrs. Colburn's anger erupted. She was determined to keep at bay a self-indulgent husband who not only committed adultery and bigamy, but suffered syphilis.

In the verbal exchanges, tempers flared. Mr. Colburn was unable to placate his wife and their relationship increasingly turned sulphurous. Mrs. Colburn dismissed her husband; her final instruction was "never to return". There could be no redemption.

Mr. Colburn travelled to Boston, a maudlin and morose man. He lounged in parks, roamed streets and slept in doorways. For once, he had too much time to think. With his talents no longer in the ascendancy, the comet that once crossed the skies above engineering's fraternity burnt itself out.

Shortly before his death, Mr. Colburn met Mr. Tyng. He told Mr. Tyng, whom he described as 'a friend for life', he had no reason to live; that he would commit suicide. Mr. Tyng endeavoured to persuade him otherwise, without success. Mr. Colburn's self-hatred had pushed him to the brink. He declared to Mr. Tyng that his life was over; that he had nothing left to give.

Your husband met another former colleague, Mr. John Winslow, of the Boston & Lowell Railroad. Mr. Colburn, in a similarly confused and delirious state, told Mr. Winslow he planned to kill himself on St. George's Day – 23rd April; St. George being England's patron saint. Mr. Winslow implored your husband to change his mind. Mr. Winslow similarly failed. It seems that in his confusion Mr. Colburn's suicide occurred on 25th April, not on the 23rd April. He may have tried to kill himself two days previously but could not bring himself to do it, or was too weak.

Thus in Belmont, not far from Boston, he came upon a deserted pear orchard and shot himself to the head. In extreme pain and delirious, he muttered various names to two boys who found him when walking a dog.

Constables, directed to the scene by the boys, examined the gunshot wound. They removed the body to hospital. Mr. Colburn expired the following day. Cadaverously thin and, faced with the promise of oblivion, he slipped into final sleep without any panic, numbed by the combined effects of a single bullet, alcohol and opium. Doctors were unable to save his life. Later, police discovered his name from initials on his magnifying glass.

At the inquest, the Coroner recorded items found about his person, including: a Dent & Company sterling silver full Hunter 'fusee' English lever pocket watch, a magnifying glass with the letters ZC engraved, and 29 dollars and 51 cents.

For the purposes of the death certificate, doctors recorded only the immediate cause of death. Any other impediment, previous contributory ailment or disease went unnoticed (or unrecorded) as doctors focused only on the gunshot wound. The coroner declared Mr. Colburn died from a bullet to the head discharged from a pistol held in his left hand while 'labouring under an aberration of mind'.

Throughout the period Mr. Colburn lived in London, Mrs. Colburn (then living in New York) had no prior knowledge of her husband's crime of bigamy; indeed even to the last, she refused to believe he would stoop so low. Immediately following Mr. Colburn's death – he died intestate – his wife sought Letters of Administration.

On a personal matter concerning your marriage to Mr. Colburn, Mr. Holley explained that in the United States of America, bigamy carries no custodial sentence, as it does in England. For that reason Mr. Colburn deemed it 'quite safe' to proceed with your marriage in New York, as witnessed by Mr. and Mrs. Baldwin. Mr. Colburn. To the end he blamed Mr. Healey for 'poking his nose' in matters of no concern to him as the reason for the unfortunate sequence of events that caused him to leave *The Engineer.*

I can but write that we have all suffered betrayal by a man who otherwise might appear a highly respectable engineer. Beyond the boundary of Mr. Colburn's professional success lurked the reality of a fractured life and a bigamous marriage, as well as deep unhappiness at a personal level. He became a disgraced human being.

I am sorry to present you with Mr. Holley's version of events, but I thought you should be aware of matters surrounding your former husband's death. I have to confess I found some of Mr. Holley's information disturbing.

On this sad note, if I can be of any help, please do not hesitate to write.

We send our very best wishes for the future, William H. Maw

That letter shed light into many dark corners. I thought, through a lucky escape, how close I came to death. Zerah could have shot me dead in London before departing for Paris, even as Emily Maw had feared many years ago.

My next thought was the reason for his death. It was obvious to me why he killed himself. Although William's letter did not refer to Zerah's moral blindness and use of prostitutes, with whom he sacrificed his professional career, surely it was the guilt of abject failure that initiated his undoing.

Lurid details of Zerah's conduct during our marriage, his ailment of syphilis and addiction to prostitution would surely attract substantial public attention in the courts, as well as Press ridicule. More information than that gathered by Mr. Bentley might emerge. Compounding this, details of his bigamous marriage in London would lead to the imposition of a custodial sentence. He would be saddled for life with the stigma of divorce. Zerah Colburn divorced and shut away in prison? Such actions would surely have tarnished the polished, impeccable, elitist image he carefully cultivated. He would face social ostracism if discovered.

My father too, would be deeply shocked. An upright accountant, he had never experienced debt, angry creditors, pawnbrokers or the prospect of the debtors' prison. Added to which, his forebears were upright men in Bermondsey.

Zerah would not be able to withstand the shame of intense public scrutiny and ridicule. Perhaps most humiliating of all would be the shame of his close friends he would have to face, particularly Mr. Daniel Kinnear Clark and with whom he was compiling a book locomotives. Mr. Clark, as a Scot and a Presbyterian churchman, had high moral standards. These, and the burden of syphilis, caused his flight to America, far from London and into the arms of his wife who, contrary to his expectation, had no desire to treat a devious and sick man.

Such burdens of shame drive men to retreat and die, like rats, in lonely places. And Zerah, being no exception, would surely experience the secret agony of his soul as he recognized his plight. He did not die from overwork, as obituaries suggest.

Zerah Colburn was an evil coward. And, had it not been for Mr. Bentley, he would still be alive today as I write these words. And I would not have met Christopher.

I then pondered on the young woman at No. 76 Henry Street, New York City, Eliza Browning. Where did she live now? Would she recall the name of Zerah Colburn and his activities? And before her, did his first flirtations with women begin with the mill girls of Lowell?

Towards the end of 1870 I received an envelope. I had seen the writing before. Redirected from *Engineering*, it contained a simple card edged in black. The printed text announced the recent death of Elizabeth Burdett Clark. The funeral would take place on 29th October 1870 at All Souls, Kensal Green. The card carried Mr. Clark's signature. Mrs. Clark died aged 46. Their marriage lasted barely eight years.

In reply, I extended my sympathies and declared that regretfully I would be unable to attend. I wondered if his daughter would be present at the funeral. I imagined she would, if only to give support to her father.

At the conclusion of 1870, I noticed a newspaper item recording the death of the well-known railway contractor, Mr. Brassey, who died on 8th December 1870. The item described Mr. Brassey as an important man for, at the time of his death, he had built one in every 20 miles of railway in the world. This included three-quarters of the lines in France, major lines in many other European countries and in Canada, Australia, South America and India. He was also a major shareholder in Brunel's *Great Eastern* steamship and for many years he was the largest employer of labour in the entire world.

The item mentioned Sir Samuel Morton Peto, another important railway contractor. He served as Member of Parliament for many years and became one of the most prominent figures in public life. Earlier he helped make a guarantee towards financing the Great Exhibition of 1851, while he and his partner (Thomas Grissell) built Nelson's Column in 1843

Following his involvement with the insolvency of the London, Chatham and Dover Railway in 1866, Mr. Peto and his associate Mr. Edward Betts (who had married Mr. Peto's sister Ann) could not pay creditors and went bankrupt. This contributed to the downfall of Overend, Gurney & Company, a London bank that injudiciously had lent the contractors large sums of money. Persistent rumours and speculation caused a run on the bank which closed its doors and ceased trading at 3pm, 10th May 1866, some five months after Zerah launched his new journal. I remember this caused him great concern and anger at the time. He did not explain what caused the run on the bank. But now I know.

As I draw to the end of my writing, I have read also an item in *The Times*. It reports the break-up of *Great Eastern* at Liverpool, the vessel having no further useful purpose. The timing was poignant. *The Times* reported that during demolition, workers found two skeletons entombed in the vessel's double hull – a millwright and his apprentice, having starved to death. The rumours that circulated so many years ago were true. The skeletons could easily represent me and unremorseful Zerah who knew much more about his life than he would ever reveal.

As for life with Zerah, I endured nearly 10 years of yielding to his moods, silences, tempers, vicious attacks and base acts; 10 years when, if he spent a moment smiling, he spent one thousand fold in deception and scowls. They were tempestuous and volatile years; years that otherwise could have been some of the best of my life. Constantly, I lived under the thumb of a truly insensitive, high-handed and ruthless man who never once acknowledged the devil lurking within. I lived with two rogues: secrecy and deceit, with both wrapped up into one man; both caused so much pain yet proved impossible to forgive.

His overpowering presence eroded my personality, and turned me into a lonely and timid woman; frightened of what he might do or say. Early in our relationship, I mused as to what extent living with someone could change a person's personality. Now I know. Later, following his departure, I am thankful to emerge from beneath his dark shadow to rediscover my former self.

As for my own sickness, mercury and iodine have played their part. For some years I suffered headaches and pains in joints and bones. And, while spared serious illness, I am conscious my body has slowly deteriorated. It is my blessing I have Christopher's unswerving support.

I do not understand what caused Zerah to make those destructive decisions that led to his ruin and a suicide now all but forgotten. Nor why he should embark on at least six liaisons that firmly placed him on the road to perdition. Like Mr. Bessemer's steel, about which Zerah wrote so fluently, I have become hardened and tempered.

Zerah finally lost all trust in his previously boundless ambition. If he searched for the positive on which to build his life, he failed to find it; unless it was death, a final sleep in which he passed from light to eternal darkness, free of misery and pain.

As for myself, in the space of 10 years, I was not only betrayed by the man who claimed to love me, but scarred by my association with him, having experienced oppression, cruelty and fear in equal measure from a pitiless, self-admiring, arrogant and thick-skinned individual. He created a life increasingly without friendship. My only friends were family and Emily, though even to Emily I dare not reveal my innermost feelings. Only with the arrival into my life of Christopher did I find a close and emotionally trusting friend.

Questions remain: Why did Zerah choose me as his second wife? And, at his deathbed, would he have uttered prolonged protestations of his love for me, and his guilt?

I was no more than a passing fancy. He enjoyed a short-lived fascination with everything he touched; a fascination that quickly burned itself out. I enjoyed no more or no less meaning than his other fancies – his wife and child, the saw mill, the land warrants, the newspapers, even the prostitutes he could dispatch after use Even now, his use of them fills me with disgust. We were all part of the shifting sands of Zerah Colburn

His life became a conundrum; on one level as an eminent engineer and author he delved into the minutiae and, using his literary skills advanced his opinions with passion; on the other, he sank to the depths of depravity. The glue holding these together took the form of his addiction to opium and alcohol that culminated in a morally-corrupt self-stupefaction. But would anyone know the whole truth about him? I do know that England gave him the opportunity to reveal his true character as an engineer, as a writer and as a husband. On the first he may have succeeded; as to the second, his torrential literary efforts were without doubt his most potent weapon in his various campaigns, most notably that of promoting the value to the world of steel. As to the third, he remained too cold to be loved.

It was the written word that counted most; he enjoyed the pleasure of assembling them based on the knowledge and understanding in his head. He enjoyed a profound and seemingly unlimited knowledge. He knew he had mastery of language and engineering the present editor of *The Engineer* did not possess.

To my knowledge, he never produced anything elegiac; his outpourings were always about engineering; no one could peer into his soul to find the real Zerah Colburn. He focused his mind on work, with the exception of one activity which preoccupied him attention and brought about our downfall. Never for a moment did I feel close to him in the way that I am with Christopher.

As such, he cast the long shadow of betrayal over every life he touched intimately, imposing a burden on his friends, his family and even the engineering fraternity of which he was a part and claimed to champion. He left ugly scars in many hearts.

Yesterday, in a local shop, I met a nice lady who, for some reason, chose me to pour out her heart. Her husband had left her for another woman. She told me: 'Some people come into our lives and leave footprints on our hearts, then their actions cause us to want to leave similar impressions on their faces.' That was just how I felt about Zerah Colburn.

Had Zerah lived longer than his 37 years to reach three score years and ten, would he have stood tall in a crowded field of engineers or been trampled underfoot by younger passing giants? We will not know.

Increasingly, I have the comfort of family nearby. Maria in particular brought great amusement to our lives when she had her photograph taken. That took place in 1885 when she was aged 38 years. Christopher remarked at the time of her beauty, at the same time reminding me kindly that she was not as beautiful as me. I thanked him for his sweetness. Maria's moral energy proved most helpful, driven as she was by a deep sense of Christian purpose; its public witness took the form of a huge cross worn on a long chain round her neck, accentuated by her hair tightly back from her forehead.

Meanwhile, as to my second question, I have no answer. But I am at peace, with the exception of flashbacks in memory of times past. I have little guilt – with one exception. For, as I near the end, I am increasingly weary, and frightened as to what the future will bring. As no one can imagine their own death I endeavor not to think about it. I feel guilt because as a Christian woman I really should not be frightened at all of my future.

And while I have almost come to the end of this life of mine, there remains much that is stored in the secret channels of my mind, as vivid now as they were over 20 years ago when they occurred. These details of my life I cannot release to be read by my family; they would be most upset. I can still feel Zerah's claws in my back; his ghost continues to haunt me from time to time. And still I ask, why did I marry him? Sometimes, I also wonder: Did Mr. Jim at The Engineer public house ever muse the sudden disappearance of one of his most regular customers? Did he ask: What has happened to that Mr. Colburn? And was someone able to provide him with a satisfactory answer? It would unlikely be the kind of place that William Maw would frequent when he became joint editor of *Engineering*. He and Mr. Dredge would prefer to obtain their information through more formal lines of enquiry.

As to the matter of adoption, only the other day Christopher and I recalled our chance meeting through the kindness of William Maw. Christopher repeated how much he wished we could adopt a child to continue our legacy. I gave renewed thought to the matter and came to the view that, by selfishly standing in the way, I denied Christopher the opportunity to experience pleasures of the child I never had.

So, on his next visit, I discussed the matter of adoption with another doctor who regularly attends my various ailments. In confidence, he mentioned a friend whose wife had had a brief intimate affair with a male friend; she is now expecting his child. The doctor's friend, while happy to forgive his wife and welcome her back into the home, would do so only if his wife had the child adopted and at the same time forsook her lover. To this she agreed. The doctor's friend asked if he knew of a good home where the child could be brought up and adopted privately.

I discussed this with Christopher who expressed joy at my change of heart; we agreed to proceed and I informed the doctor on his next visit. Meanwhile, I often wonder how Christopher will manage when I am no longer present to help. And then I console myself that, as an engineer, how he meticulously organised his work – and his life. It should be easy for him to organise *all* the tasks associated with running a lodging house.

In an occasional moment, I wonder too if he might go in search of another woman to lay at his side at night; the thought evaporates as quickly as it emerges. I dare not dwell on that prospect for long.   **ESC, December 1889**

Chapter Seventeen
The matter of adoption

S HORTLY AFTER completing her manuscript, Elizabeth unfortunately contracted further illness and did not manage to sustain long enough to witness the arrival of her "adopted" infant.

Following her tragic and untimely death on 26th May 1890, Christopher felt an obligation to proceed with his wife's wishes and arranged to meet her doctor. Christopher explained that, given recent sad events, he wished to advance with the agreement he and his wife made before her death to adopt the expected child. However, it transpired subsequently the doctor's friend's wife declared her unwillingness for the infant to be brought up by a single man and discussions were terminated.

Following Elizabeth's death and the simple burial ceremony in Cheriton – her twin brothers travelled from London to pay their respects and give the bereaved widower moral support – Christopher found it difficult to focus on life. He had been aware of Susanna's deteriorating health but felt powerless to halt her decline. He and his wife had done everything together, almost since their first meeting, sharing each and every decision as it came along. Now he was alone with his thoughts. He felt an emptiness that was hard to explain beyond the fact that he had lost the love of his life.

After the funeral and tidying up her financial affairs, such as they were, Christopher set about the task of disposing of his wife's clothes. This he found most harrowing. He had no wish to discard them, nor hand them over to the rag and bone man who patrolled the streets from time to time. In this respect he found the vicar of the local church helpful – he was aware of needy families in the locality.

As to Susanna's personal effects and jewellery he set them to one side and assigned one of the drawers in the bureau in his 'office' as a place of safe keeping. In another drawer he secreted away Susanna's journals and her manuscript.

Gradually, Christopher turned his attention to his business as lodging house keeper. He was fortunate that one of his residents, Louisa Richardson, a 38-year-old widow, had been a housekeeper and she offered willing assistance. Christopher prided himself on keeping a good quality lodging house with separate rooms for his lodgers.

Louisa Richardson, he sensed, came from good family background in Frodsham, Surrey. He knew nothing of her beyond that but she spoke with a clear diction that he assumed reflected her upbringing. His other lodgers at the time included Elizabeth Fisher, a 21 year old from Kent, and another 21 year old, Julia Brinton, who had been born in India, her father having been in the army. Finally, there was Blanche May from Devonshire who kept herself to herself.

When Susanna was alive, Christopher undertook all the heavy work about the house while Susanna took charge of the cooking – she still had her copy of *Mrs. Beeton's Handbook of Household Management* that Zerah had presented to her all those years ago. A laundry girl, Emily attended every day of the week to handle washing and ironing.

Increasingly Louisa took control of the day-to-day running of the lodging house in exchange for a small remuneration. Christopher sensed that she was a lady of independent means. Perhaps her husband had died and left her some money. Louisa remained for some time working at the lodging house.

Longford Terrace occupied a convenient position for lodging houses, being close to the sea. Mr. Harry Clark and his wife acted as proprietors of the lodging house at No. 3. Mr. Clark also took great pride in the quality of his service. Mr. Philip Gregory and his wife had lodged at No. 3 for some time. Mr. Gregory, a barrister, often undertook business in Folkestone. In addition, Mr. Clarke would take in two or three other lodgers, as well as employing a housemaid/general servant.

Next door, Mr. George Gregory likewise ran a boarding house, but the appearance of his house did not look quite as imposing as that of Mr. Clarke who took much pride in the exterior appointments of his property. He too employed several servants.

Longford Terrace, being well positioned for the harbour and its associated trade of cross-Channel shipping, inevitably attracted much custom from those who were 'passing through' either from France or those about to board a vessel next day as part of their journey to France. Inevitably, they consisted of French, Germans and Italians as well as English. Christopher was always happy to accommodate them.

In 1891, Christopher decided that he ought to put his business on a more formal footing and began place advertisements promoting the services of his lodging house; these he placed close to the ferry in an attempt to attract more trade. By doing so he considered he would give more purpose to his life. He decided also to employ a cook and a servant, in a bid to increase his trade. His thought that by providing breakfast and evening meals he could appeal also to those who might stay longer than a few nights – even a week or more.

He placed advertisements in the *Folkestone Herald* and the *Folkestone Observer* for a cook. Within a day he had already received his first applicant. Answering a knock at the door, Christopher found a young lady of about 25 standing in the doorway. Smartly dressed and slim, she was a about the same height as Christopher.

"Excuse me, Sir," she said. "I have come about the advertisement in the newspaper for a cook."

When he compiled the advertisement, Christopher had a vision that he might expect to have to interview someone of middle age; someone with experience of cooking for many mouths.

"Come in," said Christopher.

It transpired the young woman's name was Mary Bailey. She

lived in Cheriton at No. 4 Fair View Villas where she was employed as cook by Mr. Charles Steinboch, a discerning German who had become a naturalized British citizen. Asked for her credentials, Miss Bailey explained that she prepared three meals daily for Mr. Steinboch who, being German, demanded high standards of his cook; she being required to prepare three cooked meals a day and undertake all the housework and washing.

She explained, however, that as there were no others in the house this caused her some concern. She did not feel safe in Mr. Steinboch's company even though there had been nothing to suggest that he would not in any measure pose a threat to life and limb. It was for this reason that she sought a new employer.

She also declared a wish to live closer to Folkestone and the life of the seaside town. Cheriton had proved to be much quieter than she expected.

Asked if she was married or single, Miss Bailey replied that she was married but that her husband had left her for another woman he met working on the cross-channel ferries. As the woman was of independent means, her husband had chosen to go and live with her.

As Miss Bailey was the first to respond to his advertisement, Christopher felt a certain obligation. He agreed to take her on with a one-week trial. If she proved satisfactory he would employ her.

Mary proved accommodating, well organized and an excellent cook; she soon settled into the routine of the lodging house. In addition to her duties as cook she undertook extra tasks, including shopping.

As time went by, Christopher found himself increasingly attracted to his newest employee. Indeed, he was beginning to fall in love with her. He knew only too well of the dangers of a close attachment to employees but he had found himself falling under Mary's spell, no doubt aided by the faint hint of her Irish accent.

One evening, Christopher had cause to invite Mary into his sitting room to plan meals for the following day. Normally, this matter would be discussed after dinner and the chores completed, but a sudden and large influx of travellers into the town had caused extra business for lodging houses like Christopher's – not to mention extra work.

As Mary brushed past him into the room, Christopher, on a sudden impulse, put his arm round Mary's slim waist and drew her towards him. She did not resist. In the many few weeks of their working together at No. 6 the two had got on extremely well, even to the point that Christopher considered himself fortunate that Mary answered his advertisement. He could find no fault with her cooking or her judicious shopping.

Christopher pulled Mary closer, their bodies touched for the first time. Christopher lightly kissed her on the lips but Mary responded more passionately than the lodging house keeper ever expected, seemingly hungry for attention. Christopher felt himself stiffen. At 45 he remained an active man who could still admire a pretty girl. Mary undid her apron strings as if issuing a signal to the owner of the house. Clearly, a connection had been established between the two during their work together.

Their kissing became more ardent; their hands exploring each other's bodies. Christopher extracted himself and closed the door, quietly turning the key to ensure privacy. Only with Susanna had Christopher ever kissed a woman with such passion.

As the days went by, Mary began to discreetly share Christopher's bed with increasing frequency as she slid silently between the sheets, completely naked. He found her slim body and her flat stomach and firm, well-shaped breasts as deeply satisfying as their love-making. He did not feel guilty. It had been a year since his wife Susanna died.

He noticed too that Mary Bailey was an experienced woman when it came to the bedroom. Had she been like that with Mr. Steinboch? Had they fallen out – or grown tired of one another?

When Mary discovered she was with child she gave

Christopher her news; he wanted to make an honest woman of her as he had so become fond of her. He asked her to marry him, even without thinking of the consequences.

But Mary had no desire to be attached for life to an older man, however much she liked him. She had been married once and besides she had a dream that one day, if she had enough money, she would return to Ireland and settle down, perhaps with a business of her own. However, it would be impossible for her to return to Ireland as a single woman baring a child under her arms, and Christopher had no desire to leave England.

After much discussion and not a little argument, with Mary's Irish roots showing making their presence felt, they agreed on a compromise; that Mary would continue to work as cook at the lodging house until the baby arrived, shortly after which Mary would leave and Christopher would adopt the child and care for it as if it were his own. Christopher believed it best for the baby, if Mary had no wish to stay. To stay longer, mother and baby would grow attached.

Christopher also proposed to offer Mary a small dowry so that she could make a fresh start for herself in Ireland. As the child grew up, Christopher promised he would tell the child all about its mother and the brief, but loving part she played in their lives.

The baby, a little girl, was born in April and the following month, May 1892, the infant was baptized Kathleen Bailey on Mary Bailey's instructions in the parish of St. Saviour. The father's name did not appear on the baptismal register. After several six weeks, Mary Bailey returned to Ireland to start a new life leaving Christopher with a new baby to care for. Christopher and Mary had no further contact. She promised to write but did not. He had no idea what became of her.

In 1897, the nation celebrated the 60th anniversary of the accession to the throne of Queen Victoria. Christopher considered it a great misfortune that Susanna had not been alive to share in the celebrations as she had been an admirer of the sovereign.

The Diamond Jubilee, the first time the term had been used in the context of a 60th anniversary, took place on Tuesday, 22nd June; celebrations were not confined to Britain only but extended across the globe as a Festival of the British Empire.

The highlight of the day – a generally bright day in an appalling year for British weather – took the form of a procession along six miles of London's streets. Christopher could imagine having to restrain Susanna from taking the train to London to witness events for herself.

Taking part were extended members of the Royal Family and leaders of self-governing dominions and Indian states. The diminutive 78-year-old monarch, dressed in her habitual mourning black – the Queen had not only lost her husband Prince Albert but two children and six grandchildren by 1897 – was confined to her state coach by painful arthritis. Her parade from Buckingham Palace, past Parliament before crossing Westminster Bridge and then re-crossing the Thames for a service at St. Paul's Cathedral, was watched by hundreds of thousands of spectators, huddled beneath bunting and banners, one of which declared Victoria "Queen of earthly Queens". No queen had ever received such an ovation.

The following year 1898, when Kathleen was about six, Susanna's sister, Maria came to live in Underhill, on the outskirts of Cheriton, itself near to Folkestone. Maria, who had married a career army man Frederick Octavius Leggett in London on New Year's Eve 1872, was well accustomed to moving household belongings and living in different parts of the country, usually close to army barracks.

For example, some years earlier, Maria and Frederick (then a major of Assistant Commissary General of Ordnance) had lived in Frindsbury, Kent, close to Chattenden Army Barracks. The couple occupied the Ordnance Storekeeper's Residence with their two sons Eric, and Frederick.

Their latest home, Underhill Hall House, near Cheriton was

located but a few miles west of Shornecliffe Army camp, which overlooked the English Channel and the lifeboat station below. Established in 1794, the camp served as a World War 1 staging post for troops destined for the Western Front and in April 1915 a Canadian Training Division was formed there. The Canadian Army Medical Corps also had a general hospital based at Shornecliffe from September 1917 to December 1918, and during World War 11 Shornecliffe again served as an army staging post. Queen Mary visited the camp in 1939.

When Maria came to live at Underhill with husband Frederick, by that time a retired army colonel, by strange coincidence she engaged a 29 year-old servant with the surname Bailey – Alice Bailey.

When Maria first heard news of Christopher's adopted daughter Kathleen, she found it hard to come to terms with a youngster living at No. 6 Longford Terrace. Maria and Christopher's wife Elizabeth were close friends long before she acted as a witness at her sister's wedding. On her arrival at Underhill and unaware of the all the circumstances surrounding the child's adoption, Maria decided to visit her brother-in-law, whom she had met on several occasions previously. Indeed, Maria and her husband had attended Susanna's funeral when of course Christopher had made no mention of any planned adoption.

On meeting Christopher and being informed of events leading to the birth, Maria offered her help. And indeed over the coming months the two met frequently until, that is, within a short time afterwards Christopher decided to retire from the business of lodging house keeper and move to Essex. Why Christopher decided to relocate to Essex is not known. Did he and Maria have a disagreement? Did she not agree with the adoption?

Whatever it was Christopher, on reaching 65 and with Kathleen as his 'working housekeeper', decided to move away from their house in Longford Terrace, a house that he and Susanna had chosen so many years before and where they had spent many happy times.

Over the years following the adoption, father and daughter became close friends. Christopher financed all Kathleen's education and provided for her welfare, fully taking on the mantle of fatherhood. The pair moved to a house on Highlands Estate, Vange, near Pitsea, Essex, where Christopher could engage in "farming and gardening on my own property".

One cloud however darkened the sky for Christopher. On Saturday, 1st April 1905, the *Essex Newsman* reported that labourer Frederick Chambers of Vange, Essex had appeared before magistrates. Chambers had been summoned by Christopher Abelseth and charged with threatening to shoot the engineer on 21st March. No reason was given for wanting to shoot Christopher. The defendant was bound over and ordered to keep the peace for six months. He was ordered to pay costs of 7s 6d.

In Vange, a few years later, when the census of 1911 was being compiled, Christopher declared to the census-taker his birthplace as Headmark, Norway. For Kathleen, the census-taker noted down her birthplace as Cheriton, Kent – as on the 1901 census when she was aged nine. But for the first time Kathleen, then 19 and single, informed the census-taker of her 'Irish' nationality.

It was several years following his retirement that Kathleen noticed a decline in Christopher's health. He spent less and less time "farming and gardening" until on 13th August 1915, with Kathleen at his bedside Christopher died peacefully aged 73, suffering from "senility and congestion of the lungs". As Christopher slipped away, Kathleen reassuringly squeezed her father's hand and felt a limp response – a final signal of his love for her.

Christopher constantly treasured Kathleen's loving presence. He would have been delighted had he but known the certificate of death, dated 15th August 1915 and written by Robert Mathewson, MB, described Kathleen Bailey as his "adopted daughter". They had spent 23 happy years together, father and daughter.

In his will, Christopher Abelseth (mechanical engineer) directed his executor and trustee to grant £30 a year for the maintenance and education Kathleen Baily "now residing with me" and pay the same until "the said Kathleen Baily shall attain the age of sixteen years". Of the residue of his "real and personal estate" he bequeathed it to his bothers Ingvald Theodore Abelseth and Johan Frederick Haydeman Abelseth. Christopher also decreed that his funeral expenses should not exceed £15.

The gross value of Christopher's estate totalled £607 2s 10d, with a net value of £417 17s 1d.

Christopher Abelseth signed his will on 17th November 1901, when Kathleen was nine years old. She was 23 when Christopher died. She might have felt it harsh that her father left his estate to his two brothers, as she had stayed and cared for him until the end of his life. On the other hand, he had cared for her and rewarded her handsomely as 'housekeeper' over the years.

As for Kathleen, what happened to her? Well that's surely an opportunity for another book.

Some years later, Maria and her husband Frederick moved house to High Grange in North Road, Hythe, Kent, but not before they left a permanent tribute in memory of the loss of their three beloved sons killed in action in the First World War.

Brigade Major Wilfred Noel Leggett, Major Eric Henry Goodwin Leggett and Lieut. Alan Randall Aufrere Leggett all fell in the Great War; their parents dedicated the chancel screen and cross in St Martin's church, Cheriton in memory of their sons.

Maria was bereft with grief when the youngest of their three 'boys' to join the army died so close to the outbreak of war. She implored her husband to make every attempt to retrieve Alan's body from the Front so that she could grieve.

Permission was sought to bring his body to England; this was regarded as an exception rather than the rule, possibly the result of his father's influence, or because his death occurred so early in the war – 30th October 1914. He was killed in action at Chappelle d'Armentièries and it is understood Alan's father made a special journey to France to retrieve the body.

Alan was interred with full military honours at St. Martin's church, Cheriton, on Wednesday afternoon. On the previous Monday the body had been brought from Boulogne. The coffin, borne from the house to the church on a gun carnage drawn by men of the Northamptonshire Regiment, was draped with the Union Jack. A firing party, comprising men of the Northamptonshire Regiment, marched ahead of the gun carriage.

But when Maria learned that two more of her sons had been killed in action, their loss further compounded her initial grief, the more so when she was curtly informed their bodies could not be returned to England, however much Frederick tried to coerce those in authority to the contrary. Tensions in the household increased with the sharpness of the loss of loved ones; the loss exposed any weaknesses there might have been between husband and wife. Frederick, an army man through and through, knew at first hand the sharpness of death; Maria less so. Few mothers knew more than Maria the dreadful cost of war. The Great War had taken three of her sons; a toll she had to bear.

Wilfred Noel Leggett of the Royal Garrison Artillery, who died on the Somme, was educated at Wellington College and the Royal Military Academy, Woolwich. He had risen from 2nd Lieut. in 1896 to the rank of major by 30th October 1914. The previous month, September 1914, some six weeks after the outbreak of World War 1, he had married Annie Boyd Beattie, the youngest daughter of the Rev. Dr. Beattie of Belfast, a retired chaplain to H. M. Forces.

Wilfred met his bride-to-be while working at the army camp at Farnborough, Hampshire. Following her father's reposting, Mary moved with him and Mary E. Parker, her father's sister-in-law from Hougham, near Dover, to Winchelsea House on the Folkestone Road, where all three lived. Also present at their accommodation were Jane Atkins, a 22-years-old servant, and

Alice William, an 18-years-old domestic servant.

Henry Beattie, already a widower and a Presbyterian chaplain for H. M. Forces, had three daughters. Annie's elder sisters – who also lived in Winchelsea House with their father and sister – were Helen H. M. Beattie, aged 20, and Emily F Beattie, aged 17. At that time, Annie was 15 years old.

Ten years later, it is easy to imagine how Wilfred and Annie might have met in the confines of the Farnborough army camp where Annie's father remained chaplain. The chaplain's easy-going Irish personality brought him close contact with serving officers, especially those who attended Sunday services.

It was not uncommon for chaplains to invite young men, far from away their home life, to their houses following Sunday evening service for tea, cakes and discussion. It provided an opportunity for the chaplain on the one hand to gently spread the Gospel message while at the same time act as a sounding board for any who might have problems.

Within such confines it is easy to imagine Wilfred and Annie striking up an immediate rapport.

Also sharing the house in 1901 with Annie, 24, and 53-years-old sister-in-law Mary Parker in Farnborough, was another family member, namely Henry H. Beattie, Henry Beattie's 11-years-old adopted son. Emily Hogsflesh, 28, performed the duties of cook for the household while 17-years-old Edith Hammond was housemaid.

Wilfred was 36 when he and Annie married. By that age he would be seen as an attractive, confident army officer with experience of serving in many parts of the world, including Gibraltar, Sierra Leone, India and Aden. That he was killed in action by a shell when returning in his car from a reconnaissance exercise at Martinsart, did not stop his commanding officer writing that Wilfred was "unsparing of himself". His monument can be found at Martinsart British Cemetery, France.

Major Eric Henry Goodwin Leggett, DSO of the Royal Field Artillery on the other hand is buried at Longuenesse Souvenir

Cemetery, St. Omer, in France. His wife Mary Leggett lived at Stonepitts, Ryde on the Isle of Wight.

According to the Commonwealth War Graves Commission, 2,205 men died on the 30th July 1916 but Eric Henry George Leggett was the only major to lose his life that day. The 35-years -old officer served with the 188th Brigade of Royal Field Artillery. Only five years earlier in peaceful Britain, long before the onset of war, Eric (then a captain) and his wife Mary from Halifax, Nova Scotia were staying at the Grosvenor Hotel, London, when the census was taken in 1911.

Grief-stricken Maria's loss of her army sons was compounded later by the loss of her fourth son, Frederick Hugh, born in Upnor and who died in Africa at the age of 45.

Like her eldest sister Elizabeth Susanna, Maria suffered the eventual loss of all her children, her first in stillbirth – just like Lizzy.   JM

Principal characters

Elizabeth Susanna Colburn and Christopher Abelseth married at the Parish Church of St Mark in St. Mark's-road, Notting Hill, in the County of Middlesex, on 10th June, 1871. The officiating curate was Frederick Kelly; the church's vicar was the Reverend Edward K. Kendall, M.A. Witnesses were Henry C. Browning (Elizabeth's brother) and Maria Browning (Elizabeth's sister). Christopher, an engineer, gave his address as No. 2 Fairfield-villas, Birmingham. Elizabeth used her parents' home, No. 11 Cambridge-terrace, Notting Hill. Christopher's father, Johan Ulrik Abelseth, was a lawyer.

Elizabeth Susanna Abelseth died aged 53 from pleura-pneumonia and 'failure of the heart action' on 26th May, 1890. Her husband, Christopher Nicolay Abelseth, a lodging housekeeper at their home at No. 6 Longford Terrace, Folkestone, Kent, sat at her bedside as she died. The value of Elizabeth's estate, dated 4th June 1890, was 311 pounds and 10 shillings. Solicitors revalued Elizabeth's estate in November 1891 as 892 pounds, 16 shillings and nine pence. Elizabeth's brothers witnessed her will: Thomas John Browning of No. 2 Museum Chambers, Bury-street, Bloomsbury, a hop salesman, and Henry Charles Browning of No. 44 Nosette Garden Mansions, Cheyne Walk, near Battersea-bridge, Chelsea, a traveller to a white lead manufacturer.

Christopher Nicolay Abelseth and Elizabeth had no children but the year following his wife's death, in 1892, a baby girl arrived. The child, Kathleen Bailey, was adopted shortly afterwards by Christopher Nicolay Abelseth. The 1891 Census shows Christopher lived at No. 6 Longford Terrace, Folkestone. Kathleen was shown as Christopher's 'niece'. How could Kathleen Bailey be declared as his 'niece'?

Christopher Nicolay Abelseth died 11th August, 1915, aged 73; His address: Sharklands, Vange Road, Wickford, Billericay, Essex, and his occupation: mechanical engineer (retired). His 'adopted daughter' Kathleen, 24, was at his bedside. His father was Johan Ulrik Abelseth, born 1811 in Molde, Norway. His mother was Juliana Marie Dorthea Lemvik, b. 1810. The couple married in 1830. Johan died in Trondheim, Norway in 1880, aged 69; his wife died 12 years later, aged 82. Christopher had two brothers: Johan Frederick Haydeman Abelseth and Ingvald Theodore Abelseth.

Sir Henry Bessemer, famous for his invention of the converter process for making steel, was also a prolific inventor. Self-confident, industrious, energetic, infinitely inquisitive, and essentially intuitive, he was by no means modest. Capable of pique, he could be ruthless in his treatment of others. Bessemer provided the funding for *Engineering*, Colburn's London newspaper. Born 19th January, 1813 and married in 1834, he received a knighthood on 26th June, 1879. He died on 15th March, 1898, aged 85.

Elizabeth Susanna Browning was the eldest daughter of Thomas and Elizabeth Browning. Born 3rd November, 1836, she died aged 53 on 26th May, 1890.

Thomas Browning, Elizabeth's father, died 19th October, 1881, aged 90. At the time of his death his wife Elizabeth was 71. The couple, Thomas Browning and Elizabeth Wilson, married by license at St. Giles, Camberwell on 9th June 1853. My mother lived in the parish of St. Giles. Witnesses to the ceremony were Robert Foulsham, John Browning and Maria Wilson. In the years leading up to Thomas's death, the couple had moved to 37, Endlesham-road, Clapham, midway between Wandsworth and Clapham Common. Their general servant at the time, according to the 1881 census, was 27-year old Frances Ashmore; she came from +Liverpool. They also took in a 60-year-old boarder, Cordelia Hornbrook, born in France. Thomas Browning's wife, Elizabeth died 17 years later on the 31st December, 1908. At the time of her death the address given for her was 33, Westbourne Gardens, Folkestone. It is possible she lived there in 1890 when her daughter Elizabeth died, as she was widowed by then. If so, she would have lived not far from Elizabeth Susanna's residence with Christopher Nicolay Abelseth.

William and Margaret Browning, Thomas Browning's parents, married by license at Tooting Graveney on 18th July, 1782. William, a fellmonger, lived in the parish of St. Mary Magdalene in Bermondsey. There were in Bermondsey at that time some 20 or 30 manufactories called fellmongers whose business was to bring sheep-skins into a certain state of preparation before the leather dresser can commence his operation. William and Margaret had seven children between 1784 and 1792, four boys and three girls. William was born on 27th September, 1784, to be followed a year later by John on 14th November, 1785. Thomas was born on 5th July, 1787 but died shortly thereafter. Margaret arrived into the world the following year on 23rd September, 1788, to be followed by Elizabeth on 15th March, 1790. Thomas Browning, Elizabeth's father, was born on 2nd March, 1791 and baptized on 12th August the same year. Jane was William and Margaret's last child and she arrived on 28th May, 1792. In the crypt of St. Mary Magdalene, Bermondsey, 'are references to many local people and craftsmen' including William Browning, d. 1758. A monument on the wall of the church refers to William Browning, d. 11th May 1758 and his wife Elizabeth (d. 1727), and sons Rev. William browning MA, (b. 1702; d. 1740) and Stephen (b. 1712; d. 1724). Rev. Browning was Rector of St. Mary Magdalene from 1723 to 1727.

Maria Browning, Elizabeth's sister, became Maria Leggett when she married a career soldier, Frederick Octavus Leggett, on 31st December, 1872 at St. Peter's church, Notting Hill. Frederick, 23 and some five years older than Maria, was an Assistant Commissary in the Control Department of the army. By the start of World War 1, some 42 years later, Frederick had become a retired colonel. Maria and Frederick Leggett had five children, two of whom were born in Nova Scotia, Canada, and the remainder in England. Of their children, one died in infancy and likely a still born as later the couple admitted to having four children born alive. Three of their sons lost their lives in the First World War. So, of their children, Gerald A. G. Leggett, born in Nova Scotia, Canada in 1875, died in infancy. Wilfred Noel Leggett, born three years later in 1878, also in Halifax, Nova Scotia, died on 14th July, 1916. Eric Henry Goodwin Leggett arrived in 1881 in Weedon, Northants; he died a month after his brother on 30th July 1916. Frederick Hugh Beauchamp Leggett was born 1890 in Upnor, Kent and died on 21st June, 1935 in Mwanza, Tanganyika, Africa. Finally, Alan Randall Aufrere Leggett was born in 1893 in Kent. In 1911, when Alan was 17, he became a boarder at Tonbridge School, Tonbridge, Kent. Present at the same school were 18-years-old Frederick Douglas Goddard from Hong Kong and 17-years-old Eric Cope Wood from Auckland, New Zealand – such was the diversity of boys attending. Three years later Alan was dead, the first of three Leggett brothers to die in the First World War. Alan died shortly after the outbreak of the war on 31st October, 1914. So Maria and Frederick had five children all of whom pre-deceased them. The couple died at the same address, namely No. 27, North Road, Hythe, Kent. Frederick died on 23rd November, 1938 and Maria two years later on 30th December 1940 at the height of the Battle of Britain in the Second World War.

Sarah Pearl Bullard, Zerah and Adelaide Colburn's daughter, and Zerah's only known child, passed away three years before her mother at 6.10 a.m. on 7th March, 1900 aged 45. She died, a rich woman, from the combined effects of chronic melancholia and cerebral haemorrhage. Sarah Pearl Bullard's personal possessions, as itemised in the inventory declared in the Petition to the Surrogates Court, 13th June, 1900, were valued at $5,181.13. She was a rich woman. The inventory totalled 100 items. They included: seven diamond rings, a diamond cross with 23 stones, many other items of gold and silver, an 18ct lady's watch from Thos. Russsell & Sons, London – Thomas Russell signed all their watches: 'Makers to Queen Victoria', a 14ct gent's watch from the Luzerne Watch Co., and another lady's watch from L. S. Jaguin, watchmakers of New York. All items reverted to her mother.

Willard Bullard, Sarah Pearl's husband, a chief sanitary inspector, died nearly six years earlier at 9 p.m. on 1st July, 1894, aged 59. Sarah Pearl and Willard Bullard married on 1st July, 1875. They had no children. The Return of a Marriage for the Health Department of the City of New York in 1875, gave Sarah's age as 21 years next birthday. Willard Bullard was 41, 20 years older.

Mrs. Adelaide Felicita Colburn died on the morning of 21st July 1903 in Manhattan State Hospital, Ward's Island, New York. Confusion surrounded Adelaide's age. The Certificate of Death gave her age as 74, implying she was born in 1829. The Driggs family genealogy gives her birth as 19th November, 1820, suggesting age at death as 82; if so, when she married in 1858, she would be 38. The 1870 census gave Adelaide's age as 36, so making her 69 when she died at 248 West 25th Street. Money discovered in her rooms amounted to $100. She died from a 'neglected cold' and pleura-pneumonia.

Mrs. Sara Colburn, Zerah's mother and Sarah Pearl's grandmother, died 13th June, 1876, the year after Sarah Pearl's wedding and six years after her son's suicide. Aged 85, she died in Bradford, New Hampshire.

Zerah Colburn, born 13th January, 1833 in Saratoga, New York was the only child of Sara (nee Ayer) and Zebinah Colburn, a small-time farmer. Zebinah was the third child of Abiah and Elizabeth Colburn who lived in Hartford, Vermont, and later Cabot, Vermont. Abiah's ancestors emigrated from England along with early settlers. Zerah Colburn's uncle, Zerah Colburn, became known as the 'calculating child'. In his early teens, Zerah Colburn joined Locks and Canals Company in Lowell, Massachusetts. This cotton machinery maker prompted his fascination with steam and locomotives. He then worked voraciously with several locomotive builders before joining *American Railroad Journal* in New York as a writer. In New York, he married Adelaide Felicita Driggs, a woman many years older. Following a disagreement with the editor of *American Railroad Journal*, Henry Varnum Poor, Colburn created his own weekly paper, the *Railroad Advocate*. After a while, and ever restless, he sold a half share to Alexander Lyman Holley, a like-minded young man, the son of a banker and Connecticut governor. Colburn's attempt to operate a saw mill failed, as did selling locomotive tyres in competition with Lowmoor's tyres made in England. Disillusioned, Colburn returned to writing. He developed a passion for travel and in England learned at first hand the spirit that fired the Industrial Revolution. A short spell as editor of a weekly London engineering paper, *The Engineer*, rekindled his interest in publishing his own newspaper. He returned to New York to breathe new life into the *Railroad Advocate,* but without success. A three-month study of locomotive practice in England and France by Colburn and Holley provided material for a substantial report for Presidents of American railroads. This reaffirmed Colburn's love of England to which he returned as editor of his previous paper, *The Engineer*. Settling down in London in 1858, Zerah Colburn became a man about town, drawing satisfaction from the most important city in the industrial world. In London, he employed a housekeeper, Elizabeth Susanna Browning before travelling to New York and Philadelphia on Brunel's *Great Eastern*. Living in Philadelphia he published a weekly journal, *The Engineer*. Following a life of but four months, Colburn found the financial 'crash' of 1870 forcing closure of his paper. He chose to return to England when he again became editor of *The Engineer*. After some years, an event caused the publisher to dismiss Colburn from his position at *The Engineer* causing him to foster the idea of his own competing weekly journal. This he founded (with financial resources from Henry Bessemer) in 1866 and gave it the title *Engineering*. He devoted four years of his life to the paper before relinquishing the editorship and returning to the country of his birth. In a confused and troubled state of mind, Colburn attempted to end his life. Police took Zerah Colburn's body to Boston General Hospital on 25th April, 1870, following a self-inflicted gunshot wound to the head; Zerah Colburn's suicide took place in a pear orchard in Belmont. He died the following day, aged 37. His remains are in Lowell Hospital Association Lot in Lawrence Street Cemetery, Lowell, USA. The funeral took place on 4th May, 1870.

James Dredge died 13th August, 1906 aged 66. He became joint editor of *Engineering* with William Henry Maw following Colburn's departure. He first came to London from Bath in 1858 to the office of Mr. D. K. Clark. In 1863, he joined the staff of John Fowler and appointed to work on the Metropolitan District Railway. At the end of 1865, he joined Zerah Colburn at *Engineering*. John Fowler was the youngest president of the Institution of Civil Engineers between 1865 and 1867.

Alexander Lyman Holley, who introduced Bessemer's process for making steel into America, died at 7.30 p.m. on 29th January, 1882, aged 49. His remains lie in Green-Wood Cemetery, Brooklyn.

Frederick Octavus Leggett. In 1861, Frederick Leggett (born in Reading) was 12 and lived with his mother Caroline (54) the widow of Major George Leggett. He had two elder sisters, Charlotte (23) and Caroline (18), both of whom had been born in the East Indies, no doubt when their father was there on active service. Their housemaids at the time were Elizabeth Cox, 39, and Susan Crick, 35. Ten years later, aged 22, Frederick had joined the army, like his father and grandfather. Based at Portsea he held the position of acting Assistant Commissary Control Department. The army rank of Assistant Commissary is that of a Lieutenant. Frederick's living accommodation was at No. 4 Gun Wharfe, Portsea, where he had a personal servant by the name of Catherine Simpson, 29, from Aberystwith. Also present was her husband John Simpson, 33, a private in the Army Service Corps. The couple had a young son, William George, aged 2. Twenty years later, 1881 Frederick and his wife Maria (Elizabeth's sister) were based at the Barracks at Weedon, Northamptonshire, where Frederick was working at the Ordnance Store and Small Arms Department. His rank was that of Deputy Assistant Commissary of Ordnance. At that address they had their two sons, Wilfred Noel, aged 3 and Eric Henry Goodwin, under four months of age. Both Wilfred and Eric were described in the 1881 census as "officer's sons" while Maria's occupation was shown as "officer's wife". The couple had two nieces visiting them at their quarters: Ada Watkins, 18, and her sister Edith Watkins, 15. The couple also employed Eliza Blake, 28, a domestic servant and Margaret Parker, 19, a nurse maid. By 1891, the census showed Maria and Frederick, then a major, living in Frindsbury in the parish of St. Philip in Upnor, Strood, Kent. Also present was son Eric, then 10, who had been born in Weedon, Northamptonshire, The couple lived at No. 98 Honis Cottages, in the Ordnance Storekeeper's Residence where Frederick carried the position of Assistant Commissary General Ordnance in the Store Department. Maria was shown in the census as being 42 while Frederick was 44. Also occupying the property were housemaid Eliza Williams, 22, of Birling and general servant Edith Capon, 19, of Snodland. Some 20 years later, as the 1911 census shows Frederick Octavus Leggett was described a "retired colonel, Ordnance Department"; he and his wife lived in Underhill. The couple, married for 38 years, declared having "four children born alive and four still living". In the same census, Captain Wilfred Noel Leggett is shown as aged 33 and in the Garrison Artillery. He was single, while Eric Henry Goodwin, aged 30, is shown as a captain in the Royal Artillery being married to Mary, aged 29, Interestingly, bearing in mind his parents links with the region, Mary is down as having been born in Halifax, Nova Scotia, Canada. At the time of the census, Eris and Mary were at the Grosvenor Hotel in Davies Street, London. Also present at the Grosvenor were John Townsend, Lord Levian of St. Michael's Mount, Cornwall and Edith Helena Lady St. Levian. Townsend had a 90-year counterpart lease for St. Michael's Mount.

Following the death of Colonel Leggett, probate records showed his effects amounted to £2,587 11s. His wife's effects totalled £6,191 19s 9d but were resworn as £6,144 0s 5d.

William Henry Maw passed away 19th March, 1924 at his home at 18 Addison-road, Kensington, Middlesex, aged 86. In 1870, following Colburn's suicide, Maw became joint editor with Mr. James Dredge. As well as editing *Engineering*, from 1870 onwards, Maw conducted an independent practice as a consulting engineer specialising in steam plant and machinery, and the design and arrangement of workshops. He designed and laid out the print works of several important papers, including *The Daily Telegraph*, *The Standard*, *The Field* and *The Queen*. Sir Maurice Fitzmaurice said: 'He had the kindliest recollections of all that Dr. Maw had done in connection with anything he had ever asked him to do....and what Dr. Maw did not know about engineering and many other things was not worth knowing.' Maw was one of few men president of both the Institution of Mechanical Engineers (1901-2) and the Institution of Civil Engineers (1922). His hobby was astronomy. Even though an amateur, he conducted work of 'real value'. Houses in Kensington and Outwood, Surrey, both had observatories. He acted as president of the Royal Astronomical Society from 1905 to 1907, and became a founder member of the British Astronomical Association, and its president from the outset in 1890 to 1900.

Selina Dennis Pressland, of No. 92 Upper Tulse Hill Road, in the civil parish of Lambeth, for whom Elizabeth Colburn acted as companion in 1871, died on 13th April, 1891, aged 83. At the time she lived at Lindridge House, No. 98 Upper Tulse Hill Road and described her status as "living on her own means" using income from dividends and houses. In her will, probate being granted on 3rd June, 1891, Mrs. Pressland, who was born in Higham Ferrers, Northants, and for a time lived in Bedford, left £29,611 18s. 2d. (144,144)

The author

John Mortimer has an MSc in aircraft propulsion from Cranfield University, having worked for a number of aero engine companies in the early 1960s, including D. Napier & Son, de Havilland Engine Company, Bristol Siddeley Engines and Rolls-Royce. His work included liquid propellant turbopumps, small gas turbine engines, and torpedo engines, and gearbox design.

For 11 years, John Mortimer served as editor and publishing director of *The Engineer*, a London (England) weekly engineering newspaper; he acted also as pro-tem editor of *Civil Engineering* and *Tunnels & Tunnelling* during acquisitions; also editor of *Career Choice*. He followed this with five years as managing director of IFS Publications Ltd, a company specializing in books and quarterly journals devoted to robotics, sensors and factory automation.

During this time he authored *The FMS Report* and *The Ingersoll Report*, and co-wrote several books on robotics and automated assembly, as well as copy editing the English translation from German of *Automated Guided Vehicles*.

In 1985, John Mortimer established Industrial Newsletters Ltd, a company publishing monthly automotive industry newsletters and executive reports on benchmarking, simultaneous engineering, electronic data interchange and best practice product design. He generated material for the 32-page monthly, editorial-only *Auto Industry Newsletter*, which became a world-wide industry benchmark for authoritative news about the world's automotive industry – cars, trucks and buses.

Ten years later, he sold this successful activity to FTSE 100 enterprise United Business Media. He subsequently wrote news and features on diesel engines and vehicle manufacture for www.automotiveworld.com and the Institution of Mechanical Engineer's *Professional Engineering* and *Automotive Engineer*.

In 2013 he launched his blog: www.autoindustrynewsletter.blogspot.co.uk

He is a Fellow of the Institution of Mechanical Engineers and a Member of the Guild of Motoring Writers. He has won numerous awards including the John Player Management Writer of the Year Award, the Blue Circle Award for Technical Journalism, The Delphi Award for Automotive Journalism and Emerald's Literati Award for Excellence 2003.

Following many years of detailed research, John Mortimer completed the biography: *Zerah Colburn: The Spirit of Darkness*, published in 2005 by Arima Publishing. The biography concentrates entirely on Colburn's engineering and writing career. www.zerahcolburn.com

In 2014 Mortimer also wrote and self-published two semi-technical books: *A gas turbine adventure – an innovator's story*, the life story of Noel Penny, the highly regarded 'father' of the truck gas turbine in the UK; and *The 'nearly' engine*, a documentary of the development of the passenger car and commercial vehicle gas turbine engine in the UK, Germany, Italy and the USA in the 1960s and 1970s.

Mortimer's first novel, *Angel in the house*, is set in New York, Philadelphia and Victorian London between 1860 and 1870. The principal characters are from true-to-life characters of the period. The novel traces the travails of heroine Lizzy, and her life as the wife to a nefarious London engineering newspaper editor who commits suicide to escape public humiliation. Lizzy finally experiences a new romance but continues to be dogged by her 'first' husband's past.

Lightning Source UK Ltd.
Milton Keynes UK
UKHW021352231020
372106UK00008B/1853